A TYLER ZAHN PREQUEL

DAMAGED

CAUGHT IN THE UNDERTOW...

CAM TORRENS

Black Rose Writing | Texas

ISBN: 978-1-68513-566-9
LIBRARY OF CONGRESS CONTROL NUMBER: 2024947307
PUBLISHED BY BLACK ROSE WRITING
www.blackrosewriting.com

Printed in the United States of America
Suggested Retail Price (SRP) $23.95

Damaged is printed in Minion Pro

*As a planet-friendly publisher, Black Rose Writing does its best to eliminate unnecessary waste to reduce paper usage and energy costs, while never compromising the reading experience. As a result, the final word count vs. page count may not meet common expectations.

Linda – thanks for saying "yes"
in 1990 and continuing to say it after
my countless requests for rereads
of *Damaged*. I love you.

PRAISE FOR
DAMAGED

"Before he can rescue missing hikers, Air Force veteran Tyler Zahn needs to save *himself*. *Damaged* is a story of redemption; a broken man rebuilding his life, one harrowing step at a time. A gripping prequel worthy of the award-winning series."
–Gail Ward Olmsted, bestselling author of the *Miranda Quinn Legal Twist* series

"A master of the double entendre…the gifted Torrens serves up a flawed hero, a crackpot villain, and a hole in the proverbial dike in this meaty prequel to the riveting Tyler Zahn series—not to be missed!"
–Kay Smith-Blum, award-winning author of *Tangles*

"An audacious ecoterrorism plot and a military veteran's personal demons are destined for a head-on crash in this breakneck thriller where the action surges with the force of a Colorado river during snowmelt."
–Regina Buttner, award-winning author of *The Revenge Paradox* and *Down a Bad Road*

"Tyler Zahn's riveting journey from rookie rescuer to unexpected crime solver in the Colorado Rockies will leave you breathless and craving more."
–A.J. McCarthy, award-winning author of the *Charlie & Simm* mystery series

"One escaped prisoner, two kidnapping victims, and an unknown number of suspects launching an intricate terrorist plot . . . Cam Torrens ties it all together with high-octane action and suspense enriched by complex characters. I can't recommend this author enough!"
–Ruth F. Stevens, award-winning author of *The South Bay Series*

"A gripping, panoramic thriller, Cam Torrens' writing is never predictable."
–Anna Daugherty, award-winning author of the *Grace Church* series

"A captivating hero, engaging bad guys, and a superbly constructed, fast-paced plot."
–David Rabin, award-winning author of *In Danger of Judgment*

"Ex-Air Force pilot Tyler Zahn's tragic past propels his quest for a quiet life in the Rockies, but a terrorist plot forces him back into the danger zone. Another captivating novel from Cam Torrens."
–Niamh McAnally, award-winning author of *Flares Up* and *Following Sunshine*

"Tyler Zahn brings an "every man" feel to SAR and law enforcement that proves anyone can step up if it matters enough."
–Lena Gibson, award-winning author of *The Edge of Life: Love and Survival During the Apocalypse* and the *Train Hoppers* series

"*Damaged* is a gem that delivers a blend of suspense, mystery, and heroism. From the first page to the last, Torrens weaves a captivating narrative that will hold readers in its grip."
–Michelle Caffrey, author of best-selling *Bring Jade Home* and *Desire in Dairyland*

"Tyler Zahn is one of my favorite characters, and Damaged shows why Torrens should be at the top of your reading list!"
–Travis Tougaw, author of the *Marcotte and Collins Investigative Thrillers*

"Key to the appeal of this thrilling prequel to Cam Torrens's popular Tyler Zahn series is the title; we cheer for this damaged protagonist as he races against time to dismantle a terrorist plot in Colorado while fighting his own demons."
–Lea O'Harra, author of the *Inspector Inoue* series

ACKNOWLEDGEMENTS

Although Damaged is the fourth Tyler Zahn novel, as a prequel, it's the first in the series and holds a special place in my writing adventure. What you are reading is likely the 27th version of the first book I ever wrote. I've learned so much in the time in between that it's (thank goodness) a completely different story than that first version. I have many to thank for helping me on this journey:

My wife Linda to whom this book is dedicated, you set the record for the most reads of Damaged. To Susan Torrens, thanks Mom for allowing me to break the writing rule that says "never believe writing praise from a relative." My dad, Fred Balsiger, for drilling me with plot questions. My sisters-in-law Donna and Sandra for beta reads. My oldest daughter Natasha for early reviews of the original manuscript.

I owe so much to the Central Colorado Writers critique group for their patience, encouragement, and brutal honesty. You made my writing better.

Generous beta readers improved this book, highlighting errors and suggesting improvements. The early version tribe: Liz Brown, Stephanie & Bill Summers, Mary Riley, Terry Williams, Sue & Ben Paganelli, Alta Beren, Diane Haven, Jane Venohr, Penny Martin, Chris Pike, and Joy Knight. The polishers: Kathy Bowen, Kristy Beardemphl, Shane Bumgarner, Jason Brooks, Sarah Greenberg, Cecilia LaFrance, Anita "AJ" McCarthy, Travis Tougaw, Lena Gibson, Ruth Stevens, Gail Ward Olmstead, Gary Gerlacher, Anna Daugherty, Niamh McAnally, Michelle Caffrey, David Rabin, Regina Buttner, Wendy Nakanishi, Evan "Elvis" Hendricks, Jennifer Irving, Jackie Mullarky, Doreen Roger, Kristin Homer, Randy "Rudder" Kaufman, and a special, extra thanks to Kay Smith-Blum.

The members of Chaffee County Search & Rescue inspire me—especially during our busy summers—every day. I'm in awe of your technical prowess and appreciate you letting me haul your stuff up and down the mountains. We all have our talents!

A shout-out to the team at Black Rose Writing for your support, confidence, and talent!

To my sister, MaxieJane Frazier, for allowing me to break the other writing rule, "never let your family edit." Thank you for your masterful touch.

But it's the readers who bring joy to an author's heart—thank you!

DAMAGED

ZAHN

Kroenke Lake, Colorado-April 29th, 2019

Kristee Li's long black ponytail disappears around a bend in the trail. I pick up my pace, attempting to keep her in sight. My heart rate quickens, but not my speed. I halt, leaning forward on my hiking poles, gulping for air.

A sharp whistle makes me turn.

"Hold up," Rick Perez shouts from the same direction as the whistle. I turn back to let Kristee know, but she's already snowshoeing in my direction like she's kicking toward a finish line. My first search and rescue training mission—my crazy idea to get in shape while doing something useful—is foiled by the fifteen excess pounds spilling over my snow pants. The 11,500-foot elevation here in the Colorado Rockies isn't doing me any favors. I push upright with my poles and turn back toward the whistle.

Perez catches up with me at the same time as Kristee. Neither one is out of breath. Small icicles dangle from Perez's black goatee. Kristee wears a smile.

"Trailhead's trying to get a hold of us," Perez says. "Not sure if they're hearing me."

The radio in his hand squawks. *Team 1, Trailhead.*

Perez raises his radio to his mouth. *Trailhead, this is Team 1. Go ahead.*

Roger, Team 1. You're not going to believe this. We've got an actual injury. I repeat, this is actual, not training. The injured party's a female hiker at Kroenke Lake, where you all are headed.

Perez, our trainer, raises his eyebrows, grinning at us newbies before answering. I'm guessing from Perez's smile that SAR folks live for this—a real mission. *Roger that, Trailhead. So, you want us to head up to the injured party, evaluate, and call you back. See if we need to carry her out?*

Perez's radio barks back. *No. Command already determined you'll have to carry her. Hiker is on snowshoes and broke her ankle. Sounds like a compound fracture. She may be going into shock. There's no helicopter support available today. I've got the litter and sked here in the truck, but the other two training teams are out of comms right now. I need two of you to come back to the truck and carry it.*

Perez answers. *There're only three of us, Howard, and my two teammates haven't been checked out yet. How do you want that to work?*

Perez's radio stays silent for a moment before Trailhead answers. *How do you want it to work, Perez? You got the people. We got the equipment. Sounds like the hiker's in trouble.*

Perez lowers his radio, his eyes on us. "Showtime, boys and girls. You ready for this?"

Kristee and I nod.

"Zahn, you head up to the lake and provide initial first aid. You can't get lost—this trail dead-ends at the shoreline. Put all that Air Force training to use."

Perez turns to Kristee. "You come with me, and we'll start hauling the stuff up here. Even after we get the patient loaded up, we can't move fast without a bunch more people. Command's probably alerting them now."

Kristee nods, her face devoid of expression. I wonder if she's pissed Perez thinks I'm more qualified because of my military background.

My gut twists. "I'm not comfortable doing the patient assessment. Or the first aid."

Perez's eyes narrow. "What do you mean by not comfortable? You completed the SAR first aid class."

"I mean, I'd be more help hauling gear from the truck. You should do the patient."

"I don't really want to leave both—"

"I'll do it," Kristee jumps in. "I got the training. I got my wheels." She lifts one of her snowshoes in the air.

"Yeah, right. Send a trainee up the trail alone? In the snow?" Perez says.

"Hey, Zahn's a trainee too." Kristee points at the torn-up snow on the trail. "You know these tracks we've been following?"

Perez squints, as if unsure where Kristee is going with this.

"Most of them are mine," Kristee says. "I was up here two days ago by myself. Last fall I ran up here and back probably three times. By myself. So, what's worrying you most? That I won't find the lake, or that the first aid course I took for raft guiding work—the one SAR said counted for my training—isn't good enough?"

Perez says nothing, eyes locked with Kristee's. Then he turns and shoots me a look. I'm unsure if his expression means, *Can you believe this woman?* or *Why do you have to be such a wimp, dude?* He raises his radio.

Trailhead, Team 1 copies, and we're ready to respond. Kristee Li will hike to the lake. Do the initial assessment and first aid. Me and Tyler Zahn will head back to you.

Trailhead immediately answers. *Roger that, Perez. Thanks. Check in when you reach the Kroenke Lake trail fork. Have Li call in when she reaches the subject.*

Kristee gives a glove-covered thumbs up.

Roger that, Perez replies.

Trailhead continues. *Subject's name is Carrie Schork. She's alone. She texted in on her GPS locator. I'll send you coordinates on your InReach. Copy?*

Copy. Perez turns to Kristee. "What do you have for first aid gear?"

"Everything they recommended in class. All checked the night we brought our kits in."

"You got an air splint?"

"No, but I know how to use one. You got one?"

"Yep." Perez sheds his pack, rummages through his gear, and hands a splint to Kristee. After repacking, Perez shoulders his gear and jerks his head the way we've come.

"Let's go," he says. He pivots and strides down the trail.

I raise my eyebrows at Kristee before scrambling after Perez. Shit. Perez doesn't look happy. Probably not going to be a lot of talking on the hike back to the trailhead.

I settle into the rhythm of the downhill hike—gravity easing my heavy breathing—and consider whether I should have snowshoed to the patient.

Perez isn't wrong. I'm a well-trained veteran Air Force pilot. Patient assessment? First aid? I can do all that shit. But try as I might, I can't stop thinking about the last time I was in charge. Things didn't go well.

•   •   •

Fifteen minutes down the trail, Perez tosses the first shot over his shoulder. "You want to tell me what that was about?"

I don't. But since Perez is my instructor and I'm in danger of failing my first SAR mission, I figure I owe him some explanation just to get him off my case.

"It's not the first aid. I can do that. Just not comfortable without a partner yet."

Perez stops in his tracks and turns so his snowshoes point in my direction. "Weren't you some Iraq War commander or something? Top Gun fighter pilot and all that shit?"

I stop, as well. "Not fighters. I was a transport pilot. And a commander."

"Seems like taking care of an injured party would have been right up your alley. You got PTSD or something?"

I'm not talking about this. Maybe I can dazzle Perez with war stories instead.

"You ever do any military time?" I say.

"Hey, I didn't mean anything about the PTSD—"

"Perez. Relax. I'd be the last one to talk to you about what it's like to serve. You do it every day at the Sheriff's Office." I point down the trail. "Keep going? I'll tell you a bit about what I did."

Perez squints at me like he can't decide if he's pissing me off or not, and turns back to the trail.

I hustle forward until I'm just a step behind Perez. "I commanded a squadron of C-130s flying just outside the combat zone, on the border of Iraq. You familiar with C-130s?"

Perez grunts, "Yeah," without turning. "The Hercules. They fly training missions up and down the valley. They got a unit in Colorado Springs or Pueblo, I think."

"Right. Four propellers. It holds a hundred troops or six pallets of supplies. Not a sexy plane, but we got shit done. When you fly cargo— or trash, as we called it—it's a different kind of adrenaline rush than pulling G's in a fighter."

I tell Perez about getting into the runways. How our US forces somewhat controlled a four- to five-mile perimeter around the coalition airfields, requiring my aircrews to change up our normal arrivals. We'd fly directly over the runway at twenty thousand feet, well above the range of the antiquated surface-to-air missiles, SAMs, used by the Iraqi insurgents. Then, whoosh! We'd drop the C-130's nose almost straight down, flying a tight spiral at more than six thousand feet per minute, our stomachs rising to our throats like a three-minute elevator ride. Except the elevator was spinning.

Perez looks over his shoulder when I mention the elevator ride part. "Huh."

I figure he's impressed.

"Headquarters selected my C-130 squadron to lead an aerial delivery, Operation CROWBAR, parachuting supplies out the back of the plane to a drop zone near the city of Fallujah."

"Parachuting? From 20,000 feet?"

"Nope. That was the problem. We couldn't drop the stuff from that high, and going in lower put our aircrews within surface-to-air missile range. But the Marines needed the supplies. So my crews flew the missions."

"What about you? Did you fly the missions?"

I don't answer.

The radio squawks. *Team 1, Trailhead.*

Perez tilts his head at me as he answers. *Go ahead, Trailhead.*

How far out are you all?

Perez pulls up an app on his phone. *Thirty minutes.*

Roger.

I look to the side at the sun angling off the snow-covered cliffs. In my peripheral vision, Perez's head shakes before he turns and resumes the march back to the truck.

Conversation over.

•   •   •

I shove my wartime memories aside as we break at the trail junction to pull off our snowshoes. We hike the rest of the way in the mud before emerging at the trailhead parking lot. Scott Howard has the litter disassembled and helps us strap each half of the mobile stretcher to our packs.

"You heard Kristee's update on the radio, right?" Howard briefs us. "Broken ankle. Subject is in severe pain but not showing signs of shock...yet."

Perez nods, so I do too.

Howard continues. "Is the trail packed enough to use the litter with the wheel the whole way? Or do you need the sked too?"

The sked is a roll of plastic used when the snow is too deep or mushy for the wheeled litter. It unrolls like a sleeping bag. We put a pad on it, and bundle the patient as best we can. Then we cinch straps from the sides of the plastic to tighten the patient package like a shoelace does for a boot. The result is a human burrito we can slide through the snow.

"We'll need the sked from where she's at now. We can use the litter and the wheel from the trail junction to here." Perez looks at me.

I nod, assuming he knows what he's talking about.

Howard pats the two pieces resting on the tailgate of the SAR truck. "I've got support coming up to help you guys with the carry. They can take the wheel and bracket to the spot where you'll switch from sked to litter. So, just pack in the litter and the sked. Leave the litter at the spot where you'll use it."

"Got it." He turns to me. "Ready, Zahn? You take the sked." He thrusts a tube-shaped bag toward me. It's clear Perez hasn't loosened up.

"Ready." I drape the sked strap around my neck and tuck the bag under my arm.

We assure Howard we'll check in at the Kroenke Lake turnoff. I take the lead, figuring if I can get Perez talking about himself, he won't want to talk about me again.

"When are you back on patrol?" I throw the words over my shoulder so Perez can hear.

"Monday morning."

"And you're spending your weekends out here with us newbies? Why don't you relax a little?"

"Huh," Perez grunts. After a few seconds, he speaks again. "I got to make sure Howard trains you guys right. You know, so you don't show up in the field and not know what to do."

Ouch. Another dig. As if Perez has any idea what my problem is. It isn't competence. It's confidence.

"What's Kristee Li do besides guiding raft trips? Seems like that wouldn't be enough to afford to live here," I say.

"She's a go-getter. Does pretty well for herself."

I turn toward Perez, trying to determine if his observation is a veiled dig at me. Certainly, he doesn't consider me a go-getter.

Perez continues, "She plows winter roads in the higher country, like where you live out in Elk Trace. She's got a new gig going up there working gutters. A lot of those folks she plows for found gutter leaks after the last big snowmelt. Word spread in the neighborhood that she can fix them."

"Huh. Sounds like good work." Me, the master of conversation.

"She says it sucks. But it pays the bills, sort of, and you got to stay working to live downtown these days."

I grunt in agreement. Buena Vista, also known as BV, or Bewnie, sits near the headwaters of the Arkansas River with numerous fourteen-thousand-foot peaks—14ers, as the Coloradoans call them—less than an hour away. The small town used to be a hidden gem, but the secret got out over the last several years. Housing prices are climbing faster than Kristee on snowshoes.

When I decided to move here, I planned to live in town to avoid having to drive everywhere. But I found myself priced out when looking for a place large enough for a spare bedroom for visitors. Not that my ex-wife, Sheila, would be dropping by from her new home—and new marriage—in Colorado Springs, but I have hope that Daria and I can make a fresh start on our dormant father-daughter relationship. She's in school at CU Boulder—not that far away. I ended up renting a place six miles north of town in Elk Trace.

Thirty minutes in, we drop the litter halves at the trail junction and do a radio check with Howard. Another thirty, and we crest a rise. Half-frozen Kroenke Lake spreads in front of us like a hooded blue eye in the middle of the mountains. A foot of snow surrounds the water.

We follow Kristee's snowshoe prints for a quarter mile around the north side of the lake. She waves as we approach. The injured snowshoer lies bundled in a sleeping bag atop a pad Kristee must have pulled from her pack.

"Hey, guys, meet Carrie. Carrie Schork."

Carrie lifts her head off the ground and snaps, "What the hell took you two so long? I sent the text hours ago. Didn't take your gal Kristee that long."

"Carrie, I told you they had to go get the gear to carry you out," Kristee admonishes the woman, giving Zahn and Perez a shrug.

"Sorry for the delay, Carrie," Perez says in an even tone. "I'm Rick Perez. That's Tyler Zahn. You ready to get out of here?"

"I don't know. Will you be as slow on the way back?"

I hide my smile. Doesn't look like shock to me. Which is a good thing, because it'll take a lot longer to get Carrie out of here than it took Kristee to find her.

Perez turns to Kristee. "Nice work keeping her warm. Heard on the radio you gave her some ibuprofen. Do we need the splint?"

"Already done. Want to unzip the bag and check it out?"

"Was it a compound fracture? Any bleeding?"

Kristee shakes her head. "Definitely broken, but no bleeding. No protruding bone. Splint went on easy."

"Let's keep her packaged up, then. Nice work." He turns to Carrie. "You ready to go home?"

"Uh, yeah. I got better stuff than ibuprofen back home." She looks at Perez and me with a weak smile. "Alright, gentlemen. I'll ease up. I get all bitchy when I'm stressed. Tried to snowshoe around the lake and a goddamn buried tree branch took me out." Her voice softens, "Thank you for getting me out of here."

"No problem," Perez says. "I guess now would be a bad time to warn you about the dangers of hiking alone?"

"Asshole," Carrie retorts.

We lift Carrie six vertical inches, enough to pull the pad from underneath her. Kristee spreads the pad on the sked and then the three of us grab the sides of the sleeping bag and position Carrie on it. We strap her in and attach tow ropes before dragging Carrie toward the trail.

I'm relieved help is on the way because dragging a sked is a tough job for only three people. It takes us twenty minutes to get back onto the main trail. The pace picks up where our snowshoes have packed the snow-covered path on our hike up. Besides words of encouragement to Carrie, nobody talks much for the next hour as we skid our way down.

Howard sends an update on the radio. The additional help is an hour away.

We rotate positions as we slide the litter down the trail. One person pulls from the front. Another positions on the downhill side of the sked to keep it from sliding off the trail. The last person uses a guy line in the back to keep the tail end of the litter in the center of the trail and to slow the litter on the steep downhills, keeping it from running over the two people in the front. On the steepest inclines, we switch to two in the rear.

After the initial descent from the alpine lake, the trail levels off along the side of a steep slope. North Cottonwood Creek surges around sporadic ice dams a hundred feet below the path. I stay in the rear, while Kristee pulls from the front. Perez is on the front corner of the sked closest to the steep drop-off.

The hardest part about two people up front is fitting both members on the trail, especially as it narrows above the gulch. Perez switches to the uphill side, pulling to keep the sked on the center of the trail. Kristee tugs from the front, but angles toward the downhill side to avoid a boulder.

"Watch it, Li," Perez warns Kristee. "The snow on that downhill edge—"

Kristee's right snowshoe slides off the trail. The rest of her follows. Perez leaps across the trail in front of the sked to keep Kristee from sliding down the slope to the water. He snags part of her jacket, but Kristee's momentum pulls him off the trail right behind her.

From fifteen feet behind the sked, I react without thinking. I lunge to the uphill side of the trail, whipping my guy line along with me around the closest tree. I drop onto my butt with my snowshoes pointed downhill. The sked veers off to the right of the trail, and Carrie drops out of sight. My body jolts as the rest of the sked disappears and the rope yanks me back toward the tree.

Good.

The rope, the tree, and the weight of my body keep Perez and Kristee from pulling the sked down with them.

"Zahn?" Perez's voice rises from down the slope.

My spiked snowshoe toes dig into the snow. "You guys OK?"

"Yeah, we're fine. What's keeping the sked in place? Is it secure enough for us to climb around and pull it up from the trail?"

"Got it anchored around a tree up here. Come on up."

Perez's head bobs above the edge of the trail. Kristee's voice reassures Carrie she's OK. As Perez scrambles onto the path, his eyes follow the line from the back of the sked up to the tree I'm using as an anchor.

"Son of a bitch, Zahn. How'd you do that?"

"Saw you guys going over. I figured it was the only way I could stop you from taking the sked with you."

Perez pulls his guy line and the sked up as Kristee regains the trail. A minute later, they have the sked level on the path, ready to go.

"You OK, Carrie?" Kristee says.

"If you guys think you can keep this damn thing on the trail, I'll be fine. If not, give me some more drugs and I'll walk it out."

"We got you, Carrie," I say.

"You sure do, brother," Perez says. "Nice work."

"Yo, SAR Team 1!"

Seven SAR members round the bend, all smiles, and best as I can tell, full of energy.

Perez introduces them to Carrie, briefing her condition before fielding the new team's repeated questions about why he and Kristee are covered in snow, and describing their close call. Over Perez's protests, the new team insists on relieving us of the sked.

I unhook my guy line, and hand it over to a SAR member I don't recognize. "Thanks, man."

"Nice job, dude. We got it."

I've got no problem with that. Way more action and exercise than I've expected for the day. My two teammates surrender their ropes, and let the new sked team take the lead. I bring up the rear, with Perez walking in front of me.

"You got your first save, Tyler. You can just skip the rest of training," Perez jokes.

He's loosening up—using my first name. I laugh. "Yep. I'm a veteran now. Kind of cool to do something real on a training mission."

"What's the deal? You didn't get enough time serving others in the Air Force? So you joined SAR?"

"I could ask the same question of you, Deputy Sheriff."

Perez snorts. "Touché."

"Yeah, service probably has something to do with it. But I also thought SAR would give me an excuse to stay in shape and get outdoors." As soon as the words leave my mouth, I realize I should have said "get in shape," instead of "stay in shape."

"It's a good choice. But when you get done with training, it's going to slow down. It's not going to be enough for fitness."

"I do some cross-country skiing. Or at least I used to a couple of years back. I want to get back into that. What about you?"

"I run," Perez says. "Not fast, but some good distance."

"Like 5k's and stuff?" Damn. I've tried to jog a couple of times at this altitude, and after a half-mile, I'm walking again.

"Sort of. Ran a 50K race out in Utah a couple months ago."

"No shit?" No wonder Perez makes this hike look easy.

"No shit." Perez twists his head in my direction. "I can get you out on the trails if you want to give it a shot. Or take you climbing. You can show me that cross-country ski stuff if there's enough snow left. I'm a downhill guy, but my ultra buddies say cross-country is good for mixing up the training."

"I need to dust my skis off and get in shape first. Especially if you want me to run with you. Shit…50K? That's like 30 miles, right?"

"A little more."

"Yeah, I'll get back to you on that."

We hike without talking until the sked team stops to switch Carrie to the wheeled litter. While removing his snowshoes, Perez talks more about SAR. "Speaking of getting back to me, Howard asked what I thought about you taking over for him as Training Director once you're all qualified. You've got all that military background. He talked to you about that, right? After you get some more first aid training?"

My pulse quickens—the same reaction I had when my new neighbor asked me if I'd consider the board president job for the homeowner's association.

"Yeah, I don't think so. I'll talk to Howard. Kind of burned myself out on the leadership thing in the Air Force. I'd rather just be a searcher." Just in case Perez thinks I missed his dig at me, I add, "And yeah, I'll be ready with the first aid next time."

"Huh." Perez keeps hiking.

We check in on the radios with Howard before continuing toward the trailhead parking area. Conversation slows. I'm tired. I consider Perez's question. Everybody always asks the new guy—the decorated vet—to be in charge of something. I don't want to do it. Been there, done that, and I don't want to think about it anymore.

Perez halts in front of me and turns. He must sense that me being lost in my thoughts isn't a good thing. He waits for me to catch up.

"OK. I'm done flipping you shit about ducking out of the whole patient assessment thing. You saved that woman when you wrapped that line around the tree. Incredible." Perez says. "So, we good?"

I smile and put out my hand. "Yeah, man—we're good."

Perez's shake is firm but not crushing. Like the end-of-mission handshakes and high fives from crewmates I trusted.

"I got something for you to consider with all your spare time, Mr. Retiree. Why don't you do some ride-alongs with me?"

"What? Like on sheriff patrol?"

"Yeah, we're allowed to take folks out to show them what we do. Of course, if I pull anyone over or arrest someone, you got to stay in the car, but most of the time I'm just driving around checking things out. It'd be something for you to do, and you can do it more than once. I'm supposed to try to log a few of these things every quarter. My contribution to community outreach." Perez starts hiking again. "What do you think?"

I think it sounds like therapy, courtesy of Rick Perez. And I'm not really interested in all that. Except he'll keep bringing up the topic until he's satisfied poor little old me isn't just moping around the house all day. Drinking beer. Alone.

"I don't know about some, but I'll join you for one," I say. "Wouldn't mind seeing if you actually work for a living or just cruise that Tahoe up and down the county looking cool."

"How about two weeks from now? I need to run the paperwork first. I'll call a couple of days ahead when it's cleared."

"Sounds good. Thanks, Rick."

One ride. Perez hasn't asked me to put on a badge or anything. A ride-along should be kind of like Search and Rescue—I don't decide which missions to take, or what first aid to apply. I just help carry shit. A useful bystander. Perfect.

SULLIVAN

Aurora, Colorado-May 1st

Two days later, and over a hundred miles away, Galen Sullivan pushes through Front Range Brewpub's glass door, looking for the mystery contact. He nods at the heavy man in a skin-tight polo shirt manning a table just inside the entrance.

"You playing?" the trivia night host says.

"Not tonight." Out of habit, Sullivan checks the room for a table with a woman and an extra seat—his standard entrance to any bar. His mother always suggests he'll find the right woman in church. He keeps hoping he'll get lucky at places like this since he hasn't entered a place of worship after leaving home fourteen years earlier. But tonight's different. He's arranged to meet a woman here. He wears a crisp button-down shirt and new Levis. He cranked out twenty-five pushups to pump his biceps before he left his apartment. It's practically a date.

He bobs his head and offers a smile of recognition to the couple two tables away on the left. Sullivan has no idea who they are but, in his experience, women are less likely to talk to you if they think you're alone. Best to act like you know everybody.

Trivia Man belts out a question over his portable sound system. *"What's the number one selling album of all time?"*

In the back of the room near the windows, a blond-haired woman wearing a braid down her back turns from her companion. She lifts her eyebrows and smiles at Sullivan before turning her attention back to the man across from her.

Sullivan hopes it's her—the one he's supposed to meet.

Sure enough, the woman pushes away from the table. She stands and waves to Sullivan, motioning him toward her.

Sullivan cocks his head—she hadn't mentioned another guy. He turns sideways, threading his way between the tables toward the couple.

"We're thinking *Abbey Road*—the Beatles. What's your guess?" the woman says, returning to her stool. She's a couple years older than Sullivan, toned, like she works out.

"Nope. *Thriller*—Michael Jackson," Sullivan replies, glancing at the man at the table.

"Galen Sullivan, right?"

"That's me." Sullivan smiles, sticking out his hand.

The woman squeezes it. "Galen, meet Steve. Steve, Galen."

Steve nods. "Dude."

"Hey." Sullivan figures a one-word greeting deserves one back. Besides, he's unsure of the next step. This whole meeting is kind of cloak and dagger. He'd gotten a call from this woman—at least he thinks it was this woman—yesterday on his cell. She'd introduced herself as Sarah and tossed out Ron Timmons's name as a friend they had in common.

He knew Timmons when Sullivan worked for the Denver Water utility, a year back. Sarah saying Timmons was his friend threw him a bit. Timmons was a rancher from western Colorado interested in water management and Sullivan knew a lot about Colorado water. He and Timmons hadn't really hung out. Mostly they did business. Business on the sly.

Sarah snorts, as if the two men and their limited vocabularies amuse her. "I was just hanging out with Steve while waiting for you. I suspect Steve is just hanging out with me to see if I really have a blind date tonight." She smiles at Sullivan, then turns back to Steve. "Told you I was spoken for."

Steve winces. "Good to meet you, Cara." He turns to Sullivan. "Dude." He walks away.

"I think I'm supposed to meet a Sarah, not a Cara," Sullivan says, sliding into Steve's empty seat. Sarah, Cara, whatever—he doesn't blame Steve for trying to talk to the woman. He would have done the same.

"Right. I'm Sarah." She reaches across the table to shake Sullivan's hand again. Her half-smile and magnetic eyes grab Sullivan's attention. "I just gave him another name because I knew he wouldn't be staying long. Thanks for coming."

"No problem. Your mention of Ron Timmons intrigued me."

Actually, she had him at "I'm Sarah." Sullivan hasn't been in a relationship for two years. The women he liked tended to drift away after the first date. The few women who went home with him on a first date ended up being the ones he didn't want to ask out again. Not a lot of women called him out of the blue, like Sarah. And unlike the women on the website he's tried twice, this woman presents better in real life than she sounds on the phone.

"Ron said you all have spent some quality time together," Sarah says. "He trusts you."

Sullivan can see Timmons saying that. Their relationship had ended after Sullivan was laid off six months ago. Automation upgrades gave Denver Water an opportunity to cut manpower, right when he was starting to move up in the company. Sullivan and half his team lost their jobs. He hadn't heard from Ron Timmons since.

Sarah beckons the server and asks for an IPA. She raises her eyebrows at Sullivan.

"Same." A bar, a girl, and she's buying. This is already his best night out in a month.

Trivia Man's voice blasts from the speakers. "*And the correct answer…Thriller—Michael Jackson.*"

Sarah raises her eyebrows at Sullivan. "Nicely played."

Sullivan flashes a smile. He's a smart guy. Always has been, especially with remembering things. He just needs the right opportunity to capitalize on his talents.

After losing the Denver Water job, Sullivan spent a month looking for work before landing a supervisory role at a mattress production factory close to where he and Timmons used to meet in Arvada. Not his first choice of career moves, but he was running out of money. The job sucks, and he's only met his supervisor once. Nowhere near enough interaction for his boss to discover how smart he is. It's a significant pay cut from what he brought in at Denver Water. And no more added perks from Timmons.

Timmons heads up some kind of cattle rancher association. All he had asked from Sullivan was access to files from Denver Water's shared drive: upcoming meeting agendas, position papers, proposals. Nothing secret, but evidently important for Timmons's group. For Sullivan, a man on his way up, those Denver Broncos VIP tailgate passes and game tickets from Timmons were like a siren call. The kind of life he could live if his employer would just recognize his capabilities.

Sullivan gazes into Sarah's eyes without asking the obvious question. *Why am I here?* Pauses in conversation are tough for Sullivan.

Sarah smiles. "I bet you want to know why I asked you to meet me?"

"My good looks, sense of humor, and mad trivia skills?" Sullivan jokes, watching for her reaction. He hopes she laughs.

Sarah obliges. "Well, you do have the trivia thing going for you—" She pauses. "Let's wait for our beers."

The server returns after another minute with two pints, flipping out his notepad after delivering the beer. Sarah shakes her head at the server. Sullivan follows her lead.

"Let me know if you change your mind." The server leaves.

Sarah takes a deep breath. "I'm with a group that wants to unplug the rivers. Damming waterways destroys the environment and we want to stop or reverse that trend."

Oh, shit. Tree-hugger. Just when he thought he might get lucky. "An environmental group? How's that relate to what Timmons wants? If you don't regulate that water west of the Rockies, then Timmons can't use it for his cattle." He sips his beer.

"Right. Timmons started talking to me because I'm a decent-looking gal at a bar. When he found out I'm also a raging environmentalist, he was ready to bolt. But after we talked for a bit, we found common ground."

"Like what?" Sullivan can see why Timmons fell for Sarah. But she's losing him fast with the greenie vibe.

"Right now, Timmons and his fellow ranchers rely on what water remains after part of it is siphoned off upstream. We both think western Colorado water should flow its natural route to the Pacific Ocean. That's more available water for Timmons. Neither of us want water redirected east, underneath the Continental Divide, to quench the thirst of a million people in Denver and the suburbs."

Sullivan cocks his head. "Ah. You're talking about the tunnels. The Moffat, the Roberts, the Adams." He pauses, but Sarah stays silent. "So, which one is pissing you guys off? Or is it all of them?"

"You know your tunnels," Sarah says. "What do you know about the Roberts Tunnel?"

Sullivan puffs up a bit. He knows everything about this topic. "The Roberts takes water from the reservoir formed by the Dillon Dam. Runs under the mountains to the town of Grant, into the South Platte and then, on into Denver."

Sarah's head bobs, as if Sullivan is nailing a job interview.

He squints. "Not a lot of people know about that. I mean, it's not a secret or anything, but most people don't pay attention to dams. Or even know about the tunnels."

"Well, I told you, dams and rivers are kind of my group's thing." Sarah sips her beer.

"Timmons probably told you I worked for Denver Water, right? That I had access to information on what the utility is up to? Except I don't work there now. I don't know shit anymore." He reluctantly severs his chance at maintaining Sarah's interest in him. "I'm loving the beer and the company, but I don't see how I can help."

Sarah leans forward, lowering her voice. "Galen," her smile is coy, "we don't want you to spy on Denver Water for us. We don't want to give you football tickets for your efforts. How about we pay you three million dollars to actually do something about the water theft?"

Sullivan pulse quickens. He leans forward. "Like what?"

"Redirect some water."

"Redirect…?"

"Protests and letters and campaigns aren't working. We've decided to act. You know the infrastructure because of your job. And you know how to alter it, because of your Army experience. And your high school hijinks up in Washington state."

Sullivan shakes his head. She had him at three million. She lost him at the risk. He eases back in his chair, not taking his eyes off hers. "Redirect…yeah, right. Mess with a tunnel?" He pushes back his chair and stands. "You really *have* done your research on me haven't you?"

"Well…"

Sullivan scans the nearby tables, checking for listeners. Nothing. He leans forward pressing his hands on the table, "Of course I could do it. You obviously know what I did in the Army. But the whole reason I enlisted was to get out of the trouble I was in. That life's behind me."

"*Who was George Wallace's running mate in the 1968 presidential election?*" queries Trivia Man.

"We're just talking about a one-off here." Sarah says.

"No way." He slides his chair under the table before walking around to Sarah's side. "Loved the beer, and great to talk to you. Don't worry about me repeating anything you said. But you chose the wrong guy." Sullivan turns sideways, working his way out between the same two tables he passed on his way in. Then he stops and turns. He walks back to Sarah.

"Curtis LeMay."

Sarah's expression is blank.

"George Wallace's running mate. Air Force General Curtis LeMay." Sullivan turns and leaves, dipping his chin at Trivia Man on his way out the front door.

The night air is unseasonably warm for May. He strides to his truck parked in the large lot between the King Soopers and the brewpub. Two teenage kids stand between his truck and the silver BMW 525 parked next to him. Sullivan guesses it's not their car.

"Hey!" Sullivan barks, upset from his conversation with Sarah.

The kids whip their heads toward Sullivan in unison before turning toward the store. They check him out over their shoulders.

He opens his truck door, climbs inside, but doesn't start the engine. What just happened in there?

He and Ron Timmons had both shared their Army experiences, but most of their conversation centered on their current jobs. All he'd told Timmons about his own Army career related to his time in Explosive Ordnance Disposal, or EOD as the Army abbreviated it, and that he'd disarmed quite a few roadside bombs.

He might have mentioned his high school days back in western Washington running around with his friend Mitch Mandrake, blowing shit up. How they had played around with dynamite they found in an abandoned mine and used the Internet to learn how to make timers. Blowing up rocks. Starting landslides. Pretty much impressing themselves with their ability to wreak havoc.

Anybody with access to public records could find out Sullivan knows how to disarm explosives…that had been his Army job. But only Mandrake knows of his bomb-making skills. And maybe Timmons. Sullivan talks more when he's been drinking.

Mandrake's locked in a Colorado prison for a drug trafficking conviction nine years ago. Who the hell is this chick? How does she know so much about him?

Through his windshield, Sullivan can see Sarah alone by the window with a cell phone pressed to her ear. She looks straight at him.

He starts his truck. Checking his rearview mirror, he backs from his parking spot, then exits onto the highway. The two teens from the parking lot strut along the sidewalk in the same direction as Sullivan's apartment. He honks when he passes them. One kid flips him off. Sullivan taps his brakes and the kid instantly drops his arm.

He accelerates. Avalanche's Bar & Grill has two-dollar pints on Wednesdays, a promotion that draws more men than women. But who knows?

ZAHN

Mount Harvard, Colorado-May 4th

The call yesterday from Kristee asking if I want to join her on a Mount Harvard climb surprised me. In the short time we've both been a part of SAR, it's clear Kristee Li is a friend to all. I just didn't expect her invite after I wimped out of the medical stuff on the mission earlier in the week. Hopefully she won't want to talk about that.

But I'd like to be friends with Kristee, and I really want to climb a 14er. If I'm going to rescue people from the sides of these natural anomalies, I at least need the credibility to say I've summited one.

Kristee picks me up from my house at 5:30 the next morning.

I climb into the passenger seat. "I heard smart climbers are on the mountain by 4:30. You aren't thinking I'm fast, are you?"

"You got your snowshoes?" Kristee says.

"Threw them in the back with my pack."

"Good. Here's my rule of thumb. If it's early enough in the season, you need snowshoes to get above treeline, then you're not likely to hit afternoon thunderstorms. And lightning is the main reason for early starts. I checked the weather. We're good."

"Seems like it would take us longer, though, in snowshoes."

"You're right about that. After watching you last Monday, I factored that into my planning." She's teasing me. "But we're only wearing them if we need them. If the trail is packed from other hikers, we'll be good without them. And once we clear the trees, we'll cache them and pick them up on the way down. The wind, sun, and angle of the rocks keep the snow from getting deep up there."

We spend the thirty-minute drive talking about work and play. Well, she does. I don't have a job and am still looking for hobbies. I keep a steady flow of questions going to keep the conversation from turning to my life. Kristee shares a story from the previous summer where the raft she was guiding overturned, and she almost lost a customer.

"What do your parents think about everything you do out here? Are they okay with it?" I want to avoid too many personal questions in case she turns the tables on me, but can't help it. My daughter—the one I haven't seen in years—is only a few years younger than Kristee. While I want to imagine her as a strong, confident woman—like the woman next to me—I also know I'd be worried if she was taking the same risks.

Kristee turns to me, wearing the smile she started the story with. "Ugh. Do you want to trade family stories?" Her eyes squint and I realize she's forcing the smile. She doesn't want to talk about her family.

"Nope." I grin.

We ride the final ten minutes in a comfortable silence. Well, it's comfortable for me at least.

The hike to treeline takes two hours. Previous hikers have packed the trail down to where we can keep our snowshoes in our packs and get away with just wearing micro-spikes. I've caught a break. I'd be twice as tired if we'd had to slog on snowshoes to this point. My breath is ragged but I doubt Kristee can hear it from her twenty-yard lead. I pause at the last cluster of trees and face the jumbled boulders trying to block our route. My hands rest on my knees and I crane my neck to scope the trail that winds through the giant rocks.

I'm already exhausted, but the stunning contrast of granite on snow stretching toward crystal blue skies touches me. Like the earth is raising its pinnacles in praise of some higher power. The forest was pretty. These peaks are magnificent.

"How are you feeling?" Kristee has backtracked to check on me.

"Like a freight train ran over me. Did I mention I'm working on getting in shape?"

"You didn't have to." Kristee punches my arm. "I hiked with you last Monday, remember?"

I'm embarrassed about my fitness, but smile anyway. I like the fact that Kristee's comfortable enough to dog me.

"Going to get a little tougher from here. Just adjust your pace to what you can handle."

I consider admitting that this pace—the one where I'm bent over gasping for air—is about right, but simply nod instead. Finally, I throw my shoulders back, standing straight like I'm in military formation. I take a step, jabbing my pole in front of me. Then another.

Somewhere between twelve-and thirteen-thousand feet, a new problem racks my body. The previous three hours have been an aerobic nightmare, my breath chugging like a steam train. Now I've got anaerobic issues. My legs are on fire, the same burn I felt in the 400m races back in middle school track. There was a reason I dropped that event for the discus instead.

We're short of the saddle, just shy of the final seven-hundred-foot pitch to the summit, when I trip. My poles flail to the side and I hit the trail belly first. I move to my knees in an effort to get to my feet before Kristee sees me, but too late.

"Are you OK?" Kristee's expression is one of concern.

"Good to go. I just misplaced my foot."

"Are you feeling like your legs weigh twice as much here as they do at your house?"

Exactly. "Yeah. Yours too?" I'll feel better if I know I'm not the only one dying here.

"Not at all." Kristee smirks, but when my eyebrows drop in disappointment, she says, "But I remember what it feels like." She turns toward the summit, then back to me. "Listen, Z-man." She pauses when my eyes narrow. "That's my nickname for you. I've been referring to you as Z-man to everyone else. Guess I should have clued you in. Is that OK?"

I give a short nod. A nickname? Hell yes. Back in the Air Force, we had call signs instead of nicknames. You weren't allowed to pick your own. If anyone suggested a call sign that wasn't something like Turd or Stubby or Chunk, you grabbed it. Z-man is much better than ORF— old retired fuck—which is what I've earned so far.

"Z-man, we're done. Even if you make it up to the last forty feet before the summit, we need you in better condition to do the final push. It's a rock scramble. Kind of like bouldering except at fourteen-thousand feet."

"You couldn't have told me about the last part back at your car?"

Kristee grins. "Didn't want to scare you off. This is no big deal, Z-man. These mountains are our backyard. We'll come back later in the summer."

Not a big deal for her, but it is for me. I wimped out on the mission on Monday and am about to turn around less than a thousand feet from a summit. *Hell of a week, Zahn.*

The questions I expect from Kristee on our descent never come. No, *What's your deal with SAR?* No, *Do you have PTSD?* And no, *When are you going to do something with that padding around your waist?*

Kristee keeps me talking about Buena Vista, and all there is to do in and around my new home. She invites me to join her and some of the other SAR members at The Lock-up on Main Street next week. I say I'll check my schedule. I expect a snarky rejoinder about retired guys and schedules, but she lets it ride.

I should be grateful. I'm descending one of the most impressive mountains in the country with a guide I'm comfortable with.

All I can think about is the six-pack in my fridge. Kristee might find joy in these mountains, but they have defeated me. The windy trek down, forcing me to pause at every crook in the trail has robbed me of the glory I felt during our climb. When we descend below treeline, I pick up my pace. By tonight, I'll be alone at my dining room table with a pint glass in my hand, and spares at the ready. No chance of failure there.

SULLIVAN

Arvada, Colorado-May 5th

Sullivan eyes the young man in ripped jeans strolling his way from the front of the warehouse. "Dan, what the hell?"

"Had to see a man about a horse."

"That's the third time you've taken off this morning." Sullivan wipes sweat from his brow. Another warm day. "Stop drinking so much water. Get your ass in gear. We've got three trucks in line out there and you're our only forklift driver. Every time you take a piss, Mike and Bob are standing in the back with their thumbs up their asses. Move it."

Sullivan earns thirty bucks an hour with this mattress gig. These guys working for him make twenty. At least the Denver Water job had paid a salary. Not something he'd ever get rich at, but certainly more than he's pulling in now.

He likes money. Sullivan's previous salary meant he could make a new car lease payment, pay the rent, and hit the nightlife on the weekends. Working at this factory barely covers his apartment and groceries. He's had to swap his new Toyota Tundra for a used F-150.

Sullivan's past moneymaking opportunities have produced mixed results. The first one was a guaranteed gold mine. His explosives de-arming tour wound down, and he and a buddy concocted a plan to smuggle war trophies—mostly Iraqi weapons—out of the combat zone and back to the US to redistribute to their fellow soldiers. Then one of their customers got busted waving an unloaded contraband AK-47 around base housing. Military Police investigators traced it back to Sullivan and Carter. So ended his brief Army career. His supervisor had told him he was lucky to exit with an honorable discharge, but Sullivan disagreed. He hadn't stolen the merchandise. He simply moved it. And his plan was a stroke of genius: perfection. Until the gun-waving asshole screwed things up.

He earned good money as a contractor in Iraq until the war dwindled down. An ordnance instructor job at a Texas Army post kept him flush for a year, but he was let go when the contract lapsed. It wasn't his fault the drawdown in Iraq meant fewer available contracting jobs.

His smuggling partner had a friend of a friend working at Denver Water. Sullivan promised the friend a steak dinner and a case of beer for a recommendation. Two weeks later, he moved from Texas to Colorado, the same state where his Washington high school buddy Mandrake was busted for drug distribution and incarcerated.

Sullivan started as a line worker on a waterworks inspection team. After a couple of years and two different bosses, the company recognized his skills and promoted him to inspection team chief. The salary wasn't even close to the tax-free fortune he'd been making as an explosives expert in Iraq, but it paid the bills and let him play at night. And he liked the job. The complicated Colorado water system made sense to him, and he quickly gained a reputation as the guy who knew everything about all the dams, tunnels, and waterways in the state.

Now he moves mattresses in Arvada.

Sullivan has been kicking himself for walking out on Sarah earlier in the week without hearing the details of her offer. Three million dollars? He's not too excited about blowing something up for money. He doesn't want to get caught. But maybe if no one gets hurt. Like it's just an environmental message thing. He could live with that.

Dan's forklift beeps in the background. He could stay here and schlep mattresses, hoping something else pops up? Or reengage with Sarah—a woman who knows his value and is willing to pay? He reaches for his phone.

• • •

Sullivan picks The Rooster for the meet—the same bar where he and Timmons used to get together. The blue-collar watering hole isn't quite as hip as Sarah's brewpub, but it's Cinco de Mayo and he wants to avoid the crowds. Maybe he'll get lucky this time. Sarah might be a decade older than him, but she's a looker. With that braid and flower-child look, she reminds him of Jenny from *Forrest Gump,* but his online efforts to find out more about this woman have failed. He hadn't even asked for a last name.

Sullivan keeps reminding himself he's saying yes to this deal for the money and the chance to refresh his explosives expertise, not for more time with Sarah.

He parks his truck at The Rooster. Out of habit, he heads for the bar. Halfway across the room, he changes his mind and veers toward the back of the room toward a table affording some privacy. Sullivan plops into a chair facing the door and grabs a menu.

"I'll take your order up here and bring it out to you when it's ready," the bartender hollers from behind the counter. Sullivan orders two beers and a side of fries. The bartender pulls the tap and hands him two pints. "About ten minutes for the fries."

As he returns to the table, Sarah pushes through the door, scanning the room. Sullivan notes she doesn't use his head-nod-to-a-fake-friend technique. She probably doesn't realize how hard it is for a man to meet a good woman these days. Raising both beers, he catches her eye, and tilts his head toward the spot he's picked out. They converge on the table, Sullivan depositing the beers before pulling out a chair for Sarah.

"Oh, Galen." Sarah's voice assumes a Southern drawl. "You're such a gentleman."

Sullivan's face flushes as he lowers into his seat. "I left kind of quick last time."

"I'm glad you called back. I thought you might need some time to do some thinking."

"I haven't decided anything." Sullivan crosses his arms and leans back. "I didn't give you much of a chance to explain what you had in mind."

Sarah smiles. "You did kind of bolt out of there in a hurry. I just figured you're a little risk-averse."

"Bullshit." Sullivan leans forward. "If you've been talking to Timmons, then you know I'm not really the conservative type when it comes to risk."

Sarah reaches across the table and squeezes Sullivan's hand. "Why don't I just start at the beginning?"

"Go ahead." Sullivan glances at the bartender bringing the fries, enjoying the warmth of her grip.

When Sarah says *beginning*, she's being literal. Fifteen minutes later, the fries are gone. He now knows more about Sarah than he does about his first girlfriend.

Raised by middle-class parents on the Western Slope, CU Boulder dropout, living in a van when her parents cut her off, discovering her purpose in life—Sarah spares no detail. Sullivan considers asking about her first puppy, but worries his sarcasm might piss her off.

Finally, Sarah gets to the present. "We have a name," she says, "but it would be best if you didn't know that much about us. We believe that rivers are the earth's arteries. Just as blood flows through vessels to power the human body, water needs to flow unobstructed to the oceans so the earth's life cycle can continue."

Sullivan tries to stay silent, but can't. "Whoa." She seems so squared away—except for the hair—but now this *save the whales* shit comes out of nowhere, putting her squarely in the left-wing-woke category that drives him crazy.

"Galen, give me a break," Sarah protests. "I've studied this stuff. It's science. Perhaps I'm not explaining myself clearly, but behind my group stand a lot of others who really understand how this works. People who are willing to pay to fix our arteries."

"Skip the metaphors, Sarah. You mean the dams. You want to get rid of the dams. Do you have any idea how many dams there are just in Colorado?"

Sarah shakes her head. "We're not taking them all down. We're trying to make a statement. We're trying to demonstrate the good that can happen when rivers run free."

"Uh, Sarah? What about the downstream effects? Some of these dams had towns built below them after they were constructed. The dam is the only thing keeping them from being flooded."

Sarah says nothing.

"The first time we talked, your eyes lit up and shit when I mentioned the Dillon Dam. What about the goddamn town of Silverthorne on the other side?"

"Galen, listen." Sarah presses her palms to the table. "It's not just the dams preventing the water from its natural flow. There're the tunnels, too." She pauses. "We want a twofer. We want you to stop the water going from Dillon Reservoir to Denver—"

"You mean the Roberts Tunnel, right?" Sullivan interrupts. His inspection team at Denver Water used to run their custom golf-cart-sized rig through the 23-mile tunnel looking for leaks.

"Right, that's part of it. Now let me finish. We also want you to put a dent in the Dillon Dam."

"Dillon's an earthen dam, not a concrete one. You can't bomb through an earthen dam. You'd have to hit the spillway to do anything and even that wouldn't take it out." Sullivan is confused. Sarah appears confident in her plan but is clueless about execution.

"See, Galen." Sarah leans closer. "You've already got it figured out. We don't need to take out the whole dam. If we just open it up enough to flood the Blue River—you know, raise the level high enough to take out the buildings along Silverthorne's riverbanks. Then no one gets hurt. We get our message across." Sarah beams at him. "I knew Ron Timmons was right when he suggested you."

Sullivan furrows his brow. What the hell is Timmons doing mixed up with a bunch of wacko environmentalists? "He works with you?"

"No. He's a family friend. He's interested in water because of his ranching, but he doesn't know about our plan. I just told him we needed to do some research on Denver water policy. That's how I got your name from him."

Sullivan doubts that's the whole story. Part of this plan involves cutting water off to Denver. He recalls how passionate Timmons and his fellow ranchers are about eastern Colorado stealing water from the west side. And the group has the financial capacity for something like this.

He grabs a single fry he missed, while considering Sarah's plan. With a little help, he could do it. And the money? With three million, he wouldn't have to entertain women at The Rooster.

His first thought is his smuggling partner from the war. But that guy knows logistics, not explosives. He's a supply guy. Plus, the last time they worked together, Sullivan got caught.

The television above the bar flashes a banner across the screen: *Sex Offenders Use Bedsheets to Escape Correctional Facility*. Apparently, the Lookout Mountain Youth Services Center in Golden has a security problem.

If only Mandrake—his high school buddy—wasn't in prison. He'd be perfect, assuming Sullivan could keep him sober. Mandrake knew almost as much as Sullivan when it came to bombs. The operation on the dam requires getting out on the water. Sullivan isn't a boat guy. But Mandrake is.

If nothing else, he needs to run this proposal by Mandrake and see if he thinks it's feasible.

"Tell you what," Sullivan says. "It sounds do-able. Let me do some research, OK? Then get back to you."

"How long do you need?"

"How serious are you?"

"I'll give you a thousand right now, just for your research."

Sullivan waits while Sarah pulls her bag into her lap. "What's your timeline?"

Sarah looks up. "We'd like things to happen before the end of the month." She hands Sullivan an envelope.

"Give me a week. I need to check some things." Sullivan pulls up the envelope flap and sees hundred-dollar bills. He doesn't count it. She's offering millions later.

Sarah pushes from the table with a smile. "I knew you were the right guy."

Sullivan leans forward, unprepared for her abrupt departure. He's all but agreed to her plan and now she's out of here? "The night's young," he says. "Want to do something?" He raises his eyebrows.

Sarah pauses, her smile flattening. "Aren't you the smooth talker? I've got to run, but maybe we can go *do something* when you give me your answer. How's that sound?"

Sullivan's stomach sinks. It sounds like a man going home alone. Again.

He hides his disappointment. "I'll be in touch."

Sarah glides toward the door, her long hair like an arrow focusing Sullivan's eyes on her backside. Which he won't get any of tonight.

He smiles, pushing back from the table. Time to go research some bombs. Three million dollars to blow stuff up justifies the sacrifice.

Right after he tries his luck at one of those Cinco de Mayo parties.

ZAHN

Elk Trace, near Buena Vista, Colorado-May 5th
When did they start selling four-packs? Only two beers remain from my experiment with the local Eddyline brewery. Perez said these guys put out a mean IPA, and he wasn't wrong. I'll be buying more of this Cranky Yankee. It's just the math throwing me off. If each beer in a six-pack is twelve ounces and each beer in a four-pack is sixteen ounces, how much beer have I drunk? I set my pint glass on my dining room table and count fingers. Then I give up.

Just like I did on the SAR mission. Just like I did when Kristee offered me a pass on Mt Harvard. When the going gets tough, Z-man goes home. I don't deserve a nickname.

I'd been so convinced this move to the Rockies would turn my life around. Grinding away as a military contractor in Florida for five years was a convenient way to forget about my divorce, lose contact with my daughter, and—with enough beer—banish all memories of my dead son. Those five years are why I'm out of shape. And if I'm honest, that period of nothingness is how I lost my confidence. I toppled from flying planes and commanding airmen to pushing a pencil as a middle-aged divorcé. I'm afraid to do the things I know I can do because I'm out of practice.

The thing I did saving my fellow hikers from a nasty fall doesn't count. That was muscle memory. Instinct. It's when I have time to ponder that I screw things up.

I pop the second-to-last beer and pour it. The label catches my eye and when the last drop falls, I twist the can for a better look. There's a bike chain wrapped around a crank surrounded by hop buds. I examine the name of the beer again. Crank Yanker, not Cranky Yankee. I should have known a local brewery west of the Mississippi would be more likely to focus on mountain biking than poking fun at Civil War Union soldiers.

And with that astute observation, I realize I'm more than a little drunk. Continuing my study of the can, I read 7% ABV. That's twice the alcohol of the Coors Light I'd been drinking back in Florida. No wonder I got the beer name wrong.

The question I'm wrestling with is whether this move has been a simple transition from one house to another, or whether it will be the game-changer. The reboot I need for a fresh start. The goals I formulated while dragging a U-Haul trailer out here were both mental and physical. I want a relationship with my daughter Daria. She stopped coming for summer visits several years back. I need to convince my ex-wife Sheila I can act like a father figure again— something I haven't done since we lost our oldest child. My mental goal is to get over his death. But I can barely say his name.

The physical goals are proving hard to execute. I want to do something useful, both for myself, and my new community. I did nothing in Florida to help anyone, except for sending the monthly cut of my military retirement that goes to Sheila. Not that I have a choice on that, and she deserves it for putting up with me and raising our daughter alone. I spent my time shut in my apartment doing exactly what I'm doing now.

I take another sip, surprised my glass is already empty. After a refill, I study the four empty cans in front of me and then eye the wastepaper basket by my refrigerator. About a 15-foot shot.

The first can goes wide to the left, not even touching the trash container. The sound of the can rolling into my tiny laundry room is almost a taunt.

The clock on my stove reads 11:14. Way later than I should be up. I signed up for a yoga orientation tomorrow at the community center. Becky, at SAR, told me about it last week, noting it caters to an older crowd and is inexpensive. Her comments tagging me as an old guy aren't lost on me, especially since I'd assumed we were about the same age. And yes, my cargo pants have a couple of holes in them, but who wears their new stuff to search and rescue?

I line up my chair with the trash can and make another toss. I'm short, and the can rolls back in my direction.

Tomorrow's the day I'll start fresh. I might be a little hung over, but watching yoga shouldn't be too difficult. I grab one of the two remaining cans and line it up with the trash. If I make one of my last two shots, I'll go to bed and hit yoga in the morning. I shoot, following through with my wrist like my high school days. I'm left again, this time close enough that the can hits the side of the bin before bouncing to the floor.

I grab the last can. I'm overthinking the trajectory. If I just relax, my shot will fall where I want it to. I release my breath and murmur "be the can" imagining myself cross-legged on a mat tomorrow. The can arcs end over end, landing directly in the middle of the trash before bouncing off an empty milk carton and clattering to the floor.

Screw yoga. I rise from my chair and head to the fridge for another beer.

SULLIVAN

Buena Vista Correctional Complex, Colorado-May 10th
"I'm here to see Mitch Mandrake," Sullivan locks eyes with the guard manning an observation cubicle at the entrance to the Buena Vista Correctional Complex. He hands over his driver's license and wipes the sweat from his forehead.

The guard examines Sullivan's identification. The Chinese have this whole fake driver's license thing down to a science. The old smuggling partner had proved useful after all. When Sullivan needed advice on a false identity, his friend pointed him to a website offering a 5-50-500 deal. Five-day turnaround time, fifty bucks in shipping, and five hundred bucks for the fake Colorado driver's license. All he had to do was send in a picture of his actual license and less than a week later—boom! He has an official Colorado license in the name of one Alexander Buskirk. Sullivan figures he'll go by "Alex."

Sullivan wipes his brow again. He's at eight-thousand-feet of elevation in the middle of the Rockies and it's mid-May. Why is it closing in on 80 degrees already? The guard puts Sullivan's driver's license number into his computer, presumably to see if it matches the visitor reservation. He hands Sullivan back his license, and presses a button to buzz him through.

Another guard waits on the other side of the turnstile. She instructs Sullivan to empty his pockets and relinquish his cell phone. He's done a little research on phones while waiting for the Chinese company to come through on the ID. Sullivan could have bought a $30 burner phone from any drugstore, but figures he'll need a smartphone for this operation. Best Buy sells him one for $180 with a pre-paid SIM card. He told them his name was George Clooney when he forked over the cash. They didn't even bat an eye.

The guard stows Sullivan's possessions in a locker, then hands him a receipt. He stuffs it in his pocket as he's escorted to the minimum-security side of the prison.

"Stall Three." the guard points to the numbered cubicles. "You've got thirty minutes."

Sullivan walks toward the stall, noting the empty spaces on either side. A slow day. Mitch Mandrake sits behind plexiglass, his hands on the counter, wearing a huge smile. No cuffs.

"What's up, brother?" Mandrake asks as Sullivan settles into the folding chair across from him.

"Long time no see," Sullivan pulls the chair closer to the counter.

"You never write, you never call. What's up with that?" Mandrake laughs. And laughs again.

That laugh—like a sheep. Sullivan has forgotten about that. Mandrake laughs a lot. Too much. Annoying unless you are around him enough to get used to it.

Mandrake continues. "Seriously, it's good to see you, but haven't heard shit from you."

He's right about that. Sullivan hasn't reached out since Mandrake was sent away for selling drugs nine years ago, back when Sullivan still wore an Army uniform. He's not sure why Mandrake is bringing it up. Guys don't need regular hugs and kisses to know they're friends.

"I got out of the Army about a year after you got in trouble. Stayed in Texas for a while, then moved up here and started working for Denver Water. Great job, but it dried up in the end. I'm sort of in the market for something new."

"Aw, you moved to Colorado to be close to me, right?" Mandrake laughs again. Sullivan laughs, too, but Mandrake's smile fades. "So, I could ask about your folks, or talk about the Seahawks if you're still a fan. Or we could get down to business. Why are you here?"

Mandrake has always been a "cut to the chase" type of guy. Especially if it means he can get to the business of drinking, smoking, and getting high a little faster. Mandrake's probably already guessed Sullivan is here to ask for something or offer something.

Sullivan eyes the camera on the wall. "Is it just us talking here?"

"Not really. They've got a separate room for private conversations over there." Mandrake points to his right. "But that's only for lawyers and their clients. This area has video going, but the rumor is that they just store the recordings. They only listen to them if some shit goes down."

Mandrake leans forward and leers. "You wanna talk private, Galen? I'm not really that type of guy, but for you…" He lets out his staccato laugh.

Sullivan laughs too. Same old Mandrake. "OK. Here's what I got. I told you I'm between jobs. I'm thinking about branching out on my own. Got some sponsors willing to invest in my proposed business." Sullivan smiles at his own bullshit. "You're due out in a year or so. I thought you might help me get this thing off the ground. It's right up your alley." Sullivan pauses, trying to gauge whether Mandrake reads between the lines.

Mandrake furrows his brow. "Yeah, I'm interested. I got nothing lined up on the outside. Must be some serious trade secrets though if we can't talk here." Mandrake tilts his chair. "Let me see your phone."

"Uh, it's back there," Sullivan tilts his head toward the exit.

"Shit, right. What do you use to talk to your mom, girlfriend, or whichever best friend replaced me?"

"Same as everyone. Phone, Facetime, Facebook, Snapchat." Sullivan stops talking. He sees where Mandrake is going with this. But how the hell does Mandrake have access to those apps? He glances at the guard behind him. This is the wrong place to ask. "No, wait. Don't use any of those. I got a new business email. Alex B one seven one at Gmail." He pauses. "Can you remember that? The 171 is my old Army unit."

"Got it. Alex B one seven one," Mandrake says. "What did you do in the Army, anyway? I heard a rumor you were blowing shit up? Just like the old days?"

"I spent my time taking the bad guys' bombs apart. All that time I spent on your little boom-booms so they wouldn't kill us? That shit came in useful."

Mandrake brays like a donkey so loud, Sullivan checks for the guards. "Yeah, I should have done what you did. Look where my work got me." Mandrake holds his wrists together like they're cuffed.

"Never say never." Sullivan scoots back his chair and stands. "Maybe we can work together."

Mandrake's laugh rings in Sullivan's ears as he leaves the room.

May 11th

Sullivan's phone vibrates in his pocket as he walks across the parking lot away from the mattress factory. He pulls it out and checks the screen. His first email on his new Gmail account. Mandrake has a line to the outside world. The text reads:

Signal app, User: Rogera, PW: N1953YMoon

Sullivan climbs in his truck, rummaging through the center console for a pen and paper. Just in case the email disappears.

Signal? Sullivan isn't familiar with it. He pulls up the app store on his phone. *Signal* shows as a free option. He downloads the app and opens it.

The home screen asks for his username and password. Sullivan logs in with the info Mandrake has sent. Nothing happens. He waits a minute. Nothing. He shakes his head and secures the phone onto the dash mount before starting his truck. Five minutes from his apartment, his phone lights up.

Go to settings for this app, turn off all notifications, sounds, awards, select the 'disappearing messages' option. Pay for it. Answer this message when you're done.

Sullivan pulls into a grocery store parking lot. Pay for it? Shit. He's trying to go cash-only for all this and not leave an electronic trail.

Hustling into the store, he scans the racks next to the checkout counter. He spots a stack of Google Play gift cards. That'll do it. Sullivan pays cash for the card and returns to his truck. He grabs his phone, adjusts the settings, and purchases the option. When he returns to the screen for answering Mandrake, it's blank.

Shit. What to do now?

Thirty seconds later, it lights again:

Got to be quick, reply to this one

Sullivan punches a reply:

Done

The response is immediate:

Mandrake: *Alright bud, welcome to Signal, I got this set to 30 seconds then the messages disappear, OK? So you either remember what we say or write it down, got it?*

Sullivan: *Got it*

Mandrake: *Don't screenshot it. That defeats the whole purpose.*

Sullivan: *OK*

Mandrake: *What you got planned?*

Sullivan: *Got a job for a little boom boom work*

Mandrake: *Ha, it IS like old times, need me to line you up with the materials?*

Sullivan: *Yep, but I could use you for the actual work too*

Mandrake: *That ain't happening soon, still have a year left, can you wait?*

Sullivan: *No. And neither can you. Your share is a half-million.* He's thought this through. A half-million dollars is plenty for a support guy who's likely going to spend it on drugs and alcohol. Sullivan is the one running this show.

Long pause.

Mandrake: *We buying the boom boom out of our share or they paying?*

Sullivan: *We clear a million and split it.* That's a lie. But everything will be easier if Mandrake thinks it's a 50/50 split.

Mandrake: *Who's hiring?*

Sullivan: *This thing's secure?*

Mandrake: *Like Fort Knox. Who we working for?*

Sullivan: *Environmental group supposedly. Woman named Sarah. Little older than us but hot, in a hippie kind of way.*

Mandrake: *Supposedly?*

Sullivan: *Sarah knows a rancher I know. He might be behind it.*

Mandrake: *Name?*

Sullivan: *Why do you need to know?*

Mandrake: *You want my help or not?*

Sullivan: *Timmons*

Mandrake: *Sarah and Timmons. The Hippie and the Cowboy. Like a movie title. Why do you need me?*

Sullivan: *Need someone I can trust. Who can get the stuff. Drive the boat and do scuba shit.*

Mandrake: *Water demolition? Cool.*

Sullivan starts to type then stops. He's got Mandrake's attention now.

Mandrake: *OK, I'm in. Timeline?*

Sullivan: *Wait. Like you're willing to break out? Or you'll support from where you're at?*

Mandrake: *Assuming I only get my half-million if I'm with you. I can get out.*

Sullivan: *How long to line up the stuff?*

Mandrake: *Depends, we just detonating, or timing too?*

Sullivan: *Timing—but I got that—need you to get stuff for two jobs. So, two 75's*

Mandrake: *Holy shit dude, we doing a mountain?*

Sullivan: *Kind of. Make it two 75's and a 50. Second job needs some insurance. I'll work the timers. You get the bulk. Got it?*

Mandrake: *Yep, need a week to arrange, plan, all that shit. Break out's the easy part. I'll reach out to you here with an update. Or if I have to abort.*

Sullivan: *KK.*

Mandrake: *Getting the band back together, bro.*

Sullivan: *Yeah.* Sullivan pauses before sending. He needs Mandrake. But he's nervous about him too. He edits his text: *Yeah, bro!* and hits send.

Sullivan closes the app and remounts the phone on the dash. Gripping the steering wheel, he scans the parking lot. Everything looks crisper than it did five minutes ago. He lowers his window and sniffs. Fresh bread from the store's bakery. He taps the Signal app again. All the messages to and from Mandrake have disappeared. But who knows where they are out on the web? Hopefully, Mandrake knows his shit.

Sullivan needs to let Sarah know they are a "go." He also needs earnest money, plus additional funds for the bombs and gear. He tabulates what's required: explosives, timers, climbing gear, scuba gear, condo rental, boat rental, and incidentals. Probably fifty grand. And the five hundred grand he plans to ask for upfront.

Sullivan exits Signal and dials Sarah, but punches the call off before it rings. If he wants to discuss secret stuff with this woman, he'd best use an app like Mandrake. He pictures Sarah in that tight shirt, with that crazy-ass look in her eyes. Screw the app. Nothing's more secure than face-to-face. He dials again.

"Hey Galen," Sarah answers.

"I'm flattered I made your contacts. And I'm up for our planned date."

"Galen, that's awesome! I knew you'd come around."

"But how about another drink first? We can talk about specifics."

"I'm in." Sarah's voice sounds throaty. "Same time, same place tomorrow?"

"See you then."

Maybe he should have negotiated the earnest money before he pulled the trigger with Mandrake. If Sarah and her group back out, that leaves Mandrake committing to supplies, and possibly breaking out of prison with no reward on the other side. Not a major problem for Sullivan, but dangerous as hell for Mandrake.

On the other hand, Sullivan couldn't commit to Sarah's plan without knowing whether Mandrake would help. One of those Catch 22s, or, as they used to say back in the Army, damned if you do, damned if you don't. Time to quit worrying about the what-ifs and focus on the plan.

May 12th

Sullivan pulls into The Rooster's lot next to a BMW 525. Definitely the same Beemer from the first meeting with Sarah. He shakes his head and ambles to the front door. The familiar scent of hops and grease greets him as he pauses in the entryway, letting his eyes adjust to the darkness.

Sarah waves at him from the same table as last time. Sullivan saunters over and eases into a chair, like he has all the time in the world. Even though his gut churns.

"Hey." He smiles, scanning the room. No one looks suspicious. "That your Beemer out there?"

Sarah's eyes narrow. "It is. Why?"

"No biggie, I recognized it from the first time we met. Just a bit surprised to find a tree-hugging, dam-hating hippie, driving a fancy car like that."

Sarah seems to relax a bit. "I know it's against the stereotype, but it fits my budget."

"Huh?"

"It was free. My dad drove it for a couple of years. Got a good deal through one of his clients and as soon as he figured out I wasn't going back to school, he gave it to me. I'm not one for looking a gift horse in the mouth."

Sullivan laughs, "Yeah, guess I wouldn't either." He leans forward. "So, we're in."

Sarah's eyes light up, then her brow furrows. "Who's we?"

"Can't do this alone. You planning on helping me?"

Sarah shakes her head.

"I've got a buddy who's got the supply connections and he'll help execute."

"I can only guarantee you the three million."

"Plus supplies. My partner and I will split it, but I need fifty grand for everything else. And I want a half-million up front."

Sarah scrunches her nose. "We expected the down payment, but hadn't counted on the supply money."

Sullivan sighs. "Are you going to bicker over 50K? This is a complex operation. Two timed blasts, and possibly a third requires synchronized timing devices plus explosives. None of this stuff is easy to get. I can't just go on eBay and order it." The last part isn't technically true. Sullivan plans on using the internet for some of his supplies.

"Well, I need to take this info back to my side. If they give me a go-ahead, I'll bring the supply money next time we meet."

Sullivan spots the familiar glow in Sarah's eyes. She's excited about blowing the dam. He's excited too. He'd expected an argument about the half-million earnest payment, not the 50K. Even if this whole thing doesn't work out, he'll walk away with a significant chunk of change.

He just wishes Sarah would direct some of that excitement toward him. There's nothing like talking money to buzzkill a potential night of fun.

"Let's make this happen," Sullivan says. The last time he'd used that line at a bar a woman agreed to go home with him. This time he's going home alone. But that's OK. He's playing the long game.

MANDRAKE

Buena Vista Correctional Complex, Colorado-May 11th

From the outside looking in, the warden at the Buena Vista Correctional Complex is in charge. He decides who gets work release, who's allowed visitors, and who sits solitary. But from the inside, inmate Big Bobby Dorsey runs the place.

Serving a twenty-year sentence for drug trafficking, Dorsey established himself, first at the Centennial Correctional Facility in Cañon City, then at the Buena Vista prison, as the guy who can get things when you need them. Everything, that is, but a prison uniform large enough to comfortably contain his massive frame.

Dorsey's reticence, rolling expanses of flesh, and slow-moving build belie a brain operating on all cylinders, twenty-four-hours-a-day. His lungs are shot from years of smoking, so he runs his prison empire with a team of lackeys. Mitch Mandrake's cell phone comes from Dorsey. Mandrake's supply of pills comes from Dorsey.

Mandrake earned Dorsey's admiration back at the Cañon City prison, moving Dorsey's phones between two rival gangs. Dorsey labeled Mandrake a balls-of-steel negotiating guru. He probably gave Mandrake more credit than he deserved. Mandrake isn't brave, he's just willing to do anything to get high. But Dorsey trusts him. And Dorsey can get the explosives.

Big Bobby owns the picnic table on the north end of the paved basketball court. Dorsey sets up as soon as prisoners are released to the yard, rotating his callers to the opposite side of the table with a brief head nod when their turn comes.

The peaks across the valley remain topped with snow, but it's warm enough on the compound to leave jackets in the cells. Some prisoners shoot hoops while others shoot the shit. Mandrake strolls past a three-on-three match-up. He makes eye contact with Dorsey. Dorsey gives a single shake of his head. Mandrake stays near the basketball court, mingling with some other prisoners for the next forty-five minutes.

While he waits, Mandrake surveys the fence line. Then the doors. He counts the cameras in the yard. The guards have a routine and Mandrake checks for deviations. Although he's due to get out in a year, that hasn't stopped him from "what if-ing" escape options ever since he arrived. He's used his contraband phone to study the local geography.

Mandrake was the one who came up with the method for inmates to charge their illicit phones. No one ever had an excuse to be allowed behind the USB-equipped television in the common room until Mandrake asked Dorsey to request an old DVD player. Now, when someone says, "Let's watch Shawshank Redemption again," everyone recognizes it's someone else's turn for phone juice.

Dorsey glances his way. Mandrake sidles over and sits. Dorsey says nothing. Mandrake and Dorsey share at least one thing in common. They both believe in cutting to the chase. Mandrake clasps his hands together, resting them on the sunbaked concrete of the table. Fetid body odor wafts off Dorsey. Mandrake presses his lips together and tries not to focus on Dorsey's triple chin. It must be hard to keep all that surface area clean when you're only allowed two minutes in the shower, and Dorsey's probably allowed more time than others.

"I'm going over the fence. I need 225 pounds of TNT delivered locally." His voice carries a confidence he doesn't feel. But Big Bobby respects a man with a plan. Mandrake jerks his head toward town. "By next week." He chokes back his reflexive laugh. "I'll pay twenty G's, but you got to tell me how to get the money to you."

Dorsey's eyes narrow. He sucks in a breath. "Little more challenging than a fucking cell phone," he rasps. "Meet me here tomorrow."

Mandrake smiles, and stands. Dorsey glances over Mandrake's shoulder. Another prisoner brushes past Mandrake. On the way back to the main building, Mandrake passes a guard.

The guard sneers. "Get what you needed?"

"Fuck you," Mandrake mutters. These guys know Dorsey runs stuff on the inside, but they either have no clue how he does it, or they don't care.

Mandrake spends the rest of the day rehashing the Dorsey deal, and reviewing his escape plans. If Dorsey wasn't planning to help, he would have told Mandrake *no* straight off the bat. Mandrake expects twenty G's falls a little short. Dorsey will probably charge him twenty-five or thirty. He hopes Sullivan's budget has some flex.

The prison break presents an easier challenge. Inmates never try to escape this place. Not because it's too hard—quite the opposite. The Buena Vista Correctional Center is practically a halfway-house to the outside. If you get moved to the BVCC, you're likely within a couple of years of getting out. Who would want to escape that close to release?

At first glance, the work-release program seems the likeliest escape option. But the guards on those details are the ones with their shit together. If someone is stupid enough to escape, the system doesn't want it happening while the prisoners are out mingling with the local populace.

The second and third-tier level of guards, guys just trying to earn a paycheck, work the inside, the yard, and the cells. Best as Mandrake can tell, no one patrols the prison's perimeter.

The grounds hug the Arkansas River, backing against steep terrain that climbs up to ten- and eleven-thousand feet. The town of Buena Vista rests north of the prison. The small town of Johnson Village lies south on the highway to Denver. To the west, a field of scrub brush and piñon trees lead to the north-south state route to Leadville and Salida, then the airport, and four miles on, the massive fourteen-thousand-foot mountains that make up the Collegiate Peaks.

If Mandrake escapes, the roads to the interstates and big cities will be the first place they look. But Sullivan's "business" opportunity is right here in the Rockies. Mandrake plans on staying close.

He squats on the toilet in his cell, tapping on the contraband cell phone between his knees and hidden under his coveralls. He needs a local place to hole up—and he's got an idea.

Mandrake hits the jackpot on a local Facebook group's message thread. *Trash-shaming.* He hadn't even known it was a thing. Some woman pissed off at the world has posted a picture of a faded piece of trash she found outside her home owners' association dumpsters.

Losers need to clean up their game she posts.

They haven't been here in six months. They're summer residents. Get a life. Another resident answers.

Mandrake scrolls back to the picture of the trash. He zooms in on the address label.

Les & Marjorie McCorkle

39112 Yale Crest

Buena Vista CO 81211

Bingo. Mandrake saves the picture on the phone, and finishes squeezing off his loaf.

•   •   •

Swirls of snow dance through the prison yard as Mandrake strolls toward the picnic table. Snow in May is not unusual up here in the mountains. It's too cold for basketball. Groups of inmates huddle close in conversation.

Big Bobby Dorsey dominates his picnic table office, his massive gut tucked under the concrete slab, straining the seams of the canvas coat prisoners are allowed when temperatures drop below the 40s. No one sits across from Dorsey. Mandrake's gaze drifts toward the table, Dorsey catches his eye and nods. Mandrake veers to the table. The wind blows at his back, sparing him from Dorsey's cloying scent. He clasps his hands atop the table and waits.

"I can get it, but the money's not going to work," Dorsey wheezes.

Mandrake looks at his folded hands then back to Dorsey. "How much more?"

Dorsey breathes heavily before providing a semblance of a smile. "Not more. No money. I want services-in-kind."

"What exactly you got in mind, Dorsey? I'm not exactly a blow job type of guy." Mandrake brays a nervous laugh.

Big Bobby's eyes harden. "Don't press your luck, little man. I want you to accept delivery of some goods. Then deliver them. You get your stuff when you give my people their stuff. Straight swap. No money."

"What do you want me to receive? I'm not even out yet."

"Some fenty shit. Street name China Town," Dorsey says. "I just need to know when you're leaving and where you're headed. The stuff you're accepting will come through commercial delivery." Dorsey's breath is labored, as if the three sentences have worn him out.

Mandrake listens, amused. Fucker sounds like that alien, E.T., when he gets sick in the old movie. *El-lee-ut.* Mandrake presses his lips together. "That could work. I'm staying local and can get an address to you when I'm out and have confirmed it's good."

Dorsey dips his chin in what Mandrake assumes is agreement.

"Why put me in the middle?" Mandrake says, starting to take in the possible risk. "Why don't you just mail your stuff straight to your guys?"

"My guys are new. Let's just say I'm testing their loyalty." Dorsey gulps a shallow breath.

"What if they don't deliver?"

"I said they were new, not stupid." Dorsey pauses. "How're you getting out?"

"Going straight out behind me." Mandrake tilts his head toward his shoulder.

Dorsey cracks a half-smile. "Right. The generator lights don't cover that fence. What about the power?"

"Haven't figured it out yet. I want to leave in the evening, before they move us back to our cells."

"Give me a date," Dorsey breath comes in spurts. Mandrake wonders if he'll make it through the conversation. "I'll have wire cutters for you in the phone hole. Have a guy cut the power fifteen minutes before curfew."

"Thanks," Mandrake raises his eyebrows in surprise. "Next Friday? Can you work it by then?"

Dorsey grunts. "What are you up to, Mandrake? What're the explosives for?"

"Water, the new gold. Environmentalists. Cowboy ranchers. Can't share the details."

"You being smart with me?"

"No, man. Just joking with you. Seriously, not really sure who's running us." Mandrake decides to dial back on the smart-assery. He needs Dorsey.

Mandrake can't believe his luck. Dorsey's help with the escape is unexpected, but self-serving. Dorsey obviously wants his end of the deal to go through as much as Mandrake.

Dorsey shifts his gaze. Mandrake takes the hint. He's dismissed.

Mandrake stands. "Thanks again, Dorsey."

Dorsey sways his head side to side, catching his breath. "Don't thank me. Just do your end." He pauses for a few seconds. "Otherwise, my guys' second test will be the 'how fast can we make Mitch Mandrake disappear' test. Questions?"

Mandrake's eyes widen as he swallows. He's in the big leagues now.

"Nope. I got it."

ZAHN

Buena Vista, Colorado-May 13th
What kind of person feels guilty for missing an opportunity to watch a yoga class? Me. My evening pity party last week proved too much for a yoga orientation the next day. This Monday is different. I capped last night off with only three beers. Partly, so I'd make yoga. Mostly, because today is my ride-along with Rick Perez. Two activities before noon make this my busiest morning since moving to Buena Vista.

The sun peeks from behind Midland Hill, and I lower my truck visor on the drive into Buena Vista. The community center is built near the river, close enough to the low peaks that the sun has disappeared again. I grab my down jacket and climb from the truck. Yesterday we had snow flurries. Today will hit seventy degrees. This might be one of the warmest springs on record, but the air carries a chill before noon.

"Morning. I'm Tyler," I say as I approach the yoga instructor at the front of the room.

"Thought you were coming last week?" She takes in my cargo pants and belt with a smile. "I'm Ruth. You bring any shorts or sweats?"

"I had a conflict last week. Sorry." There's no way I'm telling her I couldn't get out of bed. "I just want an orientation. You know, watch and see if I like it."

Ruth tilts her head. "Usually orientation means you're trying it. But you can watch if you want." She motions her head toward the entrance. "Grab a chair."

Ruth runs her class through the wringer for the next hour, starting slow but working up to abdomen and hip work that mimics what I used to do for PT in the Air Force. Toward the end of the hour, she winds down with exercises focusing on breathing. She closes the session with a poem about hope.

I kind of get into it. When Ruth had her class concentrate on breath, and focus on the present, I did the same in my chair. I felt something familiar. The calm and the focus reminded me of my flying days, following the navigator's directions into the drop zone for a parachute drop. "Breathe in…and breathe out" becomes "on course, on airspeed…prepare to drop." I could get into this.

After class, Ruth and I talk about registration options. I sign up for a month of Mondays.

"See you next week, Tyler," Ruth says. "You can start with one of our mats. But wear something besides those cargo pants."

The coffee shop where I'm meeting Perez is only four blocks away. I leave my truck parked at the community center so I can stretch my legs after my orientation session. The sun has climbed above the mountains, warming my back as I stroll up Main Street.

Perez stands outside The Elkhead, a cup of coffee in each hand. "Need cream or sugar?"

"Black's fine. Guess you're ready to go?"

"Some of us have been working for a couple hours already." Perez hands me a cup of coffee and turns toward his Tahoe before I can tell if he's smiling or not.

I consider telling him about my early morning yoga session, but think better of it. Perez doesn't look like the yoga type. And he certainly won't be impressed if I admit I just watched. "You going to give me a brief or anything?"

"We'll talk as we drive. I figure I'm not taking out one of our high school honor students." He shoots me a grin. "You've got a military background and dealt with a lot of shit. So, pay attention, watch me do my thing, and don't be afraid to ask questions."

I hoist myself into the passenger side of the Tahoe. Radios form a tower forward of the center console. A shotgun is locked between the seats. When I turn to latch my seatbelt, I glimpse canvas bags stacked in the cargo compartment.

"What's in the back?"

Perez reverses into the street, delaying his answer until he shifts into drive. "Got a first aid kit, a defibrillator, survival gear, a crime kit. Everything needed to save the good guys and stop the bad guys." He brakes at one of the two traffic lights in town. "We're just checking things out today. No speed traps or specific tasks. We'll keep our eyes open for weird shit and respond to any calls we get on the radio. Figured we'd head up Cottonwood Pass first, then back to town, and north up 24. Head south after that."

"I was up that side of the valley the weekend before last, trying to do Mount Harvard with Kristee."

Perez glances sideways at me. "She's a little young, don't you think?"

"For a 14-er? She's done lots of them."

"No, asshole. For you. You're like twice her age."

"Pretty sure I know that, especially after I had to bail. I couldn't hang." I laugh. "But, man, I really appreciate you pointing out the age difference. Come on, it's platonic. Like I'm taking my daughter on a hike, except that Kristee's in badass shape and leaves me in the dust."

"Huh."

We pass Cottonwood Hot Springs, and the radio crackles. *Chaffee 2, Salida.*

Perez grabs his mic. *Go ahead Salida, this is Chaffee 2.*

Chaffee 2, we've got reports of an ATV headed north on County Road 4 through the Midland Tunnels. You close enough to try to stop them on the way back?

Perez slows the Tahoe and pulls into a turnoff. *Salida, we're about 15 minutes out. I'll let you know when we're at the tunnels.*

Perez explains the call to me on the drive back through Buena Vista. "We've got two hundred miles of Bureau of Land Management, or

BLM, roads and trails back there for these guys to ride their ATVs, but they all want to ride on the roads. It's legal in Wyoming and South Dakota, but not here."

We cross the Arkansas, and turn up the valley, paralleling the river. I've been here before. The old 1800s narrow-gauge railroad from South Park to Leadville used to run on this same path. Come summer, rafters, kayakers, and paddleboarders will flood this stretch of the river. I spot a few raft guides testing the water today, but this time of year it's mostly fishermen taking advantage of the recent snow thaw.

As we approach a set of tunnels carved into cliffs flanking the Arkansas, Perez points at a vehicle silhouette.

"Here we go." Perez presses the accelerator.

"What?"

"That's the ATV coming back. The road ends at the highway six miles up, so I figured he'd come back to us."

Perez flips a switch on the dash. I assume it's the flashers based on the glance the ATV driver and passenger give us as they whip past. I twist in time to catch the ATV's brake lights lighting up as it slows. The vehicle exits the county road, entering BLM land.

"Is he running for it?" I say, adrenaline rushing at the thought of an off-road chase.

"Possibly. Or he's stopping. There's a parking lot around that corner."

Sure enough, after we pull a U-turn and make the same left, our renegade ATV idles next to a trailer in the parking area. Perez pulls the Tahoe parallel to the truck and trailer and flips off his lights. The ATV driver removes his helmet. His female passenger hops off and does the same.

Perez glances my direction. "Not a big deal, Tyler, but why don't you stay in the car?"

"Got it." I check out the teenager driving the ATV.

Perez climbs from the Tahoe, leaving the vehicle running. I crack my window a couple inches.

"Morning." Perez hooks his thumbs in the top of his belt.

"Morning, Sheriff." He flashes Perez a wide smile. "Guess you're not too happy about us driving on the road?"

"Sounds like you already know what you're doing wrong. Can I see your driver's license and registration?"

"You bet." The young man stands on the foot pegs, digging for his wallet. He hands Perez his identification, then reaches for a compartment next to his seat.

"Whoa, there." Perez steps back, dropping a hand to his holster.

"Shit." The teenager's eyes widen and he yanks his hand back like he's touched a hot stove. "I'm just getting my registration."

"Go ahead." Perez eyeballs the young man as he retrieves a white card. Perez pulls a pair of reading glasses from his breast pocket and scans the documentation. "Seth Robinson? From Breckenridge? That's you?"

Seth nods.

"Are you JD Robinson's boy?"

"Yes, sir. He's not going to be too happy with me for getting pulled over." Seth indicates the girl leaning against the trailer. "Brigit wanted to get a pic of me driving out of the tunnel on the north side with Mount Princeton behind me. It's a great shot for Instagram. We were coming straight back here when you got us."

I'm curious to see how Perez handles this, especially since he has some connection to Seth's father.

Perez glances over at Brigit before returning both documents to Seth.

"Here's the deal, Seth." Perez returns his glasses to his pocket, then put his hands on his waist. "The rules are the rules. The reason Chaffee County won't let you guys on the county roads is not because we don't think you all can't handle gravel and pavement. It's because we got a bunch of wealthy, slow-driving retirees over here, just like you got over in Summit County. They don't drive like you and me do. When they round a corner or enter a tunnel and meet a teenager riding a souped-up, off-road vehicle, how do you think they're going to react? We're not that worried about you. We're worried about them. You copy?"

To my surprise, Seth hangs his head. I haven't spent a lot of time around teenagers, but I'm under the impression humility is a rare commodity at this stage of life. Unless it's an act.

But Seth probably does feel a bit bad. At least he isn't trying to use his dad's name to get out of anything.

"Got it, sir. Won't happen again."

"OK. This is a warning. Next time it's a ticket." Perez turns toward Brigit. "You make sure he stays up here. OK?" Perez points to the gravel road leading into the BLM range.

"OK."

Perez climbs into the Tahoe, shifts into gear, and circles the parking lot to the exit.

"Kids will be kids," he says, shaking his head. "You catch all that?"

"I did. Who's JD Robinson?"

"JD?" Perez checks for traffic before turning onto the main road. "JD's a real estate developer over in Breckenridge, over the pass off I-70. Known for his generous donations to the Sheriffs' Fund of Colorado for the families of fallen law enforcement officers."

"Sounds like a man with a lot of money."

"Yeah, but most of us know him because of his condos—he donates weekends in some of his timeshares to those same families. JD's a real friend to cops. We've had several inter-county sheriff meetings up at his places."

"So, that's why his boy gets off without a ticket?" I hope Perez knows I'm flipping him shit. Sort of. I'm also curious.

"Bullshit." Perez's eyes turn dark. "I'm not a big ticket writer. First time I've seen that kid up here. I didn't run his license, but I wouldn't have with anyone else either. Just want him to know he was wrong and we're watching. So, no, he didn't get out of a ticket because he's Robinson's kid."

Watching Perez over the next six hours—after Perez issues three more warnings, two tickets, and arrests a young man in possession of cocaine—convinces me that Perez is as fair as I had suspected. And his job is way more interesting than I would've guessed. You never know what's coming next.

The best part is I get to watch while Perez runs the show. I'm not responsible. I'm not in charge. I can't screw anything up.

"What do you think?" Perez says at the end of the day.

"I liked it. A lot."

"How about we try it again this weekend? Something a little different."

"Like what?"

"Show up at the same time, same place," Perez says. "It'll be a surprise."

SULLIVAN

Arvada, Colorado-May 16th

Sullivan steers his truck around the perimeter of the packed Safeway parking lot, aiming for a row of empty spaces nearer the adjoining Dollar General. Sarah said she'd find him, so he parks and waits.

In less than thirty minutes, he'll either have $550,000 or be walking away, but he doesn't really want to walk. What's he scared of?

Getting caught. That's one thing. Another is Sarah and her group. Are they committed? Or are they just a bunch of granola-munching do-gooders trying to hire the lowest bidder for their dirty work? He'll know soon.

The more he pictures that money and that new life—well, hell—it'll be goodbye mattress factory, hello fresh start. Sullivan isn't certain whether he feels so good because of the money, or because Sarah has so much confidence in him. Putting this plan together has given him a surge of energy and purpose. Like back in Iraq. It's been a while since he's felt like this. He deserves it.

A car passes in the rearview mirror. Sarah's BMW pulls into a spot four spaces away. She waves, then reaches across to the passenger seat. A moment later, she steps from her car and walks toward his truck, a daypack slung over her shoulder.

So far, so good.

Sarah opens the truck's passenger door and crawls into the bucket seat next to Sullivan.

"Hey there, big boy." She smiles. "Ready for this?"

Sullivan's mouth twitches. He's got comebacks for Sarah's double entendres, but he's just not sure she'll think they're funny. "You tell me."

"I think we have ourselves a deal." Sarah unzips the top of the backpack's main compartment before setting it on the console between them, and pulls out a bundle of hundred-dollar bills. "A hundred hundreds in each. That's ten grand. There's fifty of them for your down payment; another five for your supplies." She returns the money to the pack.

Sullivan snatches the bag and rests it on his lap. He loosens the zippers further and reaches inside, pawing through the packs of bills, and counting to himself. When he finishes, he smiles. "Yep, we got ourselves a deal."

"Shall we talk details?"

"Why? Are you planning on helping?" Sullivan arches an eyebrow. "You said you want it to happen before the end of the month—which is incredibly ambitious, by the way."

"No, no. We're not getting involved in the actual... you know, the *doing it* stuff," Sarah protests.

Sullivan shakes his head at her. "You want simultaneous blasts at the tunnel and spillway. The alternate spillway will be rigged to blow if there's a problem with the main. How we do it is up to me and my partner, right?" Sullivan fixes his gaze on her. "No help necessary. The only detail we need is where to pick up the rest of the money when it's done."

"Oh." Sarah looks flustered, but continues. "We just want to make sure it's going to happen soon. Within the next two weeks would be best."

"We're planning by the end of the month. So, about payment? How is that going down?"

"One of our members has a time-share up in Breckenridge. Assuming you do it free and clear, and no one is after you, why don't we plan on doing the exchange there? It'll be me, not the friend. If you can't make that drop point, then I'll contact you with a meet location in Denver a day later."

"Timeshare? Like for just those days or what? We need a window for pick up. Not certain what day it's going down."

"She's got the place all spring. Unoccupied."

"OK, how about me and my partner use the condo to do our prep work?" Sullivan locks in another piece of his plan. "We'll stay there prior, do the op, meet you back to collect when it's done."

Sarah appears to consider Sullivan's proposition. "That could work. Let me talk with my guys. I don't expect a problem. I'll text you the address of the place. And the key code."

"OK. Tell your guys to make sure it's open in the next two days. I want a wide window for execution."

"No problem." She eyes the daypack in Sullivan's lap. "You can keep the pack."

"This is serious shit. My partner and I are putting our asses on the line." Sullivan looks down, then back at Sarah. "If you guys have a sudden change of heart, this money ain't coming back. You understand?"

Sarah's smile disappears. "Right back at you. Don't think we don't have connections. You try to skip out of here with this money, and we'll find you," she says, like she's consciously shifting the conversation back to an even keel. "We know it's serious. We've been planning this for some time. Your work will deliver a big message. This is it."

Sullivan says nothing.

"Just do your end." She fixes her eyes on him for another moment before climbing out.

The weight of $550,000 in cash presses on Sullivan's thighs. Time to get to work.

MANDRAKE

Buena Vista Correctional Complex, Colorado-May 17th
The sun has already dropped behind Mount Princeton when Mandrake clips a hole in the de-electrified prison fence and crawls into the dark. Well, sort of. Between the almost-full moon at his back and twilight over the Collegiate Peaks, Mandrake realizes he's picked one of the brightest nights of the month to escape. He's lucky the medium security facility issues forest-green uniforms to inmates.

His elbow grazes a patch of cactus. "Shit!"

Low crawling across the field will take all night at this pace. Mandrake sprawls only fifty yards from the prison wall, gasping the thin air, his elbows bloody. He presses his nose into the sharp dry grass, tugs his arm out of the low cactus, and tries to control his breath. After Sullivan visited, Mandrake resolved to come off his oxy painkillers and start working out. He should have started a month ago.

He lifts to a crouch, checks to his right and left before continuing across the field, legs bent and back hunched, keeping his profile low. After twenty yards, his quads burn. At the next bush, Mandrake stands, shakes out his legs, and lopes toward the highway.

The field softens and his boots sink into the earth. With about a football field-length remaining before the road, he hits a marshy spot. He yanks his mud-covered boot from the muck, then freezes at a sound in the brush. The moon, perched above the ridgeline overlooking the prison, lights up the white tails on the ass ends of two deer. They bolt across the open space and disappear.

Mandrake shakes his head and wades through ankle-deep water and mud. He crosses an unused railroad track toward a small rise leading to the highway's shoulder. Scanning for traffic, he heads toward a shrub at the base of the slope, swiping his muddy boots on the dry grass as he walks. At the bush, he plops down, leaning his back against the hillside and peering at the prison. Nothing moves. Break time.

He contemplates Sullivan's offer while catching his breath. Sullivan's always been the idea man. He's smart. Smarter than Mandrake for sure. But every time he falls in with his high school pal, Mandrake ends up in trouble. Maybe he should just set Sullivan up with his explosives and skip the rest. Do the swap with Big Bobby's guys, and then keep going.

Sullivan came up with some crazy-ass shit back in their Washington teen years. Sullivan had tossed homemade quarter sticks of dynamite into the Chehalis River, and Mandrake scooped up the stunned salmon. Five or six of the prized fish would've raked in over a hundred bucks on the local market. They had thrown a couple of flashing construction barriers into the river to help light things up.

It lit up all right. The river had erupted in an explosion of white from a sheriff's spotlight, like The Flaming Lips's laser-lit entrance at the concert he and Sullivan had crashed at the Seattle Pier the previous month. Except the vocalist was yelling at him to "freeze" instead of crooning psychedelic lyrics.

That had ended Sullivan's string of great ideas. No fish, no money. Sullivan disappeared into the night, leaving Mandrake with beer and fireworks. At least they didn't nail him for the pot. He tossed that in the river.

The beer or homemade explosives alone might have resulted in a simple warning, but the destruction of government property—those fucking sawhorse construction signs—meant ninety days of juvie.

But Sullivan's newest offer? A half-million bucks? It's enough money for his dream life. Drugs to take him up and drugs to bring him down. Maybe a woman in between. A half-million would do that. He'll stick with Sullivan on this one.

•   •   •

Intermittent traffic on Highway 24, the northern backbone of the Arkansas River Valley, adds ten minutes to Mandrake's escape plan. Like playing Frogger on his old gaming console, he waits for a gap in traffic. The good news: once across, he's no longer illuminated by the prison lights and can pick up his pace. The bad news? From here on, he risks running into people.

He spent most of last week scouting this area on his contraband smartphone. The search teams will expect him to put as much distance as possible between himself and the prison, meaning they'll search up and down the highways.

Mandrake covers his mouth to keep from laughing aloud. Thanks to Facebook, he plans on holing up only seven miles away at the McCorkles' empty Elk Trace house.

Seven miles ends up taking seven hours. Mandrake speeds up after crossing the road, but he has to pick his way around the houses and roads crisscrossing the approach to the mountains. Three hours in, he pauses at a vertical white shape looming in front of him like a giant schooner sail. It takes a minute before he recognizes Buena Vista's iconic drive-in movie theater. Mandrake can almost smell the pot he and Sullivan used to light in a crushed soda can back at their hometown drive-in, before they tore it down. Who knew drive-ins were still a thing?

His pace quickens at the wails of the prison sirens. The noise triggers the neighborhood dogs. Lights pop on in the houses he's trying to avoid. Mandrake breaks into a jog.

He cuts north across the road to Cottonwood Pass, then checks his phone and confirms his planned route. Another hundred yards and he hits a creek. He scouts for a dry crossing for five minutes before muttering *fuck it* and splashing across the freezing water. A riverside trail veers toward the mountains and Mandrake tries to jog again. Another five minutes, and he slows to a walk, nursing a cramp in his calf.

He spends another hour alongside the creek before spotting the gravel road leading up the slope, and the Elk Trace sign. The retreating moon barely illuminates the words:

PRIVATE COMMUNITY, ENTRANCE FOR RESIDENTS ONLY.

Tricky. Avoiding the community road means cutting through residential property. But using the road incurs the risk of traffic spotting him. His cell phone reads 2:54 in the morning. It's too late for these geezers to be out and about. Mandrake walks up the road into Elk Trace.

At the second turn, he descends between a series of three-acre lots. Dim lights illuminate windows in several homes. Mandrake scans for a house with no cars in the front and drawn curtains. He's tired and cold. He needs rest.

Fuck that. He needs a drink.

A thin green sign at the side of a driveway reflects the number 39112. The address from the Facebook post on the trash dumpster drama. The *Bad* residents, the McCorkles are not due back until summer.

If the McCorkles haven't changed their plan, Mandrake will sleep in a soft bed tonight. He surveys the darkened neighborhood. The houses sit far apart from each other. He'll stay low until Sullivan picks him up.

He creeps down the driveway, and works his way around the back side of the house, tugging on ground-level windows, and the sliding glass doors on the lower and upper-level back porches. Everything is locked.

Mandrake would rather not break a window. Behind the house, a rear door leads to the two-car garage. He twists the handle. Locked. But it gives a little when he pushes.

"This might work," he whispers, looking for something to pry open the door. At the side of the garage, he can make out two box-like structures about fifteen yards apart. Horseshoe pits. A cast-iron rod thrusts out of the first pit. Mandrake stoops and tugs at it. The rod holds fast, but when he works it side to side, it loosens. He yanks it from the ground.

He inserts the rod between the door and the frame and exerts pressure. The door strains before splintering, the metal bolt mechanism on the opposite side shattering under the force. Mandrake pushes his shoulder into the door, it pops open and he steps into the garage.

He pauses, allowing his eyes to adapt to the lack of moonlight. A workbench stands at his left and he lowers the rod to its surface careful not to make a sound. He can make out the front garage door. No cars are parked inside, but there is an outline of an ATV parked to one side. Not looking like anyone is home.

A door at the front of the garage leads into the house. He opens it and steps inside. A short flight of stairs leads to another door. He twists the handle.

Locked.

"Shit!" One thin door separates him from rest, and hopefully, a drink. He gropes his way down the stairs, returning to the garage. Grabbing the metal stake, he retraces his steps to the locked door. The bar smashes straight through the thin wooden veneer, like a drunkard's fist through a mobile home's paneled wall, allowing him to pry apart the locking mechanism and open the door.

"Honey, I'm home," Mandrake whispers, then laughs.

He steps through a cramped laundry room. On the other side, he enters a kitchen and dining area with sliding glass doors leading to the back porch. Horizontal blinds cover the windows. Fabric vertical blinds lay flat against the glass of the sliding glass doors.

Mandrake explores the kitchen. The refrigerator contains two open boxes of baking soda and a bottle of sriracha sauce. He finds two frozen cheese pizzas and three bags of vegetables in the freezer. An inventory of the cupboards reveals shelves of canned soup and vegetables, and enough whole wheat pasta, wild rice, and quinoa to last a month.

Fuck. Fifty houses up here and he lands with the vegetarians. And no booze, except for a bottle of cooking wine up in the spice cabinet. He's not that desperate. Yet.

Another flight of stairs leads to the basement. The house is built into the hillside, the basement opening to the downhill side. An outdoor porch light penetrates the vertical blinds, striping the stairs. He steps into an entertainment room with a pool table on one end and a home theater system at the other. In the middle a wooden cabinet supports a long counter.

A bar.

Mandrake approaches and reaches for the overhead cabinet door. A movement to his left makes him freeze. He pokes his head around the cabinet door and releases his breath. A damn mirror between the two cupboards scared him with his reflection. Mandrake peers into the open cupboard, but sees nothing. He gropes in the blind and smiles. His hands caress several 1.75-liter plastic bottles—as familiar to him as fondling his high school flame's tits in the front seat of his truck.

Bingo. Vegetarians drink too. Hell, not only do they drink, but they buy wholesale.

Mandrake raises a bottle toward the curtained window and the dim light. Unopened Jim Beam. He lifts the other bottles. Full. He'll be just fine.

Perched on the barstool, Mandrake fishes his cell phone from his pocket. He twists the top off the bottle for a quick pull before unlocking it. The basement backs up to forest, and he's comfortable with the phone's glow. The whiskey burn in his gut feels like coming home.

He pulls up the top number. *I'm in*, he messages. Big Bobby's drugs are on their way.

He goes to the second number in his recent calls and sends another message. *I'm out.* Sullivan's plan is active.

Mandrake leans back, smiling at the bottle in front of him. "Hello, Mr. Beam."

ZAHN

Buena Vista, Colorado-May 18th

I step into the Elkhead, embracing the scent of fresh grounds, and scan the crowded tables for Perez. The deputy waves from the back corner, but points me toward the counter for coffee.

I order the house black, grab it at the end of the bar, and join Perez. A half-eaten slice of quiche sits in front of my friend, a fact I silently file away in case Perez razzes me about my yoga class.

"Grab a seat." Perez scowls, and I suspect it's not because of his quiche.

"What's up?"

"Change of plans. I thought we'd spend the morning shooting the shit at a speed trap. That was the surprise I promised you. Instead, some dumbass at the prison decided to escape last night."

Perez looks at me like he expects a reaction. I'm unsure what this news means for my ride-along so I say nothing. Perez drops his eyes to his breakfast.

I break the silence. "How often does that happen?"

"Not very often." Perez returns his gaze to me. "This place is medium security and most of the folks go there as a transition before release. And this guy broke out the hard way."

"What's the easy way?"

"Almost everybody in there does work-release service out in the county. Why break out of the prison when you could just stroll away from some work project?" Perez finishes the second half of his quiche in two big bites.

"So, what do they have you, or us, doing about it?" I say and take a sip of my coffee.

"Not much, actually." Perez's mouth is full of food. "They figure the guy bolted out of the county to some major highway so he can get out of state. They want us to do what we normally do, drive around and keep our eyes open. I drew the section from Buena Vista up to the county line between us and Lake County, past Granite."

"Are you sure I should go on this thing? I mean, an escaped prisoner? Sounds like a bad day for a ride-along."

"You scared of a little action, Zahn? It's not like I'm going to make you catch the guy. Get off your ass." Perez finishes chewing as he pushes back his chair. "Let's go."

I snatch a lid for my coffee on the way past the counter. We climb into the Tahoe, and Perez points us north on Highway 24.

"Here's my thinking," Perez says, keeping his eyes on the road. "If he broke out last night, he's either trying to put distance between himself and the prison as fast as he can, or he's holed up somewhere close, and we're not going to find him. We'll focus on the first option and assume he's running. He escaped at night and he's trying to move, but also stay out of sight. If he's on foot, he can't be making more than a mile or two an hour."

"What if he got a ride or had someone meet him?"

"Well, then we got the same odds as if he was holed up. Zilch. A ride would have him out of the county in less than an hour."

We spend the next twenty minutes on the highway headed north, scanning our respective sides of the road, looking for anybody on foot. An abnormally warm spring has melted the snow in the foothills, and the rivers across the state are already running high. The only snow remaining sits above 12,000 feet, like rows of white caps on the Collegiate Peaks. As we drive, the Arkansas Valley narrows, funneling the road closer to the river, and reducing the options for someone without a car or a raft.

Perez checks the shoulder and the slopes leading to the western mountains. I scan the riverbanks on my side. Three miles out of town, I see three people on foot, all wearing waders and wielding fly rods.

Perez passes Granite and turns around at the junction for Independence Pass. Neither of us has seen anything of mention. Halfway back to Buena Vista, he exits the highway, crossing a bridge over the Arkansas which connects to the same county road where we caught JD Robinson's boy on Monday.

Perez's side of the car parallels vertical rock walls. We both scour the riverbanks. After riding a few minutes in silence, Perez says, "You never finished telling me about flying those missions. For that op in Iraq. What was it called?"

Oh, shit. Here we go. I had hoped enough time had passed since that SAR training mission for Perez to forget our trail conversation. Or at least figured out I wasn't overly excited about talking about it.

"CROWBAR. Operation CROWBAR."

Perez nods like I'm supposed to continue.

So, I do. "I only flew a couple CROWBAR missions. It was just like I told you—risky, but important."

"Why did you guys stop?"

I turn toward Perez. "We didn't. I did. I had to go home."

"In the middle of a fucking war? What happened?"

"My son got sick." I turn back to the window, waiting for Perez to push the conversation further, or change the subject.

Perez steers closer to the shoulder as a vehicle passes the other direction on the narrow road. "Heard they offered you a social studies job over at the high school. You thinking about that?"

I almost smile at Perez's lack of subtlety. I can talk about this. "No teaching for me. I don't want to lesson plan every day. All those teenage problems suddenly become my responsibility. Definitely not my cup of tea. Besides, the deal they offered included me getting my teaching certificate over the next two summers. No way."

"Hmm. What are you looking at then?"

"I'm not. I've got my pension. I'm volunteering with SAR and a bit at the library. Keeps me busy." I turn from the window. "What? You don't think I'm self-actualizing or something?"

"Nah, it's not that. It just seems like after being a commander, and fighting wars, and all that shit. Well, hell. I don't know. It seems like you would be used to being in charge."

"Been there, done that. Got the T-shirt. I like what I do now."

"Hmm."

We spend another two hours searching the back roads without a sign of anyone suspicious. We pull into Buena Vista for lunch. When we finish eating, Perez suggests I call it a day. "I've got to run these roads until I'm off shift. No sense you wearing out your ass all day like me."

"I won't argue with that." I've enjoyed my time with Perez and am relieved he hasn't brought up my botched SAR mission. "Hey, it's a little late in the season for cross-country skiing, but you'd mentioned something about taking me climbing?" I'm taking a risk with this question since Perez had offered it on the very SAR mission—the one I don't want to talk about. "When's that going to happen?"

Perez brightens. "I was thinking about that. How about I see what JD Robinson up in Breckenridge has for condo availability and we do something up there for a couple of days? They've got some good climbs on the east side of Dillon Reservoir."

"I'm in. I'll need instruction, though."

"Not a problem. I'll call JD and get back to you."

I walk to my truck, picturing a weekend in Breckenridge. Just what the doctor ordered. A bit of exercise and a lot of beer. Be nice to get away.

MANDRAKE

Elk Trace, near Buena Vista, Colorado-May 18th-20th

Mandrake wakes with a dead cat in his mouth. Or close. He scrapes at the dry crust caking the roof of his mouth, then wipes it on the side of the bed. His head throbs. Between his forced alcohol abstinence in prison and the 9,000-foot elevation, he should have throttled back on the booze last night.

He stumbles to the bathroom and coughs up a solid chunk of phlegm into the toilet. The mirror reflects a crooked smile. *Today's going to be a good day.* The medicine cabinet contains a plastic bottle of Tylenol, and he washes down a handful of the tablets with water from the sink.

Downstairs, he re-inventories the kitchen, discovering a box of granola in the process. He wants eggs, bacon, or at least some god-damned Cap'n Crunch. Instead, the McCorkles have left him oat clusters and water for breakfast.

Mandrake munches through a bowl of the granola and sets the dish in the sink. As he walks toward the stairs, he hears the sound of tires on gravel. From the living room window, he watches an Asian woman climb the steps of the neighboring house, and ring the bell. She's dressed in overalls, but Mandrake knows a tight ass when he sees one. A few minutes later, she returns to her SUV and leaves. Mandrake laughs. He might be the only person home in this entire neighborhood.

He grabs his bowl and pours more cereal, contemplating his not-so-busy day ahead. Arranging for Sullivan to pick him up. Collecting his package from Big Bobby's guys. Lowering his pounding head to his hands, Mandrake reshuffles his priorities. He needs a nap already. After stumbling upstairs, Mandrake stretches out on the McCorkles' king-sized bed and sleeps.

The head pulsing has disappeared when he wakes again in the early afternoon. After a piss, he heads downstairs and grabs a box of wheat crackers—fucking health nuts—from the kitchen, before heading to the basement. At the bar, he sets himself up with another glass of Jim Beam, adding ice he found in a mini-fridge he'd missed last night. He takes a pull before turning on his cell phone.

His Big Bobby message is unanswered, but that's not a surprise. He'll know by tomorrow whether it went through. The second message shows a reply. Sullivan.

It worked. Can't believe you made it look so easy. Where are you and when can I get you? Our sponsor says we need to complete the mission in the next ten days. She drives a Beemer. Can you believe that shit? Some hippie. Anyway, we need to meet up and talk supplies. ASAP.

Mandrake grunts. Classic Sullivan. Always ready to yak on and on about logistics and planning and shit. And why the fuck is he ASAP-ing Mandrake like they're in the Army? He taps the screen and pokes out a reply.

Yah, break out worked. Hold off for a couple. We need to let things settle. I'll write when I'm ready.

He adds his street address and sends the message.

The soiled prison uniform he wears smells like ass. Mandrake climbs the stairs to the master bedroom and opens the closet. Not a lot of choices. The McCorkles must bring most of their wardrobe with them when they move up here every summer. He finds a couple pairs of cargo pants, some t-shirts, and a sweatshirt.

Mandrake tries on the pants. They work fine if he leaves the top button undone. Old Man McCorkle—he of the granola and wheat crackers—is one skinny-ass bastard.

He peels off the pants and turns on the master bathroom shower. Thirty seconds later, he laughs. Yes! The McCorkles have left the water heater on.

Mandrake spends the next twenty minutes washing off the accumulated dirt and mud from his previous night's escape. When he finishes, he dons the cargo pants, a plain black t-shirt, and a gray, tight-fitting sweatshirt with UCONN emblazoned on the front.

He wastes the rest of the day watching TV from bed, working through the bottle of Jim Beam.

Mandrake rousts himself once to heat a can of black beans, squirting each spoonful with sriracha as he eats. By one in the morning, halfway through *Return to the Planet of the Apes*, his eyes droop and he crashes.

•   •   •

The beeping of a backing vehicle the next morning jolts Mandrake from his slumber. His head pounds again. He rolls out of bed and stumbles to the window, peeking between the blinds. A brown UPS truck reverses out of the McCorkles' driveway. The truck swings its rear end into the cul-de-sac, shifts into gear, and heads up the same hill Mandrake walked down two nights before.

He farts, then glances at his watch. 10:30. Mandrake doesn't feel nearly as bad as yesterday morning. A dull drumming instead of a pulsating throb. He farts again—fucking beans. He lopes down the stairs and approaches the front door from the side. A bulky letter pouch envelope leans against the window next to the door.

Mandrake reaches for the door, then stops. There wasn't an alarm on the back door. The garage door didn't trigger anything. Who would wire an alarm to the front door only?

He steps forward again. But what about a camera? Everyone uses those front porch camera thingies these days. He peers through the side window, searching for a camera. Nothing.

As he steps to the other window, a movement flashes.

Shit.

A gray-haired man in hiking pants and a fleece pullover is walking toward the house. Mandrake pulls his head back from the window, moving behind a foyer corner, out of sight. He leans out again, checking on the guy.

"No fucking way."

The man approaches the door.

Mandrake looks left and right. He can't just hide. He's left food and booze all over the house.

He scans the room, spotting a set of pokers near the fireplace. Bolting across the carpet, he grabs the closest one and returns to his corner, expecting the door to open any minute. He sticks his head out again and watches the man walk away, swinging the UPS envelope in his hand.

"Goddammit!" Mandrake smacks the poker down on the hallway runner. "That's my shit!" He moves to the living room window, tracking the man as he strides up the driveway of the adjacent house.

It's the asshat neighbor, probably picking up the package for the McCorkles so it won't rot on the porch until they show up in the summer. That's what neighbors do.

But this fucks up his plans. *He needs that package.*

Mandrake leans against the wall, tilting his head at the house next door. *Think. Think. Think.* A minute passes, and thinking isn't working. He returns to the Jim Beam bottle he's left on the kitchen counter.

As the familiar buzz returns, Mandrake's thoughts coalesce. It's not the neighbor's package. So, it's not like the guy's going to hide it. Hell, he's probably stacking the McCorkles' mail just inside the front door.

He'll just wait for the neighbors to leave, break into the house, and retrieve his envelope. Sure, there's a bit of risk, especially if they come back before he's finished searching. He'll need a better weapon than the poker.

Mandrake hasn't seen a gun rack or a gun safe anywhere in the house. The McCorkles, with their lentils, granola, and meatless kitchen, don't really strike him as gun people.

Still worth a look-see, though.

Where's the place you'd keep a gun if you only planned on using it as a last-ditch effort to protect your wife? Mandrake hasn't seen evidence the McCorkles have kids, so they might not use a gun safe.

He heads up the stairs to the master bedroom. He jerks open the top drawer in the nearest nightstand. Nothing. Two pens and some kind of Sudoku book.

Mandrake circles the bed and checks the other one. This one contains two tubes of moisturizer and a style magazine. He pops open the cabinet underneath the drawer. Empty.

Huh. He circles the bed again and opens the lower cabinet he missed the first time. Kneeling, he reaches in, groping the sides.

Bingo. A fabric holster leans against the inside of the cabinet. Mandrake pulls it out and removes the pistol. *Smith & Wesson* is engraved on the slide. It's loaded with a 9mm clip.

That'll do. Mandrake checks the load before stuffing the pistol in the back of his pants.

Downstairs, he drags a chair next to the living room window. If he's going to watch the neighbors, he might as well get comfortable.

He grabs another drink from the kitchen before rummaging through the cupboards again. Canned corn and salsa. Mmmm. Combined with last night's beans, Mandrake has a regular taco salad building in his gut. He returns to the living room, sets his food and drink on the end table, then pulls the pistol from his pants, setting it next to his meal.

Mandrake props his feet on the armrest of the couch with a perfect view of the house between the blinds. He leans forward, grabs a magazine off the coffee table in front of the couch, and reads about how to decorate the interior of a log cabin.

Several hours pass. Nothing moves at the neighbors' place. He makes a bathroom run, refills his drink, and returns to his observation post. As he gulps his second drink, his stomach rumbles in anticipation of another snack.

Halfway to the kitchen, Mandrake stops at the sound of a car door closing. He whirls and moves back to the window. A woman sporting the same color hair as her husband occupies the passenger seat of the Toyota 4-Runner parked outside the neighbors' garage. It backs out of the driveway, turning its rear end toward Mandrake. The driver's head looks male, wide ears jutting from the silhouette. Probably the same man who picked up the envelope that morning. Dammit. He's missed them coming out of the house. Did they lock the door? Did they hide a key? He'll have to figure it out.

Time to move. And no clue how much time he has. Mandrake leaves the same way he broke in, through the laundry room and out the garage. He peers around the corner of the house. The only other home in sight is the one the neighbors just left. But a car rounds the bend of the main road. Mandrake retreats behind the house. A door slams, and he peers around the corner. The Asian woman is back. He watches her ring the bell again. This time, she cups her hands to the window before returning to her Toyota.

Mandrake counts to sixty after the woman drives away. Then, he walks across the McCorkles' property, trudges up the small embankment to the neighboring driveway, and scans for any camera or electronic surveillance system.

Nothing. No one around here seems too worried about crime.

Mandrake turns the handle of the door. It opens. These guys are idiots.

He walks through a spartan mudroom to another door and opens it. He flinches at a rush of movement, fumbling for the pistol. By the time he's pulled it out, a small dog has its front paws on Mandrake's knees, wagging its tail. He nudges the dog hard with his foot. The dog backs away but keeps its tail wagging, like it thinks Mandrake is just joking about not being in the mood to play.

Mandrake turns and scans the mudroom, searching for the envelope. Two pairs of boots and a single shoe are parked next to a coat tree holding two jackets. No package leans against the wall. He walks into the house, checking the living room to his right before entering the dining room and kitchen area. He spends extra time in the kitchen looking for the envelope.

Nothing.

Except these guys eat a hell of a lot better than the McCorkles.

He prowls down the hallway, entering the first door. It's some kind of study. A bare desk pushes against the far wall. He opens the large drawer on the right.

What the hell? He pulls something that looks like a garlic press from the drawer and twists it in his hands. It's not a garlic press. It's a pill crusher.

He peers back into the drawer. There's also a pill-splitter. His mom used to use a splitter like this for Mandrake and his brother, taking adult medicine and cutting it down to a child's portion.

He returns the pill crusher to the drawer and opens the large drawer on the other side to find another kind of pressing machine. As he pulls it out, tires crunch on gravel outside. *Shit!* The neighbors are home.

Mandrake shoves the press back in the drawer, then peers out from the side of the hallway window. The gray-haired woman swings her legs out of the car preceded by a pair of crutches. Her husband exits the driver's side with a handful of envelopes and waits for her on the porch stairs.

Mandrake checks the safety on his gun, then returns to the window. The couple work their way up the steps. Mandrake shakes his head and moves to a chair at the dining room table.

The woman hobbles through the mudroom, the dog jumping at her crutches. The main door slams shut, and the woman's husband helps remove her coat. As he hangs it on the rack, the woman freezes at the sight of Mandrake at the table. He can almost hear her suck her breath in.

"What the hell? What're you doing in my house?" she barks.

"What—who's that?" Her husband rushes through the doorway.

Mandrake palms the pistol with the grip showing out one side, the barrel out the other. He taps it up and down on the table, indicating the chairs opposite him.

"Why don't you all come on over and take a seat? Let's have a little chat."

"Why don't you tell us what you're doing in our house?" The man's voice trembles as he steps in front of his wife.

She grabs his arm. "Move over, Jim. I want to hear this." Lifting a crutch, she points it at Mandrake. "Stop banging the table with that thing. You'll scratch the finish."

Mandrake pushes his chair back and stands. He rotates the pistol in his hand so it points directly at the man.

"Sit. Down. Now," he commands. "I'm doing the talking and when I tell you to talk, you'll talk. Do you understand?"

Jim swallows. Keeping his eyes on Mandrake, he attempts to guide his wife to the chair closest to the window. She shrugs off his arm and uses a crutch to lower into a chair. Jim slides into the chair across from Mandrake. The dog looks up, turning his head toward each person as they speak.

"If you want money—"

"Shut up," Mandrake says.

Jim stops talking and lowers his hands to his lap.

Mandrake sits. He returns the pistol to the table and rests his hand atop it.

"Breathe," he says. "I don't want your money. I want the UPS package you picked up this morning from that house down there." Mandrake points toward the McCorkles' house.

Jim opens his mouth—probably to argue—then glances at the gun and appears to reconsider.

"What's your name?" Mandrake says.

"Jim Schork."

"So, Jim, where's it at?"

"In the kitchen. In the cupboard behind the breakfast bar."

"Great." Mandrake picks up the pistol. The one cabinet he'd missed. "Jim, why don't you get up and go get the envelope while me and—what's your name?" Mandrake turns toward the woman.

"Carrie," she snaps. "What's yours?"

Mandrake ignores her. "Jim, Carrie and I are right here watching you and if you bring your hands out of that cupboard with anything besides my package…" Mandrake snorts. "I said 'package.'"

Jim and Carrie don't even smile.

Mandrake is unimpressed with the Schorks. No sense of humor. Doesn't anybody outside of prison tell dick jokes anymore?

"Right, so anything but my envelope and you will hear a little 'boom, boom' over here by me and Carrie. Do you understand?"

"Yes." Jim raises his hands from his legs, thrusting them in the air as he stands.

"Go ahead now." Mandrake motions toward the kitchen. He flicks a glance at Carrie, then returns his gaze to Jim. "What'd you do to your foot?"

"What do you care?"

"Oh goodie, should I bang Jim around a little just because you want to be a smartass?"

"I caught a snowshoe. Search and Rescue had to drag me out on a litter."

Jim pauses behind the breakfast bar. He bends and reaches to the cabinet underneath, saying, "I'm pulling it out now."

Mandrake chokes back a laugh. "You didn't laugh when I said 'package.' I'm not laughing at your jokes."

Jim pauses, his eyes expressionless. This is not a man Mandrake will be sharing a beer with anytime soon.

When he stands again, Jim holds the McCorkles' package. He raises it to eye level before cautiously walking back toward Mandrake, slowing as he steps over the dog.

"Give it here, then sit down."

Jim lowers the envelope to Mandrake's side of the table and inches back to his chair.

Mandrake sets the pistol directly in front of him before reaching for the envelope.

"It's all there," Jim says. "We didn't even open it yet."

"Shut up, Jim." Carrie glares at her husband.

Mandrake pauses. "What the hell are you two yammerin' about? What's all there?"

Jim opens his mouth, but Carrie interrupts. "It's Les McCorkle's. From next door. It's medicine for his back. We pick up all their packages."

Mandrake squints at Carrie. What the fuck? He rips open the perforated tab, lifts the flap, and peers inside. Another envelope—manila. He opens it. Three pouches of dirty white powder. More than what he is expecting.

Beep. Beep. Beep.

Mandrake lifts his eyes to the Schorks. Both look toward the window facing the McCorkles' house.

"Stay here." Mandrake waves the gun at the couple while moving to the window. He peeks around the window frame at a FedEx truck trundling up the hill in front of him. A white shipping envelope leans against the McCorkles' front door.

Mandrake turns to the envelope on the kitchen table, then back to the McCorkles' doorstep. "You've got to be shitting me." He returns to his chair and sighs.

"What the fuck are you talking about, 'back medicine?' What is this?" Mandrake lifts the envelope on the table and drops it.

"It's—" Jim starts.

"Jim," Carrie interrupts.

"What?"

"Let me explain, honey."

Jim shrugs and leans back.

Carrie turns to Mandrake. "I'm a pharmacist. That's Les McCorkle's pain meds that I order out of Denver. It comes here in raw form. I make the pills, and when the McCorkles get here, it's ready to go."

Mandrake shakes his head. "That sounds like a crock of shit."

"What?"

"Why doesn't he just bring his meds from wherever he lives in the winter? And why is it being mailed to someone's house? Why not your office?" Mandrake pauses, then speaks again before Carrie can answer. "And why not send pills? Why powder? Something's not on the up and up here."

"Oh, you're a fine one to talk about 'up and up' Mr. Break-Into-My-House. Waving your gun all over the place."

"Carrie!" Jim looks panicked.

"Shut up and answer my questions." Mandrake pats his palm on the gun. "Want me to use it?"

Carrie's head twitches. "It's complicated. Les has chronic back issues. But New Mexico—that's where he and Marjorie are right now—is cracking down on opioid prescriptions. He can't get his meds there anymore. Nobody will prescribe him anything like what he needs."

"Why the home delivery? Why not your office? Or at least your own house?" Mandrake sees what looks like a flash of fear in Carrie's eyes. The story's coming apart, and she knows it.

"OK. I *am* a pharmacist. But I don't work in a pharmacy anymore. This is freelance. Just helping out my neighbor."

"Ah, now I see. Not quite legal, is that?" Mandrake leers at Carrie.

"I have a license, and—"

"Right. And you're so confident that what you're doing is legal that you have the shit mailed to someone else's house. Someone who doesn't actually live there now. And then after you pick it up, you bring it here and process it back in your little pill packaging office." Mandrake tilts his head toward the hallway.

"You bastard. You went through our house?"

"Carrie, stop." Jim aims his eyes toward Mandrake's gun.

Carrie leans in her chair, folding her arms across her chest and pressing her lips together.

Mandrake raises the envelope. "Jim?"

"Yes?"

"You got any booze in this house?"

"Yes. We've got beer, wine, and some hard stuff. Over in that cabinet." He points toward the end of the kitchen.

Damn. Another missed cabinet. "You go pour me a jigger of the hard stuff. I'll stay right here and keep an eye on Ms. Carrie."

Jim returns to the kitchen and pulls a bottle from the cabinet. The dog follows.

Mandrake glances at the bottle. "Crown Royal. Now we're talking."

Jim pours a shot, then looks at Mandrake for approval.

"Keep it coming, Jimbo. Can I call you Jimbo?"

Jim pours another splash into the glass and brings it to Mandrake. Mandrake tilts the glass to his lips and swallows as Jim sits.

"Oh, that's some good shit. Jimbo, you hold up. Got another task for you."

Jim stands again, waiting for Mandrake's direction.

"I want you to head on over to the McCorkles' and pick up that other envelope. Can you do that? I'm going to watch you from that window." He waves at the window where he had watched the FedEx delivery. "I'll have one eye on you, and the other aiming this gun at your bride here. I'm talented that way. You fuck around and I will shoot her. Then I will chase you down and do the same to you. Got that?"

Jim glances at Carrie, then back at Mandrake. "I'll get the package and come straight back." He heads toward the front door.

Mandrake stands and moves to the window, keeping his gun pointed in Carrie's direction. "Carrie, Carrie, Carrie. What am I to do with you folks?"

"How about taking whatever you're looking for and leaving us alone? Just take the pain meds there." Carrie snaps. "You already figured out I'm probably not going to run to the cops and say you stole my drugs."

"Carrie, you misunderstand. My question was one of those—what's that called? Metaphorical questions. I already know what we're doing with you."

"It's *rhetorical*, you dumbshit."

Mandrake glances out the window. Jim scurries back with the envelope. Mandrake turns back to Carrie. "Listen up, bitch. Respect. That's what I expect out of you. The quicker you show it, the better chance you have of coming out of this alive."

Mandrake doesn't plan on killing Jim and Carrie. Drugs and bombs are one thing, but he doesn't need to add murder to the list. Of course, Jim and Carrie don't need to know that.

He can't let them go, though. They'll call the cops before he can meet up with Sullivan. Unless he ties them up. But what if someone stops by and finds the couple before he leaves?

They're going to have to go with Sullivan and him.

"Bring me that envelope and pour me another drink, Jimbo," he says, as Jim enters the kitchen.

Mandrake sips his Crown and tries unsuccessfully to loosen up the Schorks. They're not even interested in enjoying a jigger with him. When he finishes his drink, he stands. "Time to blow this joint." He looks down at the couple. "What do you think? Your garage got a back door?"

Jim nods.

"Well, lead on, Jimbo," Mandrake stuffs the FedEx envelope and the UPS envelope into a cloth grocery sack Jim has pulled from the kitchen. Turns out Big Bobby used FedEx, not UPS. The envelope Jim retrieved from the McCorkles' holds fifty small baggies of fentanyl, or, as Big Bobby calls it, China Town.

Mandrake grabs Carrie by one arm while pointing down the hallway with the pistol in his other hand. Carrie hops then reaches back toward the chair for her crutches.

"Shit." Mandrake drops her arm. "Grab those things and lead us out to the garage." He turns to Jim. "You follow her. I'll bring up the rear."

Jim follows Carrie down the hallway, reaching in front of her to open the interior door leading to the garage.

Carrie stops and turns. "When are we coming back?"

"What the fuck? Move your ass." Mandrake pushes Carrie forward.

"Scottie. He'll need food." Carrie points with her crutch back down the hallway at the small dog watching their exit.

"Screw the dog." Mandrake herds Jim and Carrie through the door and into the garage. The Schorks have another Toyota parked inside, surrounded by racks of bikes and skis.

"Aren't you all the sporty ones?" He pushes Jim in Carrie's direction toward the back door, then suddenly stops. "Hold up there, boys and girls."

Jim grabs Carrie's arm and they both pause.

Mandrake surveys the workbench next to the back door. "You all got any of those plastic zip-tie things? You know, like if you were putting wire bundles together or holding up a loose muffler under your car?"

"No." Carrie shakes her head. "Maybe some bungee—"

"—Carrie, we bought some of those zip-ties in case Kristee needed them for the gutters. Over by the garbage cans," Jim blurts, twisting his head toward the front of the garage.

Carrie glares at her husband. Mandrake snorts. "All righty then, let's grab those. Jimbo, how about you go around and bring them back to me?"

Jim edges around the Toyota, grabs the bag of zip-ties, and returns to the group.

"Open them up and grab one."

Jim pulls a zip-tie from the bag.

"Now I'm going to stand behind Carrie here with my gun," Mandrake says. "I want you to zip-tie your left hand to Carrie's left hand."

Jim moves so he and Carrie stand side-by-side—Carrie with her crutches wedged in her armpits—and starts fumbling with the zip-tie.

"No. I said left to left. So, Jim, you face Carrie, reach across her, and tie them with your right hand."

Jim turns and faces Carrie. After a minute of fumbling, he locks the zip-tie in place, binding their left wrists together. Mandrake releases Carrie's arm and reaches between them, yanking the end of the zip-tie tighter. Jim winces. Mandrake grabs the bag of zip-ties from the hood of the car and stuffs them into Jim's coat pocket.

"Let's move." Mandrake reaches around the couple to open the door and pushes them outside. One of Carrie's crutches drops as Jim's weight pulls her in the opposite direction.

"I got that." Mandrake stoops to grab the single crutch. "You guys need to figure this shit out."

As they shuffle toward the McCorkles', Jim adjusts their movement so that Carrie leads facing one way with one crutch and Jim trails facing the other direction. Mandrake scans left and right for nosy neighbors, but sees no one. Just another balmy spring day. A minute later, they're inside the McCorkles' garage. Mandrake marches them up the steps, and through the house to the living room couch.

"Take a seat."

The Schorks lower themselves awkwardly to the couch with Carrie on the front edge of the cushion, and Jim, twisted around, wedged in behind her. Mandrake sets the pistol on the coffee table.

"Now Jimbo, I'm going to reach into your pocket for those zip-ties, OK?" Mandrake reaches into Jim's pocket and retrieves the bag. He pulls out another tie, fastening their other hands together, and putting Jim behind and under Carrie.

"What do you think, Jimbo? You like that position?" Mandrake sneers. "Your wife's got quite the mouth. Guess you're used to her being on top?"

Carrie glares at him. Mandrake stands and looks at the couple. He hasn't put them in a sustainable position. But it will have to do for now.

He grabs the gun and Carrie's crutches and walks around the corner into the dining room. Before sitting, he reaches into his pocket and pulls out his cell.

What to do about his unexpected guests? It's one thing for him to hole up at the McCorkles'. Nobody would even notice him unless he stayed here until summer. But how long will it be before someone figures out the Schorks are gone? That could happen anytime.

He pulls up his *Signal* app and types a message to Sullivan:

Got the stuff. Problem in delivery and now have company with me that I have to babysit. Need pick up now instead of later.

Mandrake presses send. The half bottle of Jim Beam from last night perches on the kitchen counter. He smiles. The Schorks haven't really been in the mood for a drink. Imagine that.

He drops some ice from the freezer into his glass and pours the bourbon. A buzzing sound comes from the dining room. His phone. Mandrake drinks, allowing the bourbon to rest on his tongue a moment before swallowing. This is better than that fancy Crown Royal shit. He walks into the dining room to check the phone.

Sullivan has responded: *Company? WTF? I can be there between 8-9 tonight.*

Mandrake replies: *That'll work, you got the address, park your car at the easternmost bend of Princeton Hill Drive, we'll be there at 8.*

Hang on. How many with you?

2

OK. Got the pickup. I'll be there.

Mandrake closes the app and swigs another drink. When he checks on the Schorks, he finds them piled on each other on the couch. He smiles and waves before returning to the table.

He pulls both envelopes from the grocery sack, opens them up, and stacks the contents in separate piles on the table. His hands tremble, ready for a little pick-me-up. He probably should hold off until after Sullivan gets them out of here tonight. He swivels his head between the two piles, noticing how similar the product looks. It's hard to tell the two drugs apart.

Mandrake considers this. What was that fortune cookie thing? Every crisis presents an opportunity?

He grabs a large baggie of oxy in one hand and a couple baggies of China Town in the other, balancing each up and down like a human scale.

The crisis?

A middle-aged couple he doesn't know how to get rid of.

The opportunity?

What if he cuts the oxy into the China Town and keeps half the original China Town for himself? The street value for the China Town runs twice that of the oxy.

Hell, yeah. He's getting a quarter-million from the bomb job. Add that to over a hundred grand selling this shit? He'll be set. Sullivan won't even have to know.

Mandrake stands and looks around the corner at the Schorks again. They're still playing Twister. "Hi guys." He laughs before heading for the kitchen. Rummaging through drawers, he grabs the smallest measuring spoon he can find. Back at the table, he pauses before mixing the drugs.

What should he call his invention? China-Oxy? Choxy? Mandrake snorts.

It's time for some chemistry.

ZAHN

Buena Vista, Colorado-May 20th

The sun slinks behind the Collegiates as I pull into the SAR bay parking lot for weekly training. Monday is turning into my social day with morning yoga and evening SAR. I force myself to arrive early so I can chat a bit with my fellow trainees—get to know them. It was a big step suggesting a climb to Perez the other day. But I'm a self-aware guy, and I know that part of the reason I've been in such a funk is because I've been spending too much time alone.

When I push through the door, Scott Howard is setting up Google Slides on his laptop. Kristee taps on her phone in the second row back. In the rear of the classroom, two young women I don't recognize have their heads together laughing. I wave at Howard and offer a round of hellos to the rest of the students. Kristee pats the chair to her left and I slide in beside her.

"What's up, old man?" Kristee extends her fist for a bump.

I tentatively push out my fist. Kristee bumps it and I laugh. My junior airmen were doing this fist bump thing as I was transitioning out of the Air Force. Not with me, though.

"Living the dream. Perez says you're doing gutters?"

"Yep. I've got two places I'm working on. I'm supposed to have a third up your direction but can't quite seem to make the connection. Every time I go by, they're gone."

"Traveling?"

"I don't think so. You've met the woman. Carrie Schork?"

I know the name but can't place it.

"The gal that broke her ankle up at Kroenke Lake? You kept her from going off the cliff?"

"Right. Got it. You think something's wrong?"

Kristee frowns. "I don't know. They're never there. At first, I thought they were probably off hiking or walking, right? Then I remembered she's got to be on crutches. No car in the driveway, but the curtains are open. I can see the dog inside."

"I'll keep my eye out. Might catch them at the mailboxes."

"I left them a note with my number. They might not be interested anymore. Anyway, the husband's name is Jim. Same last name as her. Schork. Second house from the end down Yale Crest. One of those downhill spurs off Eagle Ridge."

"I know that road, but don't go down it much. I'll keep my eyes open."

"Thanks, dude. Appreciate it."

I press my lips together to keep from smiling. *Dude.* Another difference from the military. Kristee talks to me like an equal, instead of an elder, or a boss. Hell, she talks to me like a friend. My Air Force friends are all a little long in the tooth like me, either rocking toward a general's star or retired and working for a contractor. Friends I've flown with through some serious shit.

I smile, remembering these lifelong friends I'm reminiscing about are ones I'll reach out to once a year on their birthday. None of them are willing to drag me up a mountain and not laugh when I can't make it. None of them are the fist-bumping, "dude" type. If the rest of the SAR team is anything like Kristee, or Rick, I'm going to be OK.

Training is quick. An hour of knot-tying skills and we're done. As I move to the exit, Howard calls from behind the podium.

"Tyler, are you thinking about a SAR position?"

"No." I consider leaving it at that, but I don't want to be the crusty guy who won't explain himself. "I mean I'm a hiker. I told you guys that. I might look at snowmobile or ATV quals later on. After I get my feet wet with this stuff."

"No, man, that's not what I meant. I mean a staff position. You got all that military experience. I thought you might consider being the next Training Director."

"Your position?" I remember Perez bringing this up on our training mission. "It would be pretty tough to fill your shoes."

"I've been doing it for four years now. I'm ready for a break. I think you'd be a good fit after you get a couple of missions under your belt."

I'm quick to answer. "Sorry, man. I'm flattered that you are asking, but I'm not interested. I'm just here to hike and climb. I'm not ready for anything else."

Howard gives me a look I can't quite decipher. Somewhere between disappointed and understanding. Not understanding like he empathizes with how I feel, but rather he understands I'm just here for the fun outdoors stuff and not willing to take on any responsibility.

"Alright then," Howard says. "I thought I'd ask. Let me know if you change your mind."

I depart the bay in a funk. First, the high school asks me to teach. Now SAR wants me to be the SAR Training Director. What's next? Everyone expects me to be in charge of something.

I pull into City Market on the way home for a pre-roasted chicken and a six-pack of beer. As I stand in front of the cooler, surveying my options, I change my mind. I'm buying two six-packs.

MANDRAKE

Elk Trace, near Buena Vista, Colorado-May 20th
"OK, Jimbo, Carrie, time to move." The sun hides behind the mountains shading Elk Trace. The McCorkles' clock reads 7:30.

Mandrake crosses the living room packing scissors in his right hand, Carrie's crutches under the same arm, and the pistol in his left. Wearing a winter jacket from the hallway closet and a day pack where he has stuffed the drug envelopes, he stands over the awkwardly sprawled couple and spells out the ground rules.

"We're going for a ride, but we're taking a stroll first. Through the backyard, down the hill to the road." Mandrake points toward the back of the house with the gun. "I'll cut you loose, Carrie, and you limp your ass in front of me and your man. Me and him, we'll be strapped together with a zip-tie. If you try to get away, I'll shoot you. If you swing one of those crutches at me, I'll shoot you. If you manage to get away without me shooting you, then I'll just shoot Jimbo. Got it?" He laughs, then stops abruptly. Sullivan told him once he laughs too much.

Carrie scowls. She opens her mouth, but Jim nudges her. She says nothing.

Mandrake reaches into Jim's pocket for the bag of zip-ties and pulls one out. Then, pointing his gun at Carrie, he snips through the tie binding her to her husband. He stows the scissors in his pocket, and switches the pistol to his right hand, and hands the new tie to Carrie, who rubs her wrist with her other hand.

"Alright, Carrie. Strap us up."

Carrie runs the tie around Mandrake's wrist and through the tie her husband wears.

"Tighter."

Carrie pulls on the end of the tie and it snugs up close to the two men's wrists.

Mandrake pulls Jim upright. He has already checked the house, making sure the cops won't find any clues. But it wasn't a spring cleaning either. If the McCorkles show up early, they'll figure out someone has been here.

Mandrake laughs out loud again. Hell, he doesn't even know their destination, so it's hard for him to leave any clues behind. North first, Sullivan said. That's why Mandrake has arranged to pick up the supplies they need at Twin Lakes.

He waves the pistol toward the kitchen. "Let's go. Through the garage and out the back."

They exit the garage, descending a slope layered with the pine needles and rocks that make up a backyard in this part of the Rockies.

Mandrake considers using his phone's flashlight, but decides against it. The moon in the east shines bright, although less full than his escape night. Carrie's fucking crutches are a pain, but noise shouldn't be a problem—there are enough deer and elk up here moving around that it would be odd *not* to hear noises from the woods every night.

Five minutes later they reach the road. When they descend into the drainage ditch, the white ribbon of road highlighted in front of them, Mandrake tugs Jim to a stop and whispers to Carrie.

"Back up. To those trees." He motions over his shoulder. They duck between the branches. Mandrake points at the ground with his pistol while looking at Carrie. She drops her crutches and sits.

Mandrake pulls Jim down next to him. He checks his watch. 7:57.

They wait.

Lights, riding high above the road, flash around the corner toward the bend where they wait. As the truck reaches the curve, it slows and turns off its lights.

Mandrake waits.

The truck waits.

Mandrake gives it a minute. The truck remains motionless, no doors opening or closing. It must be Sullivan. He tugs on Jim, pulling him to his feet, then waves his gun at Carrie, beckoning her to lead them toward the road. They cross the drainage ditch onto the gravel, and walk to the driver's side of the vehicle.

Mandrake recognizes Sullivan behind the wheel, window open. He pushes Carrie forward, while tugging Jim closer to the truck.

"What's up, man?" Sullivan whispers. "Who're your friends?"

"I'll do introductions later." Mandrake's voice is low. "Let's put this lady in the front next to you." He turns to Jim. "Me and him, we'll take the back, me first."

"Got it." Sullivan opens his door and walks Carrie to the truck's passenger side. He leans her crutches against the bed before boosting her up into the seat. "Ladies first."

While Sullivan situates Carrie, Mandrake pushes the driver's seat forward with his gun hand and climbs onto the bench seat in the back, pulling Jim along behind him. He taps Carrie's shoulder with the pistol. "We're right back here, no worries."

Carrie stiffens but says nothing.

Sullivan closes the passenger door, tosses the crutches in the truck's bed before returning to the driver's seat. As he drives away, he flips on his headlights. Within five minutes, they are off the back roads and headed north toward Leadville on Highway 24.

SULLIVAN

Twin Lakes, Colorado-May 20th

Sullivan glances in the rearview mirror, trying to catch Mandrake's attention. It's too dark to make out Mandrake's face, but he's definitely back there. The smell of booze leaches from his pores.

"Who do we have here, Mi—brother?" Sullivan fumbles, as he realizes he and Mandrake haven't discussed the future of these guests. Best not to use names.

"Your shotgun guest is Mrs. Carrie 'Smart-ass' Schork." Mandrake's hand reaches forward, patting Carrie on the shoulder. "And this guy I'm tied to is Mr. Jim Schork." Mandrake turns to Jim. "Why the fuck are we holding hands?"

Sullivan hears Mandrake moving around and then the distinct snip of scissors.

"You're probably wondering how we met," Mandrake says.

"Yup."

"Interesting story, isn't it, Jimbo?" Mandrake continues, "I was just squatting at the neighbors' house minding my business when Jim here walks on down and steals my mail. Or at least I thought it was my mail." Mandrake pauses. "That's another story. Anyway, can you believe it? Mail stealing? That's a federal offense."

"I was j-j-just—" Jim stutters.

"Shut up, Jimbo," Mandrake says.

"What was so important about the mail?" Sullivan can't imagine his friend is using mail as a metaphor here. Not Mandrake.

"It's what we need in exchange for tonight's pickup," Mandrake says. "While they are out, I stroll up to their place to retrieve what I believe is my rightful property. Then they decide to come back home right in the middle of the whole thing. I considered getting rid of them right there. So messy though." He laughs.

Sullivan cringes. That laugh.

"Who knows, they might come in handy." Mandrake's hand appears on Carrie's shoulder again. "Hell, if they behave, we might even let them go."

Sullivan says nothing. He can't fault Mandrake for his decision to keep the couple. Not much choice if the neighbors had taken whatever Mandrake needs to get the explosives. But his friend's talk about "getting rid of them" makes him nervous. He's never killed anyone, not even in Iraq. This whole plan of Sarah's is supposed to be about sending messages. He might have to remind Mandrake of that.

The couple has seen their faces. But they don't know their names, what they are doing, and where they are going. They can let them go. But not now. They need to wait until after the bombs.

He brakes momentarily, then speeds up again after three deer bound across the highway.

"Pull off up there at that brown sign." Mandrake leans over the seat, pointing straight ahead.

Sullivan slows. "Why? What's up?"

"Got to take a shit. Take that left up there and park. I think we're next to the river."

"There's nothing here."

"All I need is some trees. Sorry, man, got to go." He hands Sullivan the pistol from the back seat. "You watch our guests while I'm gone. Back in a sec."

Sullivan switches off his headlights, watching as Mandrake directs Carrie to move her seat forward and open the door. Mandrake pushes the seat, pressing Carrie against the dash, and slides out the door.

"Wait a sec," Sullivan calls. He unbuckles his seatbelt and switches the pistol to his left hand, rummaging around at Carrie's feet with his right. He grabs an empty Subway bag and pulls out some napkins. "TP, man," he says, reaching across Carrie and thrusting the napkins at Mandrake.

Mandrake laughs, grabs the napkins, and disappears into the darkness.

Sullivan twists in his seat, keeping both Carrie and Jim's silhouette in sight. "You all just hold tight." He glances in the direction Mandrake disappeared. A cell phone glows between the trees.

When Mandrake returns, Sullivan climbs from the truck and meets him by the hood. "What's the deal with the mail? What's your plan?"

"It's drugs, man. I'm giving them their fenty order, they're giving us the boom boom."

"You sure? I brought money."

"I worked this all out. You can thank me later by cutting me half of the money we didn't have to spend tonight."

Sullivan considers Mandrake's plan. It's not like he has a choice at this point. He just wished he would have known ahead of time. He hands the pistol back to Mandrake and the two men climb into the truck.

Sullivan maneuvers back onto the highway.

"No hurry," Mandrake says. "The pickup isn't for another couple of hours."

"Right. You know where to go?"

"Another ten miles up the road. You just drive, I'll show you."

They continue in silence. Sullivan glances at Carrie. She is stiff as a board. But she seems to be handling this pretty well, all things considered.

Twenty minutes later, Mandrake tells Sullivan to turn at a sign for Independence Pass. After a half-mile, Mandrake points left again to a gravel road. They follow the road for another half-mile along the roaring river flowing from an unseen reservoir. As they crest a small rise, moonlight reflects off the lake's surface. The water level of the huge lake is high and within three feet of the road.

"There, in that clearing to the right of those trail signs," Mandrake says. "Pull in, shut down, and we'll wait."

Sullivan parks the truck, turns off the ignition and the lights, and unbuckles his seatbelt.

Mandrake leans through the gap between the front seats. "We got about four hours. You need some shuteye?"

Sullivan rubs his eyes, He has driven the three hours from Denver to BV, picked up Mandrake and party, and now another hour to the pick-up spot. "Yeah, I could use a bit."

"OK, I'll keep an eye on things. Jimbo, you and Carrie might as well rest. We're going to be here a while." Sullivan hears rustling. "Jim, hand me those zip-ties would you?"

Sullivan watches shapes move in the rearview mirror as Mandrake zip-ties Jim's hands to Sullivan's headrest.

It will not be a comfortable rest for Jim.

Sullivan leans his seat back, giving Jim a bit more slack on his arms, and himself a more comfortable position. He closes his eyes and pictures a different Galen Sullivan three weeks from now: 2.5 million dollars, plus change, thanks to Mandrake.

New life.

New car.

No more of this shit.

MANDRAKE

Twin Lakes, Colorado-May 21st

Mandrake jerks in his seat. A flash of headlights illuminates the truck's window from a distance as a vehicle climbs the gravel road toward them. Mandrake reaches for Sullivan's shoulder.

"Wake up. It's showtime."

Sullivan flinches. "What's up?"

"They're here. Right on time. See them coming up the hill? Got to be them, at this hour."

"So." Sullivan rubs his eyes before turning to Mandrake. "Here's how I want it to go down. You stay here. Watch them." Sullivan waves at Carrie and Jim. "I'll do the meet and check our stuff."

"Wait a minute—" Mandrake set this up. Why's Sullivan strutting out there like he's the man?

Sullivan cuts him off. "Let me finish. If the explosives are good, then we swap places and you make the other exchange. No need to tell these guys we have guests." He turns, pauses, then swings his head back to Mandrake. "You got their 'mail?'"

"Right here in my bag." Mandrake pats the daypack. "Sounds like a plan." He grabs the zip-tie binding Jim's wrists to the front headrest and twists it. Jim winces. "You be good now, Jimbo, understand? These guys we're meeting are even meaner than us." Mandrake laughs, giving the tie another twist.

"Stop it. We get it," Carrie says from the front seat. She sounds more annoyed than scared.

Mandrake flicks the back of Carrie's head like he's shooting a marble. Carrie jerks forward. Jim flinches.

"Seriously?" Mandrake shakes his head.

"Keep them quiet," Sullivan warns. He pulls a flashlight from the glove box, climbs out, and stands in front of the truck. As the headlights sweep across Sullivan's profile, Mandrake picks out two vehicles, not one. An SUV, pulling a small U-Haul trailer.

"Shit," Mandrake mutters. "Looks like rich Texans moving to their summer home in Colorado. Nice wheels."

Sullivan approaches the car and leans in the window, engaging the driver. After a moment, Sullivan points his arm toward his truck. Then he backs away as all four doors of the vehicle open. Four shadowy figures climb out, stretching arms and legs. The interior lights illuminate a figure in the passenger seat, head turned away from everyone.

The driver walks Sullivan to the U-Haul, another man following them. The other two men split up, one taking the SUV's front, the other disappearing behind the trailer.

Mandrake grunts in approval. Professionals. They're setting up some kind of perimeter.

The rear door of the U-Haul swings open. Sullivan disappears inside with the driver. A minute later, Sullivan exits the trailer and walks toward the truck.

He cracks the driver's door open and leans in. "We're good. Enough for all three. Beemer Babe's going to be happy. You do the swap."

"What? You still think it's Sarah running things? My money's on Cowboy Timmons." Mandrake seriously doubts BMW-woman who Sullivan is so hot after is the mastermind behind the plan.

"Shut up, man." Sullivan glares at Mandrake in the back seat. "Go do your thing."

Touchy, touchy. "Got it. Going out this side. Carrie, move your ass up." Mandrake mashes the seat forward and crawls out of the truck while Sullivan climbs into the driver's seat. Mandrake tucks his pistol into the waistband of his pants, leans back into the truck over Carrie toward Sullivan. "Who's the guy who stayed in the car? In the passenger seat?"

"I don't know. He's Asian, though. He turned away when I showed up."

Mandrake nods. "If these two give you any trouble just use that knife on Carrie here." He pats Carrie on the thigh. She jerks away from him. Mandrake has no idea if Sullivan brought a weapon. But then again, Jim and Carrie don't know whether he did or not either.

He strolls to the U-Haul doors. "Who's in charge here? You, or the guy in the car?"

The SUV driver stands between the open trailer doors, unsmiling, wearing black slacks and an open black jacket over a bright white shirt. A shine from black leather shoes glints in the moonlight. The man looks like a cross between Johnny Cash and a pimp.

"I'm Robert," the man says in a thick Hispanic accent. "You got Dorsey's stuff?"

"Right here." Mandrake unslings the backpack. He hands it to Robert.

Another man steps from the shadows and stands next to Mandrake. Mandrake shifts his feet, keeping his eyes on the backpack. Robert digs into his pocket and pulls out a penlight. Switching it on, he sticks it between his teeth and opens the pack. He raises his eyes to Mandrake as he extracts the envelope.

"Look inside," Mandrake says. "Fifty packs. Looks like a piece per pack."

Robert removes the light from his mouth. "Better be fifty. Better be exactly a piece in each."

He lowers the pack to the trailer's floor and removes his jacket, spreading it like a picnic blanket next to the envelope. Turning the envelope on end, he empties the contents onto his jacket. He arranges the baggies in five piles, counting the bags, and holding each up to the penlight before returning it to the jacket.

Mandrake silently counts the piles. *Damn. Better be fifty.* Robert finishes his inspection. He retrieves a single baggie, using both fingers to open it. He sniffs the contents.

"What's it smell like?" Mandrake says. He hadn't smelled any odor when he mixed the drugs.

"Smells like nothing. If it had a smell, you'd be doing some explaining." Robert turns to the man at Mandrake's side. "Bag."

The man reaches into a pocket, pulls out a gallon zip-lock bag, and hands it to Robert. Robert seals the little baggies into the larger bag before transferring it to the backpack.

Robert pivots to the other man. "Start loading the stuff in their truck." Then he disappears. Back to the SUV, Mandrake assumes. Not even a handshake. This Robert is a cold bastard.

Mandrake turns to the other man. "We'll move our rig down here." As he hikes back to Sullivan and the Schorks, a shadow moves behind the truck's tailgate.

"Hey!" Mandrake calls.

The figure steps into the open. It's one of the perimeter sentries. "What the hell are you doing?" Mandrake says. Sullivan steps out of the truck, looking from the sentry to Mandrake. "What's happening here?" The sentry points two fingers at his own eyes then aims them at Mandrake followed by Sullivan. Then he walks back to the SUV and the trailer.

"Found him behind the truck," Mandrake says, crawling in the passenger side behind Carrie. "Creepy fuck."

"We good?" Sullivan says.

"We're good. Move us down next to the back end of the trailer."

Sullivan moves the truck forward, aligning the rear of the bed with the trailer. After turning off the ignition, he turns to Mandrake. "I'm going to help load. Make sure they don't short us."

Fifteen minutes later, the SUV and U-Haul trailer pull around the truck, the bouncing headlights disappearing toward Highway 24. Sullivan waits another five minutes, then starts his truck.

"Stop," Carrie says.

"What do you want, woman?" Mandrake leans forward in his seat, speaking close to her ear.

"I need to pee. I don't know where we're going next, but I'm not going to make it."

"Uh, me too," Jim adds.

Sullivan sighs, turning off the ignition. "I'll stay with the truck. Have fun."

SULLIVAN

Twin Lakes, Colorado-May 21st

Mandrake takes Carrie, and then Jim, to relieve themselves. Sullivan flinches when Mandrake slams the rear door after shoving Jim into the truck.

"Where're we going now?" Carrie says.

"Shut up, Carrie," Mandrake says, "or I'll zip-tie you back up again."

"Hey." Jim's voice is barely audible.

"Oh, now you're stepping up again, Jimbo? Really? How about I bitch-slap you?"

Silence.

Sullivan doesn't turn at Mandrake's comment; he cranks the engine instead. Going to be a long week. Mandrake will need watching. He maneuvers the truck back to the highway. Twenty minutes north, he pulls in for coffee at a 24-hour gas stop in the old western town of Leadville.

He heads into the store leaving Mandrake to watch the Schorks. When he returns from pre-paying, he pumps the gas, swapping guard duty with Mandrake, who decides he needs the facilities after all.

Mandrake strides back two minutes later, bee-lining to Carrie's side with a scowl on his face. As Sullivan hangs the gas nozzle on the hook, a car pulls away from Carrie's side. The driver's eyes fixate on Carrie and he almost hits a pump exiting the station. Sullivan looks from the driver back to Mandrake as he climbs behind the wheel. Mandrake is slapping the back of Carrie's head. Jim squirms in his seat.

"What the hell?" Sullivan says.

"Bitch signaled that car," Mandrake says. "I walked back from the john and saw her lips moving through the window. That other guy saw her."

"Stop it! I was—I was—" Carrie stutters.

"You were what? Dammit!" Mandrake cuffs Carrie's neck with the back of his hand.

"OK, Mitch," Sullivan says. "Why don't you hold off for a minute and explain to the Schorks their key role in our plan?" Mandrake glares at him in the mirror. Sullivan realizes his mistake.

Oops. Just called him Mitch.

"That's right Carrie, Jim," Sullivan continues, "you don't have a role. You got in our way and that's why you're with us. But we don't need you. Not to slow us down or get us caught."

Carrie and Jim say nothing.

"So, I guess we can give you a choice. Option A is you come with us and we'll deal with you later. Or there's Option B. We eliminate you right now. That's easy. Isn't that right, Mitch?" Sullivan can't imagine acting on his words, but tries to use his slip with Mitch's name to their advantage. If the Schorks hear him use the name without fear, they'll assume their demise is a real option.

Mandrake pulls the pistol from his waistband and rests it in his lap. Carrie can't see it, but when Jim sucks in his breath, she twists her head toward him.

"That would just break my heart." Mandrake gives his laugh. "What's it going to be, girls?"

Jim does another breath suck before answering. "No, we'll come with you. We won't do anything, see anything, or tell anything. Promise." He looks from Mandrake to Carrie. "Tell them, honey. Tell them we'll do what they want."

Carrie hold's Jim's eyes for a moment, then says, "We'll be good… but you're both assholes." She whispers the last words.

Sullivan raises his brows at Mandrake, then eases out of the station, and pulls into the lot in front of the convenience store. "Be right back."

A few minutes later, Sullivan emerges carrying a plastic bag. Inside the truck, he pulls a handful of neck gaiters out of the sack, separating two and tossing them to Mandrake in the back seat.

"Lay him down and put these over his eyes. They don't need to see where we're going, anyway."

Mandrake laughs. "Oh great, you get the girl's head in your lap and I get Jimbo. It's 'cuz I was in prison, right? That's why I get the guy?"

Sullivan reaches across the center console, unbuckling Carrie's seatbelt. "Lay down."

Carrie leans in his direction and Sullivan spreads the neck gaiter, pulling it over her head. He repeats the process with the second gaiter.

"See anything?"

Carrie shakes her head and gives a muffled, "Can't breathe."

Sullivan pulls the material up from the bottom, so her mouth shows. Then he raises his hand above her face and shadow-punches her covered eyes.

No flinch.

"Put both of them over his eyes," he says over his shoulder to Mandrake, "and make sure he can breathe."

Sullivan pulls out of the station. Forty-five minutes later they've crossed Fremont Pass and turn at the Frisco exit. Dillon Reservoir reflects the moonlight.

Sullivan points at the massive, man-made lake as they drive through the town of Frisco. "Hell of a lot of water, isn't? Look how high the level is."

"Sure is… dammit."

Sullivan doesn't answer.

"Get it? Dam—it?" Mandrake presses, then bursts out laughing.

"Got it, man. Got it." Jesus. That laugh.

In Breckenridge, they pull up to the address Sarah provided—Alpine Meadows Condominiums. Sullivan passes the darkened office and follows Sarah's directions to the back of the complex.

They park and pull the blindfolds off the Schorks. Sullivan helps Carrie with her crutches, as they herd the couple inside. Mandrake stands guard over them in the living room while Sullivan checks out the condo.

"Only two bedrooms. They're sweet. Duvets instead of comforters." Sullivan says.

"What the hell is a doo-vay?" Mandrake says.

"Big cloth bag with feathers that you lay over the top of yourself when you're sleeping. Fancy hotels all got them," Sullivan answers. "Looks like one bedroom for me and one for you and we'll each keep one of them for company?" He nods toward the Schorks.

"I call Carrie here," Mandrake responds. "I think we bonded at the gas station."

"Don't even think about it, son. I'm the same age as your mother," Carrie growls.

"Ohhh, love me an older woman with a mouth."

Sullivan shakes his head, wondering how long it's been since Mandrake has slept with a woman. "OK, I'm going to unload the truck and bring the stuff inside. You keep an eye on things in here." He walks to the door. "When I'm done, we have some planning to do. You know. Food. Clothes. Those guys are starting to stink." He wrinkles his nose. "And we need to talk about the actual plan."

"You got it," Mandrake says. "We need booze, too." He leans back on the living room recliner. "Careful with those boxes. Don't hurt your back."

•   •   •

Sullivan unloads the truck, transferring the boxes to the condo entryway, while Mandrake moves them into the master bedroom inside an empty walk-in closet.

The condo setup is sweet. No one pays attention to guys moving stuff in and out of vacation rentals.

Next on the agenda is a food and clothes run. Sullivan has brought stuff, but Mandrake clearly never gave the Schorks time to pack a bag. He eyes his partner's ill-fitting clothes, obviously lifted from his hole-up house. The UConn sweater is two sizes too small and either the clothes or Mandrake stinks.

The Schorks won't smell so good before long. He can take that for a while—he's used to gym rat funk from the desert—but it's his firm opinion that girls, including Carrie, shouldn't stink. Folks might label his thinking sexist. Whatever.

The staggered sleep schedule in the truck last night has left Sullivan worn out. He considers using Mandrake for the shopping run, but sending an escaped convict out in public less than a hundred miles from where he broke out of prison is too risky. Sullivan gathers clothing sizes from everyone and leaves Mandrake in charge.

Shopping at Goodwill and Walmart takes an hour and a half. He returns with underwear and socks, faded jeans, and shirts. And groceries. He tosses Carrie a plastic grocery sack to tie around her foot cast and sends her to the shower. Jim puts the food away. When Carrie finishes, Sullivan has her fix lunch while Jim showers.

Sullivan goes next. In and out. Mandrake spends twenty minutes showering when it's his turn. Just past noon, the four share the small table adjoining the kitchen, eating Carrie's sandwiches.

"Not bad, Carrie," Mandrake jokes, his mouth full. "Any other talents I should know about besides turkey sandwiches?"

Jim glares at Mandrake. Carrie chews her food.

"What's the matter, Carrie girl, you get some soap in that bitchy mouth of yours?" Mandrake goads, his eyes shining.

Carrie says nothing.

"Jim, Carrie, why don't you all follow me into the living room and I'll get you set up with a little TV? My friend and I have some business." Sullivan says.

He leads them to the sofa and turns on the television. MSNBC. Of course. Long-haired snowboarders running the lifts for minimum wage or rich Denver liberals out for the weekend. They all love their talk shows. He cranks up the volume, then zip-ties Jim's wrist to Carrie's ankle.

"Sorry. Need to make sure you all stay put." He points toward the dining room. "We can watch you from the corner of the table there. See my friend, with his little friend?" He yells at Mandrake, forming a gun shape with his fingers. "Give us a wave!"

Mandrake twirls the handgun on his finger, smiling at the couple.

"Understand?" Sullivan says.

The Schorks nod. Carrie raises her foot to the couch so Jim can lay beside her. They turn their heads toward the television.

Sullivan joins Mandrake at the table. "Shit. It's hard to plan with company around all the time."

Mandrake shrugs. "Would you rather I'd have shot them?"

Sullivan shakes his head. "No. You did right. No sense upping the ante with murder on top of what we got planned."

"So, what *do* we got planned?" Mandrake's voice is louder than usual. "What are we blowing up? When do we get the money?"

Sullivan squints at Mandrake. "You high, man?"

"Fuck that. A little buzzed. Still got that Jim Beam I've been sipping on. That a problem?"

"You remember that dumbass joke you told about the dam back there at Dillon reservoir?"

"Sure do, dammit." Mandrake howls. "Get it?" He pauses. "Is that the one we're going to blow?"

"Yep, that's part of it. Actually, we're doing a twofer. First, we're going to plug an outlet shaft from the lake behind the dam. The Roberts Tunnel."

"What's that?"

"The tunnel is under the lake. It takes water from the reservoir and runs it under the Continental Divide down into Denver. We'll plug that first. Then we're going to blow the outlet at the bottom of the dam here at the lake. Enough to flood the town pretty good."

"What do you mean, pretty good? Are we blowing the dam or what? We trying to break things or send a message? I don't get it."

"We can't blow the dam. It's what's called an earthen dam. Made out of dirt. You'd need a nuke or something."

"Oh." Mandrake appears to process Sullivan's explanation. "You ever figure out who's paying us?"

"They say they're environmentalists. Pissed about Denver stealing water that should flow into the Colorado River, and they're against all dams, period. I'm trying to remember how Sarah phrased it. They want to make a statement powerful enough to start a *discussion*."

"Well, this ought to do it. I've never heard anything like that before. Where do environmentalists get the kind of money they're offering?"

"Right? They've got to have outside funding."

"That the Cowboy Timmons theory you mentioned before?"

"Might be. He gave Sarah my name… so she says. Those ranchers are pissed about Denver stealing their water, too." Sullivan cocks his head. "I don't know where the money comes from. Sarah has the money, so who cares who's behind it?"

"I guess I don't care either. Hell, you had me at a half-million," Mandrake says. "The rest is just noise. So, explain this twofer."

"Hang on." Sullivan disappears into the bedroom and returns with a map. He checks on Jim and Carrie on the way back. Sullivan turns the TV volume up. Rachel Maddow's spiky voice fills the room:

And here's what the president had to say at his Pennsylvania rally yesterday. Sullivan pauses to watch the video replay. A familiar voice drones, *I had such an easy life. People say, I had such an easy life. Who the hell knew it was going to be this difficult, but I love it.*

"Have fun with this one, Jimbo," Sullivan says.

Jim says nothing.

Sullivan returns to the dining room and spreads the map on the table. "I'm not sure Jim goes by 'Jimbo' out there in the real world."

Mandrake laughs. "Yeah, I don't think so."

Sullivan points to a blue lake on the map. "Here's the reservoir. There's the dam." He moves his finger to one end of the blue on the map. "The west end is here. The tunnel goes this direction," he draws his finger in a straight line through tightly packed contour lines, "all the way under the Divide—twenty-three miles. Comes out here." His finger rests on a river blue line. "The North Fork of the South Platte River. The water empties into holding reservoirs down in Denver."

"Which end are we blowing? I ain't diving, am I?" Mandrake taps on the reservoir on the map.

"No diving. We're going to blow it in the middle." Sullivan jabs his finger near the town of Montezuma, about halfway along the tunnel. "When they built this thing, they started at the ends, here and here." He points to each end of the tunnel. "But they also dug a shaft in the middle, digging opposite directions toward the ends. Close to a thousand feet deep."

"Uh-huh." Mandrake's eyes shine. "All we got to do is cave in the shaft and plug the water?"

"Yep. Going to rappel down about twenty or thirty feet and set up our stuff on the support structure. I've got timers and detonators on their way to us at a post office box here in town. We'll set up the explosives, wire the detonators, and then set up cell phone repeaters just to make sure it gets a signal."

"You control the timing with the phone? Is there like a fail-safe time where it blows, anyway?"

"Nope. If these guys pull the plug or something happens, then it doesn't blow. Gives us the option of bugging out with no damage done."

Mandrake studies the map. Sullivan drums his fingers on the table and looks back at the Schorks.

"What do you think?" Sullivan says.

"I think it'll work. But what do you need me for?"

"I need you to make sure I don't die when I got my ass hanging down that hole. There's no way I can do that shaft on my own."

"OK. And…?"

"And the shaft's the simple part. I really need your help on the main dam."

"What did you mean when you said you'd need a nuke to blow a dam made out of dirt?"

Sullivan pokes his finger on the Dillon Dam. "Right. If it was concrete, then we could just target the right spot and cause a structural failure. But there's no concrete, at least on the outside."

"So, it's concrete on the inside? Can we blow up that?"

"No. There's a concrete core that we can't get to. Everything else is fill. And the dam runs almost a mile long."

"Shit, what's the plan?"

"Where would you guess the weakest part of the dam would be?" Sullivan doubts Mandrake has a clue.

"Fuck if I know, I ain't no engineer."

"It's going to be the outflow valve." Sullivan moves his finger to the dam's south side. "See down here, at the bottom of the dam, is where the water comes out. It's just a continuation of the old Blue River." Sullivan tilts his head toward the window where the Blue River flows next to their condo.

"So, we blow up the mouth of the outlet? At the base of the dam?"

"I think that would work. But it's too hard to get at. And valve stations, like this one, have people working in and around them." Sullivan points to where the river re-starts at the dam's base. "And I don't know how we'd get upstream into the outlet."

Sullivan reaches into his pocket for his cell phone and pulls up a map of the area. "But how about this?" He scrolls the map up until Dillon Reservoir fills the screen, then zooms to the dam. "Take a look. The paper map doesn't show this."

Mandrake rounds the table, and looks over Sullivan's shoulder at the screen. Sullivan zooms in, and a concrete-lined hole appears in the water about fifty yards from the shore. "What's that?"

"That, my friend, is the Morning Glory Spillway."

"I see it, "Mandrake says. "So, the reservoir water goes down that drain hole thing and then comes out down at the base? By that pump station? It's like an overflow drain?"

"Right. It's like your toilet. That tube comes up the middle of the tank and keeps the water from overfilling." Sullivan glances over his shoulder again, checking on the Schorks. "There's a minor channel that comes into the river at the bottom of the dam from this section up here," he jabs his index finger on the dam's north end. "We'll come back to that. It's our backup." He returns his finger to the dam's south end. "When the water is high, like right now, the main flow is out the Morning Glory Spillway."

Sullivan taps the spillway. "If we get our bomb down that spillway tube, and then blow it, they can't close their shutoff valves. Then you'll have some serious outflow. The top of the overflow valve will collapse and it'll be underwater, so more water will start pouring in. The debris from the blast will suck inside and fuck up the shutoff valves. It will force all the lake water out of the outlet at the bottom. Like a 100-foot diameter fire hose."

"So, we *do* wipe out the entire town?"

"They aren't going to drown anyone to send their message, just buildings. It's going to flood the river, crest the banks, but when folks see the water rising, they'll bug out." Sullivan pauses. "It'll take out everything on the banks for sure; condos, houses, restaurants, that kind of stuff. The town's going to be pissed. And if it doesn't flood enough, we'll blow the backup charge on the north end."

"How the hell are you going to blow up that drain hole… what did you call it? The Glory Hole?"

Sullivan punches Mandrake's shoulder. "That's where you get to do that water shit you're so good at," he says, pointing to the shore near the Morning Glory Spillway. "You'll raft from here with the explosives. I'm getting you a wetsuit for this. You'll be roped to me on the shore here." He taps on the shoreline.

Mandrake's eyes widen.

"You steer the raft to the spillway over these barriers here." Sullivan points to roped orange barrels marking the no-boat zone. "When you got it headed for the hole, hit the detonator timer, go overboard, and head back to shore. I'll be pulling you in on the rope."

Mandrake studies Sullivan's cell phone for a good twenty seconds before laughing out loud.

"You are one crazy-ass son of a bitch." He shakes his head and laughs again. "And I must be crazier, cuz I can see it. I see it going down."

ZAHN

Elk Trace, near Buena Vista, Colorado-May 21st-22nd
I pull on my windbreaker the next morning before my morning walk. The forecast calls for seventy degrees, but the temperatures hover just above freezing in the mornings.

At nine-thousand-feet elevation at the base of Mount Columbia, Elk Trace offers a sweeping view of Mount Princeton and Mount Yale. The first week I moved in, I strolled the roads around my new home, pausing every two hundred yards to catch my breath in the thin air. Now fully acclimated, I can maintain a brisk walk for most of my routes. Depending on how much beer I consume the night before.

I push it today, propelled by my failure to make the top of Mount Harvard with Kristee. The scent of ponderosa pine overpowers the sour beer taste in my mouth. I angle toward the mountains and the higher lots where Kristee said the Schorks live. I pass the Yale Crest turnoff twice a week, but have never veered down the dead-end road.

I follow Yale Crest down, passing several houses on either side of the wooded drive before descending into a cul-de-sac. A sign reading *Schork* juts upright from the driveway's edge.

I scope the circle. These are sweet lots. The pines on the uphill slope block most of the mountain view, but to the east, you can see the Arkansas River Valley. The San Luis mountains show their snowcapped peaks to the south.

The Schorks and one other house occupy the cul-de-sac. The other lots sport realtor signs.

I note the 4-Runner parked in the Schorks' driveway and climb the porch steps. My watch says 8:00 am. Not too early—most of the Elk Trace folks have a good seventy years under their belts and wake at the crack of dawn.

Through the glass-paneled front door, I spy coats hanging on a hook in the mudroom. Movement flashes through the picture window. I spot a terrier jumping on a couch in the living room. It appears the Schorks are home.

Except Kristee's note is still jammed between the doorframe and the door.

I ring the bell and wait. No one answers the door. I ring it again. Nothing. What time had Kristee come knocking? Perhaps they run errands in the mornings.

I glance again at the dog cavorting around the living room. Would they leave the dog? Not for a mail run. They might if they were headed downtown for groceries. But that would mean they have another car. I clip down the steps and head back out.

·　·　·

The next day, I retrace my steps, stopping in on the Schorks. Kristee's note hasn't moved. The dog jumps at me through the window. I ring the doorbell again and wait.

Nothing.

I press my face against the living room window for a better look. A blanket lies on the floor. Three piles of dog crap decorate the hallway. As the dog scratches at the sill, it leaves bloody paw prints.

This dog hasn't been out for days. Something's wrong.

I pull my cell phone from my pocket and check for a signal. One bar. Not bad. Cellphone service sucks in Elk Trace. I bring up Perez's number and dial.

"What's up?" Perez answers.

"Out for a walk. Where are you?"

"Just south of Nathrop, on Highway 24. Pulled off on the shoulder waiting for an accident to happen. Everyone's slowing down to gawk at this herd of elk. Must be four or five hundred." He pauses. "Elk, I mean. Only thirty cars."

"You got time to run up here? To Elk Trace? I've got something you might want to see."

"You alright?"

"I'm fine. No hurry. Just a weird situation with a neighbor that Kristee Li noticed. I verified it while out walking. Best case, I think we might have an abandoned dog in a house. Worse case, well, I don't know. Some folks missing?"

"Give me an address, I'll be right there."

"How about you pick me up at my house? That'll give me time to finish my walk."

"Pick you up in twenty minutes or so, and we'll take a look. I'm not going to call it in yet."

"Got it. See you in a few." I hang up and turn back to the dog. "Hang in there, buddy. We'll see what we can do about getting you some food."

•　　•　　•

Perez pulls into my driveway twenty-one minutes after my call. I lock up and climb into his Tahoe.

"It might be nothing," I say and point toward Mount Princeton, as we pull onto the main drag. "The house is up the hill just over a mile on a dead-end called Yale Crest."

The Tahoe climbs the hill and Perez glances at me. "You run up this? I'm impressed."

"Walk. I'm working up to the running part."

"I need to get you out on some trail runs. Speaking of which, what are you up to next weekend?"

"Thinking about a hike up toward the Buffalo Mountains. All the snow's gone already up there. Or I might talk Kristee into taking me up on another 14-er attempt."

"How come she never calls me for that?" Perez doesn't pause for my answer. "Anyway, want to head over to Breckenridge on Friday evening? I talked to JD Robinson—you know, ATV kid's dad—and got one of his condos for the weekend. We could climb on Saturday, and hike on Sunday. Hit a brewpub in between."

"I'm in." Exercise. I need it. Beer. I need that too.

"OK. Friday and Saturday night. Two-bedroom, in downtown Breck. Nice setup."

"You want me to drive?"

"Nah, I got it. I'll pick you up Friday after work about six-thirty. That'll put us there about eight and we can go eat." Perez points at the street sign ahead. "Is that it?"

"That's it. And I'll be ready on Friday."

"Good." Perez turns and slows as the road descends. "Only thing that would keep me from getting the time off, would be a couple of dead bodies here. Hope you didn't ruin our weekend with this call."

Perez parks the Tahoe in front of the Schorks' house. "Might as well join me since you called it in."

I climb out and follow Perez as he scans the yard and exterior of the house on the way to the door. The terrier waits for us, nose pressed against the window, paws scrabbling at the couch. More blood stains the sill.

Perez rings the doorbell, but no answer. Perez pushes the bell again. Nothing.

Perez shrugs. "No indication of harm. No probable cause for a crime. I don't have enough to go inside without a warrant or cause."

"So, what do we do? Look at that dog shit in there. That's not normal."

"Let's check the neighbor. See if they know anything," Perez says, motioning toward the house at the end of the cul-de-sac. "We'll start close and work our way up the street. They might have seen them out walking."

We cut across the slope directly behind the Schorks' 4-Runner. The neighbor's house looks less occupied than the Schorks' place, with an empty driveway and drawn shades. We cut between a set of horseshoe pits. Perez points out a missing post on the pit closest to the back of the house.

"Hard to win if you got nothing to aim at." We round the house and cross the driveway. Perez gives the front porch doorbell a ring. A minute passes. Perez pushes the bell again. Nothing.

"This doesn't seem as strange," Perez says. "No cars, no sign of life. You said some folks winter down south and just show up in the summer, right?"

"That's what I've heard. A lot of houses up here look empty all winter."

Perez turns, hands on hips, and studies the road leading to the two houses. "Tell you what. How about you head back over and do a walk-around the back of the Schorks' place and I'll do the same here? Meet me up at the Tahoe when you're done. Don't go inside. Call me if you see anything unusual."

"Got it." Perez is giving me a bit more action than he did on the ride-along.

Perez disappears behind the house while I trudge back to the Schorks. I aim for the rear of the house, scanning the home as I walk. I zero in on the doors and windows. Nothing is open. Nothing appears broken. Unlike the last house, no blinds cover the Schorks' windows.

I circle to the front of the house, cutting across toward the Tahoe. As I walk, I glance at the other house. Perez gestures at me to join him. Reversing course, I walk back between the horseshoe pits to where Perez stands in front of a half-open door.

"Check it out." Perez lowers his voice, pointing at a damaged door jamb. "Break in, it looks like."

"What do we do next?" I say.

Perez says nothing for a few seconds. Then he says, "OK. Listen up. I got enough reason to go in now. But I don't want to do it by myself. And I sure as hell can't do it with a ride-along. There might be someone in there." Perez appears to weigh his options. "I need to call for support. But I can't guard this exit and run my handheld radio without possibly alerting the perp. So, how about you go make the radio call for me out of the Tahoe? Can you handle that?"

"Yep." I've got twenty-five years of talking on radios to air traffic controllers. Two-way radio isn't a problem. "I've made a few radio calls before. What's your call sign, who am I calling, and what am I asking for?"

My precise questions seem to confirm Perez's confidence in me. "I'm Chaffee 2. You're calling Salida. We've got a possible ten fourteen at... what's the number of this place again?"

"Not sure, but the Schorks' is 39110. On Yale Crest."

"Close enough. A possible ten fourteen next door to 39110 Yale Crest in BV. Request backup for an entry."

"Okay, so it's 'Salida, this is Chaffee 2. We've got a possible ten fourteen in the house directly east of 39110 Yale Crest, Buena Vista. Chaffee 2 wants backup so he can make an entry.'"

"That'll work. The frequency is already set. Just grab the mic, press the button, and talk. Wait in the Tahoe and watch the front of the house until they arrive."

"Got it."

Twenty minutes later, a white Crown Vic with flashing rollers and Sheriff decals coasts around the bend and pulls in behind the Tahoe. An officer walks to my window.

"You don't look like my deputy." The officer doesn't smile, but his eyes tell me he knows what's up.

I read his name tag. *Larkin.* This is Perez's boss.

"Hi, Sheriff. I'm Tyler Zahn. I know Rick from search and rescue. We're not sure what's up with the missing neighbors over there." I point past Sheriff Larkin toward the Schorks' house. "But Perez found a broken door over at that house when he went to ask them questions."

No reason to mention I was with Perez when we went next door. "He's in the back right now. He thinks that whoever broke in might still be in there."

Sheriff Larkin gives me a long look. "That was a tight radio call. You a cop?"

"No, sir. Air Force pilot. Used to be. Just retired now with too much time on my hands."

The Sheriff laughs. "I got a relative in the Army. Military does a good job teaching radios." He glances at the house Perez entered, then turns back to me. "OK. You stay here and monitor the front of the house. If you see anybody leave, use the radio to let us know. Don't try to stop them."

"Got it." I'm a lookout. I can handle that.

•   •   •

Fourteen minutes later, Sheriff Larkin and Perez exit the back door and trudge in my direction. Perez opens the Tahoe's rear hatch while the Sheriff fills me in on what they discovered.

"The house is empty. A couple named McCorkle owns it," Sheriff Larkin explains. "At least one person has been living in it for a day or more. Got food cans in the trash, liquor bottles, and they used the bed."

The Sheriff glances back at Perez, who is rummaging through a large plastic case. He turns back to me. "You stay up here. We're getting gloves and stuff out of the crime investigation kit and going in for another look."

A half an hour passes. The two officers step from the back door again and head toward me, faster this time. Sheriff Larkin goes straight for his Crown Vic. Perez pokes his head in the window of the Tahoe.

"Give me a hand with the crime scene tape." Perez's mouth turns up slightly at the corners. "You'll never guess what we found."

"What?"

"A prison uniform. Looks like our escapee from BV Correctional might have used this place as a hideout."

I gape at Perez. "And you think the Schorks are involved?"

"Not sure yet. As soon as we found the uniform, it changed the dynamic. We can investigate the prison break, but if we got the potential for kidnapping or homicide, that's something else. Me and the boss, we both think we need some help on this one. Sheriff's calling it in to the Colorado Bureau of Investigation, you know, the CBI. You and I need to cordon it off while they figure all that out."

I climb from the Tahoe and spend the next twenty minutes following Perez's instructions, taping off the entranceways to the McCorkle house and the exterior of the property. When we finish, we rendezvous with Sheriff Larkin for an update.

"CBI is sending out an investigation team. They're activating the Colorado Fugitive Task Force. You know what that means, right?" Sheriff Larkin focuses on Perez.

"Don't touch anything?" Perez quips.

"Yep. Also means the US Marshals out of Denver are going to be on this one for the prisoner. And probably the FBI for the possible kidnapping. They're on the Task Force, anyway." Larkin hooks his thumbs in his belt. "We're going to need to secure the scene until they get here. Which won't be for another five or six hours." He turns to me. "Sure appreciate your help, but there's no need for you to hang out here that long."

I'm dismissed.

He turns back to Perez. "Rick, I got a call in to Jesse to come take over monitoring duty. You stay here until he relieves you." He looks at me again. "You live up here, right?"

"Yep, just over a mile. I can walk home."

"Bullshit. I'll run you home. Take me three minutes." He puts his hand on Perez's shoulder. "After I drop him off, I'll start talking to the rest of the neighbors. When Jesse relieves you, find me and we'll split up the door-knocking."

"Got it," Perez says. He pivots to me. "Glad you raised the alarm. We wouldn't have found that prison uniform until the McCorkles returned this summer."

"What about the dog?" I say.

"Let's wait for the team," Sheriff Larkin says. "Need to be sure the Schorks aren't just out running errands. Come on. I'll run you home."

MANDRAKE

Breckenridge, Colorado-May 23rd

The Schorks stare at the television. Twenty-four-hour MSNBC would normally drive Mandrake nuts—but he's too loaded to care. After he finished Mr. Beam, Sullivan has graciously replaced his beverage with a fifth of Mr. Daniels. First name, Jack.

Mandrake keeps himself in a low-grade buzz as a coping mechanism. Drinking drowns out the television and dulls Carrie's smart-ass comments. And it's something Mandrake is good at. Sullivan takes his shift with the Schorks, and Mandrake decamps to his bedroom. TNT advertises a *Fast and Furious* marathon and he figures that will take up the rest of the day.

Sullivan picked up the booze when he made his mail run. They expect the timers and detonators by tomorrow. Sullivan tells Mandrake to be ready to place the shaft charges by tomorrow night.

Sullivan.

He's pissing Mandrake off. While he works on the charges, Sullivan keeps harping on him to throttle back with the drinking, so he'll be on his game. Mandrake has two problems with this. First, a little buzz is exactly how he stays *on his game.* Second, why buy the booze if he doesn't want Mandrake to drink it?

No matter. It's not hard to pace himself through the new bottle, seeing how he has an extra something to keep himself sharp—the oxy-

China Town combo he'd secretly mixed for resale. Before they left the McCorkles' house, he had set some aside for product testing purposes. And the first test's results? When you're mixing it with Jack Daniels, just a little dab will do you.

ZAHN

Elk Trace, near Buena Vista, Colorado-May 23rd

"Hey man, thought you'd like an update."

Perez's call interrupts my gutter repairs. My landlady is giving me a rent cut to fix these for her, and Kristee coached me on all things gutter. "Yeah, more than a little curious."

"They matched prints in the house to our prison escapee Mitch Mandrake. He was definitely there."

"And…?"

"And the Schorks were there too. The team found other prints and ran them through the national database. No match. Then they went up to the Schorks and—"

"Took care of the dog?" I interrupt. I know Perez is sharing something serious, but that mutt's bloody paws have been on my mind since I left.

"The dog is in caring hands," Perez replies. "Anyway, they pulled prints at the Schorks. They matched. The Schorks were in the McCorkles' house with Mandrake. Not only that, we found prints from Mandrake at the Schorks' house. Like they were having a little block party."

"What do they think happened?"

"No clue. It doesn't make sense that the Schorks assisted in the escape. If they were in on it, why wouldn't Mandrake just stay at their place? It's more like they discovered Mandrake staying at the

McCorkles' and he either took them or eliminated them." Perez pauses, then continues. "We brought dogs, and they were going wild at the place. Just can't tell why. The dogs will go off on drugs, explosives, and dead bodies. They searched the place and found nothing."

"Well, how'd they leave then? Did they take the McCorkles' car? Did the Schorks have another one?"

"Not sure. We called the McCorkles. They're in shock and are driving home. They said they left nothing but the ATV in the garage. The rest of their cars are with them in New Mexico. The neighbors up the hill say the Schorks just have the 4-Runner and another Toyota RAV-4. Both still there. The same neighbors said they doubted anyone came and got them unless it was the middle of the night. The only traffic they've seen passing their place is Kristee, who they all know, and delivery trucks. I think Mandrake, and maybe the Schorks, got picked up. The team agrees. Some broken brush behind the house could mean they hiked down to another road for pickup. It's only about a hundred fifty yards and the road's pretty secluded there."

"Holy shit," I say. "Big trouble in little Buena Vista."

"That's not all. We found some drug equipment over at the Schorks. Looks like it belongs to them."

"Like what?"

"A pill press, pill splitters, that kind of stuff. Neighbors say Mrs. Schork is a retired pharmacist. None of that stuff is illegal, so it might not be a big thing."

"What's next?"

"We're not doing diddly." Perez sighs. "Except for helping arrange rooms for the CBI, FBI, and Marshal teams rolling in and taking over. It's a shit show with all the different agencies. I walked some FBI guys to their room and there was almost a brawl right in the hallway."

"What do you mean?"

"I mean the US Marshal—they only sent one—is setting up the command-and-control structure. He puts his agency, the Marshals, in the lead because it's a fugitive case, right?"

"Right."

"The FBI guys hear that and spin up. They say it's a kidnapping and drugs involved, so the preponderance of criminal activity puts them in the lead."

"The FBI took charge?"

"No. The CBI guy hears them arguing, steps in and alpha-dogs them."

"Huh?"

"Yeah, he tells them all to shut the fuck up and listen. Surprisingly, they do. He tells them the Marshals, the FBI and any other fucking federal agency that shows up are only advisors, and work for him until anybody can prove any crimes crossed state lines."

"What do the feds say?"

"Nothing. This CBI guy, Hedley, tells them the primary focus on the case is the kidnapping, and secondary areas of interest include the drugs and the fugitive. I talked to the US Marshal afterward, a guy named Williams, and he was pissed. He was wondering why he even bothered showing up."

"Man, I thought military politics were bad."

"Oh, back to the dog. I picked up the dog crap at the Schorks, and took the dog down to the animal shelter. Got his paws taken care of. On my way, I gave Kristee a call just to see if she liked animals. She's going to watch him."

Finally, Perez has found an excuse to call Kristee. "Let me guess. You dropped the dog off yourself?"

"Of course. She didn't invite me to go climb a 14-er, though."

I like that Perez isn't afraid to get his hands dirty. He's transitioned from potential double homicide and confirmed prison escape investigation to arranging interagency room assignments and scraping dog shit off the floor in a stranger's house. Whatever it takes. He reminds me of the folks I used to work with in the Air Force. No complaining or trying to tell anyone *it's not my job.*

"So, our Breck trip tomorrow. Still on?" I say.

"I'm not sure. We'll have to see how this thing shakes out. I'm guessing the CBI and Feds will run it all, so there's a good chance I can take off."

"If you're tied up, any chance I could go up alone tomorrow and you come up on Saturday?"

Perez waits a beat. "Maybe. The condos are supposed to be for cops and family. I'm trying to set us up for drinks with Robinson tomorrow night. Wouldn't want you to do that alone, not without even knowing the guy."

"Let me know." It surprises me how much I've been looking forward to a weekend away. Be nice to have Perez there. But I don't mind drinking alone.

MANDRAKE

Breckenridge, Colorado-May 24th

Friday afternoon, Sullivan picks up the detonators and repeaters. They'll prepare for the first-phase execution that evening, planting the bomb in the midpoint of the Roberts Tunnel. Sullivan spends the day sorting out which explosives are necessary for the shaft. Mandrake eases back on the drinking.

He tries convincing Sullivan that tonight's operation will be easier if they just tie up the Schorks and leave them at the condo, but his partner isn't buying it. Sullivan claims he's already worried about leaving the rest of the explosives behind. Leaving the Schorks where they might escape or possibly suffocate will just add to his concerns.

That evening, they move the remaining explosives to the outdoor storage unit that comes with the condo. Sullivan's paranoid about leaving anything important in the condo. They stuff the couple into the truck in the same seat configuration: Carrie up front, Jim in back. Mandrake wedges Carrie's crutches with the equipment in the truck bed. Carrie looks relieved to get out of the condo.

"What? You need me in the front to navigate?" she says.

Mandrake cuffs the back of her head.

"Asshole," Carrie cries.

"Jimbo, you got to teach your woman some respect," Mandrake says.

Sullivan pulls out the makeshift blindfolds and tosses two back to Mandrake. Then he turns to Carrie. "Hard to navigate if you can't see." He peers outside at the dark. "The good news is you don't have to lie in my lap again."

The drive to the shaft takes thirty minutes, skirting the reservoir on Swan Mountain Road and intercepting the highway feeding east from I-70. Mandrake points at the moonlight reflecting off the patchy snow-covered slopes of the Keystone ski resort as they fork to the east. "Pretty," he says. Let those blindfolded idiots imagine his sensitive side.

Only two cars pass them, heading in the opposite direction. Another car follows them out of Keystone but continues straight when they turn off the highway.

Sullivan had warned Mandrake that access to the shaft might be a challenge. It is. A half-mile off the highway, a cable blocks the road, the wire padlocked to a metal post. They bolt-cut the lock, drop the cable, and leave a new lock on top of the post to resecure the cable on their way out. The odds of anyone checking on the shaft before they remotely blow it tomorrow night are slim, but Mandrake admires Sullivan's caution. No sense leaving the cable down and advertising their presence.

A light flickers on the road behind them then disappears.

"What do you think?" Sullivan says.

"Traffic from the main road," Mandrake replies. "Probably headlights reflecting in the trees."

They ease up the road another three hundred yards and park the truck next to a chain-link fence surrounding a cinder-block structure. Patches of snow glisten in the moonlight, and drift against both sides of the gated entrance.

"It's on the back end of that building," Sullivan says. "Let's get these guys situated and discuss the rest outside." He loops around the car to the passenger door and catches Carrie's elbow as she stumbles out. "Keep the blindfolds on."

They push Carrie into the back seat.

"Use this for Jimbo." Sullivan tosses a bike lock to Mandrake.

Mandrake loops the lock around the steering wheel, then stretches Jim's arms around the front bucket seat, and zip-ties his wrists together. Mandrake threads the bike lock through the zip-tie loop and around the headrest bar, locks the lock, and shoves the small key in his pocket.

"How you liking that, Jimbo?"

Jim's face presses against the front headrest. He says nothing.

Mandrake positions Carrie's arms around Jim's right arm and zip-ties her wrists together. Carrie's injured ankle ends up wedged in with Jim's feet. It looks awkward, but bearable. *Who cares?*

Sullivan sweeps the flashlight along the fence and adjacent structure. "The gate's a keypad lock. Can't use the bolt cutters. I don't see any cameras. Let's cut through the fence there." He points to the far side of the enclosure. "Where it's not so easy to see from the parking area. Then we'll set up the cell phone repeaters. What do you have for signal?"

Mandrake pulls out his phone. "One bar."

"That's what I got too," Sullivan checks his phone. "Probably enough for this all to work, but we'll put the repeaters up to make sure. You put one on the roof. I'll place the one above the tunnel."

Mandrake takes a step toward the fence.

"Wait. Put these on." Sullivan thrusts a pair of surgical gloves at Mandrake.

Mandrake grabs the gloves and puts one of them to his mouth, laughing. He inflates it, then pinches off the opening with his fingers.

"Look. It's Chicken Buddy. We used to make these back in the pen. Almost as much fun as a Sock Buddy." Mandrake laughs again as he lets the air out of the glove.

Sullivan shakes his head. "You got issues, man."

The two men don their gloves, and tramp to their planned entry point. Mandrake snips a vertical slit in the fence, then pushes it apart, wide enough to get through.

"Want to start hauling the stuff?" he asks Sullivan from the other side.

Sullivan edges through the fence. "Let's check out the shaft first. See what we're working with."

They circumvent the building to find a four-foot-high single rail, surrounding the perimeter of the shaft. The moon hangs two-thirds full, illuminating the area behind the maintenance building.

Sullivan switches from the flashlight to a headlamp and scans the yard before focusing on the shaft. Mandrake straps on his headlamp, pointing his beam down the shaft. They both peer over the edge.

"Glad you're going down and not me," says Mandrake. "It's a fucking black hole."

"Nah, look over there." Sullivan points his flashlight beam toward the edge of the shaft closest to the building. "There's an access ladder right there. I'll strap up and we'll use the ropes to lower the bomb. It's not as bad as I thought."

"What did you think?"

"I thought I was going to be hanging from one rope with all the explosives shit dangling from another, and trying to find a good spot to place them. With the ladder, even if there's no platform, I can just wedge the stuff around the rungs."

"How far down are you going to go?"

"Not sure yet. Need to check out the sides. If it's solid rock up here, then I want to get down low enough to find some looser rock that will fill the shaft and plug the bottom. If it's loose up here, near the top, we'll set it down a little way, twenty feet or so."

"Let's go get the stuff," Mandrake says.

They cross the yard and duck through the fence opening. At the truck, Mandrake opens Jim's side and points his headlamp inside.

"What's happening, Jimbo?"

Jim turns his head toward Carrie, then back to Mandrake. "Can you retie Carrie? She's got her ankle wedged. It's hurting her."

"Tough titty, little biddy," Mandrake says. He leans over Jim toward Carrie's bound arms. "Give me a hug, darling."

Carrie turns her blindfolded head toward Mandrake. "Dick," she whispers, then turns away.

Mandrake closes the door and rejoins Sullivan at the rear of the truck.

"Problems?" Sullivan says.

"Nope, let's roll."

It takes them four trips between the truck and the shaft to move all the material. Mandrake ponders what Jim and Carrie have guessed about all this. They probably figured out he escaped prison. But they're likely clueless as to why Mandrake and Sullivan would kidnap a middle-aged couple, hang out with them in a condo, then move a bunch of boxes into the middle of the Rockies.

After they position the gear, Sullivan hands the truck keys to Mandrake. "I don't want to drop these while I'm down there." He steps into his climbing harness before handing the repeater box to Mandrake. "Get up on that maintenance building roof and find a spot where it won't move around, would you?"

Mandrake grabs the small box and walks around the perimeter of the building looking for an easy way up.

No ladder. Shit.

The top of the large utility box beside the building is within three feet of the roof. Looks doable. He tucks the box in his jacket pocket, and scrambles up the side of the box. Once on top, he pulls the repeater out and positions it on the sloped shingles, leaving room for him to hoist himself onto the roof. Mandrake presses his palms on the roof at chest-level. It should just take a little jump, then a press up like doing dips at the gym.

He pulls his pistol from his waistband and lays it at his feet. Then he counts to three and jumps. His belly hits the edge of the roof, but the arm press technique fails. *Fuck.* The prison had a gym. Why had he never used it? He slides backward an inch. *Fuck.*

He thrusts his arms higher, pressing his palms flat against the shingles while inching the rest of his body onto the roof, and drags himself over the edge. He lies motionless for a full minute, catching his breath. Then he grabs the repeater and stands.

A one-foot vertical vent pokes from the midpoint of the roof. *Perfect.* He orients himself in the reservoir's direction from where they will send the signal. The repeater needs to go on the downhill angle of the vent and he needs something to keep it from sliding off the roof. He pulls Jimbo's bag of zip-ties from his pocket and threads one through the vent bracket and the casing on the repeater.

After taping the antenna wires to the side of the vent, Mandrake presses the power button and waits for a green light. Then he crawls to the edge of the roof and works his way back to the ground. Two minutes later, he stands next to Sullivan at the edge of the shaft.

"All set," he says. "How's it going here?"

"I just secured the repeater over there." Sullivan points toward the barricade. "Here's my safety line." He grabs the rope attached to his harness and traces it to where it is anchored on the perimeter barrier. "I'm going down the ladder, but plan on using this as the backup if the ladder gives. Or, if I need to move away from the ladder, then this will be my primary and I won't have a safety."

"So, if that line goes, you fall?"

"Yeah, but I don't plan on leaving the ladder. It's a just-in-case thing." Sullivan tilts his head toward the box of explosives. "You see, I've got that thing all strapped up with the two pulley mechanisms."

He picks up the rope on top of the box. "When I call or give the rope a shake, you walk the box to the edge with the rope on top. When you set it down, you grab the rope and pull out the slack. Then you just nudge the box over the side and start lowering. Got it?"

"Yep. Next to the ladder, right? So you can reach it?"

"Right. The box has a safety anchor there." Sullivan points to another rope next to his anchor. "But if you need that, we're in trouble. Just don't drop the rope."

"Got it."

Sullivan rechecks the ropes and his harness and looks at Mandrake. "You ready, man?"

"Shit yeah," Mandrake says. "You're doing all the hard stuff."

"Yippee-kye-yay, mother fucker." Sullivan disappears over the edge.

ZAHN

Between Leadville and Breckenridge, Colorado-May 24th
"What's a weekend look like for you?" I have to raise my voice. We're heading east out of Leadville in Perez's Jeep Renegade, climbing up Fremont Pass toward the Climax mine. Carved walls of snow border the highway, casting shadows from the setting sun across the passing lane.

"I work half the weekends in a month," Perez complains. "I'm the middle-ranking deputy of three. Can't just pick my schedule. When I'm off, I usually hit the range and shoot, or do the SAR thing." Crossing Fremont Pass, our conversation snags as we gape at the snow-covered mine. Colorado's largest producer of molybdenum has scraped at these mountains long enough that it looks like they might actually level away the peaks someday.

I pick up where we left off on the descent to I-70. "And the dating life?"

"I'm still in recovery from the last one. I could afford my own weekend condo if I wasn't making monthly payments to my ex."

"Ugh. Sorry to hear it."

"What about you?"

"Nothing on the dating front." I decide to reassure Perez. "Divorced too. The only women I've met are in SAR—and they're all my daughter's age." I shake my head.

"You like music?"

"Yep."

"I go down to The Lariat sometimes. Or the Deerhammer, or the Surf Hotel if there's somebody good playing. I'll give you a call next time." Perez pauses. "We could invite Kristee along."

I doubt the places Perez mentions hold my future heart's desire, but listening to a band resonates. I turn my head toward my window. "Why not? I've got nothing better to do but sit around and wonder why an escaped convict would kidnap a middle-aged couple."

I wait for Perez to process my words. It's not my smoothest segue.

Perez is silent. As I turn back in his direction, he says, "What do you mean? You thinking about the case?

"It doesn't make sense." I rest my hand on the dash. "You pointed out the first odd thing about it. Why escape when he was probably getting out in a year or two?"

"Right."

"Holing up at the McCorkle place, up in Elk Trace. That's not bad. Smart idea. No one was looking for him locally. All he had to do was steal a car or have someone pick him up."

"No one reported a missing vehicle."

"Right, and half the neighborhood folks are weekend warriors or only live there in the summer. All kinds of opportunities to steal a car."

Perez tags on. "And he could have made the Schorks tell him who was home and which houses were empty. They probably know who keeps cars up there while away."

"Possible," I say. "But here's what's got me thinking." I glance at Perez. "Do you really think Mandrake planned on escaping from prison just so he could kidnap the Schorks?"

"Not really."

"So why take them?" I say. "There's something more than a prison break going on here. Figure out why he took the Schorks, then you figure out what's really going on."

Perez shoots me a grin. "Don't hold your breath waiting for the Task Force to give us an answer. The US Marshal guy, Williams, he's focused on catching Mandrake. The FBI guys want to bring the Schorks home. I'm not sure they're doing a lot of talking to each other."

"If they did, they might figure it all out."

"So, following your train of thought, I see a couple of ways it could have gone down," Perez says.

"Let's hear them."

"Worst case? They might be dead. The Schorks caught Mandrake in the house and he killed them and stashed the bodies."

I pause, then answer. "Could have. A lot of work to find a car and figure out how to move the bodies with no one seeing him."

"Right. So, alternatively, the Schorks could be in on it somehow? What about that drug stuff CBI found?" Perez appears to ponder his own question. "I mean if Mandrake was in cahoots with the Schorks, why would he break into the house next door, and why would the Schorks leave their dog?"

"Right. Doesn't add up. But someone ought to take a hard look at the Schorks."

Perez agrees. "If the Schorks are bad, the Task Force will figure it out. They've got teams in the house and all those tech geeks combing their computers and shit." Perez is silent for a full minute. "So, that brings us back to where we started. He took them. Hopefully alive. Why would he do that?"

"Well," I say. "None of the prisoners at BVCC are murderers or rapists, right? All drugs and other offenses?"

"Right."

"So, what if the Schorks interrupted Mandrake's plan? I don't know what kind of plan. An escape plan, a drug plan, something that's on a timeline, and Mandrake took them because leaving them after they had seen him would mess up the plan. Mandrake is a con—well, I guess he's an ex-con now—but that doesn't necessarily mean that murder is his go-to method for resolving issues."

Perez glances at me, then slows, rolling to a stop on the shoulder. "Holy shit, Tyler. That one makes a lot of sense." He shakes his head. "I should have thought of that."

"I'm not saying I'm right. I know nothing about criminals. But I spent over twenty years in the military examining courses of action. And it seems like a course of action Mandrake *might* have taken."

"I like it. I like it enough that I'm going to get on the horn when we get to Breck and let the guys back there chew on your theory. That all right with you?"

"Sure. Whatever helps. But feel free to tell them it was your idea. I don't need to be involved."

Perez bobs his head, and steers back onto the highway.

•　•　•

Twenty minutes later, we pull into the Alpine Basin condos and park the Jeep. Perez taps in the door code, and we survey our living arrangements for the weekend.

Fancy. Two bedrooms in the loft, a master on the main floor, and an open kitchen, dining, and living room floor plan with windows opening towards the forested hills behind the complex.

"This is sweet." I tour the condo, admiring the setup.

"You're probably used to 5-star hotels being a pilot and all. You can have the master bedroom if you want."

"No way," I protest. "You set us up. You get the king-size bed. And I'm no Gucci pilot. The plane I flew in the Air Force? Bunch of canvas covering metal rods for seats. Blue-collar."

"So, no Hiltons in Hawaii?"

"Before all the shit hit the fan in the desert, we used to stay in some decent places on cargo trips around Europe. But once 9-11 hit, it was all Middle East stuff. The only time we didn't sleep in a tent or the back of the plane was on the way to the desert and on the way home."

Perez smiles. "No wonder you fit in with those young guys at SAR. They slept in the back of their van. You slept in the back of airplanes. You're kindred spirits."

"Right." I laugh, but I'm thinking I don't have much in common with those hard-chargers on my SAR team. "Where're we going to eat?"

"We'll walk to a brewpub just down the road. JD and his wife will meet us for a drink after dinner. Let me call back to the department and pass on your Schork theory and then I'll send him a text we're heading out."

"Great. I'm starved."

. . .

The Blue River Brewpub displays varnish, metal, and clientele that work against its attempt to look rustic. Fancier than anything in BV. But I haven't gone looking for fancy in my town.

We grab a table by the bar and I order a bacon burger for me, and one of the new-fangled fake meat burgers for Perez.

"What's up with that?" I say as the waitress departs to place our order with the kitchen. "I saw you eating eggs in that quiche at the coffee shop. So, you can't be one of those vegans."

"Vegetarian, brother, not vegan. Just don't eat meat."

"Why?"

"Plants are good for you. Meat, not so much. Plus, I discovered when I stopped eating meat, I could drink an extra beer now and then without gaining weight."

I treat for dinner. Perez springs for the drinks—two pints of the microbrewery's signature IPA. As we finish eating, a silver-haired man in a down jacket opens the main door for the woman he's with. He tosses a silent hello to the bartender and smiles to the room like a king entering his court. He and the woman wind their way toward us.

Perez waves. This must be our host, JD Robinson, with his wife. Robinson looks about ten years older than me, and his wife is definitely more Perez's age. Possibly a bit younger. Backslapping his way through the bar, Robinson owns the room.

The woman with Robinson is not a stereotype. No wallflower waiting adoringly in the face of Robinson's larger-than-life personality, she laughs alongside her husband, reaching out and punching the arm of the guy at the table closest to Perez and me. A good-looking woman with penetrating eyes, her thick hair is gathered in a tight ponytail running past her shoulders. I'm guessing the down jacket, like her husband's, is designer.

"Rick, how are you?" Robinson claps Perez on the back. I stand and pull out chairs.

Perez gives Robinson a half-hug, then grabs the woman's hand. "Leanne. Good to see you." He turns toward me. "This is Tyler. He was with me when we ran into Seth the other day."

Robinson shakes my hand. "Hey, good to meet you."

Leanne smiles at me. "Hi, Tyler."

Robinson shakes his head. "Yeah, sorry about Seth. He knows better. I told him he's banned from Chaffee County for a month."

Perez laughs. "Come on man. An ATV on county roads? Ain't no felony. Lots of worse things a teenager could be up to. He's a good kid."

"He is. He sure is," Robinson agrees. "I told him he should spend more time out on the lake. Warmest spring in years. Did you see how high the water is?"

"Our county too," Perez says.

We spend the next hour drinking beer and small-talking. Robinson dominates the conversation, but the topics don't center on himself. Instead, he quizzes me about my military time and grills Perez on the latest happenings in the Sheriff's department.

Perez and I both try to pick up the drinks tab, seeing how we're staying in Robinson's condo, but the server knows Robinson's unspoken rules: no one else can pay, and Robinson should never hold an empty glass. Robinson even picks up the bill for the neighboring group, where Leanne love-socked the guy.

Robinson emanates an aura, accompanied by a deep voice that blankets the room. People turn their heads when he gets going on a topic. Not annoyed—just interested in what the man has to say. And beer doesn't have any effect on him. I've downed three beers in the two hours and Robinson is out-drinking me at a rate of two to one.

The noisy table next to ours stands to leave. Leanne's friend walks over to shake Robinson's hand.

"Thanks for the beers, JD. You didn't have to do that."

Robinson booms out a reply. "Can't help it, Rich. I see a group having a good time and just want to facilitate."

Rich laughs. "Well, it worked. I told these guys that you were like the Rob Tolliver of Breckenridge. You're the king!"

I'm not a pop culture expert. Perez shrugs at the "Rob Tolliver" reference.

Robinson's normally ready response freezes. He narrows his eyes at Rich, pressing his lips together. "Hope you guys had fun. Take it easy."

Rich's eyes widen. He's obviously been dismissed.

"Right, see you, JD. Good night, all." Rich tips his hat to the rest of our table and departs.

"I'll be back." Leanne stands and heads toward the restrooms.

I glance at Perez and then at Robinson, whose eyes follow Leanne's path. Something is going on here. Something that isn't my business.

Perez lacks my propriety. "What was that about?" he asks Robinson.

Robinson turns to Perez. "Nothing. Rich just picked a bad night to bring up Tolliver is all."

"Who's Tolliver?" Perez says.

A braver man than me. After watching the couple's reaction to Tolliver's name, there's no way I'd ask these questions.

Robinson glances back at the bathroom doors again. "You know how the four big towns show on the map, right? Like a backward question mark, with Dillon at the top in the north, Silverthorne and Frisco curving around the west side of the reservoir, and Breck down at the bottom where the point would be." Robinson arranges beer coasters on the table showing each of the towns.

"Rob Tolliver owns all the condo developments in Dillon and Silverthorne and about half the ones in Frisco," Robinson points at the coaster above the one representing Breckenridge. "I've been trying to expand up toward Frisco for a couple of years. Every time I put a bid in on open property, Tolliver sees it coming and swoops it up. He owns those towns. And the worst part about it is that after he outbids me, he usually doesn't even develop the property. He's just taking them so that I can't."

"A land baron war," Perez says. "No wonder you're pissed at him."

Robinson shakes his head. "It's part of business. And yes, it pisses me off. But Leanne takes it personally. She hears Tolliver's name, and it's instantly Ice Age. As you just witnessed."

Leanne exits the restrooms and heads in our direction. Robinson nudges Perez. "New topic."

Leanne approaches the table, lifting her eyebrows at Robinson. He stands, grabs his coat, and dons a smile before addressing us. "Gentlemen, we're going to have to hit the road." He turns to Leanne. "You ready, honey?"

"Ready."

Perez gives me a look that says he's ready to go too. We push out of our chairs and grab our jackets.

"We'll leave with you," Perez announces. "We're doing some climbing tomorrow and need our beauty rest."

We walk to the parking lot with Robinson and Leanne. After saying our goodbyes, we take the path leading to our condo.

"You all need a ride?" Robinson's voice booms from the passenger side of a sports car.

"Thanks. We got it," Perez hollers. "Nice of you to build a condo so close to the brewpub."

Robinson laughs, and waves us off before lowering himself into the car. Leanne backs out and exits up the slope toward town center.

I turn to Perez, as the headlights disappear. "That guy's in control,"

"What do you mean?"

"I mean your friend JD just drank a six-pack, soothed a pissed-off wife, recognizes he's over the driving limit, and lets his wife drive him home."

"He knows I'm a cop?" Perez jokes.

"Maybe, but I think that guy likes running things."

SULLIVAN

Roberts Tunnel near Montezuma, Colorado-May 24th
Sullivan grasps the ladder handles and threads the safety rope to the side to keep it from tangling on the descent. He puts a foot onto the first rung, testing his balance and pointing his headlamp between his legs to check the ladder's condition.

We're doing this.

Sullivan isn't sure why setting the bomb feels like opening day at the ballpark, but this part—planning the operation, scouting the terrain, and executing—brings back the rush of his bomb-disarming days in the desert. He'd almost forgotten how much he enjoys the adrenaline surge.

Back in the sandbox, the high from cheating death and the satisfaction of the job only lasted a day or so. Between missions— boneless chicken breasts at chow, no booze, same movies on a laptop hard drive—the rush faded. But this? This money will change his life. The reset he needs for a fresh start.

Sullivan counts as he descends. At rung forty, he checks his surroundings. Two metal channels, like vertical railroad tracks, run along the shaft's right side. The rails are remnants of an elevator rig used to move tools and materials up and down the shaft.

On the other side of the shaft, smooth, solid stone lines the wall— too solid for what they are trying to do. He isn't deep enough.

Sullivan lifts his chin. His headlamp barely illuminates Mandrake's face, peering at him. The moonlit sky casts a blue aura around the shaft's opening. "Gotta go deeper."

Mandrake shoots him a thumbs up and Sullivan aims the light between his legs, He spots a shelf attached to the wall at the end of his beam. He descends another forty or fifty feet, pulling up even with the shelf. The platform juts from the rails. Three metal girders thrust out four feet with weathered wooden planks lying crosswise on the support beams, unevenly spaced.

Definitely not something that would hold his weight. He pushes a plank with his free hand. The wood is aged and dry, but the girders appear strong and are spaced close enough to hold the dynamite's weight.

Sullivan surveys the walls. The rock consistency is different at this level—chunks of boulders rather than the smooth sides from above.

He trains his light down the ladder. Nothing visible between himself and the end of the beam. This is the spot.

"Mitch." His voice echoes. "Send down the stuff."

"What?" A faint reply.

More muffled words trickle from above. Sullivan grips the safety rope, whipping it twice. The rope whips back at him—then tightens. Mandrake got the signal.

Sullivan gazes upward. The starlit sky a dime of light, like looking through a soda straw. On the edge of the circle. Mandrake is lowering the box.

The rope next to the ladder swings like a pendulum, bumping the container against the wall at three-second intervals, each thump louder as it nears Sullivan's head. The rope twirls and swings from side to side. He times the swing, clutching the edge of the container with his left hand, and pushes it against the shaft wall to stop its momentum.

He yells to Mandrake. "Got it!"

Muffled response.

Shit. Should have had Mandrake anchor the lowering rope. Sullivan grasps the ladder with one hand while pressing the case against the shaft wall with the other. The platform is only a few feet to his right. He eases the pressure on the box and it slips several inches.

He needs both hands on the container if he wants to move it onto the platform. He'll need to use the safety rope. At least he knows that rope is secure—he anchored it himself before descending, and Mandrake has taken up the slack.

He sucks in a breath and leans back in the harness before releasing his right hand from the ladder rung. He drops an inch or two, but the harness holds. Swaying left, Sullivan grabs the case with both hands and kicks away from the wall. Hugging the box, he uses his legs to press off the rocks, moving a couple of inches per push along the boulder face of the shaft toward the platform.

Maneuvering past the ladder, he bumps into the first girder. A board splinters. A chunk of the plank separates from the girders with a loud crack, echoing as it tumbles down the shaft.

Sullivan waits for it to hit bottom.

Nothing. Not even a thud.

The remaining planks are plenty of space for the explosives.

Hanging just below the platform, he inches the box over the edge until it rests on the remaining boards. With his feet pressing against one girder, he reaches above his head and slides the container closer to the wall of the shaft.

When he can't move it any farther, he kicks off the girder and swings back to the ladder, grabbing it firmly with both hands. He gathers himself and tilts his head back. "Coming up," he calls. His words echo down the shaft and the dark hole swallows them up.

Good thing he hadn't tried to do this alone.

MANDRAKE

Roberts Tunnel near Montezuma, Colorado-May 24th

Mandrake peers over the edge of the shaft as he lowers the box of explosives. A moment later the line slackens. Sullivan must have it secured. As he follows the rope with his headlamp beam, it goes from slack to full taut and begins swinging back and forth.

What the hell?

He pivots from the shaft to check the pole securing the lines. As he turns, he catches a flash of movement near the break in the fence. His mind races. Did the Schorks get out?

He grabs for his pistol in his waistband. *Shit.* He's left it on the utility box next to the maintenance shed roof.

Shit. Shit. Shit. He's unarmed—naked and afraid. He squints into the moonlit yard. Two figures move toward him. He peels off his gloves and tosses them down the shaft.

"What's up, *hombre*?" a man in the lead calls.

Mandrake doesn't answer.

"Doing a little maintenance work?" the man says. He trains a gun on Mandrake.

The moonlight reflects off the man's loafers. He looks familiar.

"Let's take him to Robert," says the second man.

Robert? Fuck. Big Bobby's guys—the ones he traded the drugs to for the explosives. Mandrake struggles to understand why they are here. Headlights thread the trees.

The first man waves his pistol at Mandrake. "Let's go."

Mandrake walks forward, forcing his eyes away from the shaft, and ducks through the fence. The two men follow close behind.

Two more figures stand next to the open doors of Sullivan's truck. The SUV from the Twin Lakes meet-up, minus the trailer, blocks the rear of Sullivan's truck. A silhouette of a man shows in the passenger seat.

A voice calls out, "Roberto…"

A man on Jim's side of the truck steps away from the door, his pistol pointed at Mandrake. It's Robert from the drug exchange.

"Robert, what's up? What are you guys doing here?" Mandrake laughs. Then he laughs again. He's nervous.

"I should ask you the same thing. Except I don't care. Where's your partner?"

Mandrake shrugs. "Just me and my friends here. Not with the other guy anymore."

"Friends, huh? Why are your friends tied up and blindfolded?" Robert looks over Mandrake's shoulder at the fence. "Jesse, what's back there—where you find this guy?"

"A big fucking hole," Jesse answers, "A mine or tunnel or something."

"Go keep an eye on it while we deal with this piece of shit."

Jesse leaves. Mandrake's heart pounds hard enough that his fingers are throbbing.

"Julio, search him," Robert commands. He eyes Mandrake. "Dorsey says your name is Mandrake, that right?"

While Julio pats down Mandrake, Jim's eyes shine from the back seat. Robert has taken off the makeshift blindfolds.

Mandrake nods.

"OK, Mr. Mandrake, here's the problem. We gave you your stuff. But you messed with our stuff."

"What are you talking about?"

"I mean it's not pure. You cut it with some shit."

"Bullshit," Mandrake sputters. "I gave you what I got in the package."

"No, amigo. It's been tampered with." The man patting down Mandrake shakes his head. Robert continues. "By someone like you, I'm thinking."

"No, I—"

"Shut up." Robert gazes at Mandrake. "You pulled some of our China Town out and cut in some other shit. We want the rest of the China Town." Robert moves his face closer to Mandrake. "Where were you from the time you got our shit to the time we met you at the lakes?"

Mandrake sizes up the men. It's like a bad movie. His heart races as he struggles to keep up with his situation. They're bluffing, not entirely sure what happened when. If he starts talking now, they'll kill him.

"Robert, blow me. I didn't take your shit," Mandrake says.

Robert stiffens, before turning to the truck. "Mr. Jim. Do you know where Mr. Mandrake here got the other shit?"

Jim says, "They came in an envelope to our next-door neighbor's house. I grabbed the envelope because I always pick up the mail for the McCorkles. Then he—" Jim's body jerks toward Mandrake, his temple pressed against the headrest. "He broke into our house looking for the envelope. We came home while he was there and that's how we ended up here."

"Have you all been with Mr. Mandrake ever since?" Robert says. "Do you know every place he's been?"

Jim tries to turn his head toward Carrie but can't.

Carrie spits, "Except from Leadville on. The bastards blindfolded us after that."

Mandrake glares at the couple through the open door.

Robert steps toward Mandrake. "Keys, phone."

"What?"

"Give me the keys to the truck and your phone." Robert moves the gun closer to Mandrake and holds out his other hand.

Mandrake digs into his pocket and holds out the keys. Robert grabs them. Mandrake reaches into his back pocket and hands over his phone.

Robert cocks his head, and Mandrake senses Julio shift behind him.

Mandrake laughs.

Robert shoots Mandrake in the head.

SULLIVAN

Roberts Tunnel near Montezuma, Colorado-May 24th
Sullivan finishes prepping the explosives, then works the touchscreen with his thumb, calling up the detonator-cellphone link. He keeps one hand on the ladder and a foot on the platform, breathing easier now that his body weight isn't solely supported by the safety rope.

Once Sullivan sets the detonator, he unties the rope from the box and gives it a tug to signal Mandrake. He scans the platform and walls one more time, then aims his light up the shaft toward the exit. He hears voices. More than one.

Fuck. Who would Mandrake be talking with?

He powers off his headlamp and freezes. Beams of light cross the hole above him like a disco ball.

Shit. Sullivan steps down three rungs. After he passes below the platform, he swings off the ladder on his safety rope and leans back in his harness while grasping the bottom side of the structure. His new position keeps him out of sight.

The voices go silent. Then a crash almost knocks him from the platform supports. The shelving above him buckles from an impact, planks splintering above his head. A dark shape sags between the broken wood and solid girders.

Sullivan flicks on his headlamp. The beam catches a face with open, blank eyes and a hole in the forehead, as it slides past him, gathers speed, and pinwheels down the shaft. He sucks in his breath.

Mandrake.

Sullivan's hand shoots back to his headlamp switch. In the pitch-black darkness, he senses the tension in his climbing harness release. The rope slithers against the platform, the sound like a rat in a crawlspace, as it drops from above. Sullivan hangs from the bottom girders, the length of safety line now dangling below him like an anchor. Legs bicycling in the air, all thoughts of Mandrake disappear.

They cut my fucking ropes.

Sullivan waits. The shaft has gone silent. He kicks one leg up to an adjoining girder, then the other, relieving the burning in his arms. He pauses, hearing nothing but his own breath.

After a slow count to sixty, Sullivan guesses whoever dumped Mandrake has left. Hanging by one hand, he reaches with the other and turns on his headlamp. He waits a few seconds. Nothing.

Half the platform has disintegrated. Sullivan's legs curl around the remaining bare girders. Hand over hand, Sullivan works his way toward the remaining wooden planks. Gripping a girder with one hand while pressing a wooden plank with the other, he pulls himself onto the edge of the splintered platform.

The box of explosives remains pressed up against the shaft wall, the rope dangling down from the case. Sullivan can't trust the remaining board to hold him—hell, Mandrake had broken right through it. Sullivan scoots toward the ladder, grabs the rungs, and swings his body off the platform onto the metal frame leading up the shaft.

What the hell just happened?

Mandrake is dead. Whoever killed him probably thinks Sullivan is dead, too.

Or maybe, they don't know about him.

It's not the cops. Cops don't throw bodies down shafts. Cops don't cut ropes.

Someone else is on to Sullivan's operation, but who?

Sullivan pulls himself up the ladder. He pokes his head over the rim, scanning left and right. No one is in sight. Frayed threads from the cut ropes glimmer white in the moonlight. He steps from the pit and stands at the perimeter, looking for signs of life. Nothing.

He ducks through the fence and heads for his truck.

It's gone.

Fuck.

They took his truck and the Schorks. They killed Mandrake. Sullivan's mind races.

Then he gets it. This is prison shit. This is about Mandrake, not Sullivan. Whoever killed Mandrake doesn't care about Sullivan's bombs.

It's the drug guys. Besides Sarah's people, who else could have tracked them to the shaft? He remembers the perimeter guard Mandrake caught behind the truck during the transfer. The "creepy fuck." He needs to move.

But if he can blow the dam alone, he'll no longer need to split the money.

Back to three million bucks, baby.

Sullivan returns to the hole and steps out of his climbing harness. If the shaft is deep enough for Mandrake, it's deep enough to dump everything else. He tosses his gear down the hole.

His mind spins as he walks away from the shaft. He has to get to the condo and finish the job before someone figures out what is going on.

The Schorks can identify him but don't know his name. Are they even alive? If the druggies have no compunction about killing Mandrake, then they certainly won't have any concerns over getting rid of the Schorks. Why didn't they get thrown down the shaft?

He needs to finish the job. Too many loose ends.

Sullivan mulls this over on the way to the highway. The main road comes into view. He checks his watch. 4:26 AM. Too early to hitch a ride.

He angles off the shaft road, looking for a resting place in the dark woods. A few steps in, he bumps into a large log. He kneels next to it, running his hands over the ground. Relatively flat. Good enough for a rest.

He props his back against the log. *This is fucked.* Then he pictures the potential payoff now that Mandrake is out of the picture and the job practically half done.

Half-a-million more for him.

Bye-bye mattress factory. He smiles, closes his eyes, and sleeps.

•   •   •

A truck's air brakes wake Sullivan a couple of hours later. He rolls over and watches taillights flickering through the trees. The sunrise backlights the peaks to the west but needs another hour to crest the mountains.

Sullivan shivers. It's 7:09 AM. Time to find a ride. He works his way through the woods toward the highway, pausing in a gully adjacent to the road. All quiet. Sullivan scrambles up the loose dirt. He checks for traffic left and right, before crossing the road and shuffles toward Dillon. Hobbling is more accurate. Between the shaft work and sleeping outside he's pretty beat up, but his joints loosen as he moves. A westbound truck pulls over to his raised thumb. The driver offers him a ride to Dillon, near I-70 and drops him at the nearest gas station.

Sullivan strolls to the restrooms. Sitting on the toilet, he pulls out his cellphone and opens his Uber app, on the off chance the ride-service company has penetrated the Rockies. Sullivan types in the condo's address, and arranges for a car to pick him up in ten minutes.

Halfway through taking a shit, Sullivan groans. *Fuck.* He's left the cable gate down, back at the shaft access road, with that new lock on top of the post. Might not be a big deal. The road to the shaft didn't look like it got much traffic. Until last night, that is.

He exits the restroom, grabs a package of white donuts—the kind with powder on them—and fills a cup with coffee from the industrial machine next to the checkout counter. Sullivan pays with cash before walking outside to wait for his ride. The sugar rush from the donuts and the hot coffee provides a shot of confidence.

He looks across the road at the dam separating him from Frisco and his condo. The small town of Silverthorne straddles the Blue River at the base of the massive earthen wall. By this time tomorrow those residents might be knee-deep in water.

A red Nissan Altima pulls up. Sullivan climbs in the rear seat. He doesn't feel like talking. Evidently, neither does his driver. Fifteen minutes later, he exits the car at the condo office and walks the rest of the way. What would the Schorks have told the druggies? What if the men who killed Mandrake are waiting for him at the condo?

If his truck isn't here, the bad guys probably aren't either.

But no truck means no transportation for tonight's op. He's going to have to rent one.

He walks through the complex, checking vehicles and looking for his truck. Nothing, but the condo door is wedged a half-inch forward in the splintered frame. Did they ditch the truck and come here with another car? He wishes he had Mandrake's gun.

He puts his ear to the door. Silence. He shoulders the door open and steps inside. He checks the condo from end to end. Pillows, sheets, and the other set of clothes lay strewn about the hallway. The contents of the refrigerator decorate the kitchen floor. Sullivan steps outside and strides to the storage units, checking the parking lot for anyone watching. He taps in the code and opens the door. His boxes remain untouched in the center of the closet. He opens the top box for confirmation and sighs in relief. He has what he needs to blow the dam.

Whoever trashed the condo was looking for something. They didn't find his explosives. Not yet, anyway.

He smiles. If he can get his ass out of here before they come back, this might still work.

ZAHN

Breckenridge, Colorado-May 25th

I ride shotgun the next morning as Perez weaves through the bustling weekend traffic. We head north to a site he's picked out at Swan Mountain.

Perez takes a sip from his to-go coffee. "We'll start with simple top-rope work to get you going."

"Top-rope?"

"Like in those indoor climbing walls. You fasten your harness to a safety rope running to the top of the climbing route. If you miss a step or a hold, the rope will catch you. The difference from indoors is that I'll use an existing route up the first time, set the top rope, rappel back down, and be your safety belay."

"So, if I fall, you're going to be strong enough to hold my body weight?"

"Physics, brother, physics. Show you when we get there."

We spend three hours practicing on two different routes before stopping for a lunch break. Perez's fitness level is off the charts. Mine, not so much. The altitude isn't helping things, but cramps in my fingers slow me down.

The spring sun has heated the rock wall and sweat soaks our shirts. I finish my lunch and lean against a rock with my eyes closed. The climbs have energized me. I need less beer to do it right. The drinks last night with JD and Leanne don't help. I open my eyes. Perez is studying me.

"I can't figure you out," he says.

"What's to figure?"

"Whether you're like on a path of self-exploration to become a better you, or you're heading down the slow road to falling apart."

I squint at Perez. "Deep words. You sound like Ruth at that yoga class." Perez doesn't respond, so I force it. "What the hell are you talking about?"

Perez pushes an unopened baggie of cheese toward me. I nudge it back. "It's like there're two Tyler Zahns." He holds out his left hand. "On the one hand, you've got the Zahn who's researching yoga. I mean who researches yoga?"

Perez can't miss the surprise in my eyes. "Ruth told me. I told you I know everybody in town." He smiles. "So, potential yoga guy and power-walking around his neighborhood at nine-thousand feet trying to get back in shape. This Zahn joins Search and Rescue. Volunteers at the library."

"You have a problem with this guy? Sounds like a real Boy Scout." Inside, my head screams, *Where's he going with this?*

Perez's eyes meet mine. "But what are you actually *doing*, man? You rent a three-bedroom house, but never mention any visitors. You don't go out at night. Hell, you've never even heard of those bars I mentioned on the way here."

Perez takes a breath. "Howard offered you the training job at Search & Rescue, and you turned it down and the job teaching at the school, too." Perez shakes his head. "And I don't think you're hiding a girlfriend in your place."

This side of my new pal surprises me. I didn't expect Perez to be a connoisseur of human nature, peering into my life. But he's not doing a terrible job of it. Next thing you know, Perez will be digging through my trash, finding the empty beer cans—a sure-fire Zahn's-an-alcoholic clue. And certainly enough for him to see how I spend most nights.

Screw him. A bit of nightly numbness helps me face my tomorrows. The ones where I try to be the better Zahn and make up for the past.

Perez continues, "So, I'm back to not being able to figure you out. You did all those things in the military. Running what? A battalion? Of planes?"

"Squadron," I say.

"A squadron of planes. Leading people into combat. You were a fucking big deal, man. And here? Well, it's like you hiked up to 10,000 feet to swim in a mountain lake and then stand in it at knee-level afraid it's too cold. Why do all that work to get there if you're just going to stay on the shore all afternoon? What are you afraid of?"

I'm pretty sure Perez respects me, or at least respects my past. I don't think he's trying to give me a hard time. He's just concerned.

I'm not impressed with the timing, though. I can't pour my heart out about something I don't fully understand myself. Not now. Not yet.

"More metaphors, Rick? My sad life and alpine lake swimming?" I'm getting huffy, so I try to balance my next statement with a smile. "Give me a stinking break. I just moved here, dude. Give me some time."

Perez shoots me a skeptical look and grabs his harness. "Daylight's burning if we want to get one more route in."

Well, shit. It's not even noon. Perez's cheer sounds about as forced as it can get.

And how many chances am I going to get with him?

So, I tell him. Everything. Almost.

•　　•　　•

Perez already knew I had to go back home during Operation CROWBAR—back to my family because my son Jacob was sick. So, I tell him about the late evening incoming phone call from the desert. How it was night in Texas, but morning in Kuwait. The grim news that followed.

"Plane down. No survivors."

Perez stares up at the mountain, avoiding eye contact. "What happened exactly?"

"RAVEN 24 had been hit after parachuting a load of supplies into the drop zone. The missile took out one of their outboard engines and part of the wing. But those Herks, man, they're workhorses. It just flew on. They limped the aircraft back to Kuwait, but the damaged engine caught fire."

I shot a glance at Perez. His face was expressionless. "All hell broke loose. The rest of the wing burned off." I cast my eyes down. "They crashed just twenty miles north of the runway."

My body shudders. Thanks to my relationship with beer, I haven't relived this in years. But now the guilt I felt for leaving the desert in the middle of combat barrels through me.

Perez almost whispers. "Your family needed you. And your aircrew was following orders."

"But they were using my tactics and died, while I sat in the comfort of my home three thousand miles away."

"What could you have done if you'd been there?" Perez has hit the crux without even knowing it.

I stand and walk away, then pivot, my finger pointing. "I failed to put eyes on the mission before it launched." I shout, "I could have adjusted the timing or the routing, or the crew composition."

Perez stands. "So you think you could control enemy missiles?"

I shake my head, "No, but—"

"Someone else had to be in charge, who?"

"My deputy, Brett 'Mac' McDonnell, a top-notch leader. He ended up commanding his own squadron a year later." I scraped my hands over my scalp. "But just as it was my responsibility to take care of my family, it was also my responsibility to lead my airmen, especially when tragedy strikes. That's what true leaders do."

The rest spills out. "I wasn't there, man. I should've jumped on the return flight to Kuwait. Helped Mac pick up the pieces. Recover the bodies, tell the parents and spouses, and bring the fallen home. The missions weren't stopping just because the squadron reeled with grief. They needed me."

"So why didn't you?"

"Sheila was already exhausted from our own trauma." I flash back to when I broke the news. Her face sagged like she might break at the thought of nine families dealing with the loss of their loved ones. But her brown eyes had narrowed, into a silent question. Would I leave her when she needed me most? "She knew I wanted to leave. I knew I couldn't leave her."

"She said that?"

"Not out loud, but we stopped sleeping in the same bed. Eleven days later, Sheila came into the guest room. Told me to go. Said she couldn't deal with Jacob and me at the same time."

"So you left?"

"Flew out the next morning. Was back by the time the crews returned from their night time missions."

I explain to Perez that I ended up leading my airmen through the most successful resupply of a forward ground unit in the history of the Iraqi conflict. And brought the rest of them home after their year was up. "No one else died. But I couldn't make up for the rest."

"So because your family needed you, you think you failed your troops?" Perez sinks back down to the ground. To his credit, he says none of that shit about understanding, how cops know what it's like to lose another cop. He just returns his eyes to the mountain.

I fill his silence. "So, I finished my time in the desert. Did the grind at the Pentagon, then contracting bullshit." I grimace. "And I left my family. Now I'm just trying to figure things out. That's what I'm doing here."

Perez keeps his voice steady, as if he doesn't want to set me off again. "Hey, I'm not questioning your right to do whatever you want, I'm just saying—"

"You're just saying that I'm not doing what you'd expect, right?" I know I'm being defensive, but I can't stop. "Just let it go, Rick. I appreciate your efforts to get me out and about. You're a good friend. But I'm not giving you a sloppy kiss for it."

Perez shakes his head slowly, looking at my untouched bag of cheese. "Alright, brother, but I'm not sure I understand your strategy." He points back to the rocks. "You got enough gas in you for another route?"

I snatch up my climbing harness at my feet. "See if you can keep up." As I step into it, Perez's cell phone rings.

"Perez." He listens for a moment. "Yeah, we're still here. East side of the Dillon Reservoir."

Pause.

"What? You're shitting me!"

Pause.

"Hell yes, I can be there in…" Perez looks at his watch. "About an hour. Call you when we're on scene."

Perez punches off his phone and turns to me. "Forget the harness, we're moving out."

I loosen the straps on my legs. "What's up?"

"They just found Mitch Mandrake. He's washed up on the North Fork of the South Platte River—where that tunnel from this reservoir comes out—with a bullet in his forehead." Perez strides toward the parking lot.

I hustle after him and shove my gear in the Jeep before climbing into the passenger seat. "Help me out with the geography. Where's the North Fork of the Platte?"

"Over on Highway 285. It drops down off Kenosha Pass on the way to Denver. Just before Grant." Perez pulls out and turns toward Breckenridge.

"So, we go through Breck and over Hoosier Pass?"

"Right. Come out at Fairplay and join 285. About 30 minutes northeast of there," Perez explains. "Park County sheriff is on the scene and has jurisdiction. When they found Mandrake's body, one of the deputies recognized him from the prison break 'be-on-the-lookout' notification—"

"I know what a BOLO is."

"OK. From the BOLO. So they gave Chaffee County a call. Thought we might want to have a look."

"Is the FBI team coming up too?"

"Nope. It's just Mandrake. There's no sign of the Schorks, so the Task Force is sending up Williams—the Marshal I told you about." He turns to Zahn and smiles. "We're about 30 minutes closer and the boss—my boss, not the Task Force boss—thought it wouldn't hurt for us to have a look."

We pass through Breckenridge on our way over Hoosier Pass. Perez is silent. As we crest the pass, I turn to Perez. "How do you think he got in the river?"

"The real question is how he got in the tunnel. They found the body about thirty yards outside the opening, just before it feeds into the South Platte. So, he either washed out of the tunnel, or someone dragged him up that way to make it look like that's where he came from."

"What do you know about this tunnel?"

"Not much," Perez says. "I know they built it back in the '50s or '60s when they built the Dillon Reservoir. Water from the reservoir flows through it to help supply Denver."

I twist toward the mountains we've just driven over. "Really? Dillon Reservoir's all the way back behind us. That's a hell of a tunnel."

"Yep. Goes under the Continental Divide."

Flashing lights of a Park County sheriff flanked by a beater Honda Civic and an ambulance mark the scene. I glimpse the tunnel's mouth as Perez passes the line of cars. He pulls over onto the shoulder and shuts down the Jeep.

Perez beelines toward a small group of people standing on the bridge between the tunnel and the river. I lope after him.

The sheriff introduces himself as Bill Engstrom and as he shakes Perez's hand, the two men realize they already know each other. Perez introduces me.

A young woman with a nose ring and downcast eyes stands next to Engstrom. She shifts her feet before stealing a glance at Perez and me. She looks more girl than woman. I glance over her shoulder. A team of paramedics stand in the water between the tunnel and the bridge, grouped around a form clothed in bright blue.

Engstrom introduces the woman. "Gentlemen, this is Alta. She spotted the body. Lucky for us. It might have been days before we found it if she hadn't stopped."

Perez smiles and moves to shake her hand. The woman's eyes drop to the road.

Perez doesn't lose a beat, sweeping his outstretched hand toward the tunnel. "Why did you stop here?"

Alta mumbles, "Waterfall pictures."

"You stopped to take pictures of a waterfall?" I say, thinking something's off.

Alta bobs her head but keeps her eyes down.

Perez turns to Engstrom. "What's at the other end of this thing? This is the tunnel coming from the Dillon Reservoir, right?"

"Yup. My uncle worked on this thing," Engstrom says. "Only two ways to get something in this tunnel besides this exit here." He points to the water spewing from the mountain. "There's the opening where it starts, which is up at the reservoir. I think the hole itself is underwater, controlled with valves from a building on shore. Probably just a metal grate underwater to keep debris from flowing down the tunnel."

Perez glances at me. I raise my eyebrows. Perez turns back to Engstrom. "Doesn't sound like a likely entrance point for the body. What's the other way?"

"It could have come from the shaft."

"What shaft?" Perez says.

"My uncle said when they built this thing, they started in the middle. Sunk a shaft nearly a thousand feet deep and then dug out both directions toward the lake and toward this river. I'm thinking that's where the body might have come down the shaft and out to the river."

Engstrom adds, "Not our jurisdiction, though. Probably Summit County."

Perez turns toward the tunnel, then looks back at Engstrom. "How about you call it in, and I'll head up there with my partner? Give it an initial look-see. You tell Summit County they can either meet us up at the shaft, or we'll give them an update when we're done."

Engstrom lets loose a half-grin. "Sounds good to me. We're running incident command out of our headquarters in Fairplay. If you all find anything, call it in to us as well."

"Will do," Perez touches his forehead. "Oh yeah, you got a US Marshal—Randall Williams—on his way up here. Probably here any minute. Tell him what we're up to. Have him give us a call if he wants to discuss."

Engstrom agrees.

We say our goodbyes and scramble down the bank for a closer look at the body. One of the paramedics joins us and Perez introduces himself.

"What do you got?" Perez says.

"Pretty straightforward—but not something we see every day. We're guessing the bullet to the head killed him. Haven't checked for water in the lungs yet—we'll wait until we get him up to the hospital— but probably dead before he hit the water. We think all the scraped skin is from the drop down the tunnel. There's no bruising in those areas, which indicates they occurred after death."

Perez turns to me. "Up for checking out a thousand-foot hole in the ground?"

My body aches from climbing, but we're just looking, not spelunking. "I'm in."

•   •   •

We ride in silence for most of the drive. Perez is keeping his thoughts to himself and I am, too. But as we skirt the east end of the reservoir, I point at the dam on the far side.

"Check out the water level. Is that normal?"

"Lots of snow this past winter. And it's a warm spring. I never really thought of it until now, but the technicians controlling the reservoir must bust their ass trying to control this runoff from the melting snow. Probably have that tunnel Engstrom mentioned flowing at max capacity. Same with the river coming out the bottom of the dam—full throttle."

The road winds between hills and trees on the shoreline. I strain to keep the lake in sight, trying to spot the tunnel control building Engstrom mentioned. A thin layer of snow covers the frozen reservoir behind us, but when I look at the dam, I see open water. Another week and the ice will be gone.

"I think that's the finger of land that juts toward the start of the tunnel." I point toward a ridgeline overlooking an inlet of water.

"Huh. Can't see it from here. Should we check it out before the shaft?"

I can't tell whether Perez really wants my opinion or is just being polite. "Engstrom made it sound unlikely, but we could stop by on the way back if we don't find anything at the shaft."

"Agreed."

After merging onto Highway 6, we take the Keystone exit onto the narrow road winding up the pass. Perez checks his phone and eases off the gas for a right turn. A hundred yards down the gravel road, he rolls past a cable laying on the ground between two gate posts. He brakes.

"Let's take a look." Perez throws the Jeep in park and hops out. He circles each gate post in turn before climbing back in the Jeep. We continue up the road.

"Weird. Brand new lock left on top of that post," Perez says.

"Should we grab it? Evidence?"

"Evidence of what? We don't really know what's going on here. If it's nothing, then I've stolen their lock. If it's something and I grab it, then I've screwed up the fingerprints."

Perez parks outside the fenced complex. We exit the Jeep, each of us scanning the area.

I point toward the fence. "Someone cut through."

Perez eyeballs the damage. "Let's put some gloves on." He retrieves a first aid kit from the back, rifles through the pouch and tosses a pair of surgical gloves my direction, keeping a pair for himself.

We hop out, and duck through the fence hole. Perez circles the building, and I follow, searching for anything that looks out of place. At the shaft, Perez steps over the barricade surrounding the pit and peers over the edge. I join him. A ladder and rails fade into darkness about ten to fifteen feet down.

"Need a flashlight," Perez says, stepping back over the barricade. I survey the yard again. I head over to the building and try the back door. Locked. I circle around and try the front door. Locked.

As I round the building to meet Perez, I pass a large utility box on the side of the building. A muddy footprint on the box's side makes me pause. Glancing Perez's direction first, I touch my finger to the very edge of the print. The mud is wet. I step several paces back and gauge the distance between the box and the roof. Do-able, with a little effort. I step back two more paces. No visible footprints on the roof. But I spy a small box resting in front of a vent.

Everything about the building screams 1960s, but the box looks modern. I walk around the building and yell to Perez, who stands with his flashlight pointing down the shaft. "Hey, I'm going to check something out over here."

I return to the utility box and grab a metal bar to pull myself up, carefully avoiding the mud on the side of the box. As soon as I crest the edge, I see a pistol lying on the flat surface.

Holy shit.

Now I see why Perez had us don gloves. Grabbing the gun, I lower myself to the ground. "Rick," I yell, "check this out."

Perez rounds the corner of the building "What you got?"

I dangle the pistol by the barrel, and motion toward the top of the utility box. "Found it up there. And look at this." I motion with my free hand to the mud streaked on the box's side.

"What the fuck, Zahn?"

"I know, right? It's got to be related to Mandrake."

"No, Zahn. I mean why did you pick it up?"

"I've got gloves on. Isn't that why you had us wear them?"

"Did you snap a picture before you picked it up?"

Oh shit. "No. After you mentioned the lockdown at the gate, I was only thinking about fingerprints." I glance up toward where I found the weapon. "Sorry."

Perez opens his mouth, and I prepare for a dressing down. His mouth closes, and he's silent for a moment. "Right. Let's put it back where you found it, but we'll have to explain what happened when we get a team up here."

I'm an idiot. I should have realized the position of the weapon might have been a clue in itself. Now I'm hesitant to bring up the box on the roof. What if it's nothing? I step back to see if I can see the box from here.

"What?" Perez says.

I can't keep this from Perez. Even if it's nothing.

"There's a weird box strapped to the roof vent."

Perez climbs the utility box and turns to me. "Give me that."

I pass the gun to Perez with my thumb and forefinger on the end of the barrel. He pinches it just below my fingers and lays it down out of my sight.

I don't move. I'm not doing anything else until Perez tells me to. Perez continues onto the roof to check out my "weird box." I step back until I can see him. He crouches next to the vent and squints at the zip-tied device.

"I think it's a repeater." He raises his voice. "A new one. You're right. It's odd."

"What would it repeat?"

"See these wires running up the vent?" Perez points at the taped wires on the side of the sheet metal. "I've seen this before. Antenna wire. The repeater picks up a cell phone signal and pushes it out. It's on, too. Can you see the power light from down there?"

I shake my head. "Why so close to this facility? If you needed to call out, you'd set it up down the hill."

"I'm not sure." Perez turns toward the gate, then scans the fence line. When he faces the shaft, he pauses and points. "Look at that. On the other side of the barricade. Looks like another one." He gets to his feet and walks to the edge of the roof. "Let's go check it out."

Perez climbs down from the roof, skirting the pistol on the utility box, and we approach the repeater hanging from the barricade. The same green light winks from the corner of the box.

Perez says, "Same green light as the roof. You thinking what I'm thinking?"

"What?" I'm thinking it's a way to communicate to or from the shaft but I'm hesitant to voice my opinion after my buffoonery.

"Looks like a comm setup for people in the shaft."

Shit. Should have spoken up. "Maybe for an inspection team so they can talk to whoever is down there?"

"Could be. Seems like a legitimate team would come up with a better system than zip-ties though." Perez snaps his fingers. "I don't think it belongs to an inspection crew. First, you saw the water flow barreling out of the tunnel where we found Mandrake, right? No way there's a team down there this time of year unless they're on a raft and have a death wish."

"Wait. I think I know your other reason." I forget about my earlier errors. "Batteries."

Perez's head pumps. "Yep, no power lines coming out of these repeaters, so they are only good as long as the batteries last."

A temporary comm link. A convicted felon dead at the other end of the tunnel. Why did Mandrake escape in the first place?

He was on a timeline.

Shit. No way...

"Rick, we got to go down there."

"What are you talking about, man?" Perez's expression makes it clear he thinks I've lost my mind. "Whatever phone he had probably washed into the river with his body."

"No—here's what I think. I think Mandrake was doing something else in the shaft. What if the repeaters aren't for voice communication? Couldn't they relay a signal instead?"

"For what? Blowing up the shaft?" As soon as he says the words, Perez's mouth falls open. "Holy shit, that Park County guy, Engstrom—he said this thing supplies water to Denver."

I bob my head, "And if Mandrake blew up the shaft that would plug the tunnel, right?"

"There might be a live bomb down there." Perez walks around the edge of the shaft to the ladder. He grabs curved rungs and shakes them. The ladder rattles, echoing down the chasm. "I've got go down that?"

"I could use the ladder." The words are out of my mouth before I realize what I've said.

Perez gives me a thin smile. "Neither of us are using that ladder without a safety rope. And you're not going anywhere down that shaft."

"I just meant—"

Perez interrupts, "I got the climbing gear in the Jeep. I'll just put on my harness with a line, tie another as a safety, and then go down the ladder. I can use these barricade posts. Technically, I wouldn't even need the ladder."

"We could call it in to the bomb squad," I say, giving him an out.

"What if we're wrong?"

"You could blame it on me. I'm screwing everything else up."

Perez aims a thin smile at me. "Don't beat yourself up. Pretty sure I wouldn't have made the leap to possible explosives." He strips off his surgical gloves. "I'll get the gear out in the Jeep." Perez beams at me. "We'll know in five minutes if we're right."

• • •

Perez leans over the edge of the shaft, wearing a climbing harness, and tying up his ropes. His helmet perches on his head, a headlamp wrapped around it. I remove my medical gloves, replacing them with a leather pair from Perez's climbing bag. He gives me belaying instructions and we practice rope-pull signals for communication.

I'm nervous as hell about belaying, but don't dare say that to Perez. No time for a lecture on accepting responsibility.

Perez pulls on his gloves and lowers his foot to the first rung. Into the shaft.

He points to the rail structures on his right. "For hauling stuff up and down," he notes and continues down the ladder. After fifty feet, he disappears.

"Everything OK?" I call.

"I don't see anything yet." Perez's voice echoes in the shaft, then dies out.

A minute later, Perez yells, the sound fainter than before. "Got something down here. A box. With a blinking green light on it."

"Then get your ass back up here and we'll call it in."

"I'm going a little closer to check it out."

"Dammit," I say, knowing Perez can't hear me.

Three long minutes pass and I feel panic setting in.

Perez's voice floats up. "I'm coming up." A minute later, Perez pulls himself to the top of the ladder. "This is serious, man. I didn't get a look inside the box, but it's wired to go with what looks like a detonator."

"Can you disarm it?"

Perez shakes his head. "Not my area of expertise. Can't mess with it anyway without letting you clear the area first. I have an idea though. Something we could do after we call it in."

"What's that?"

"We can disable the repeaters. I mean, clear it with the bomb guys first, but I think if we take these repeaters out, there's no way a signal can reach down the shaft."

"And it's not like we think anyone's going to blow it, right? I mean Mandrake is dead."

Perez disagrees. "I'm not so sure. I mean, yes, I'm sure he's dead, but Tyler—I found blood all over the platform down there next to the bomb."

"No shit. Mandrake had a bullet hole in the center of his forehead."

"Yeah, but think it through. Let's say Mandrake set up the bomb and armed it to blow. When did he get shot?"

"Well, obviously after he armed the bomb. What's your point?"

Perez pauses. "No one would go down that rickety ladder without a rope. Right?"

"Not unless they were crazy."

"So Mandrake didn't get shot while he was setting it up because if he did, we would have found a harness on his body."

Now I get it. "Right. And who would go down there to kill him, if they could just wait until he came up?"

"Exactly," Perez says. "They could have cut the rope while he was down there, but Mandrake might have been able to climb up the ladder. So, they just wait until he crests the top and pop him then, right?"

"Wrong. I see where you're going with this. Why would they wait for him to come up and then make him take off his climbing harness? They would just shoot him and drop him back down the shaft."

"Which means—"

"There's more than one person involved here." My voice rises in pitch. "And that means there are still dangerous people out there who may have the controls to blow this tunnel up." I look around. Technically, they could blow us up too. We need to get out of here.

Perez finally speaks. "OK. I don't want to call the bomb guys first. I'm a little nervous about using a cellphone this close to all this shit."

"Yep," I say, relieved Perez is in charge.

"Okay, priorities," Perez says. "Let's get the repeaters down the mountain and away from here. Get to better cell coverage, and call in the cavalry."

I offer, "Bomb guys first, then the Task Force bubbas, then Sheriff Larkin?"

"Exactly. Once I got the calls made," Perez continues. "We'll head back to BV. I'll drop you off, grab my Tahoe so I got all my stuff, and head back here." He pauses. "Shit, I need to update Park County and coordinate with Summit County to let them know what's happening in their jurisdiction. Best get some permission to be here." Perez smiles.

Excitement courses through my body. A familiar feeling from my past—and not a terrible one. We have faced danger and lived through it. I imagine Perez is feeling it too.

"You're not cutting me out of this thing now, are you Rick?" I ask, trying to not whine while untying his climbing ropes from the barricades. I feel stupid about moving the gun, but I'm still glowing a bit for thinking of the bomb.

Perez dons a fresh pair of surgical gloves. He disconnects the repeater from the rail and turns to me. "It's not personal. I can explain your involvement so far because we were on off-duty time, but once I get my uniform on and climb into the Tahoe? Well, that's an actual mission. I can't really have you on a ride-along on a real mission. A liability thing, you know?"

I sag a bit, disappointed. "I'll go get the other repeater—as long as you're sure it's okay for me to move it?"

Perez laughs, handing me a pair of gloves. "Do it. This is a safety thing."

I cross the grounds to the utility box and climb to the top, avoiding the pistol lying next to my feet. *I don't want to go home.* The dopamine rush from just holding the damn rope during Perez's climb clings to me like when my crew dodged a missile in Iraq. And I didn't even do anything. But I felt a part of something. Like coming in high above SAM range, then rolling the lumbering plane into a steep spiral to minimize exposure to the combat zone. Nervous enough to pucker the seat of my pants, but in a good way—senses hyper-aware.

I'm not ready to give up on this mission. My brain is operating at warp speed, as I pull myself up to the roof and walk to the repeater. This entire shaft is only a cellphone call away from blowing up. Someone out there has the phone providing the signal. I snip the repeater from the vent with my multi-tool's small scissors and carry it back to the roof's edge, holding it by the corners with my surgical gloves. By the time I reach the ground, I've made up my mind.

Perez waits for me at the fence. I join him and we walk to the Jeep.

"Drop me off in Frisco," I say.

"Why? What's in Frisco?"

"Nothing. But I feel like I'm in the middle of this. I don't want to go home. I understand why you can't bring me back. I get it." I stop at the Jeep and help Perez position the repeaters in the back. "But I want to do some thinking about this entire setup. There's something missing. Not like a physical thing. Just some piece of the puzzle that we're not seeing."

"Why Frisco?"

"Because it's on the way. And if I think of something, I'll already be in the area. It's not like you'll get in trouble if I come up with a lead and you follow up on it, right? And if I come away empty? You can give me a ride home when it's all over."

"OK," Perez shoots me a funny grin. "You figured out a piece of this thing already, and I like the idea of you staying close." Perez hoists himself into the driver's seat. "But you shouldn't have to pay out of pocket, man. Let me see if JD can hook you up with a place in Breck."

I slide in. "Cool."

Perez reaches to turn on the car, then pauses and pulls the keys from the ignition. "You drive, and I'll start making calls on the way back, OK?" He hands me his keys.

We switch places and I navigate the winding gravel road to the highway. Perez's phone shows one bar, and he makes calls on speakerphone.

The Summit County dispatcher spins up as soon as she hears the word *bomb*. Perez waits while she puts the sheriff on the phone. His voice is so loud it's hard to understand.

"You found what? Where is this thing?"

The sheriff assumes the bomb response coordination, allowing Perez to concentrate on updating everyone else.

Next, he calls the Task Force based in BV and updates them on the shaft and the accomplice theory. He explains a possible second party might have helped Mandrake escape and might be the one trying to blow the shaft. Perez reminds the Task Force to call Marshal Williams.

Then he dials Park County and updates them on the situation at the shaft. I sense Park County's relief that Mandrake's death likely occurred in Summit County. "Let us know if they need any help," they say, but it sounds half-hearted.

Sheriff Larkin back in Chaffee County is the next call, and he agrees with Perez's plan to retrieve his patrol car and augment Summit County's force. Perez doesn't mention my plan to stay in the area to anyone. Folks might not be so agreeable about that.

Perez finishes updating everyone as we pass the east end of Dillon Reservoir. He turns to me. "Think of anyone I might have forgotten to coordinate or liaison with? I'm about all talked out."

"Three counties, the FBI, and the US Marshals. I think you covered your bases." Then, I remember what we're forgetting. "The repeaters."

"Shit. Forgot about those," Perez says. "Let me call back Summit, and they can ask the bomb guys." He pulls his phone from the charger and gets the Summit sheriff back on the line.

"Remember I told you about pulling the repeaters?"

"Right?" the sheriff says.

"Can you ask the bomb team what they want us to do with them? They're in my back seat right now."

"Shit. I'll call the bomb guys. Plan on dropping them somewhere here in Dillon. I'll call you back."

"Roger," Perez says. "I'll stand by." He glances at me and dials another number. I recognize the booming voice from the bar. Perez turns off the phone's speaker and presses it to his ear. He thanks JD for the condo stay and then gets straight to the point.

"JD, got to ask another favor."

Pause.

"Well, we've found ourselves doing some actual sheriff work up here and we'd like to see if we might use one of your Breck condos for another night or two."

Perez glances at me as he waits for a response.

"Uh-huh. No, we really appreciate it."

Pause.

"Sure—same one is great." Perez listens, raising his eyebrows at me. "Well, it's ongoing, so this is just between us but it's kind of a big deal. Murder slash possible terrorism."

Pause.

"Yeah, no shit is right."

Pause.

"We're right in the middle of it, JD."

Pause.

"Uh-huh. Much appreciated."

Perez turns to me. "He offered you the same one we used last night up in Breck."

"Right, he doesn't own condos in Frisco," I say. "Remember that Tolliver guy drama?"

"Right." Perez's cell phone rings. He puts the phone back on speaker. "Perez."

"You said you're going back to Buena Vista, right?" the Summit County sheriff says. "Pull in at the Burger King on the right just before you get on I-70. My deputy, Stan Muziak, will wait for you in a Summit County Sheriff rig. He'll take the repeaters off your hands. The response team is an hour out."

"Okay, but we're only three minutes out."

"If you beat him there, just wait."

"Got it."

I turn to Perez. "Just drop me at BK with the repeaters. I'll wait for Muziak. You stay on the road so you can get back.

Perez points to the Burger King sign ahead. "There—first right after the light."

I pull into the back of the parking lot. I leave the keys in the ignition. Perez pulls the repeaters from the Jeep's rear.

"How are you going to get up to the condo?"

"I'll figure it out. You just get your stuff. I'll text you where I am in a couple hours."

Perez stacks the repeaters in my hands. "I feel like I should deputize you, man. Sure you don't want a career in law enforcement? Plus, extra training on evidence handling."

I give Perez a half-smile, taking the ribbing. "No thanks. Too much coordinating and liaising for me."

Perez laughs and drives away.

I look at the bomb repeaters in my hands. So much for not getting involved.

SULLIVAN

Breckenridge, Colorado-May 25th

The dull roar of the Blue River wakes Sullivan from his power nap. He stumbles to the kitchen. No bread remains from the supply run. He squirts mustard on the turkey slices, rolls them up, and eats three naked turkey burritos. Should he patent the idea?

Everything has to change with Mandrake dead. The original plan had them positioning the backup explosives at the dam's north-end runoff channel after dark. Then Mandrake would have driven the two-man motorized raft full of explosives to the spillway on the south side, and timed the detonator to go off after he bailed.

Sullivan thinks through the steps requiring two people. With Mandrake, Sullivan would have run the safety tether to the raft. They would have worked their way to the Morning Glory Spillway in tandem. Once the current caught the raft, Mandrake would have activated the detonator, dove overboard, and Sullivan would have pulled him to shore.

The timer would be set with just enough time for the raft to drop to the spillway's bottom before it blows. The massive spring runoff has required the dam operators to run the spillway drain at max capacity, so there's little danger of any shutoff valves or obstructions blocking the raft's plunge down the drain.

It's a "dam"—Sullivan snorts, remembering Mandrake's stupid joke—good plan. For two people.

He can eliminate the north-side backup explosives. His partner is dead. The condo is compromised. The north-end bomb—the one they never planned to use anyway—is just another chance to get caught. Hell, Sarah won't even know if he ditches the backup plan.

First things first. He needs to rent a truck. He can wire the explosives in the condo. He already has the raft and the wetsuit. All he needs to do is figure out how to get all the gear from the truck, over the water, and down the spillway—by himself.

He pulls up Google Maps and zooms in to where he and Mandrake had planned to launch. The far south end of the parking lot is closest to the spillway, a dimly lit spot with low probability of detection at night.

He expands the view of the shoreline near to the spillway. There is nowhere to unload the truck without drawing attention. A security guard monitors the area around the spillway and the road crossing the dam. Everything between the spillway and Frisco looks clear, though. The shoreline is unguarded until the inner set of buoys that barricade the spillway. Where the buoys meet the shore, a fence surfaces from the water, running up the rock-strewn bank.

The raft portion of the plan worries Sullivan. He's not a water guy—that's what Mandrake was for. Google Maps makes it look like he can hand-tow the boat from the shoreline, instead of navigating across open water to the spillway. He can park at the far end of the lot like the original plan and transfer everything from the truck to the shore. He'll need to figure out how to work around the fence and the buoys when he nears the spillway.

Sullivan likes it. He can even ditch the motor. Once he has the raft beyond the fence, he can anchor a rope on shore and just use a paddle to get the raft on the right trajectory, then bail, and pull himself back into shore with the rope.

He's nervous about the detonator timing, especially since he'll be pulling himself to shore. Maybe he should add some time, so the explosives don't blow while he's in the water.

Sullivan calls three recreational rental companies, but they only rent Jeeps and ATVs. His fourth call succeeds. Blue River Rentals offers a two-wheel-drive Chevy Silverado.

"No off-roading," the agent warns.

"I'll take it," Sullivan says. "See you shortly."

The sky is cloudless, the temperature in the upper forties, as he strolls to the rental facility. The Blue River roars through the rest of Breckenridge, the rising water pushing its banks. He smiles. If the local residents think the river is running high up here, they should check out Silverthorne tomorrow after the dam blows.

The Silverado is parked out front, ready to go.

"You sure you only need it for one day?" the agent says.

Sullivan hands him the fake Alexander Buskirk license. "Yep. One day. My car's in the shop and they don't have a loaner."

"And I'll need to burn a copy of your license and run your credit card."

He meets the agent's eyes. "Lost my card the other day, though. Gotta use cash."

The agent wrinkles his nose. "I don't think that'll work. It's a $500 deposit, plus you'd have to pre-pay the daily rate. For the truck, that's another $95."

"Right. Do it." Sullivan peels six hundreds from his wallet.

The agent zips inside and is back in less than a minute, returning Sullivan's license. "Need it back by three tomorrow afternoon."

"You bet," Sullivan lies. He'll be out of Colorado by three tomorrow. Fuck the six hundred bucks. He pulls the truck out of the lot and drives a quarter mile to the hardware store. His fence snippers were in the truck when it was stolen. Breaching that fence at the spillway is a new addition to the plan. Plus, he needs an air pump, cigarette lighter adapter, and extension cord for the raft. As he parks the truck in the store lot, his cell phone rings. He checks the screen.

What the hell? It's Sarah.

ZAHN

Dillon, Colorado-May 25th

Stan Muziak exits his Ford Expedition and introduces himself. "What are these things again?" Muziak says, pointing at the boxes in my arms.

"We think they're repeaters—to relay a cell phone signal somewhere it normally wouldn't reach. They were lined up near a bomb in that old shaft—at that tunnel's halfway point between here and the river flowing into Denver."

"North Fork of the South Platte—that's Roberts Tunnel," Muziak squints at the mechanisms. "Did you check these things for explosives?"

I shake my head. "No. We powered them down. I think they're safe."

Muziak glances past me. I turn. A black SUV parks next to Muziak's Expedition.

"You expecting anyone?" Muziak says.

"Nope."

As the driver, a black man, steps from the vehicle, his sports jacket flares, exposing a holster containing a weapon. Muziak, steps beside me, and opens his stance. The man stops, raising a set of credentials.

"Hey." His smile is thin. "United States Marshals. I'm Randall Williams."

Muziak stays at the ready. "Nice to meet you. Mind walking over and letting me have a closer look at that badge?" He mutters my way. "Black SUV? Of course it's the feds."

I say nothing.

Williams hands Muziak his badge and offers me his now-empty hand. "Randall Williams."

I shake Williams's hand. "Tyler Zahn. I know your name. Perez said you're working the fugitive case back in Buena Vista. You've been checking out the body on the other side of Kenosha Pass?"

Muziak relaxes and returns the badge. "Randall Williams? I'm Stan Muziak." His voice turns apologetic. "Sorry if I looked antsy, we got this bomb thing—"

Williams laughs. "And it's pretty darn white this side of the mountains, isn't it?"

Muziak shakes his head.

Williams smiles. "I would've reacted the same way if you walked into a bomb investigation on my Detroit turf."

Muziak gives a half-smile. "You go by Randy?"

"I prefer Randall."

Muziak flicks his eyes my direction. I keep my expression neutral.

Williams turns back to me. "I got to the body about ten minutes after you and Perez left. I'm pretty sure that's our guy, but need an autopsy to confirm."

"Are you here to talk to me or Stan?" Williams isn't treating me like a civilian, but I'm not complaining.

Williams turns to Muziak. "Stan, if you've been talking to Perez, then you know that the fugitive aspect of this case hasn't been the top priority—it was always about the kidnapping. Until today."

Muziak grunts. "I've heard of Deputy Perez. Haven't met him. But I assume there's a link between an escaped convict and this potential bomb."

"Right," Williams says. "A possible terrorist angle to this thing. I'm on the Task Force and my boss doesn't want me coming home until we figure this case out." He points at the repeaters. "I heard the call about these devices. Volunteered to come check them out. Where are you taking them?"

"I'm meeting the other EOD team—the ones not headed to the shaft—over at our outdoor range in Silverthorne. You're welcome to come along."

"I'll follow you."

"OK." Muziak takes the repeaters from me. "You need a ride?"

"Nope. Appreciate it though." I need to think through this thing. I can do that walking to JD's condo. I think better when I walk.

"If we got questions," Muziak says, "I guess we can reach you through Chaffee County Sheriff's Office, right?"

"That'll work. Perez knows how to get a hold of me."

Williams digs into the inside pocket of his sports coat and hands me a card. "Perez said you got a good head on your shoulders—that they wouldn't have found Mandrake's hideout without your help. You think of anything else, call my cell."

Muziak pulls out of the parking lot. Williams follows. I use my phone to check the best walking route to JD's condo. It's too far to walk the whole way. But Frisco's at the halfway point. I can grab an Uber or Lyft from there. I zoom in on the route. It takes me on the road on top of the Dillon Dam.

I retrace the route Perez and I drove to Highway 6, then veer towards the water, passing an empty security building between the two-vehicle lanes where the dam starts. A bike path parallels the road across the dam. I cross the shoulder and pick my way between the rocks until I hit the path.

My muscles ache from our morning climb. Or maybe it's from holding Perez's safety rope while he descended the shaft. Regardless, it's a good sore. I've done something. Helped discover a bomb.

Useful. And I haven't felt useful in a while.

Halfway across the dam, I pause to admire the view. Stretching my legs has loosened up my joints. My brain goes into question mode. What the hell were those guys trying to blow up? I continue walking, reviewing the facts. Mandrake escaped. Mandrake took the Schorks. Someone helped Mandrake. Mandrake was murdered. The Schorks are gone. Those are the facts.

What am I missing? Planting a bomb in that shaft took planning. Which fits with my theory about why Mandrake took the Schorks. They must have discovered him at the McCorkles' place. Mandrake needed to keep them quiet until the shaft blew.

Unless…Mandrake didn't take the Schorks. What if the Schorks needed Mandrake for the shaft bombing? They could have helped him escape and had him stay in the neighbor's house so that when they disappeared, it would look like a kidnapping.

I slow my pace. Mitch isn't the alpha dog here. He's the Schorks' accomplice.

Are the FBI guys thinking about that?

I call Perez.

"Where are you?" I say.

"Halfway between Leadville and BV. What's up?"

I tell Perez about my theory. "It's the only thing that makes sense if you go with the assumption that Mandrake broke out to help with this bomb thing."

"Really? What's the Schorks' motive?"

"I don't know. But I also don't know Mandrake's motive. Or anyone else's. I just can't think of any other way it could've gone down. Can you?"

"I'll mention it to the FBI. And yes, I can think of another alternative."

"What?"

"Someone from Mandrake's past. Maybe the Schorks do know him. But it could be someone else. I'm going to look at the files for Mandrake's visitors while he was incarcerated. Why else break a random guy out of prison to help with your plan?"

Perez's theory makes sense. I wish I would have thought of it before I called. "You're right. I hadn't considered that."

"You at the condo now?"

"Not yet. Working my way there. The repeaters are in Summit County hands. Just doing a little walking."

"What? Not enough exercise for you today?" Perez laughs. "Call me if you think of anything else. This is good stuff."

"Roger that." I grimace. Perez is just trying to keep my spirits up.

I end the call. At the south end of the dam, a hundred yards offshore, a large concrete-ringed drain, like one used on a giant's bathtub, sucks in lake water. Lots of water. I turn the opposite direction toward the road that crosses the dam. The water draining behind me must emerge at the bottom of the dam. Another security building monitors this side of the dam, between the road and the bike path.

I wave at the security guard out front.

"So, are you guarding road access or the drain hole?" I point to the opposite end of the dam from where I came. "There's no guard on the other side."

"We're just here to monitor suspicious activity," she answers. "We don't control road access unless something is going on." Her eyes move up and down like she's sizing me up. "Why do you ask?"

"Just trying to understand how this whole water system works. I heard about the water tunnel to Denver this morning. Then I saw the drain hole out here. Does that water come out down there?" I point across the road toward the dam's edge.

"Yeah, that drain is the Morning Glory Spillway. It's how they control the level of the reservoir. Reservoir overflow empties it into the Blue River down there." She points the same direction I did. "The Blue River flows through Silverthorne. That tunnel you mentioned—the Roberts Tunnel—helps release the water, but the main outflow is through here. Especially now because the backup release isn't working."

"Huh. Can I cross the road and look over the edge?"

"Well, technically we're not supposed to allow pedestrians or bikers to loiter here." She does that sizing-up thing again before smiling. "But if you look both ways for cars and don't take long, it's not a problem."

"Thanks. I'll just be a sec."

I cross to the opposite shoulder and peer over the steep drop. At the base, water roars into a riverbed, then underneath I-70, before winding through Silverthorne. The interstate crosses on a 40-foot-high bridge, probably to avoid rising water. A large dry concrete spillway feeds into the riverbed from the north. Must be the backup release the guard said was inoperative.

Cool.

Before Mandrake popped out of the Roberts Tunnel, I had never given water management a second thought. After hearing the history of the tunnel, discovering the Morning Glory Spillway's function, and learning of the behind-the-scenes work that goes into controlling runoff levels—well, I'm somewhat fascinated.

I return to the security building. "I appreciate your time," I call to the guard. "Thanks." She waves and turns her eyes back to the dam.

I pass another security building a couple hundred yards later, this one empty and apparently designed to control access to the roadway. At the parking lot just past the building, the bike path veers from the Dillon Dam Road and hugs the shoreline. The main road runs directly toward Frisco. I pull out my phone to check the map again. I've got another two miles until I hit the main part of Frisco.

My phone rings. My screen shows *Rick Perez*.

"What's up?"

"You're not going to believe this."

"Try me."

"They found the Schorks." The words spill out of Perez. "I was driving past that launching area on the Arkansas—you know, where they start The Numbers. You know where I'm talking about?"

"I know it." The Numbers is the most challenging stretch for rafting on the Arkansas River. I've done it once with a guide from the rafting company Kristee works for.

"The other BV deputy's Tahoe was down there and two BV police cars, lights flashing. I pull in to see what's happening, right?" He sucks a loud breath. "Turns out, I just missed the ambulance taking the Schorks to the hospital."

"What were they doing there? Did they arrest them?"

"Uh, no. They found them hog-tied with zip-ties in the back of a pickup truck behind the public restrooms. No one else was there.

They're going to be OK—just kind of dehydrated, hungry, and of course, worn out."

So much for my Schorks theory. "Did anyone talk to them before they went to the hospital? Mandrake couldn't have left them there. Someone would have found them sooner."

"I'm back in my Jeep right now, heading to the hospital to ask them more questions." Perez pauses again. "But it's weird. They said someone kidnapped them from the two guys who kidnapped them first."

"So Mandrake plus someone else took them?"

"Yep. They said Mandrake and the other guy took them up in the mountains somewhere. Left them tied up in a truck. Then some other guys—Hispanic, they said—showed up. The Schorks saw them kill Mandrake and drag his body away. The only reason they didn't kill the Schorks—or at least this is what the Schorks guess—is because the Schorks guided the Hispanic guys to all the places Mandrake and his partner had taken them."

"What?" I can't help asking useless questions. Perez's story is blowing my mind.

"Yeah, the Schorks said the Hispanics killed Mandrake because he stole drugs from them. They must have found the drugs because they let the Schorks go."

"What about Mandrake's partner?"

"They didn't have a clue. Last they saw him was when they got left in the truck. Which we think is the shaft area. My guys are checking out the truck." Perez stops talking, like he's giving me a chance to speak.

I don't.

He jumps back in. "Hey, I got another call coming in. Let me call you back after I interview these guys and I'll give you an update, OK?"

"Yeah, yeah," I say. "That means Mandrake's partner is probably on foot—"

"Got to go, Tyler." Perez hangs up.

SULLIVAN

Breckenridge, Colorado-May 25th

"Galen, what the hell's going on?"

Sullivan's mind races. What does Sarah know? How can she know anything about Mandrake? She can't. He presses the phone to his ear, turning back to the truck.

"Not much, sweetheart. On time, on schedule." He climbs behind the wheel.

"That's bullshit, Galen. They know about the stuff in the shaft. They're on their way to get it right now."

"Who's they?" Is she talking about the guys who took out Mandrake?

"The cops! The cops are on their way."

"How do you know what the cops are doing?"

"Never mind that. We have someone on the inside. The point is, it's a bust. They found a body at the end of the tunnel and traced it back to the shaft. When they went down to investigate, they found your stuff. They're on their way now to de-arm it."

Sullivan considers this. "Do you want me to try to blow it right now, before they stop it?"

"No! That's not the publicity we're looking for—a bunch of dead cops. I need to know what your plan is. Are you going to run? Or are you going to do the rest?"

"Well, I guess that depends on whether you're still paying. I don't see how they can trace the shaft to me. No one's expecting anything down here at the reservoir. I can get it done. But it's a little riskier. You got the money ready?"

"I do. But you didn't fill your end of the deal. You get the dam blown and we'll give you a million on top of the half mill we advanced. That's fair. Especially since you don't have a helper anymore." Sarah takes a breath. She's not finished. "What the hell was that, anyway? An escaped prisoner for a partner? Why didn't you just put out an APB on yourself—*please catch me and my prison buddy*?"

"Cut the bullshit, Sarah." Her snark pisses him off. "We put a lot into this. You're making the call not to blow the shaft, not me. I can blow it right now. I want the money from the deal. Two-and-a-half mill."

Sarah's breath sounds like she just ran a hundred-meter dash. "One-point-five million. Take it or leave it."

Sullivan runs the numbers. A half-million in his pocket already, plus the leftover money for supplies. And now he doesn't have to share with Mandrake. That's over two million. Plenty for a fresh start. Goodbye mattress factory.

"Deal. I'll pick it up tomorrow. Pick another place though for the meet. When I leave the condo tonight, I'm done with it."

He isn't telling Sarah about the guys who killed Mandrake and tossed the condo. Let her pick up those pieces. Another thought occurs to him. What if the cops have found the condo? Nothing at the shaft ties him to the place. But something pokes at his subconscious. What? Then it hits him. The Schorks. If the Schorks are alive, they know about the condo. He needs to get out of there.

"Starbucks in Breck," Sarah says. "Parking lot. Just south of your condo. What time?"

"Early. I'll see you there at six tomorrow morning."

"I'll be there."

Sullivan tosses his phone on the passenger seat and rests his hands on the steering wheel. What kind of eco-terrorist group has contacts with the cops? He bets this whole thing links back to Ron Timmons and his rancher buddies. They're probably using tree-hugger Sarah as a conduit to move water around and send a message.

Sullivan purchases his supplies at the hardware store before returning to the condo. He leaves it all in the truck while he cleans the place out. He moves the remaining gear from the condo to the truck, then goes room to room with a roll of paper towels and Windex, wiping every surface. He empties the refrigerator contents into a grocery sack. He grabs the bag of trash, the food, and heads out to the truck.

Sullivan considers a motel—somewhere to hole up until dark. But that involves checking in, unloading, and trying to sleep. Then reloading. Before he starts the engine, he runs the seat recliner back as far as it will go. He can sleep in the truck. Definitely more comfortable than sleeping in a Humvee in the desert. Sullivan raises the seat and screeches out of the condo lot.

The Frisco Bay Marina parking lot is the perfect hole-up spot. He can hide in plain sight, and it's only a ten-minute drive from where he'll launch the raft. A mixture of restaurant patrons and winterized boats on trailers pack the lot. Sullivan pulls the truck to a stop between two large cabin cruisers and leaves the engine running.

Just like he did for his Iraq missions, he needs to run through his gear before the actual operation. He pushes the adapter into the cigarette lighter and tests the air pump. He reviews the required changes for doing the mission solo. Most important is timing. He is paddling instead of using the raft motor, he needs to add extra seconds for the detonator.

The explosives and detonator are nested in a long Pelican case to distribute the weight in the raft. All Sullivan has to do is set the timer, shut the case, and bail out. His watch reads 14:45, the military format.

He has six hours before go time. Eight hours before he blows the Morning Glory Spillway. Time for dinner and sleep.

Sullivan rummages through the grocery bag from the condo. Turkey burritos again. He rolls up three, using the last of the mustard, and chokes them down. By this time next week, he'll be sleeping in the Four Seasons and dining on steak. Sullivan sets the alarm for 20:45 on his phone and reclines his seat. He has a knack for falling asleep anywhere, any time.

ZAHN

Frisco, Colorado-May 25th

The bike path along the reservoir leads to a vantage point. The outskirts of Frisco pop into view. Perez's story about the Schorks has me thinking. Smart move for Perez to return to BV. Something new from the Schorks might break this thing wide open.

Curious how the bomb de-arming is going up at the shaft, I kick myself for not asking Perez to text updates.

My phone rings. I snatch it from my pocket, assuming Perez has more news, but the screen shows a Colorado number I don't recognize.

"Hello?"

"Hey, Tyler," a female voice says. "It's Leanne."

"Leanne…?"

"JD's wife? We met at the brewpub on Friday. Rick said you guys might stay another night with us?"

I put it all together. This getting old thing isn't making me happy. Leanne is the best-looking woman I've encountered all year, and I can't remember her name? "Leanne. Sorry, I didn't recognize your number. Yeah, is that OK? Using the condo? I'm on my way there right now."

"Of course," Leanne says. "I wanted to see if you needed a ride? Rick said you were meeting a deputy, but that was over an hour ago. Is everything alright?"

"Yep. Just taking a stroll to stretch the legs. I'm walking into Frisco now from Dillon. Probably an hour fifteen from the condo."

"Longer than that if you're on foot. Let me pick you up."

"I planned on grabbing an Uber or Lyft once I got into Frisco—"

Leanne interrupts. "Tyler, you're a guest. Where are you exactly?"

"Just cut off the bike path from Dillon. I-70 is to my right and the Valero gas station is in front of me."

"Okay. Turn left at the Valero and walk two hundred yards until you see the Walmart. I'll pick you up at the entrance and drive you up to the condo. I'd love an update on the bomb. Scary."

I say nothing. Perez didn't say anything to JD about a bomb. He said "terrorists."

"Uh… okay. Much appreciated, I'll be out front. Got a bag over my shoulder." I can't reasonably decline the ride but dread the inevitable questions. Might be an awkward trip to Breckenridge.

"See you in ten."

I beat Leanne to the Walmart by a minute. I search the lot for a sports car. She pulls up in a white Range Rover SUV instead. I stow my duffel in the back seat and jump into the passenger side. I catch a whiff of smoke and Leanne notices.

"JD's car. He's on his way back from Denver with mine." She looks at me, her eyes aglow. "I can't believe you walked all this way. Why didn't you just give us a call?"

"I needed the exercise. It clears my mind."

"Well, I can understand that." Leanne steers us out of the parking lot and heads toward Breckenridge. She doesn't waste time. "So, dying to know. How did you guys find a bomb? That kind of stuff never happens around here."

I don't answer right away, not wanting to confirm or deny the bomb. "I really can't talk about it. Local law enforcement guys are taking care of the situation. The feds are involved. It's an active investigation."

Leanne frowns. "JD thought they might base you guys out of Breck for this, so I just wanted to get an idea, you know?"

I do know. Leanne wants the inside scoop. Who wouldn't? "Rick really appreciates the setup you're giving the department. I appreciate it too. But please keep the info you have to yourself, OK?"

"Got it."

On the outskirts of Breckenridge, my phone buzzes again. This time Perez's name shows on the screen.

"What's up?" I say. "I'm riding with Leanne up to the condo. We're almost there." Leanne glances my way and I hope Perez picks up on the fact someone else is listening.

"I haven't talked to the Schorks. I'm at the hospital waiting in line with all the other agencies to speak to them. I got some info on the truck, though."

I pull the phone from my ear and lower the volume. "Like what?"

"It's registered to a Galen Sullivan out of Denver. Manages a mattress factory in Arvada. The Task Force is all over this. And guess what?"

"What?"

"We were spot-on about the past history. This guy grew up with Mandrake back in Washington State. He visited him in the prison last week, three days before the escape. Different name, different ID. But the same truck. Parking lot cameras got it."

"No shit?" Nice of Perez to say "we," since I distinctly remember the past history theory being his idea. Leanne gives me another glance. I turn toward the passenger window.

"Yeah. He's probably running now—so not much chance he's up where you are. No way he's down here where I'm at. My talk with the Schorks might be our only chance for additional intel. Might be awhile, OK?"

"I'll just hang tight up here." I sneak a peek at Leanne. She's focused on the road. "I met Williams—the US Marshal. He's looking at the stuff we found."

"Ha. You didn't call him Randy, did you? He hates that."

I laugh. "Nope. Figured that out right away."

"OK. I'll call you back after the Schorks. Or if I get a shaft update. I haven't heard how that's going. If I finish late tonight, I might come up in the morning. The shaft is sort of our last lead if we can't get anything useful from the Schorks."

"Right. I'll probably grab some dinner in Breck and just hang. Thanks for the call." I click off.

"Sorry Leanne, I—"

"I'm not asking questions," Leanne reaches out, grabbing my arm. "But I did hear that you're solo in Breck tonight and eating dinner. So, JD and I are joining you."

I keep my face expressionless. There goes my thinking time. But they are providing the condo. I am a guest.

"Very kind, Leanne. Thanks."

Leanne pulls up to the condo and produces the keys from her purse.

"I'll walk you in. Make sure they prepped the place." She smiled at me. "Good to trust, but verify, with housekeepers, you know?"

"Right." I try to sound like I've had a housekeeper.

Leanne unlocks the door. When she pushes it open, the lingering scent of Pine-Sol tingles my nose.

"Someone's been cleaning." I'm hoping this counts as the verification, because I'm not exactly comfortable touring my sleeping quarters with JD's wife.

"Let me do a quick walk-through."

Leanne ducks in and out of the rooms.

"Did you like the sheets in the last place?"

"Great." There were sheets. I remember that.

"That's the thing about condos. You try to turn a profit with them, but you can't go cheap on certain things. Sheets. Duvets. And double- or triple-ply toilet paper. Never skimp on toilet paper." We end up in the dining room, Leanne gazes across the table at me like she's thinking about something.

"I can't believe all this drama happened so close to Breck. It's crazy." She shakes her head, locking her eyes on mine. "Shower?"

Oh. My. God. I feel a stirring I haven't felt since Sheila. One I thought might be lost. Nope. Suppressed maybe, but definitely there. One word has brought it to the surface.

I look at my shoes. Am I reading too much into her question? I do need a shower. Is she—?

"I mean, you're probably ready for one after all that walking, and climbing, and de-bombing or whatever you call it, right?" She flashes a grin. "So, JD and I'll see you at Jose's at seven. You sure you don't want us to pick you up?"

Holy missed signals. If she meant something by *shower*, I delayed my response too long.

"I'll be there. Thanks, Leanne. It's not even five blocks, I'll meet you there."

Leanne leaves, and I head straight for the shower in question. Peeling off my clothes, I glance in the mirror. Working out is helping— a little—but I still pack a gut. A two-pack instead of a six-pack. My hair isn't thickening either. Did I misinterpret her question? What would she see in me? She's married. I like JD. I give myself a sad smile in the mirror, glad she left.

After the shower, I wrap a towel around my waist and gaze at the river out the window. *What now?* The investigation fills my thoughts.

I survey my options. If Perez doesn't return tonight, that leaves me on foot. Perez might not come back at all. The interview with the Schorks might point him in another direction. I'd be stuck in Breck until I could find a ride to BV.

I need wheels. And a nap. Finding a dead body in the morning, discovering a bomb in a tunnel shaft in the afternoon, and then walking four miles, I'm beat. I poke around my phone and find a rental car place, closing in an hour. Forget the nap.

I change clothes, and call to book a car. They say half hour. I flip through the TV channels for thirty minutes before walking up the street to the rental address. The agent stands next to an economy model—a Hyundai Elantra—waiting for me. I'm happy. Anything fancier would cost over a hundred a day. I drive the Elantra back to the condo and park out front. I glance at my watch. *Shit.* Time to meet my hosts. Jose's is only five blocks away, but after today, there's no way I'm walking.

Leanne waves from across the room as I enter the restaurant.

"Zahn!" JD Robinson's voice booms. Just like the brewpub, Robinson's presence fills the room. I notice several patrons turning their heads to see who called my name. Leanne smiles at me, then glances back at Robinson, like she is assessing his enthusiasm. Robinson jumps out of his seat and strides toward me, his hand extended.

"Good to see you, man. Staying up in Breck for the investigation, huh?" Robinson appears to be trying his best to lower his voice with the second question—but it isn't working.

"Great to see you guys, JD. Appreciate the condo for another night." We walk back to the table together. "I'm not really involved, but Perez is coming back this way, and he was my original ride home. I thought I'd hang here rather than go back to BV."

Leanne gives me a quick hug.

"You smell better," she whispers in my ear.

Robinson says, "Can't say I blame you. Exciting shit. Hope we figure out who is behind it." He leans close to me. "You think it was some Middle East terrorism?"

"JD," Leanne says.

"Oh yeah, Leanne told me you can't talk about what you know. Sorry man."

"Yeah, ongoing investigation and all that," I agree.

"JD, there're plenty of folks that could be interested in messing with water," Leanne says. "They've been arguing over it for years. Should it go to Denver? Should it go to the Western Slope ranchers? Should anyone even control it at all? Lots of folks get crazy about that water stuff." Leanne pauses, but her husband remains quiet. "And this year, with all the runoff—that's a lot of water."

Robinson shakes his head. "Yeah, but are they crazy enough to set off bombs? That's wacko crazy. Not good for tourism either."

Robinson flags the server to order drinks. "Tyler?"

"IPA?" I say to the server.

"Sorry sir, just Corona, Tecate, and Negro Modelo."

I wince. Why do Mexican restaurants always have such great food and such lousy beer? Especially one in Breckenridge—six local breweries and they're serving Corona?

"A house margarita is fine—thanks."

"Make that three," says JD.

The server returns in under two minutes with the drinks and takes our orders. I missed lunch today. When the food arrives, I tear into it. Robinson—thank goodness—doesn't bring up the bomb again.

I'm about halfway through my meal before I realize I haven't spoken a word since our order arrived. Mainly because Leanne is still talking about water, and what happened today—a topic I'm trying to avoid.

It takes just one question from me about the status of Robinson's business to get him going. He launches into an update on his holdings in Breck, the future of the town, and his plans to influence that future. When he finishes describing his Breckenridge dreams, he leans back as if to take a breather.

Leanne's eyes shine. "Tell him about your plans for the rest of the county." She turns to me, wonder in her voice. "JD's got ideas—he's got a vision for the future of these towns—Frisco, Dillon, and Silverthorne."

I glance at Robinson. The last time Frisco came up, it involved the rival real estate guy Tolliver, and Leanne had got all worked up. I'm hoping there's no repeat episode tonight.

Robinson smiles at Leanne before turning to me. "You interested in hearing about it? I don't want to bore you."

I get a twenty-minute earful on the prospective development of Summit County. Leanne's right. Robinson has a vision, and he possesses the ambition to match. Leanne's eyes darken when Robinson describes his efforts to get a foothold in the other towns.

"That fuckin' Tolliver," Robinson says. "What he doesn't realize is that there's room for everyone. He's got his finger in the approval process for everything in those towns. He only allows small-fry investors in. If he senses any competition—anybody with the potential to develop big—he freezes them out."

Robinson describes his plans for developing the east end of Frisco, despite Leanne's darkening expression.

We finish our meal and Leanne suggests we hit the same brewpub where we first met for a nightcap, but I decline. Margaritas always make me crave more alcohol, and the one I've finished tonight is no exception. Combining tequila with the come-down from the day's high? This would be a perfect night to tie one on.

But this case has me going. And I don't need beer clouding my thoughts.

"It's been a long day," I say. "I need to get some shuteye." What I really need is some more alone time. As interesting as Robinson's plans sound, and despite my urge to keep drinking, my mind keeps returning to the case.

We say our goodbyes. As I walk to my rental car, I check my phone. No texts from Perez.

Shit.

I need guidance. The more I mull over this case, the more I think about getting involved. And that never turns out good.

I also need rest. But that's not happening anytime soon.

SULLIVAN

Dillon Reservoir, Colorado-May 25th

It's past nine when Sullivan arrives at the south dam parking lot. The six solid hours of sleep were both unexpected and needed. He backs the truck into the furthest slot from the entrance, one with a downward slope to the reservoir banks, and minimal visibility from the main road. He unloads the explosives first, stacking them on the lake-side of the truck, then moves them crate-by-crate to the sandy shoreline.

Setting up the raft proves more complicated. Sullivan runs the power out of the rental truck's cigarette lighter with two twelve-foot DC extension cords that fit into the air pump. Then he lugs the deflated raft to the end of the cord. The whine of the motor echoes in the darkness, but Sullivan doubts it's audible outside the empty parking lot.

Inflating the raft takes almost twenty minutes. He uses the time to squeeze into the wetsuit he'd bought for Mandrake. After the bottom raft baffles are full, he loads the oars and wire snippers, and secures the rope to the boat's prow.

He wishes his bosses at Denver Water could see him. They knew he was smart. But what everyone overlooked was his ability to plan, prepare, and execute. He wags his head. Their loss.

The sides of the raft bulge with air. He unhooks the pump, caps off the filler hole, and drags the raft to the shore next to the Pelican case. He loads the case diagonally leaving enough room for him to paddle from the middle. Then he shoves the floating bomb into the water while he remains on shore holding the rope attached to the bow. Moonlight reflects off the rubber sides of the raft. He glances up and smiles. A waning gibbous moon. How many people know that?

Sullivan glances back at the truck. It's still the only vehicle in the parking lot. He'll grab the pump and cord on his return. It's time to go make some *boom boom*.

He walks toward the spillway, dragging the raft behind him while he picks his way across the rocks in the sand. He makes it twenty yards before stopping. Tugging with the rope alone is a pain in the ass. The boat keeps drifting back to the shore and running up on the sand. He pulls an oar from the boat and uses it like a cattle prod, poking the raft back into the water.

Finally, he gets a system going. Pull ten steps. Go back and push the raft back out in the water. Pull ten steps. Once he falls into the rhythm, he makes decent time.

Forty-five minutes pass before Sullivan reaches the fence running from the road to the water. He's ahead of timeline. Fine. Buoys extend from where the fence disappears into the water, warning boaters of the approaching spillway. He lets the raft beach itself while he checks out the barrier.

Lights shine from the roof of the guard shack. As he predicted, the glare illuminates the spillway, but doesn't reach the buoys or the fence.

The eight feet of chain link in front of him is topped with three strands of barbed wire running at an angle. Climbing isn't an option.

Seizing the snippers, Sullivan clips a hole in the fence three feet up the shoreline from the water. The hole-snipping operation takes less than five minutes. While snipping each link, Sullivan is reminded of Mandrake's recent prison escape. Despite his friend's obvious flaws, Sullivan wishes he was here. So he didn't have to do this alone.

He stows the snippers in the raft and pushes it offshore, allowing the attached rope to drift until about fifteen feet remains. He throws that section over the fence. The rope's end catches in the barbed wire. The raft isn't going anywhere.

Sullivan crawls through the hole and turns back. He grips the chain links and pulls himself up high enough to release the line. Back on the ground, he pulls the raft toward his side of the fence.

All he has to do is guide the nose around the point where the top of the fence disappears underwater and—*fuck*.

The raft's nose stops moving.

The boat has cleared the warning buoys but is stuck against the barbed wire near the water's surface. Sullivan guesses if he yanks hard, he can pull it to his side of the fence. But if he tugs too hard, he risks puncturing it, and sinking the explosives.

Sullivan flings the rope back over the fence, then dives through the hole to grab the end. Tugging from the opposite direction, he frees the raft. As he beaches it on the original side of the fence, Sullivan realizes he's going to have to pilot this boat around the barrier.

He piles the tow rope in the raft's bow, grabs the oar, and climbs aboard, stepping around the Pelican case in the front. Then he pushes off with the oar, allowing the vessel to drift away from the fence edge. He dips the oar in the water and paddles, maneuvering around the fence and buoy line where the raft had stuck before. It's basic fucking paddling. He doesn't even need Mandrake. After beaching the raft on the other side of the fence, Sullivan wipes his hands dry on his pants.

He can do this.

ZAHN

Breckenridge, Colorado-May 25th

Too wound up to just lie around the condo, I cruise the rental down the valley from Breckenridge toward Frisco. No Perez updates, but with what I've learned about tunnels, dams, and spillways today, I decide to drive along the shore.

The route takes me between Main Street Frisco and the marina. At the Valero, I turn toward the dam—reversing my route from earlier today. I pass the manned spillway guard station, and start across.

At the midway point, I glance at Silverthorne nestled beneath the dam. You couldn't pay me to own a house at the bottom of a pile of earth holding back five square miles of water.

I exit the dam at Dillon and follow the shore for a mile. My headlights light up a sign for Marina Park. The large parking lot next to an amphitheater has a sidewalk that winds toward the reservoir. I take a seat on a bench with a view of the lake. Frisco's lights wink in the distance.

Discovering the Schorks were missing led to finding Mandrake's hideout in Elk Trace and the bomb in the shaft. Picking up the gun was stupid, proving I've got a lot to learn about investigating. But I might be the only one with more than fifteen spare minutes to put some thought into this case. My pocket vibrates, and a faint ring breaks the night's silence.

"What's up, Rick?"

"Sorry for the delay. Just finished up with the Schorks an hour ago."

"It's all good. I had dinner with JD and Leanne over in Breck. Now I'm down by the reservoir, just thinking."

"I heard you guys went out. How'd you get to the lake?"

"Rented a car. Decided I needed wheels. Especially, if you don't come back."

Perez laughs. "I'm coming up, but it'll probably be late or first thing in the morning. Not sure yet. The Schorks showed me on Google Maps where they were held hostage. Like five hundred yards from us."

"No way." Mandrake and Sullivan probably drove right past our window on the way to the shaft.

"Yep. I've called it in. They're securing the place now. Randall Williams is on his way up from Dillon, too. JD owns the complex. Gave JD a heads up—that's how I knew you went to dinner with them."

"Think they'll find anything?"

"That's why I'm coming back. The Schorks said Mandrake and Sullivan didn't pack up their clothes before they left. So, I figure—"

"They were coming back." I interrupt Perez. "But why?"

"The road over the pass beyond the shaft is pretty rugged. Maybe they left their stuff because they figured they had to come back through here, anyway."

"It doesn't make sense to set a bomb and sleep it off in your condo only twenty miles away from the crime scene."

"Right?" Perez says, "Leave the door unlocked up there. If I come up tonight, I'll try not to wake you up."

"I took the master. Figured you wouldn't be back so soon."

"I'm so beat, I can sleep anywhere."

I'm about to disconnect, when Perez's says, "One other thing. I ran into Kristee while I was in BV."

"Nice. Did you finally work up enough nerve to ask her out?"

"Not. But she told me an interesting tidbit. Said the word around is that the Schorks can get you pain meds if you need them."

"I thought Carrie Schork was retired—not doing pharmacy anymore?"

"She is. But sounds like the Schorks got something going. Remember that drug equipment we found?"

"You're saying they're involved in this whole thing?"

"Not sure, but something's going on with them. I'll dig into that when I'm back in BV."

We sign off and I stuff my phone back in my pocket, wondering why Mandrake and Sullivan would drag the Schorks up to the shaft and then back to the condo. Why didn't they just leave the Schorks at the condo, set the bomb, and take off? Pretty obvious they didn't want to kill the Schorks, but they could have called in an anonymous tip from the road after the shaft blew. Told the cops about the couple. Were the Schorks in on it, or in the wrong place at the wrong time?

I yawn. Perez isn't the only one who is beat. I stand, stretching my arms over my head before returning to the car. I'll think through all this in the morning. I turn the key in the ignition and head toward the dam.

As I cross the giant wall of dirt, an almost half-moon lights the water's surface just a few feet below the road and the bike path. The reservoir is like a too generous cup of coffee, a tad too full. The other side of the wall is a black drop-off with Silverthorne in the distance.

My gut twists. What if the dam *did* give away? Or worse, someone made it collapse? The bomb Sullivan planted back in the shaft operated on remote detonation. Mandrake and Sullivan were coming back to Breck for something. What if there are more explosives?

I slow the car, preparing to stop on the narrow shoulder. Then I accelerate again, realizing stopping the car in the middle of a dam might draw every guard's attention—even though there's probably just one—within sight.

In the Air Force staff college, I'd studied the Allied efforts to destroy dams in Germany during World War II. Earthen dams are a bitch to blow up. In hundreds of sorties, bomb after bomb rained down on those dams and never made a dent in the giant structures, until the Allies stumbled on a method that would at least chip away the dirt.

The bombers would release their payload early, from extremely low altitude, and the combination of high speed, low altitude, and flat-shaped bombs caused a skipping phenomenon that horizontally impacted the dams. The skip bomb used forward momentum to take out the top part of the dam where the layers of earth were the thinnest.

As I think through the realm of what's possible—no way Sullivan can skip bomb this thing from an airplane—the knot in my stomach loosens. But there has be something else I'm missing. I edge past the guard shack on the Frisco-side of the dam and follow the road toward the shoreline.

Where's the weak spot? Is the spillway the proverbial Dutch boy's finger in the dike? Where does it empty? After emerging from the dam, that flow essentially restarts the Blue River, the largest of the three rivers that feed the reservoir. The river flows through Silverthorne and runs another thirty miles before emptying into Green Mountain Reservoir where it is metered to flow on into the Colorado River.

The spot where the river emerges from the bottom of the dam— news flash—that's a weak spot. Set off a charge in that opening—widen it—and the water flow would surge like an erupting volcano. The reservoir can't hold much more water.

I pull into the empty parking lot a quarter mile past the guard shack to check my phone for the shortest route to the dam's base. I'm tired, but I can't shake this weird feeling about the dam. I have to check the outlet down in Silverthorne.

I park the car facing the line of trees between the parking lot and the reservoir. Google Maps tells me the quickest route is to reverse course back across the dam to Dillon, skirt the hill into Silverthorne, and approach the base of the dam from the town.

Am I chasing ghosts here?

Honestly, I'm unsure if I could sleep now. I'm too wired. There are lots of places where Sullivan can mess with waterworks, but working close to the condo makes the most sense. No harm in doing a drive-by.

As I maneuver out of the empty lot, I spot a lone vehicle parked at the far end. I continue onto the highway, accelerating back toward the guard shack. Then I ease off the gas and pull a U-turn.

Must be my post-9-11 military service, seeing terror plots everywhere.

Circling back into the lot, I pull up next to the driver's side of the lone unoccupied truck. I'm guessing it's probably someone camping by the lake, except there's a *No Camping, No Boating, No Fishing* sign dead ahead.

I loop around the truck to head back to the highway, and hit my brakes. An extension cord runs out the top of the passenger-side window.

What the hell?

I park the car, grab my headlamp from my bag and follow the cord into the darkness, donning my headlamp as I walk. Ahead of me rests a small plastic box. I recognize it as an air pump as I get closer. I bend to pick it up, then freeze as I remember my mistake with the gun earlier today. I study the adapter in the beam of my light. The hole is the size of a quarter—like the kind you use to pump up an air mattress or paddleboard or raft or something.

The water laps against the shore in a steady rhythm. My headlamp provides a good thirty yards of visibility. But I see nothing.

I glance back at the truck and consider what's on the other end of the lot. The guard shack. More importantly, the spillway. Shit. Is this just some guy out night fishing, or did I just stumble upon Sullivan's second act?

Impossible.

A professional bomb squad is dismantling the shaft bomb. Multiple police departments, the CBI, FBI, and at least one US Marshal are looking for Sullivan. *And I just happen to find him on the shore of Lake Dillon?*

OK. Not impossible. But certainly not likely. Yet…

What if Sullivan messed with the spillway above the dam instead of at the base?

I double time it back to the truck, capture the plate number with my cell phone camera and jog to the shoreline. Right or left at the water? I turn toward the dam. Has to be.

The sandy shoreline, peppered with large rocks, parallels the back of the parking lot. As I traipse along the edge of the reservoir, the sand thins out, and the route becomes more of a rock hop. The parking lot disappears, replaced with a stand of trees. I see nothing unusual. No boat. No people.

After twenty minutes picking out a path along the rocky shore, the lights of the guard facility shine through the trees along the shoreline. My headlamp spotlights a chain-link fence running from the shore into the water, with a line of safety buoys warning boaters to stay away from the spillway attached. I point my headlamp toward the spillway drain hole, but the beam doesn't extend far enough.

I put my beam back on the fence, and spot a two-foot hole in the bottom.

Holy shit. This is real.

The spillway perimeter is breached.

Someone likely came from the truck.

I didn't see anyone on my walk along the shoreline.

Which means…someone is out here now, right in front of me.

Time to bring in the cavalry. I have to call Perez. My hand trembles and I drop my phone. Dropping to my knees, I extract it from between two rocks, relieved it still has power. The time on the screen reads 10:43 p.m. When I look up, the shoreline is framed by the hole in the fence. If Sullivan is here, I don't have time to mess with my phone.

I scramble through the fence hole and scurry along the shore, my headlamp pointed over the water. The cone of my beam finds the spillway opening, and I spot movement. A rubber boat floats on my side of the drain hole, a figure crouched in the center.

SULLIVAN

Dillon Reservoir, Colorado-May 25th
(Five minutes earlier)
Sullivan loops the rope around a large boulder wedged among the piles of rocks lining the shore before tossing the remaining coil in the raft. He checks his watch. 22:38. Just past 10:30 p.m. for all those civilians down in Silverthorne who will soon be evacuating.

He sucks in a deep breath. And another. He's ready.

Armed with the paddle, Sullivan pries the raft off the gravel bank and floats into the lake. He dips the oar into the water, turning the raft toward the spillway. Turning is about the extent of his water skills. Damn Mandrake. Sullivan paddles, alternating sides while aiming for the spillway, which looks like a grand prize from the lights next to the guard shack.

He calculates he has about a hundred yards to go. Probably only seventy until he can set the timer and bail. He pulls the paddle into the raft and gauges the current. He expects the current will pull him toward the spillway in just a few minutes, but the raft drifts to a stop. He dips the oar back in the water. The recovery rope uncoils behind him as he zig-zags toward the spillway. Three strokes on the left. Three on the right.

At fifty yards, he pulls his oar out again, and the raft continues forward on its own, sucking it into the spillway hole. Breathing hard, Sullivan steers the raft's nose toward the hole, then pulls out his phone.

"Hey!" A shout reverberates behind him. Sullivan lowers his phone, peering over his shoulder through the darkness.

Nothing.

"Hey! What are you doing?" The same voice echoes across the water.

Shit. Sullivan's fingers shake as he fumbles his phone into the waterproof bag. He jams it into his pocket, then swivels to the Pelican case. He opens both clasps and yanks the box open. Good thing he has planned this to the second. The timer is strapped on top of the payload for easy access. Sullivan mashes the button. The LED numerals flash 90, 89… It's an earlier countdown than he wants, but—*fuck! Who is out there?* He grabs the rope in his right hand, tossing the remaining coil into the water before rolling overboard.

Even with the wetsuit, Sullivan's heart rate spikes at the shock of the freezing water. He sucks a huge breath as his head breaks the surface. His left hand finds his right on the rope and he begins pulling toward the shore. The timer countdown flashes in his head.

85, 84…he's got to move.

It doesn't matter who shouted from shore. He needs to get out of the water before this thing blows. He tugs five arm lengths, then surfaces for air again. As he checks the distance to the shore, he spots movement in the water. Twenty feet away from him a swimmer splashes his way.

"Hey!" The shout comes from the shore, but in a different voice. Treading water with one hand clinging onto the rope, Sullivan looks past the swimmer toward the faint outline of a guard running toward the shore from the security shack.

Shit.

He makes a quick check over his shoulder at the raft drifting toward the edge of the spillway. He's got to get out of the water.

Now.

ZAHN

Dillon Reservoir, Colorado-May 25th

"Hey!" I shout.

The shape straightens, whipping its head toward me.

"Hey!" I call again. "What are you doing?"

The figure turns away and huddles over something in the raft. I bend and tug at my laces. The boat is pointed straight at the spillway. Is this guy on a suicide mission?

The silhouette flips over the raft's side and disappears underwater. I dig in my pockets for my cell phone, wallet, and keys, tossing them by my shoes. Cold slams me as I wade down the steep drop-off until my feet can't touch anymore. Not just cold. It's ice water. My head isn't even underwater and my breaths come twice as fast as normal. I flail forward in an attempt to swim.

"Hey!" This time it's not me yelling. I turn, treading water and gasping with the shock of the cold. A figure emerges from the guard shack, barreling toward the water. Looks like I've got help.

I turn back and spot the first figure splashing toward me. My brain isn't focusing. I take a deep breath, treading water, and zero in on the shape. Definitely a male. And he's not exactly swimming. He's using some kind of line to pull himself toward the shore. Behind the figure, the raft continues steadily drifting toward the spillway.

I estimate the distance to the empty vessel. Can I reach it in time? I have to try.

Ignoring the man splashing my direction, I swim toward the boat, my form improving as I adjust to the weight of my clothes.

Stroke. Stroke.

I should have taken off my cargo pants. My legs are like frozen tubes of ground beef. My arms are lead blocks.

Stroke. Stroke.

I swim for another thirty seconds before stopping for a progress check.

Fifty feet away, the raft gains speed as it approaches the hole in the middle of the spillway. I don't know what I'll do if I catch it. A concrete structure surrounds the spillway. Can I anchor the raft and myself to the side of the hole? Then what? Is the bomb wired for a cell phone detonation like the shaft?

I make a quick check on the swimmer. There's no way that guy is using a phone anytime soon.

I keep swimming.

Stroke. Stroke.

I'm nine-thousand feet above sea level, crawl-stroking, fully clothed in an alpine reservoir fed by snowmelt. Every muscle in my body burns. My body moves faster in the current created by the spillway. Another thirty seconds passes. I look up, ready to grab, but the raft is gone—and the spillway hole looms in front of me, less than ten yards away.

Oh shit.

I spin in the water and swim, opening my eyes between head swivels to find the shore. Zero progress. The spillway is sucking me in.

This is it. I can't save myself. I rock back in the water, my heart pounding, and tilt my head back and roar in anger. Not at my certain death but at my inability to prevent it. Just like before. The rest of the story I kept from Perez. How I couldn't stop my son from dying.

"Jacob!"

A muffled roar shudders the water like a cannon fitted with a silencer, freezing my limbs in place. A huge geyser of water erupts from the hole, reversing the current that had been sucking me toward the spillway. Water pours on me from above, and my body surges toward the shore.

The son of a bitch has blown the spillway.

Instinct kicks in, and I swim for the shore, riding the blast current radiating out from the erupting spillway. As I seize the possibility of living through this nightmare, my son's face disappears, replaced by my daughter Daria's smile. I keep swimming.

The wave I ride will peter out and start sucking me back to the spillway. I need maximum distance between myself and the hole.

Stroke. Stroke.

The numbness and fatigue disappear, replaced with a euphoria that propels me toward shore. Ahead of me the security officer's flashlight pans over the water.

Stroke. Stroke.

The current slows. I swim harder. Then it changes. I power through the water, straining to beat the current when my hand brushes against something thin and coarse. The bomber's rope. I grab it.

The current tries to rip my fingers from the rope. I don't have the strength to pull myself to shore. Just enough to hang on. I cling to the rope, my feet trailing behind me and my head bobbing as I try catch my breath.

The current eases. But that doesn't make sense. If the spillway is destroyed, the current should increase. Right now, it seems to have stopped. My body moves toward the shore even though both my hands remain frozen on the rope. I raise my head. The security guard is reeling me in.

After forty feet, my feet brush the bottom of the reservoir. I struggle to stand. The guard drops the rope and draws his weapon.

"Sir, get out of the water. Put your hands behind your head and lie face down on the shore."

I stagger forward in knee-deep water. "But I'm—"

"Save it. I wasn't quite ready for your partner. Didn't know what was going on. Actually helped him out of the water before he took off. I ain't making that same mistake twice."

I slowly clasp my hands behind my head. "He's not my part—"

"I said save it." The guard circles behind me as I step from the water. "Down on the ground."

I lower myself to my knees, then pull my hands forward to lay on the ground. When I return my hands behind me, I taste the coarse shoreline sand.

I've screwed this up.

I let the bomb blow and Sullivan—got to be the same Galen Sullivan who owns the truck from the shaft—I let him get away.

I close my eyes and press my face into the sand.

SULLIVAN

Frisco, Colorado-May 25th

"Sarah, it's Galen."

"Why are you calling me? I told you—"

"Shut up. It's done," Sullivan hisses into his phone. "We need to change our meet-up plans. I can't wait until six and I'm not going back to Breck."

"Galen, it's almost midnight. I can't just—"

"The hell you can't. Get your ass in that little Beemer and meet me down by I-70. The parking lot behind Walmart in Frisco, where the shuttle buses pick up and drop off people. Know where I'm talking about?"

"I know it, but I need you to wait until morning. I can't leave right now."

"Turn on the fucking news, Sarah. You asked for this shit, and you got it. They're shutting off traffic toward Denver on I-70 right now. I almost got caught when it blew—they're going to be looking for me." Sullivan pauses. "Don't make me play hardball. I need my payoff now and then I'm out of here."

"What do you mean, hardball?"

"I've got your picture."

Sullivan smiles as Sarah's breath quickens.

"I'll be there. Give me twenty minutes," Sarah says.

Sullivan disconnects. He's shaking, in soaked clothes—the wetsuit hadn't prevented that—in the rental truck, scanning the mostly empty lot in Frisco where he'd parked after he bolted from the dam and that damn security guard.

He had a close call on the drive here. Flashing lights from two oncoming patrol cars momentarily blinded him on his way to Frisco. But they whipped past him on their way to the dam.

Sullivan digs a pair of pants and a shirt from his duffel. The truck's seat reclines almost horizontally, and he changes into the dry clothes. His hands are so numb he can hardly maneuver the shirt over his head. His seat is drenched. The shaking ceases.

Who the hell was that swimmer? The events at the dam replay in his head. He'd always known the security guard could turn into a problem—but had planned on surprise and chaos to deal with that contingency. He hadn't counted on an outside party. Who could have known his spillway plan? Mandrake did—but he's dead. Sarah knew as well—but not in detail.

It doesn't make sense. Fortunately, the swimmer went after the raft and not Sullivan. Could the swimmer recognize him? Sullivan exhales. Hell, the guy's probably dead. He obviously didn't make it to the raft. *What a dumbass.*

He reviews his exit plan. Drive west out of Colorado. Ditch the rental truck by day's end. No one will even know he's rented a truck until the company counts it as late this afternoon. He'll get rid of it in Vegas.

He planned to head to Seattle. But if the cops put everything together—and they likely already have after finding Mandrake's body— they'll probably look for him there. Vegas is a city made for disappearing. And it will be easy to deal with a sizeable amount of cash. Plus, it's got penthouse suites, those white, terry-cloth bathrobes, and the buttery taste of lobster. Vegas it is.

Sullivan checks his watch. Sarah is due in eight minutes.

He considers the woman, Sarah. Sullivan senses she is just as worried about getting caught as he is. Her panties are in a wad about this late-night meeting. He shakes his head. *I Just blew your fucking dam, lady. How about a little flexibility?*

Her giving him up wouldn't make sense, politically speaking. Her tree-hugging wackos will want the credit for blowing the dam. Doesn't serve their purpose to blame it on some low-level former employee of Denver Water. Plus, Sarah's group wouldn't put up all that cash and then fail to take the credit.

Sarah's BMW flashes in his rearview mirror as it enters the parking lot. She pulls in next to him, leaving a space between the cars.

Sullivan waits.

Sarah waits.

Their eyes meet. Finally, Sullivan exits his truck and saunters over to Sarah's car, peering at her through the six-inch gap in her window. The interior smells like a woman scent or something.

"Let's go, Sarah. The money. I need to move."

Sarah's eyes are expressionless. "I've got it right here." She pats two bags in the passenger seat. "Give me your cell phone."

"What the fuck?"

Sarah presses her lips. "Galen, don't make such a big thing about it. Think about it. You've got to get rid of it anyway, right? When they figure out it was you, they'll be tracking it. You have my picture on it. So, give me the fucking phone, and I'll give you the money."

Sullivan considers what Mandrake would have done in this situation. He would have sucker punched Sarah through the window and took the money. Sullivan has the capacity to blow up a dam above a town full of people, but he can't strike a woman. Besides, she's right. He needs to dump it. And there really isn't any risk in leaving the phone with her. Anything that incriminates him on the phone also implicates her.

"Show me the money," Sullivan says.

Sarah grabs one of the unzipped bags. Bundles of bills flash green under the dim parking lights. She lowers her window the rest of the way and pushes the bag to Sullivan. "Take it. Count it. That's half. I'll give you the other bag when you give me the phone." She returns the window to the six-inch position.

Sullivan spreads the bag's sides, exposing bound stacks of hundred-dollar bills. He counts the bills in one bundle. Then he counts the bundles, confirming Sarah's claim this was half. He zips the bag closed and holds it with one hand while reaching into his pocket for his phone.

"Show me the other bag."

Sarah retrieves the other open bag and sets it on her lap. More bills are visible inside.

Sullivan extends the phone, then yanks it back. He needs Sarah for something else.

"I got extra dynamite," he says. "Two boxes. You think your group might want it for another op or something? I'm just going to ditch it, otherwise."

Sarah leans forward, as if curious. "I thought you were using it all?"

Sullivan doesn't want to get into the details about ditching the backup plan on the north side of the dam. "We didn't."

The trunk pops behind him. He turns at the sound, then pivots back to Sarah.

"Stick it in the back," she says. "You're right. We can use it."

Sullivan returns to his truck. He pulls the two boxes from under the tarp. After he stows them in Sarah's car, he shuts the trunk and returns to the driver's door. She still has the money in her lap.

He rests one hand on the top of the half-open window and hands Sarah his phone with the other. Sarah grabs it, lowers the window, and pushes the bag through the opening. Sullivan snags it. Sarah reverses the BMW.

"Wait, let me count—" Sullivan protests.

"It's all there. We're done," Sarah calls from the window.

Sullivan spreads the bag open. It's filled to the zipper with greenbacks. He turns the key in the ignition, the engine hums. Sullivan laughs. He's earned this.

He pulls out of the parking lot, jogs onto I-70 West, and lets out a long breath. He's gonna need a new phone.

ZAHN

Frisco, Colorado-May 26th

The Frisco police department buzzes with a tension I'm guessing is unusual for one o'clock in the morning. The smell of burnt coffee hangs in the air. Uniformed personnel barrel in and out of a station that is designed to handle tourist misdemeanors rather than terrorist plots. As the arresting officer marches me to the station's rear, I catch snippets of conversation trying to ignore the fact my clothes are dripping a puddle on the floor beneath me.

"Bomb…"

"Tried to blow the dam…"

"SWAT team…"

"Bomb number two—not sure how many more…"

What I don't hear is anything about the authorities nabbing Sullivan. I sit facing the officer.

"You need a lawyer. You want to make a call?" the officer says.

"You need to look at the photo on my phone. I got the plates."

"So no lawyer?"

"I told you when you arrested me, I don't need a damn lawyer. I need you to call the Chaffee County Sheriff's office. Or even the Summit County Sheriff's office." I try to recall the name of the deputy who collected the repeaters. A name like the baseball player—but not quite. "Muziak. Stan Muziak. He knows me. The Chaffee deputy sheriff and I found the bomb in the shaft this afternoon. I delivered the repeaters to Muziak."

The officer's head jerks up when he hears the Summit County deputy's name. "You know Muziak?"

"Met him today. Listen, we're wasting time if you think I'm one of the bad guys here. Call Muziak. Ask him about Tyler Zahn from Buena Vista."

The officer reaches for his cell phone. "Judy?" he says into the phone. "Yeah, could you patch me into Stan?"

Pause.

"Yeah, Judy. Stan Muziak."

Pause.

"Yeah. Everyone and their brother are out at the reservoir right now. I'll wait."

The officer holds the phone to his ear for a full minute, his eyes never leaving me. Two more minutes pass.

"Stan? Walt Tucker here, Frisco PD."

Tucker listens. To Stan Muziak, I presume.

"Wouldn't have called if it wasn't important," Tucker continues. "We pulled a guy out of the water over by the Morning Glory Spillway. Claims he's on our side, and the other guy—the one who got past the security guard—is the one who did it. Says he knows you."

Pause.

"Tyler Zahn."

Pause.

"Well, he knows you. Said he gave you some repeaters today that came out of that shaft," Tucker looks at me. His eyebrows raise in surprise. Tucker covers the phone. "You meant yesterday on those repeaters, right?"

Right, it's morning. I open my mouth, but Tucker holds up a hand to stop me.

"Really?" Tucker says, taking a hard look at me. "Yeah, this is him. OK—hang on." Tucker covers the phone mouthpiece. "Stan wants to come debrief you—can you wait?"

A minute ago, this guy is ready to lock me up. Now he's asking if I can wait? "Sure."

Tucker returns to his phone, "Yeah Stan, he'll be here… uh-huh… yeah, I'll tell him."

Tucker hangs up and addresses me. "He'll be about fifteen minutes. How about we take the cuffs off? Got any other clothes in your car? I can have an officer swing by and grab them."

Tucker fishes a key out of his drawer and I extend my hands. "Nope. Left them in the condo I'm staying at up in Breck."

"OK. You can borrow some of mine. Or I can hook you up with some coveralls we use for guys staying in the jail. It's temporary."

"Yeah, I'll borrow the civilian clothes," I say, thinking I've already been mistaken once today. "I've got a rental car parked close to the dam."

"Nobody but law enforcement is getting in and out of that area right now. When we finish up, we'll get you back to Breck."

Tucker walks me back to his locker, and I choose a pair of Crocs, sweats and a long-sleeved shirt. While I change, he sets me up with a cup of coffee and a microwaved Hot Pocket.

No longer a suspect, I slide into normal mode. "What? No doughnuts? You call yourself a police station?"

Tucker snorts, "Enjoy." Tucker leaves me in a side chair and turns back to his paperwork.

I'm swallowing the last bit of my Hot Pocket when Stan Muziak bolts through the door out of breath. Tucker pulls another chair next to his, and Muziak and plops into the seat.

"What the fuck, Zahn?" Muziak says. "We're assholes and elbows up there trying to figure this out."

"Did the bomb blow out the bottom?" I say.

Muziak shakes his head. "It exploded. I guess you already know that, since you were there."

I bite off my *no shit* reply and say, "And?".

"We should have uncontrollable water surging out the bottom of the dam right now." Muziak pauses. "But we don't."

I recall the steady stream emerging from the dam. "Same flow as before?"

"Nope. That's the bizarre thing. There's no water coming out at all now. Zero."

I'm no waterworks expert, but this sounds like positive news. "That's a good thing, right? If the bomb plugged the outlet instead of destroying it, then you don't have to worry about flooding."

"That's what we're all thinking, at least in the short term," Muziak says. "We're blocking off I-70 below the dam, where the interstate crosses the river. Engineers are looking for damage. But the base of the dam seems to be in good shape."

I lower my eyes and exhale. The town hasn't flooded after all. I should have tried to catch Sullivan instead of chasing the raft.

Muziak's expression is grim.

"What are you worried about?" I say. "Something's still wrong, isn't it?"

"The reservoir is high this year. The water guys have been using the spillway at max capacity because the other runoff channel needs repair."

"Other runoff channel? You mean the drain outlet that runs under the shaft? Where we found the first bomb."

"No, that's already running at max capacity. There're some other outlet pipes over at the north end of the dam by Dillon. But the main valve in that one has been stuck for a year. So, the spillway is all we got."

Realization hits me like a two-by-four smacking my face. "So, with the spillway plugged, and no way to get rid of all the snowmelt flowing into the reservoir, right?"

"Right. Water's rising."

"How long to unplug the drain hole?"

"Won't know until it gets light. They're bringing in more water guys. But they are saying it'll crest the dam in three days if they don't unplug the drain."

"But the overflow would be controllable, right? Just go over the top of the dam instead of through the drain hole."

"It's what the water will do to the dam when it crests. It'll start washing the dam away."

My mouth drops. "Holy shit. Erosion could take out the whole dam?"

Muziak bobs his head. "The entire valley is in danger."

"What about Sullivan? Any word on him?"

"Nope. They found that truck of his and recovered that couple he kidnapped last night down by Buena Vista—that's where you're from, right?"

I nod.

"So, we're guessing he found a vehicle for last night's work."

"That's what I've been saying." I stand and look at Tucker. "You've got my cell phone, right?"

"Yeah, back behind the counter," Tucker says. "We were going to process everything."

"I took a picture of Sullivan's plates last night."

"Well, hot damn," Muziak says. "Go get the phone. Might be just the break we need."

SULLIVAN

St. George, Utah-May 26th

Sullivan follows the speed limit on his westward dash out of Colorado. He's almost to the Utah border when the inevitable wave of fatigue from his action-filled night hits him.

Grand Junction was two exits back. Plenty of gas stations where he could have taken a break, but if he can make Utah, he'll have a better shot at staying under the radar of Colorado's State Patrol.

Eastern Utah is a bunch of nothing. Sullivan's hand chafes raw from seventy miles of biting on it to stay awake. When the signs for Green River and a gas station flash by, he pulls over. He pays cash for gas and pulls behind the station for a two-hour nap.

An employee taps on the window. Sullivan considers arguing about his sleeping rights before remembering he shouldn't draw attention to himself. He drives west on I-70, then south on I-15 for a couple of hours before fatigue creeps up on him again. He has enough gas to make it to the border and on to Vegas, but he can't stay awake. He pulls into a Maverick station close to the Nevada border and wedges his truck between two semi-trucks.

Sullivan wakes with a start at the sound of a megaphone.

"Sir, exit the car, turn around, and put your hands on the roof," a voice blares. "You're surrounded."

Sullivan's stomach drops. Stupid, stupid. He should have dumped the rental sooner. Sullivan checks his rearview. A Utah State Patrol cruiser is parked sideways twenty feet behind his truck. Two patrolmen crouch behind the car's open doors. One of the officers holds a megaphone. The other aims a shotgun at Sullivan over the car door. Sullivan exhales. They're not here to tell him he can't sleep in the parking lot.

Shit. It's over.

Sullivan suspects these guys don't patrol Utah in pairs. Too much space. Not enough patrolmen. How many other cops are spread out around the parking lot?

"Sir!" The megaphone echoes tinny, like a lifeguard warning beachgoers about sharks. "Keep your right hand raised and open the door with your left. Nod your head if you understand."

Sullivan exaggerates his chin-to-chest movements. That's a fucking shotgun behind him. He slides out.

The two patrolmen bend him over the patrol car while yanking his hands behind his back.

"Hey. How about that thing where you read me my rights?" Sullivan's voice sounds muffled, even to himself.

The cop working the cuffs snorts.

"What about my rights?" Sullivan repeats.

The other cop lowers his radio. "You don't meet the 3C criteria."

Sullivan has no idea what the cop is talking about, but says nothing.

The cop explains anyway. "The 3Cs are *cops*, *custody*, and *cwestions*. I'm a cop. You're in custody. But we don't have any questions. We'll save that for the feds."

Sullivan fights an urge to point out the cop's spelling error. *Dumbass worker bees.*

The two patrolmen—Sullivan is wrong about them not driving around in pairs—stuff him in the back of the squad car, before joining the other officers checking out his bags of money. On the drive north, the officer in the right seat runs the radios. They look pretty enthusiastic about their catch, and waste no time letting everyone and their brother know they have the suspected domestic terrorist in their custody.

"Right, Command. Plates are a match." The deputy is practically shouting. "Same guy that plugged up that dam."

Sullivan's eyes go wide. What the fuck does *plugged up the dam* mean? He taps on the combination of wire mesh and glass separating him from the two officers.

"What are you talking about? Plugging the dam?" he says.

"Save it for your lawyer, buddy," the officer driving says, glancing over his shoulder at Sullivan. "No backseat negotiations."

What the fuck? Sullivan heard the bomb explode. Sure, the geyser had surprised him—he'd predicted the subsequent surge of water—like a mini-tidal wave or something, but not the accompanying water eruption. The bottom of the dam should've blown wide open.

Plugged?

An hour out of Salt Lake City, the deputy turns up the radio volume. A news broadcast crackles from the front speakers. Sullivan leans forward again.

The communities of Frisco, Dillon, and Silverthorne have mobilized in response to a terrorist attack on the Dillon Dam.

A bomb exploded last night in the vicinity of the Morning Glory Spillway, causing significant damage to the primary outlet for snowmelt runoff to leave the Dillon Reservoir.

Denver Water engineers are on scene, evaluating the damage, but the more immediate danger is being addressed by city maintenance crews from all three towns.

The Dillon Dam road remains closed to the public and efforts are underway to raise the height of the dam.

If engineers cannot restore the outflow in the next seventy-two hours, the water from the reservoir could breach the dam and cause it to wash away.

An evacuation advisory is in place for the city of Silverthorne. We repeat, residents of Silverthorne are being advised to evacuate.

Sullivan leans back in shock. Instead of severe flooding like he planned, an entire city could be wiped out. He's in some serious shit.

The deputy turns his head and raps on the glass. "That get your rocks off, asshole? Or did you actually need dead bodies to feel good?"

The left-seat officer glares at his partner. "Shut up, Miller."

Miller doesn't turn from Sullivan.

Sullivan composes himself and meets Miller's eyes. "I'll wait for that lawyer."

ZAHN

Breckenridge, Colorado-May 26th

Banging on the bedroom door jolts me from sleep. My head aches.

An afternoon wake-up brings back memories of long-haul supply missions. Coasting into the UK from the States just before sunrise. Offloading cargo as the nights morphed into gray dawns. Crew buses to hotels. Downing a few morning beers, ignoring the glares of the others trying to enjoy an English breakfast. Calculating takeoff times so we know when to pop that last can—eight hours bottle to throttle—that rule was sacrosanct. Reveling in our last real bed until we returned to base after delivering supplies to our brothers and sisters deployed in the desert.

I pull a pillow over my face. Glory days—leading a crew like a fine-tuned watch. That was then.

Rap. Rap. Rap.

The thin bedroom door rattles in the frame. If this had been a military operation, then I'd say I'd failed to meet my objective.

I missed it. Spent most of last night figuring out where the bomber might strike next—and my hunch took me right to the heart of the action. But a day late and too indecisive after I arrived. The bomb exploded—and the bomber got away, thanks to me.

An entire community faces destruction.

"What?" I yell, pulling the pillow from my face.

"It's Perez. Can I come in?"

"Not like I'm still asleep. Thanks for that."

Perez pokes his head in the room. "Holy shit, Z-man. You almost got him. I can't believe I was in BV sleeping while you were up here in the thick of it. Why didn't you call me when you figured out his next move?"

I sit up, fully clothed, and check my surroundings. Two beers remain from the six-pack I bought this morning at the gas station next door. The room smells like a brewery. I squint at Perez. "*Almost* got him. That's the key phrase. I surprised Sullivan in the middle of it. Probably messed up the timing."

"What do you mean?"

"The bomb plugged the drain hole, or spillway, or outlet—whatever the hell you call it. How do you plant a bomb to plug a spillway?"

Perez looks puzzled "Hell if I know. Put the bomb in just the right spot?"

"I don't think you can plan to plug it. It was an accident. He was trying to blow out the bottom of the dam from the spillway by timing it to go off when it hit the bottom."

"So, what happened?"

"I did. When I yelled at him, it threw him off. Accelerated the process, I'm guessing. Probably activated the timer sooner than he planned to, bailed, and swam to shore."

"You couldn't catch him," Perez says. "Why didn't you just wait and nab him when he got on shore?"

"Like an idiot, I thought I could stop the bomb before it went down the hole. But wasn't fast enough."

"You tried to swim to the bomb? And your plan if you had caught it?"

"Rope it to the top of the hole. Figured less damage if it blew up on top of the water."

Perez gives me that same expression he gave me when I told him I wasn't comfortable treating Carrie Schork's broken ankle. Except this time, it doesn't radiate disappointment. It's something else—

something even he can't seem to decide. "And if you had secured it, the bomb could have exploded while you were in the water."

"Oh, I didn't miss out on that fun," I say, dropping my eyes. "I got sucked into the spillway hole current when the bomb blew, but the blowback popped me out of it. Just dumb luck the waves from the blast pushed me toward shore."

Perez's jaw drops. "Tyler Zahn, you are either the stupidest guy I've ever met or a fucking hero for trying to do what you did."

I shake my head. "You miss the point. It would have turned out better if I hadn't got involved. The bomb would have blown out the bottom of the dam instead of plugging the spillway. Sure, Silverthorne might have flooded, but I'm guessing it would have been manageable." My throat is crusted from a bad morning's sleep. I cough, and glance at the nightstand for water. There's nothing but the beer and I'm not going for that in front of Perez.

"Sullivan would have probably still got away," Perez says.

I shake my head. "I'm not so sure about that. If I hadn't sped up the entire process, the security guard and I might have got him. Bottom line—I tried to help but I screwed it up."

Perez's voice is soft. "I think your perspective is a bit warped. You didn't cause all this. Sullivan did."

"Whatever." I lie back in the bed.

"Listen. I'm going into Dillon to check where they're at on finding Sullivan. Nice job on the plates by the way. You stay here." Perez eyes the empty beer bottles. "Sleep it off."

I say nothing.

"When we get Sullivan, I want you in on the questioning, buddy. You've read him like a book every step of the way. Need you to help wrap this thing up."

I jerk back up at Perez's words. "I'm done, Rick. I'm not a deputy sheriff. I have no responsibilities here except for the mess I've already created." I meet Perez's eyes. "Sorry."

Perez shakes his head and shuts the door on his way out.

I lie back and close my eyes. Perez is right about something. I need more sleep. I also need some food—and a ride home.

•   •   •

It's the doorbell this time. Not that much better than someone pounding on the door. The persistent chime rouses me from my slumber. I open my bleary eyes and check my watch. It's 4:37 p.m.

Shit. If I rest any longer, I'll never sleep tonight. I groan and pad to the main entrance, peering through the side window as I approach.

It's Leanne. JD's wife.

What day is it? Am I supposed to leave today? I can't remember.

"Leanne!" I force a smile as I open the door. "How are you?"

"Are you okay?" Leanne's eyes are wide. "I heard you tried to stop the bomb?"

I'll be forever known as the guy who almost stopped the bomb. I shoot Leanne another thin smile. "Yeah, I was involved. It didn't do much good though."

Leanne steps closer and I involuntarily step back, my hand remaining on the doorframe.

"You must be exhausted," she says. "Did I wake you?"

"Nope," I lie. "I got some sleep earlier in the day."

Leanne's eyes shine, and she leans in.

I'm tired—but not so exhausted I can't read Leanne's signals. She wants to come in. Again? I'm not up for more shower banter.

"Uh—would you like to come in?"

"Just for a second. I don't want to bother you."

I step to the side, allowing Leanne through the door. The same faint smell of perfume accompanies her. Leanne perches on the couch.

"I'd offer you something to drink, but I haven't had time to get anything." I taste the remnants of the four beers I finished before bed and remember the two full ones on my nightstand. Definitely not offering her a warm beer.

Plus, I'm unsure what Leanne wants. We've only known each other for four days. Is it me she wants? Now is not the time.

"I guess you and JD are probably trying to figure out how long we'll be here, right?" I say, going into apologetic mode. "I'll talk to Perez. Now that it's a full-blown investigation, I think he can move us to a hotel in town."

"You guys can stay as long as you need. Don't worry about it."

"Thanks. I know the Sheriff's Department appreciates it." I pause and run my hand through my hair. "And I do too. This place beats a hotel room any day."

Leanne smiles.

I smile. This is awkward.

Finally, she reaches forward, resting both hands on the edge of the coffee table, and looks directly at me. "Tell me about it. What happened?"

Oh shit. I've forgotten about Leanne's desire to get the inside scoop on the bombing plot. How could I forget after yesterday's grilling?

"Well, I think it is an ongoing—"

"Oh, come on." Leanne leans in. "I mean, I heard you saw the bomber. Is that true?"

"It was dark…"

"Could you recognize him if you saw him again?"

Now that's a weird question. "Leanne, I don't think me recognizing him will be the clincher in this case. We've got a name. We've got his license plate."

Shit. Another slip, just like the information Perez shared. Spouting *we've got this* and *we've discovered that*. Hell, I'm not even a member of the Sheriff's Office.

Leanne appears stunned at my revelation.

"Look, I probably shouldn't have told you that. My point is, I think it's probably only a matter of time before they catch this guy."

"Well, what's his name?" Leanne blurts.

"Come on Leanne. I told you. Ongoing investigation. Can't reveal details. I shouldn't have even told you what I did."

Leanne's stunned expression fades and turns contemplative. "Well, I hope you guys catch him fast. It's terrible what he's trying to do to our community. What's your next move?"

I shake my head. Enough already. "I don't have a next move. I'm no longer involved. Perez will stay here, but I'm headed back home to BV either tonight or tomorrow morning."

Leanne's eyes widen. "Tyler, don't take this the wrong way—you've done so much already—but how can you leave?"

"Well, I—"

Leanne interrupts. "Silverthorne is on the verge of being washed away. They're mobilizing volunteers to fill sandbags."

"Sandbags?" I squint. "They think sandbags will stop all that water?"

"They have every bulldozer in the area building up the dam with fill material: dirt, and rocks, and stuff. The sandbags are the last-ditch effort if it comes to that. JD's down there helping with it. You should stay."

I can fill bags. Done my share of that in the desert. It's mind-numbing work, but useful. Besides, I'm the one who created this problem. Leanne is offering a small way to help fix it.

"I'll think about it." I'm too exhausted to consider doing anything right now. And I've got those beers in the bedroom.

Leanne smiles nervously, reaching across the table to grab my hands. "And if you need anything—anything at all, you call me, right?" Then her expression hardens. "And you'll let me know when you have information you can share, OK? This guy needs to pay."

•　　•　　•

At two in the morning, I wake up thinking I'm done with the whole R&R thing. I spent most of a previous day sleeping off the early morning beers and now am paying the price for too much sleep. I roll from my bed and wander into the kitchen. Perez's backpack rests on a chair at the dining room table.

I brew a pot of coffee, feeling like ass. Not so much from the beers, but from constantly replaying my role in creating the disaster facing Silverthorne.

If volunteers are filling sandbags, they're likely running a 24/7 operation. I exchange my coffee mug with a travel mug from the cupboard and fill up. I might as well go find out.

Fifteen minutes later, I'm at a standstill in traffic on the main road through Frisco. Cars pack the thoroughfare. It's 2:30 in the morning, and the road congestion confuses me. As I approach the end of the main street, flashing lights at the intersection with I-70 reflect inside my Hyundai. Of course—the bomb has forced a major reroute of Colorado traffic. When the police let me access my rental car last night, I had to detour around the east side of Dillon Reservoir to get to the Breckenridge condo.

I turn off at the I-70 roadblock, and pull next to the patrol car monitoring entry to the Dillon Dam road. A patrolman approaches my window, shining a flashlight in my face.

"Help you, sir?" he says.

"I heard there was a need for sandbaggers?"

"Can I see your driver's license?"

I show him my driver's license and retired military ID card. The military ID always seems to help in situations with the authorities. The patrolman examines both, then hands them back, while bending closer to squint at me.

"Hey, aren't you the guy who tried to stop the bomb?"

I might as well get used to this. "Yep. Didn't succeed, though. Obviously."

"Screw that—good on you for having the balls to try. Can't believe this happened on Memorial Day weekend. We've been talking about you on the net. Hell of an effort."

"Thanks. Are they still filling bags this time of night?"

"You bet—but you got to go around the lake." He points over the top of my car in the opposite direction of I-70. "They've established a command center at Dillon Fire & Rescue. The sandbag operation is set up in the parking lot next door. They can use all the help they can get."

The patrolman guides me through a three-point turn, I join the flow of traffic rolling through Frisco. It takes me an hour to circumnavigate the reservoir, a drive that usually lasts twenty-five minutes. I enter Dillon, and follow the lights to the command center, and check in at the volunteer table. Training lasts less than a minute, and soon I'm filling bags.

I partner with Gene, a local in his mid-sixties. I shovel and Gene holds the bags open. We quickly fall into a rhythm, our combined breaths forming a small cloud in the brisk morning air.

I fill ten bags. Gene ties the tops. We each make five trips to stack the bags at the edge of the parking lot. Another group of volunteers loads bags onto a flow of flatbed trucks arriving at ten-minute intervals.

"Where they taking the bags?" I say, after Gene and I switch roles. "Any idea?"

"I think over by the security shack at the north end of the dam."

I recall my walk from yesterday. No, wait. That was two days ago. "What's the update on the dam?"

"The engineers started working it yesterday, but not a lot they can do from above the water. The spillway tube collapsed in on itself. The obstruction is about two hundred feet down."

"What's the plan?"

"Some kind of floating drilling platform, I heard," Gene says between shovelfuls, "Something that can support a well-digging apparatus. They plan to drill from the Morning Glory Spillway side. Try to break through whatever is clogging it up."

"How much time we got before they think the dam might breach?" My breath comes hard. I'm impressed with Gene's ability to shovel sand while keeping up a conversation.

"About forty-eight hours. That's if we don't get rain. But the forecast is clear, so we got that going for us."

Two days. Not much time.

We work at a steady pace for several hours before breaking for coffee and donuts provided by another set of volunteers. As the sun pokes above the reservoir's shore, more and more people trickle in to help. Gene and I finish our fourth hour, and find ourselves more valuable as instructors. Some volunteers have never used a shovel for anything but snow.

Midmorning arrives. My back and shoulders ache. Gene has headed home for some sleep. As I shuffle to my rental car, Perez pulls alongside me in his department Tahoe.

"Hop in. I want to show you something."

"I need a nap. Had an early start this morning."

Perez peers over my shoulder at the lines of people filling bags. "Good for you, brother."

Curiosity wins. "What do you want to show me?"

"Over by the roadblocks. I want to show you what the engineers got going. Plus, I got news." Perez smiles.

I raise an eyebrow. "Yeah?" I climb in.

Perez steers to the north-side roadblocks where a patrolman waves us through. An overloaded dump truck idles in front of us. Lights silhouette Perez and I. When I turn, I spot another dump truck on our bumper waiting for the traffic to move. The steady dull roar of heavy equipment vibrates our windows.

"You sure we're not in the way?" I say.

"We're fine. There's a wide spot over by the spillway where cars are parking. The engineers are there, and the Task Force guys are checking out your crime scene."

"Right, my crime scene—so what's the news?" I crane my neck, trying to see if the traffic ahead is moving.

"They got him. They picked up Sullivan last night in Utah. Just north of Vegas."

I whip my head toward Perez. "No shit?"

"Yep. He had two sets of ID. One of them says Galen Sullivan. The other is what he used for the rental truck. Plates match the picture you sent in. And he just happened to have a couple bags full of cash as well."

I focus on the truck ahead which finally moves. *Cash?* I turn back to Perez as we pull into parking next to the spillway. "Cash?" I say aloud. "That would imply—"

Perez cuts me off. "Someone hired Sullivan and Mandrake. We thought that might be the case, right? Neither one of them quite fit the domestic terrorist profile."

"Right," I agree. "But frustrating to know you got the guy who did it, but not the guy who wanted it done. Any clues?"

Perez backs into a parking spot, but doesn't answer my question. "I went into Incident Command early this morning for the update. Good thing you were helping with those sandbags because we might need them to stop this thing."

"Aren't they going to drill through the clog?"

"They're going to try. The floating barge should be on the water before noon. The crane apparatus with the drill should be operational by this afternoon. Hopefully, it will work."

"And if it doesn't? Use the sandbags and pray the water doesn't rise anymore?"

Perez shakes his head. "If it doesn't work, they'll blow a corner of the dam. Use sandbags on the Dillon end, and blow an outlet on this end."

"But won't that—"

"Yep—it'll flood the river banks in Silverthorne. They figure dealing with the damage along the lowlands is better than the reservoir breaching at the dam's middle and washing the whole dam away. That would flood the whole town."

"I think I'll stay and keep filling bags."

"No. I brought you up here to show you they had a plan. I need you with me. I've talked to Sheriff Larkin and the Task Force guys and got the approval. I want you with me while I interview the folks involved."

I groan. "Rick, I told you. It's been great being your pseudo-deputy, but I got in over my head and screwed things up. I'm done. I'll help here—fill some more bags. But after that, I'll stick to looking for lost hikers with SAR."

"Don't make me fucking beg, OK? I've been on this case since you first made that call about the Schorks' dog. Now it's national news and everybody and their brother has fingers in it. They're only letting me work it because they know I was involved from the beginning."

"Right, and you need me because…?"

"Because a few of the key breaks we've had in this case have been from your ideas. This is my chance to do something big for the department. Make a name for myself. I'd have a hell of a lot better chance of breaking this case if you'd help."

I say nothing. I know Perez cares about his job—but I hadn't realized he was so passionate about it.

Perez continues, "I promise you. No action. Just interviews. OK?"

I'm surprised it only takes five seconds of thought. "I don't want a title. I'll do the interviews, but you just introduce me as your associate. You're the lead. Got it?"

"Got it!" Perez punches my shoulder. "That's all I'm asking. You just provide your insight. For a couple of the interviews you won't be in the room. We'll have you listen in."

"And the ones I join you on?"

Perez grins knowing he's sucked me in. "You can ask a question if you got one, but there's no requirement to open your mouth. Just listen, absorb, and most importantly—debrief. We'll hash out the interviews together after they're over."

"OK. Who are we interviewing first?"

"We're going back to BV. Give the Schorks another once over, now that we know about their little drug operation. Then head to the prison where Mandrake was. The prison staff says Mandrake talked to a Robert Dorsey, a.k.a. Big Bobby, twice in the forty-eight hours prior to his escape. They've got video from the yard cameras. Maybe he'll give us something." Perez pauses. "You'll probably have to listen in on that one from the outside."

"Alright. When do we go?"

Perez grips the steering wheel. "Now. Let's pack it up. You turn in your car. I'll give JD a call and close out, and then we'll hit the road. We'll interview the Schorks this afternoon. Already set up."

"You must have been pretty confident I'd say yes." I smile.

"Brother, I'd be interviewing these guys with or without you. But, yeah. I feel a lot better having you along. Thanks."

I say nothing. All I have to do is listen. I can't screw things up.

SULLIVAN

Salt Lake City, Utah-May 27th
Jail in Salt Lake City sucks.

Sullivan tries channeling his inner Mandrake without success. He shares a large cell with the guys picked up for minor charges, vagrancy, and public intoxication. He dreads his impending move to a penitentiary.

They've got him. No question. The security guard who pulled him ashore can identify him. They tracked his rental truck. Bags of money are always suspicious. And the Schorks. He'll be behind bars in record time.

The question remaining is *for how long*? His only bargaining chip is Sarah, and he hasn't a single reason to protect her.

He runs through what he knows about Sarah—or at least what she has shared over beers. Western Colorado. Middle-class parents. Eco-activist. And she owns a Beemer. There are plenty of BMW's in Colorado, but an environmentalist driving one around? That should stick out like a dick on a doughnut.

He spends one night in the Utah jail before moving to the Chaffee County jail in Salida, Colorado. The trip includes an ironic twist; when they turn off I-70, climb over Tennessee Pass, and thread down the Arkansas River Valley, they pass within a quarter mile of Mandrake's old prison.

Mandrake had explained the Buena Vista Correctional Complex serves inmates with minor offenses. Sullivan blew up shit and kidnapped old people. There's no way he'll end up there.

Sullivan in-processes to the Chaffee County jail in the early afternoon. He'll remain in this jail until trial. The staff supplies a list of local lawyers, but Sullivan ignores it. He read the green sign at the edge of town: *Entering Salida, Population 5,963*. No lawyer from this podunk town can help him.

The jail staff allows him the use of a computer, and he researches big-name firms in Denver, ones whose names he recognizes from working with Denver Water. After thirty minutes of research and two phone calls, he realizes he needs those local lawyer names after all. He doesn't have the money to pay the big firms and they aren't interested in *pro bono* for terror and kidnapping. Imagine that.

The Schork kidnapping made national news and proved a hot topic in the valley. The locals breathed a collective sigh of relief when the Schorks returned unharmed. Phil White, the first Salida lawyer Sullivan dials, jumps at the opportunity.

"I'll be there in thirty minutes," White says.

Sullivan squeezes his eyes shut. Phil White sounds more interested in the publicity than keeping Sullivan out of jail. But he figures all these shysters out here will be like that.

White is four inches shorter than Sullivan, sporting running shoes and a pot belly held tight under a polo shirt. They spend an hour in a meeting room reviewing the case. The jail staff interrupts with a five-minute warning.

"What's your best guess?" Sullivan says. "Can I get this thing reduced?"

White squints at Sullivan. "Galen, what do you think it would get reduced from?"

"I don't know. Twenty years?"

"The kidnapping alone is twenty years. At least. But the real problem is that dam. Have you been watching the news?"

Sullivan shakes his head. "Not since about an hour after they arrested me. Did it overflow?"

"Not yet. But it's looking like it might. If the dam goes, that's domestic terrorism. And we're talking a life sentence for a terrorist attack designed to wipe out a town."

"But it wasn't supposed to—" Sullivan's hands tremble. This is not how it's supposed to turn out. Bye-bye penthouse suite. Bye-bye terrycloth robe. "Life?" Sullivan looks up at his lawyer. "I can't do that. And the girl who hired me—Sarah? Can't I give her up to get less?"

"We'll use it, of course. But you need to be prepared for the worst. I can't promise you anything. Just keep your mouth shut about anything to do with the case. Don't talk to your cellmates. Don't talk to anyone who comes to visit. No one but me. Do you understand?"

Sullivan nods.

He's screwed.

ZAHN

Elk Trace near Buena Vista, Colorado-May 28th-29th

Perez runs through the sequence of events with the Schorks one more time, his mini-recorder running. "So, you didn't actually see Mandrake hide anything at the rest stop along the river?" I'm beside him on the couch in the couple's living room, petting Scottie and contemplating how much has happened since we rescued Carrie from Kroenke Lake.

Jim snorts. "That was when you first had to pee, right, Carrie?"

"Hell, you were too scared to ask, Jim. Or should I say, Jimbo?" Carrie says.

"Shit. I hated him calling me that."

Perez tries steering the conversation back on track. "After the rest stop, you all drove up to Twin Lakes?"

"That's right," Carrie says. "At first, we thought it might have been Clear Creek Reservoir. But we Googled it the other day and confirmed it as Twin Lakes. You know, that spot over on the south side past the campground? The last place before the road gets bumpy?"

"Right. You met a group of men. Driving an SUV and pulling a trailer. Any more details?"

"We're not sure what make of SUV, but kind of fancy. Dark color. The trailer was a U-Haul, with a picture of Yosemite or Yellowstone on the side," Jim says.

"Anything else?"

"Carrie and I remembered a couple things that we didn't bring up yesterday."

"Go ahead."

"What was the name of Mandrake's partner?" Jim says.

"Sullivan. Galen Sullivan," Perez says.

"Right. Sullivan mentioned an Asian guy in the passenger seat of the SUV."

"What about him?" Perez glances at me. I shrug.

"Nothing, really. We never heard anything more about him. But when they killed Mandrake later and took us? Someone was in the passenger seat of their SUV. Maybe it was the same Asian guy."

Perez scribbles a note. The Schorks had told Perez before the men were all Hispanic.

Jim continues, "And it wasn't like Mandrake and this Sullivan were just taking the boxes from the other guys. We heard them say the word *swap*. Plus, later on, the guys who shot Mandrake talked about getting cheated and drove us back with them to the lake and the rest stop. It sounded like a drug deal gone bad."

Carrie snorts. "Like you'd know."

"You could be right." Perez says. "Our dogs at the rest stop signaled on a hidey-hole."

Jim turns to Carrie. "Told you."

"What happened after the swap?"

Jim continues. "Sullivan moved the truck beside the U-Haul, and he and the other guys loaded the boxes onto the back. After that, the other guys drove off. Mandrake took us on a potty break and then we left."

"Then you went to Breckenridge, stopping in Leadville for gas on the way, right?"

"Hang on." I can't help interrupting. "You said Sullivan loaded the stuff? He did the whole thing? Checked out the load, did the swap, and loaded the truck? Mandrake never got out of the truck?"

Jim and Carrie exchange glances.

"Mandrake left once," Carrie says. "I remember leaning the seat forward to let him out."

"That's right," Jim agrees. "After Sullivan came back, he told Mandrake to go do his thing."

Carrie snaps her head toward her husband. "And he told him to shut up, too. Remember, Jim? When Sullivan came back, he said something about how some woman would be happy. What was the name he said?"

"Right. Damn—wait. Sullivan called her Beemer Babe. Remember that? Then Mandrake said her name, something starting with an 'S.' But Mandrake thought it was a guy running things, not the woman. Sullivan got pissed when Mandrake—"

"Cowboy Timmons," Carrie blurts.

"Cowboy Timmons. Right. That was the guy's name Mandrake said."

"Cowboy Timmons?" Perez glances at me before turning back to the couple. "Who's that?"

Jim and Carrie look at each other and shrug.

Carrie says, "I mean, looking back on it, they must be related to the bombs? The S-girl slash Beemer Babe and Cowboy Timmons. But that was the only time we heard their names. Those assholes got pretty careful with names after that."

"Right," Jim agrees. "We never heard those names again. We heard Sullivan call Mandrake by his first name—Mitch—when we were at the gas station. That's where Carrie tried to signal a guy that we were in trouble. Things got a little dicey after that." Jim beams at Carrie with what Zahn guesses is a trace of pride.

Perez has the Schorks retrace every event from Leadville until their rescue. I jump in several more times with questions, but the couple provides nothing new.

Perez switches gears, trying an angle he and I discussed while driving back to Buena Vista. "Carrie, the dogs up at The Numbers— they signaled on oxycontin. Did you know that?"

Jim glances at his wife. She eyes Perez. "So, they must have had drugs up there. You said that made sense."

"It might. But the dogs signaled the same way when they searched your house after you disappeared. When we found your pharmacy stuff back there." Perez glances toward the hallway.

"We knew you saw that," Carrie says. "You know I'm a pharmacist, right?"

"We know you're not a practicing pharmacist."

The room goes silent. Carrie looks at Jim then back to Perez. "Is this the part where you ask me if I want a lawyer?"

"Do you need one? Anything you can tell us about your connection to Sullivan and Mandrake will obviously help your case."

"Our case?" Carrie explodes. "Screw you, asshole—"

"Carrie," Jim's voice pitches up at the end, like he's cautioning her.

Carrie takes several deep breaths. She extends her hands toward Perez. "Lock me up, Sheriff. Or Assistant Sheriff—whatever you are. But it won't be for terrorism, or bombs, or whatever drug deals those guys had going."

"What should I charge you with then?"

"Illegal distribution." Carrie drops her hands to her lap. "I've got four people in town I get painkillers for. Each of them is sick. But with the opioid crackdown and the doctor shortage out here, these people can't get what they need." She sighs. "And they need it. The doctors are waiting for an amputated limb, or a gunshot wound these days before they will prescribe painkillers." Carrie pauses. "I get the stuff delivered next door while the McCorkles are gone. They don't even know about it. I get the painkillers in various forms and use the equipment in the office to package it for these people." Carrie sticks her arms back out. "So, sue me, or arrest me… or whatever."

Perez studies Carrie. I watch Perez.

"How much are you making from this?" Perez says.

Carrie sucks in her breath.

Jim says, "No money. She's got connections in Denver. This is a medical thing. She's doing it for folks that need it. In doses less likely to cause addiction."

Perez looks my way with blank eyes. I match his expression.

Neither of us speaks. Finally, Perez stands. I join him.

"Let's circle back to that issue, Carrie," Perez says. "Another visit."

Carrie says nothing, her breath heavy.

"I sure appreciate the help you've provided." Perez shakes Jim's hand. He smiles at Carrie whose injured ankle remains propped on the coffee table. "They'll ask you about all this again at the trial, so please keep brainstorming. Let us know if you remember anything else."

"We hope today helped," Jim says.

"The names were especially helpful," Perez says. "Think about the S-girl's name, OK?"

As Perez's Tahoe crests the hill, he smiles. "Told you I needed you, brother Zahn. We got some research to do on this Cowboy Timmons."

"Don't forget S-girl," I add, just so Perez knows I was paying close attention.

Neither of us bring up the Schorks and their unauthorized drug operation.

•   •   •

Sweat beads on my forehead as Perez and I step through the security entrance at the Buena Vista Correctional Complex. The forecast calls for eighty today, unusual for June in the Rockies. Buena Vista's eight-thousand feet elevation negates the need for air conditioning, which means this interview, in a meeting room with three white walls and another made of one-way glass, promises to be sweltering.

I take a chair outside, behind one-way glass, as Perez steps into the interview room. A giant of a man in prison coveralls dwarfs a normal-size chair. I don the headphones in front of me.

"Mr. Dorsey? I'm Deputy Sheriff Rick Perez." Perez reaches across the table to shake the prisoner's hand. Big Bobby doesn't stand but thrusts his hand forward. "First things, first. I'm going to read you your rights, OK?"

Dorsey grunts.

Perez pulls out a card and reads from it. "Do you understand?"

"Uh-huh. You called me Mr. Dorsey before. In here they call me Big Bobby." Dorsey takes a big breath.

"Right." Perez wipes his brow and wrinkles his nose as he takes a seat. "Did anybody tell you why I'm here?"

"Nope."

"Have you heard about the bomb at Dillon Reservoir?"

"News. On TV."

"Do you know who did it?"

"Nope."

"It was a friend of one of your friends. Your friend being Mitch Mandrake. Do you remember him?"

I lean forward to gauge Dorsey's reaction. I don't see one.

"Yep. I know Mandrake."

"I thought you might. He's dead. Did you know that?"

"Nope." Dorsey's eyes register no emotion.

"Mandrake spent some time with you just before his escape. That true?"

"Nope."

"Are you sure?"

"Yep." Dorsey's voice wheezes.

"Well shoot. That's just a shame." Perez shakes his head. "The warden thought if you helped us, you might have a shot at getting out of here in months instead of a year and a half."

I spot a flicker of something in Dorsey's eyes.

"Yeah?"

"Yeah," Perez replies. "Why did Mandrake come to you? Did you help him escape? Did you set him up with something on the outside?"

I wince. Too many questions, too fast. This isn't Dorsey's first rodeo. The man is smart enough to know if he incriminates himself, he'll be in prison longer—not getting out earlier.

"Sounds like I need a lawyer," Dorsey whispers.

"Did you provide the bombs?"

Dorsey remains silent.

Perez glances at my window. He obviously needs a lifeline. I type a text.

Bring up the videos.

Perez reaches for his pocket a second after I hit *Send*. He ignores Dorsey as he scans his phone. Dorsey glances at my window and smiles.

To Perez's credit, he doesn't make excuses for the phone. Dorsey has our game figured out.

"Mr. Dorsey, we know you met Mandrake. We've got it on film."

"OK."

"Could you tell us what you talked about?"

Dorsey squints. "If I cooperate, I might get time off?"

"That's right."

Dorsey leans back, sucking in a couple of breaths. I worry about the strength of Dorsey's chair.

"Yeah, OK. Mandrake came to me because he was nervous, I think. Needed somebody to talk to." Dorsey stops and catches his breath. "You ask around. Lots of guys in here come to me to talk. Every day. I'm a good listener."

Perez interjects. "They say you're a good fixer—that they come to you so—"

"Rick," I whisper my friend's name to myself in a soft voice.

Perez stops talking. He looks at the glass. My eyes widen. *Wow. How'd that work?*

"Sorry, Mr. Dorsey. Go on."

"Yeah, so Mandrake. I think he wanted to get things off his chest. He told me he was getting out. Going to do a job."

"Did he tell you what kind of job?"

"Nope. But he mentioned water. Guess we know now he meant the dam, huh?" Dorsey gasps the question.

"What exactly did he say about water?"

Dorsey leans back again and I wince as the small chair flexes.

"He said water was the new gold. Environmentalists and ranchers, that's all I remember. Yep. That's what he said." Dorsey reaches forward, grabbing his knees, and tries to catch his breath.

"Did he say if any of those groups hired him?"

Dorsey's chest heaves, as he tries to get more air. His breath rasps in my headset. "I don't think he knew for sure. He called the ranchers *cowboys*. I remember that."

Perez's eyes flick my way. Cowboy Timmons. Dorsey doesn't miss Perez's glance either.

"Did he say anything else? I'm trying to figure out how his friend got the supplies. Was it a swap, like drugs for bombs or something. Know anything about that?"

"Nope. Mandrake just needed to get the stress off his chest. I already told you what he told me."

Perez checks his phone. "Mr. Dorsey, I think that's all we've got for today. Do you have questions for me?"

Dorsey leans forward, grabbing the edge of the table with his meaty hands while pulling himself off the small chair. "Yeah. You'll tell the warden, right? Tell him I helped you. I told you about the *cowboys*, right?" He tosses his head toward my window.

Perez doesn't bother shaking Dorsey's hand. "You bet, Mr. Dorsey. We'll let him know."

•   •   •

I've made the drive from Buena Vista to Salida, along the Arkansas River Valley, many times. But today seems different. After our conversations with the Schorks and Dorsey, I sense we're gaining traction. The excitement sharpens my senses, making everything out my window pop with color. To the east, rocky outcrops and red sandstone jut skyward, reminiscent of Moab in Utah. To the west, jagged snowcapped 14ers extend the horizon even higher. The foothills of these massive mountains cascade straight to the edge of our valley, then slant like a table with one short leg toward the river.

I peel my eyes from the passenger window. "What did you think of Dorsey?"

"He smells. Like coffee grounds and fish left together in a garbage can. And it was hot in there."

I snort. "I meant the interview."

"I thought he was full of shit. Even the warden admits Big Bobby is the big boss on the inside." Perez glances my way. "I bet he hooked up Sullivan and Mandrake with the bomb. Hell, he's the one who probably helped Mandrake escape."

I focus on the road, hoping Perez will take the hint and do the same. "Even if that's how it went down—and I'm not doubting you—he couldn't really tell you. He can't get time off for cooperating if he incriminates himself for additional offenses, right?"

"I know, I know." Perez sighs. "Where'd a pilot learn this interviewing thing?"

"Some of the units on my last deployment were kind of non-standard."

"Like how?"

"We had this prisoner-of-war camp just over the Kuwaiti border in Iraq. It was a hodge-podge of units. The Army did the interrogations. I got a chance to watch some of those."

"Like waterboarding and shit?" Perez glances at me sideways.

I shake my head. "Never saw any of that *enhanced* stuff. These interrogations were just like interviews. Strategized beforehand. Picked up some stuff just listening."

Perez wags his head and says, "Back to Dorsey. What'd you think about that *cowboy* shit?"

"Something there." I pause. "And Mandrake called water the *new gold*. What if this whole thing is about water rights?"

"Possible." Perez laughs. "My grandma has lived in Colorado her whole life. She used to say, 'Whiskey is for drinkin' and water is for fightin' over.'"

"We should google water rights Colorado. See if Cowboy Timmons pops up."

"Do it," Perez says.

"What about the environmental wacko Dorsey talked about?"

"There's only a million tree-huggers in Colorado." Perez grins and slows the Tahoe as we enter Salida. "We're like five minutes out from the jail. Any tips?"

"Sullivan lawyered up, right?"

"A Salida local."

"So, if he lets Sullivan talk, that most likely means he's looking to bargain. He might give up who's pulling the strings."

Perez brakes. Six deer cross the road between us and the courthouse parking lot. Perez pulls in by the county jail side.

"Same plan as before?" Perez says.

"If I got something to add, I'll text."

SULLIVAN

Salida, Colorado-May 29th

"Who are these guys again?" Sullivan and his lawyer, Phil White huddle in a cramped conference room outside Sullivan's cell block. The Chaffee County jail clientele are slightly less seedy than his previous cellmates. And the food is better. Neither of these improvements change Sullivan's mind about trying to minimize his time behind bars.

"It's a deputy sheriff from the county and his associate. They discovered the bomb in the shaft. One of them tried to stop the raft from going down the drain hole. Sounds like they were one step behind you the whole way."

"No shit? One of them was the wannabee swimmer?" Sullivan enjoys this attorney-client privilege thing.

"Too bad he didn't stop the bomb. It might have helped your case."

"Yeah? Well, hindsight's 20/20. That's what we used to say in the Army." Sullivan scratches his nose. "And why agree to talk to them?" White's expression pisses him off. Like Sullivan's the dumb one here, and White considers himself smarter.

"It's just to show you're being cooperative. You shouldn't say anything. Let me do the talking."

Sullivan fights the urge to tell White what he really thinks.

The door opens and a law enforcement officer approaches the table. He extends his hand toward Sullivan. "Mr. Sullivan, I'm Deputy Sheriff Perez from Chaffee County."

Sullivan doesn't stand, but awkwardly thrusts both cuffed wrists toward Perez. Perez shakes his right hand. Sullivan says nothing.

White steps forward, offering his hand to Perez. "I'm Phil White, Mr. Sullivan's attorney."

Perez shakes it with a grunt.

Sullivan senses Perez isn't a fan of lawyers. He looks over the deputy sheriff's shoulder. "Where's Michael Phelps? Your Olympic swimmer associate?"

White coughs, shaking his head. Perez says nothing.

The deputy sits across from Sullivan and reads him his Miranda rights. Sullivan thinks back to Utah. Here it is. Cops. Custody. Questions. With a *Q*.

"I'd like to ask you a few questions about the bombing up at Dillon Reservoir. Is that OK?"

Sullivan gives Perez a half-smile, then turns to White.

"Deputy Sheriff Perez," White says. "Mr. Sullivan will listen to your questions. However, he is facing trial for his alleged actions and will reserve his responses for that trial."

Nice. Phil's big-city lawyer act impresses Sullivan. He notes the deputy doesn't look too happy.

Perez turns back to Sullivan. "Were you associated with Mitch Mandrake?"

Sullivan says nothing.

"Were you involved in the kidnapping of Jim and Carrie Schork?"

Sullivan leans back and remains silent.

"Did you trade drugs for bomb material?"

This bit of detective work surprises Sullivan.

"Did an individual at the Buena Vista Correctional Complex—a Mr. Dorsey—help in the escape of Mandrake and, or, supply your bombing efforts?"

Sullivan says nothing. But his mind races. *Who the hell is Dorsey? Did Mandrake leave loose ends?*

"Who hired you to bomb the reservoir and the shaft?"

This guy hasn't a clue. Maybe he *can* throw Sarah under the bus for a reduced sentence.

"Was it someone you and Mandrake referred to as *Beemer Babe?*"

Oh shit, he's got a little bit of a clue.

"Or was it someone named Timmons—a rancher?"

Timmons? Timmons? Do the cops actually know more than he does about who hired him? All Sullivan is certain of is Sarah's involvement.

Where could the deputy have gotten Timmons's name? He glances at White. This local yokel lawyer hasn't a clue how to play this. If Sullivan can steer this guy toward Timmons, then perhaps he and his lawyer can save the big "Sarah reveal" for the trial.

"Ron Timmons?" Sullivan blurts. "Now why would he be interested in water in this part of the state?" He watches the deputy scribble notes on his pad while White jerks in his seat.

"Galen," White admonishes.

Sullivan stops talking, leans back, and plasters a half-smile on his face. He's planted the seed.

After thirty minutes of questions without answers, Perez checks his cell phone. Sullivan looks from the phone to the camera in the room's corner. Sullivan shifts his chair to line up with the camera. He leans forward. "You might want to look at swimming lessons, dude. They got all kinds of programs for middle-aged men now."

"Galen!" White interjects.

Perez's eyes move from Sullivan to the camera. He looks pissed. "Time for me to go, gentlemen." He turns and walks toward the door. Sullivan notices Perez didn't thank him for his cooperation. Or shake his hand goodbye. But now Sullivan knows law enforcement has Timmons's name. They don't have Sarah's.

Sullivan turns to White. "Not sure I really needed you for that, Phil."

ZAHN

Between Salida and Buena Vista, Colorado-May 29th-30th
The power of the Internet amazes me. We used to joke in the C-130 that duct tape and baling wire were tools that could get you out of a jam when options ran low. Now the answers are online. While Perez drives up the valley to Buena Vista, I use my cell phone to find Timmons.

It was a good thing Perez kept me outside the interview. That crack about swimming lessons got to me. I wouldn't have wanted Sullivan to see my expression.

Big Bobby Dorsey had mentioned water being the new gold. I type *Timmons, Colorado* and *water rights* into my browser. I strike gold on my first search. Ronald J. Timmons, 42, from Montrose, Colorado, has been arguing for ranchers' rights to water west of the Rockies for years. A member of the Colorado Cattlemen's Association, his name features prominently on cattle ranching advocacy forums.

I read the results to Perez. "I think this is the guy. Says he's from Montrose. I bet we can track down his address."

Perez scoffs, "You think? Man, we're so wired into databases at the department, I can probably tell you where he took his last crap after we run his name through the system."

"We got time to check him out?"

"Not today. Too far. I'll need my Montrose County contacts to confirm he's there before we make the drive." Perez pauses. "Tomorrow, first thing?"

"As long as there's no action and you're in charge. What time you want to leave?"

"I'll pick you up tomorrow morning at six."

• • •

We retrace our route back toward Salida, then turn west over Monarch Pass, and head through Gunnison, skirting the Black Canyon. The sun takes its mid-morning spot in the sky.

Perez updates me on the dam. "I called last night, and it's going to be a close-run thing."

"They haven't cleared the blockage yet?"

"Nope. The platform is in place and they've dropped the drilling mechanism. No breakthroughs though. Water is rising. They expect a breach by tomorrow afternoon unless they bore through the blockage. Their last-ditch plan if that doesn't work is to blow out the corner of the dam by the spillway."

I shake my head. "I feel like I should do something to help."

"What do you think you're doing right now?"

"I'm not helping the people below that dam. At this point, the dam, and our case are independent. The dam's going to go, or it isn't. We're going to figure out who's behind this or we won't. Neither impacts the other."

"I'm not a deep thinker," Perez says. "You probably figured that out."

Perez keeps glancing my direction like he doesn't think I'm listening. I keep my eyes on the road in front us. Someone should.

"Go ahead," I say.

"No one is dying if the dam goes—they've evacuated the town. But I'll tell you what will happen. Millions of dollars—possibly even a billion—of damage. Businesses will fold. Homeowners will lose houses. And what will those people need?"

"Money," I say. "They're going to need financial aid to get back on their feet. And this will destroy the developers. Like that guy. JD's competitor?"

"Tolliver—Rob Tolliver. Yeah, it will wipe out guys like him. But it's not just money."

"What else?"

"Justice. They'll want justice. Government aid money, insurance claims, bailouts—that's going to help. But justice—that's what brings closure to this disaster." He smacks the steering wheel. "And justice, brother, is what we're going to bring to them. Right?"

I'm impressed. Perez claims he's not a deep thinker. But he's definitely thought this through. He's right. If the dam fails, economic recovery and justice loom as the two most important things on those victims' minds.

The silence feels awkward. I slap the dashboard. "You're right! I'm ready, coach—put me in."

Perez's eyes narrow.

I realize I've made things more awkward. Perez thinks I'm poking fun at him. "Seriously, Rick—I hadn't thought of it in those terms." I'm trying to paddle my way out of my mistake. "I'm making a joke because I'm embarrassed you had to remind me why we're here."

"Screw you, Zahn," Perez says, but I can tell he's holding back a smile.

I'm licking my fingers when Perez turns off the main highway, following the directions to Montrose he got from the local sheriff's department.

"He expecting us?" I say.

"Yep. Montrose County Sheriff gave him a heads up and then kept a loose watch on his place to see if he went anywhere. Nothing suspicious. They say he's more than willing to talk."

Perez turns the Tahoe onto a gravel road, passing through a three-log square arch bearing a *Silver Bar Ranch* sign. A mile later we stop next to a large log cabin built in the middle of two outbuildings and a large barn.

"Heck of a spread," I say.

Ron Timmons strides from the front porch and meets us in the driveway. A smaller man, Timmons wears the leathery skin that comes from years of working in the Colorado sun at eight-thousand feet elevation. I can picture him on a horse, tossing a rope over a steer. He's a cowboy.

"I'm Ron Timmons. Welcome to the Silver Bar."

"Mr. Timmons," Perez says, climbing out of the Tahoe. "Good to meet you. I'm Deputy Sheriff Rick Perez. This is my associate Tyler Zahn. Chris Martin, over at Montrose County should have told you we were coming?"

"Come inside? Want some coffee?"

Perez looks my way, and I decline. Perez says, "I think we're good. I could use the facilities though."

Timmons leads us through the entranceway, and points to a hallway. "Two bathrooms down there. Meet you out here when you're done." He points to a large room with cathedral-style windows which open to a view of the mountains in the distance.

I beat Perez to the living room and sink into a cattle-hide chair across from Timmons, noting the deer antler chandelier above. "How long have you been ranching, Mr. Timmons?"

"Call me Ron." Timmons smooths his hand across the sofa arm like he has a story he wants to tell. "The Timmons family has been running cattle on this land for 123 years," he begins. "We're native Coloradoans. Well, at least one of the first white families."

I nod. Timmons appears politically aware enough to recognize the issues rankling society.

"We run twelve hundred head of cattle," Timmons says. "More than my daddy or granddaddy, but less than we need to turn a profit. Tough go out here on the Western Slope. You got to navigate grazing rights, environmental rules, not to mention water."

"Water's what we want to talk about, Mr. Timmons." Perez takes a seat next to me. "Have you heard about the Dillon Dam?"

"Yeah. Someone tried to blow it up, right? And the tunnel to Denver, too?"

"We got to the tunnel explosives before they blew," Perez says. "But the Dillon Dam blast plugged the spillway and the reservoir is rising. If the water breaches the dam, everything could wash away."

Timmons squints. "Crazy. Why would these guys do it? And why are you talking to me about it?"

"We think it's someone trying to direct attention to the water issue," Perez says. "You know, the argument over western water going to the eastern side? Or even more basic—if the dam goes, the west side will get more water."

Timmons's eyes widen. "You're not thinking I had anything—wait a minute, this stuff is terrorism, right? I'm a goddamn rancher trying to make a living." Timmons sucks in a breath. "There's no way I'd involve myself in something like this. Why're you here?"

I study Timmons's face while the rancher argues with Perez. If Timmons is lying, he is certainly skilled at it. He seems genuinely offended.

Perez continues. "Your name has come up during the investigation. Are you familiar with a man named *Galen Sullivan*?"

"Yes. He used to work for Denver Water until about six months ago. I used to meet him for drinks on my Denver trips. Is he involved?"

"He bombed the dam."

Timmons's mouth drops.

"Did you ever ask him questions about his work? Talk about water issues?"

Timmons snorts. "Hell, yes. That was the whole reason I kept meeting him. The first time we met down in Arvada, and he told me he worked for Denver Water, I stuck onto that guy like white on rice. He was just the contact I needed."

"What do you mean?"

"I'm the President of the Western Colorado chapter of the Colorado Cattlemen's Association—you've heard of that, right?"

Perez glances my way. Neither of us had heard of the group before yesterday's internet search.

"I used Sullivan to keep abreast of what Denver Water was planning to do with water each year. Sullivan would bring me draft agendas and internal minutes of the meetings and I'd use that information to brief the Association on what to expect for the year."

Perez scribbles a note. "Did you pay for this information?"

"Not in cash. I'd throw some Broncos or Avalanche tickets Sullivan's way, but that's about it. Some tailgate passes too."

Perez says nothing.

Timmons continues. "Listen, I realize that might sound like corporate espionage or something. That's probably what Sullivan is saying. He got into that whole cloak and dagger thing. But it wasn't like that. I mean, these were just meeting notes. Not classified, not intellectual property—nothing like that. Hell, they posted the edited minutes for public record later on. All I was getting was advance notice."

"Did you ever use that information against the Denver Water Authority?"

"What do you mean *against*? If you mean, did we use it to argue against their proposals—yes, we did. That's why I wanted the information—to keep up with their plans."

"I guess I'm asking if your group ever took any physical actions against Denver Water."

"Never."

Perez leans back, glancing my way.

I say, "Do you or your association have any relationship with any environmental groups?"

"Well, I guess that depends on what you define as a relationship." Timmons's gaze drifts to the window. "We talk to some of these groups. Most aren't happy with us. Especially with grazing rights. You know we lease land from the Bureau of Land Management—the BLM—for grazing, right? A couple of environmentalist groups aren't too happy about that. So, we talk to them periodically. Would you call that a relationship?"

"How about a cooperative relationship?" I say. "You ever work with a group trying to push for getting rid of dams or letting water run its natural course?"

"Nope. We aren't happy with the east side siphoning off our water, but we also wouldn't be happy with anyone telling us we couldn't control the water over here on the west side. For example, getting rid of dams or prohibiting irrigation. Yeah, eliminating dams wouldn't help us." Timmons pauses. "Back to your question. No. I don't know anybody in those circles."

I ask the oddball question. "Ever heard of anyone referred to as Beemer Babe?"

Timmons cocks his head. "Beemer like the car? The BMW?"

"Maybe. Ring a bell?"

"Nope."

"Do you know anybody who drives a BMW?"

Timmons smiles. "Well, I know it sounds strange coming from a cowboy like me, but yeah, I got friends with Beemers. They all live in the cities—Denver, Breck, Aspen…" Timmons scratches his chin. "And one down in Pueblo—Johnny Hernandez. But nobody you would call a Beemer Babe."

Perez shrugs at me. Timmons admits his relationship with Sullivan. That explains Sullivan's use of his name.

"Mr. Timmons, er, Ron," I say, "have you ever heard of a Mitch Mandrake?"

"Nope."

"Mr. Mandrake escaped from the Buena Vista Correctional Complex last week."

"I heard about the escape. Missed the name. I've never heard of him."

Perez stands and puts his hands on his hips. "I guess that's all we got, Ron. Sorry if this line of questioning offended you. We had to ask. Your name came up with the suspects."

Timmons huffs. "I don't know why. Let me be perfectly clear with you gentlemen. I had nothing to do with this. Neither did my organization. Yes, I'm offended that you suspect me. But I also want you to know I'm available for any more questions you think might help. Whatever it takes to put that son of a bitch away."

Timmons walks us to the front entrance. We say our goodbyes, and Perez pulls forward, looping the Tahoe around the circular driveway.

"Stop the car," I say.

"What?" Perez steps on the brakes.

I lower the passenger window. Timmons walks toward us. I poke my head out. "Where did you say you met with Sullivan when you were in Denver?"

"Arvada. You know—that suburb west of town on I-70. Why?"

"Different places, or same place every time?"

Timmons scratches his nose. "Mostly the same place. Once or twice over in Aurora, but mostly we met at The Rooster on West 64th. It's a drinking place close to Eldridge."

"The Rooster?"

"That's right."

"OK—thanks." I put up my window. Timmons waves in the passenger-side mirror as Perez rolls down the driveway again.

"What was that about?" Perez says.

"Not sure. But something I think we ought to check out."

"What? The Rooster? Do you think Timmons was involved?"

"Not really. But we know Sullivan said he was. You remember what Timmons said about Sullivan? How he got into that cloak and dagger stuff?"

"Yeah?"

"I don't know. Sullivan used The Rooster to meet Timmons for semi-secret stuff. Maybe he used the same place to plan the bombing?"

"A bit of a stretch. It's possible, I guess. That's a five-hour drive, though, for a weak lead."

"We can call. We could send them a pic of Sullivan and see if they recognize him?"

"Do that." Perez checks his watch. "It's only nine. He called The Rooster a drinking place. You might have to wait until afternoon."

"Sounds good. We can get a dam update on the drive back."

"I'll call now." Perez glances at me. "Hopefully they're making more progress than we are. We're running out of leads."

ZAHN

Grant, Colorado-May 31st

Perez is reluctant to make the Denver trip, but doesn't have any problem sending me. US Marshal Randall Williams no longer has a fugitive to chase and volunteers to join me. We crest Kenosha Pass on the way. Williams downshifts his Explorer on the sharp downhill corners, before straightening out to guide us through the town of Grant.

"There's where it started." I point to the Roberts Tunnel outlet on the left.

"Except for Mandrake. That's where it all ended for him," Williams counters.

Following the Timmons interview, I gave The Rooster a call. I talked to a bartender who passed me on to the manager who told me they don't video their customers. But he had the name of the bartender working the dates in question.

I thought it was worth checking into, even though Perez didn't. Especially after Randall Williams called and gave us an update on the dam. The next twenty-four hours will determine whether Silverthorne washes away or whether the engineers will prevail.

"So, humor me," Williams says. "Where do you think we're at on this case?"

"Yeah, I've been thinking about that," I say. "We know *who did what* with the bombs and the kidnapping. Sullivan and Mandrake sabotaged the shaft leading to Roberts Tunnel while holding the Schorks against their will, right?"

"Right."

"Someone else—somebody likely involved in drug trafficking—killed Mandrake and ultimately released the Schorks. But we don't know who."

"Also right."

Williams has proven to be a man of few words, but at least they are affirming words. I continue. "So, Sullivan continues the mission and bombs the Morning Glory Spillway on the Dillon Dam. He's caught twelve hours later with bags of cash. Probably a payoff. Which leads to the obvious question."

"Yep," Williams says. "Who's the brains behind this whole thing? Who's the sponsor?"

I consider this. While alive, Mandrake was an unlikely ringleader. The investigative team pulled the visitor logs for everyone who visited him at the prison. One person. Galen Sullivan using a fake ID. It's possible someone could have hired Mandrake from the inside—maybe Big Bobby Dorsey—but why? Besides, the warden at the complex seems to think Dorsey's field of expertise centers on information and drugs, not terrorism or bombs.

So, yes. It's possible someone hired Mandrake for the bombings, and he talked Sullivan into helping. But it doesn't seem probable. It makes more sense that someone hired Sullivan instead.

I mentally run through the interactions Sullivan would have with a sponsor. There would be the approach—the initial proposal presented to Sullivan. That would probably happen face-to-face. Then there would be a follow-up planning meeting or two. In person? Maybe electronically?

I review my musings out loud with Williams. "The Rooster's a long shot, but it's all we got. Maybe we'll get lucky."

Williams maneuvers the last of the tight curves on Highway 285. Denver's handful of skyscrapers jut through the haze in the distance. We loop north to a bypass road which leads to Arvada. Ten minutes later, we pass a Shell station and pull into the next entrance. A large white sign with green lettering and an orange and black chicken plastered on the front advertises The Rooster.

I expect an empty bar at four in the afternoon, but I'm wrong. The Rooster must have one hell of a Happy Hour. The place is packed and reeks of stale beer and French fries. The bartender glances our way as we grab seats at the counter. After a minute, she works her way in our direction.

"What can I get you?"

"Glass of water, please. No ice," I say.

The bartender turns to Williams. "You?"

"Same. But I'll take the ice." Williams places his credentials on the counter. "Are you Sandi? We're the ones your boss told you about—coming to ask questions?"

"That's me," Sandi says. "Let me grab your waters first."

Williams and I remain silent until Sandi returns. She props her elbows on the counter.

"So, what do you want to know?"

Ice cubes bob in both glasses. Attention to detail might not be Sandi's thing.

Williams shoves Sullivan's mugshot across the counter. "Do you recognize this guy?"

Sandi studies the photo. "I hate these things," she says, looking up from the picture at Williams. "You ever notice that a mugshot looks nothing like the actual person?"

She's right, but I don't say anything. I smile. Williams doesn't.

"It's the only photo we got," Williams says. "Look familiar?"

"What did he do?"

"He's a suspect in the bombing up at the Dillon Reservoir."

Sandi's eyes widen. "Yeah, I've seen him in here, but don't know his name. Or anything about him."

"His name is Galen Sullivan. When did you see him last?"

"Not sure—within the last couple of weeks."

"Anything about him stand out?"

Sandi doesn't speak for a moment. "Not really. I mean, I usually just pay attention to what everyone drinks. This guy, for example, I think he was a beer drinker. But not your Bud Light or Coors Light type of guy. He liked the craft beers."

Williams writes on his notepad. "Anything else?"

Sandi frowns. "He always came in alone, but he never sat alone. Not in a weird way, like he was on the make or something." Sandi surveys the bar. "Look at this place. No one comes in here to pick up someone, you know?" She laughs. "Anyway, yeah. He was always joining someone. Not a group, but someone. Sometimes he'd meet with this guy. Sometimes it would be with a certain gal."

Williams slides a newspaper across the counter. "This guy? Recognize him?" I had pulled the piece with Timmons's photo from the Colorado Cattlemen's Association website before we left Buena Vista.

Sandi squints. "Possibly? I'm not one hundred percent sure. You got any pictures of the gal I mentioned?"

Williams shakes his head. "Do you remember anything about her?"

"Actually, I do. She was kind of new-agey or hippie something. Not sure what you call it. She had her hair pulled back, you know?"

"Like ponytails, or in a braid?" I say.

"Definitely some kind of braid thing. I just remember it because the other guy—what was the mugshot guy's name?"

"Sullivan," Williams says.

"Sullivan didn't seem like the hippie type. They made for an odd pair." Sandi points across the room. "They sat back there."

"And you all don't have any interior video here?" Williams says.

"Nope."

"Do you know what kind of cars any of them drove?" I say.

"No. I'm behind the bar until quitting time."

I'm stuck on the cars. "How about external video?"

Sandi shrugs. "No video here at all, sorry."

Williams sighs. "Anything else you can recall about any of the folks we talked about?"

"I'm surprised I remember the guy in the photo, let alone the people he met."

I've seen Randall Williams smile, but he doesn't seem to use it much at work. Today is an exception. "You did good." He hands her one of his cards. "Call me if you think of anything else, OK? Anything."

Sandi almost beams. "Thanks. I'll try to remember more."

I follow Williams out the door. While he aims for his Explorer, I turn and study The Rooster's roofline, in case Sandi was clueless about the surveillance cameras. I see nothing.

"I need gas." Williams backs the Explorer, then cuts across the lot to the adjoining Shell station.

"I'll pump," I offer. As I fill the tank, I look back at The Rooster, only fifty feet away. Almost instinctively, I tilt my head toward the awning covering the gas pumps.

I see cameras.

The twenty-something cashier's eyes light up when Williams flashes his badge.

"Oh yeah. We gonna bust someone?" Anthony, the cashier, says. When Williams mentions the security cameras, Anthony instructs another twenty-something to watch the register and leads us into a back room. The station has four cameras covering the eight pumps. I zero in on Camera 2 which is aimed to cover the customers at Pump 3 and Pump 4. The angle is broad enough to cover six of The Rooster's eight parking spots.

"How long do you keep the footage?" Williams says.

"Well, we used to keep it for just twenty-four hours. That's when we were saving it all to the hard drive. But now we're on the cloud. I think we just max it out and when we bump up against our storage limit, it automatically dumps the oldest day and tapes a new one." Anthony puffs up a bit and I'm unsure whether it's because he's proud of his workplace for the cloud upgrade, or if it's because he can see I'm processing his techno explanation. "The security camera shit is all we keep on there. We use a different account for office work stuff."

"Can you show us footage from three weeks ago?" Williams says.

"I think so. Let me check. What time?"

Williams glances at me. "Oh, let's say six in the evening?"

Anthony moves the cursor and types in the date and time. "Yeah, man, look at that. It's there." He grins as he looks over his shoulder at Williams. "You guys trying to catch someone from three weeks ago? Someone who came to our station?"

Williams seems to pick up on Anthony's enthusiasm. "Yeah, Anthony. But we're not a hundred percent sure when they came through your video. If they're on there, your video could break this case open."

"Shit, man, that's cool. So, you guys are going to like commandeer the computer? Take it away? I need to tell the boss so we can set up something else." Anthony looks excited and nervous at the same time.

"You know, with this cloud thing," Williams says, "I don't think we need to take anything. Any computer could access it, right? If they were logged in?"

Anthony bobs his head. "That's right. We've always got it running on this computer so I don't have to log in or anything. But yeah, I could just give you guys the login info and you can look at it from your own computers."

I try to keep a straight face. Our man Anthony is offering usernames and passwords?

Williams stays stoic. "Yeah, Anthony. If you provide account access, that would be a huge help. We won't delete any files or mess with your setup."

Anthony grabs a piece of paper and scribbles the information. He pauses after the username and looks at Williams. "Hey, dude, if you guys break this thing, can you put in a good word for me with my boss? I've been asking for a raise for the last two months." He finishes writing and hands the paper to Williams.

I look over Williams's shoulder: *www.safeviewcam.com*

WilloughbyC

W64thShell2602

"You bet, Anthony," Williams says. "This is great. Put your full name on here and your boss's name and number so I can make that call."

Anthony adds the information. "Thanks, man. Hope you get the guy. If it's a guy." He holds his hands out, gesturing. "Cuz you never know, right? It could be a gal. Or it could be a guy dressed as a gal because he identifies as a gal, but he's really a guy. You know what I mean? There's some crazy shit out there, man."

Willams tilts his head. "Thanks. Hopefully, we'll get someone. This video might help."

I follow Williams to the Explorer. It's possible this trip wasn't a waste of time after all. If we assumed Sullivan wouldn't have met anyone during the day while he worked at the mattress factory, then that eliminates a third of the video right there. The Rooster doesn't open for lunch and it closes by one in the morning. We can focus on the hours from about five in the evening until closing. Eight hours. And Sullivan wouldn't have met anyone here in the last six or seven days.

"Mind if I update Perez?" I say to Williams. "You think this is legal footage?"

"Oh, we're legal. Yeah, call him. Tell him what we got. Ask him if he's got something we can watch it on."

I pull up my recent calls and tap on *Perez*.

"No shit?" Perez says, after I debrief him. "You got a witness saying Sullivan was meeting a woman at The Rooster? Same place as he was meeting Timmons?"

"Yep."

"And video? You think you might have this woman on video?"

"We're not sure about that," I say. "We've got access to the video. We just need a computer to watch it."

"We'll set you up when you get back in town. Come to the department."

"I'll let you know when we're fifteen out."

ZAHN

Buena Vista, Colorado-May 31st

"Williams is right. It's not illegal to look at the video," Perez hovers over my shoulder as I study the computer screen. "It only gets sketchy if you're using it for an arrest."

I swivel my chair toward the deputy. "And we're not using it for that—yet. We're just using it to find a suspect, right?"

"That's what I'm thinking. Any luck?"

"Nope. I've been through two days of footage in three hours." I'm tired. My coffee buzz from Williams's stop at the Bailey gas station wore off an hour ago.

"Tell me again what you're looking for," Perez says.

"Two things. I'm searching for Sullivan's truck—and there're tons of those coming in and out of The Rooster's lot—and I'm also looking for a BMW."

"I don't get how finding Sullivan's truck helps. We already know he goes to that bar."

"Right. But I'm whipping through this footage pretty fast. If I find the truck, then I slow the search and look harder for a BMW." I swivel back to the screen. "What's the update on the dam?"

"The engineers are prepping the south side for a pressure relief blast. The drill isn't working, and the water is too close to breaching to risk another day. They're setting up the explosives tonight—actually, right now. If the drill hasn't worked by midmorning tomorrow, they're going to try the controlled release."

"This relief blast will flood the river? Not the entire valley?"

"Yep. If it works as planned, the Blue River will only rise three or four feet. All the stuff along the banks gets flooded. But most of the town will be OK."

"What's in the flood zone?"

"Couple of city buildings. A nursery. Two or three restaurants. The primary structures are the condos. They've got like four in a row down there that they call Tolliver Town."

"Let me guess. JD's rival owns them all?"

"That's right. Hope he's got those things insured."

. . .

Just past one in the morning, I get lucky. Something about the curve of a vehicle on screen jerks me in my chair. A parked car—half-on, half-off my monitor—looks closer to a BMW than anything else I've seen.

I stop the video, set it to double speed, and reverse it. Hot damn. A woman walks backward from The Rooster's entrance and enters the car. Actually, she is getting out, because the video is running in reverse. I pause the footage and run it forward at normal speed. The car pulls into parking. A woman exits and walks into the bar.

I groan. It sounds like the start of a bad joke.

I study the grainy black-and-white screen. She wears what looks like jeans. Running shoes. A light-colored blouse. Nothing that stands out. I can't see her face.

I replay the video, pausing as the woman turns and walks toward the bar's entrance. Something about the way her hair falls on her shoulders. Not just in a single wave, but like long strands of hair clumped together. Like a braid.

I rewind again and replay the car's arrival. The angle is off. But it's enough to confirm it's a BMW. I can't tell which model. That's not really the fault of the video quality, but more because I don't know my cars that well. I freeze the video and play it frame by frame. Zooming in, I focus on the license plate partially visible on the screen. It looks like a Colorado plate. I squint and make out the last two digits on the Beemer's plate. A *2* and a *4*. Not much to go on.

Adrenaline erases my fatigue. This is the first BMW I've seen in over five hours of scanning. I speed the tape forward.

Whoa, cowboy. My finger jams on the mouse button, stopping the video. I switch to normal speed and reverse.

The vehicle arriving two minutes later looks familiar. Galen Sullivan steps from the truck and walks toward The Rooster's door.

Jackpot.

A Beemer. A woman. Possibly a braid. Sullivan. I've got something here.

I switch back to high speed and advance the footage to watch the woman and Sullivan leave. Sullivan exits first. He climbs into his truck and departs. I can't read his plates, but I definitely recognize him. The woman leaves shortly after Sullivan. I rerun the segment three times but find no more clues.

It's time to wake Perez's ass up and bring him in.

• • •

"Better be worth it, old man," Perez grunts. "Waking me up from a good sleep."

I smile. The past week's events have bonded us. Perez trusts my judgment. "I guess it depends on how good your database is."

"What do you mean?"

"We've got a gal in a BMW at The Rooster, with our man Sullivan pulling into the same bar close behind her. We've got them leaving at nearly the same time. And we have the last two digits of her Colorado license plate."

"Hot damn. But only the last two digits? That's thousands of plates."

"That's why I said it depends on your database. If you can filter by number and car type, then we could have our suspect list whittled down pretty quick. Like within the hour."

Perez's eyes light up. "No sense waking anyone else. I've got a database account and just enough training to be dangerous." He grins. "Scoot over. Let me in."

I surrender my seat. Perez grabs the mouse and clicks on the licensing icon. As the program loads, he rifles through his wallet for his username and password.

The database interface is relatively simple. Perez clicks the *Plate Nbr* filter.

"OK. I remember this one. You use asterisks for the numbers you don't know." Perez pulls a sheet of paper from the desk and a pen from his uniform pocket. "So, if you know the first digit is *C* and the last digit is *4*, then you type in *C*, an asterisk four times, and then *4*." Perez scribbles what he's explaining on paper:

*C****4*

"So, we just need four asterisks, then *two-four*?" I say.

"That's what I'm thinking." Perez types the search parameters I provide.

The computer instantly produces results. *57,655 records found.*

I snort. "You knew that would happen. Now you're just messing with me. Use the *Make* filter and put in *BMW*."

When Perez enters *BMW*, I see *Model* as an option below. "What about *Model*?" I point at the option. "Should we hone it down further?"

Perez selects *Model*, and frowns at the drop-down menu. "*Commercial truck, truck, van, sedan, coupe, hatchback...* damn. I was hoping it was advanced enough that we had drop-downs for types of BMWs."

"A BMW is a sports car, right? I don't see that option. What about sedan?" I say. "Because it has a back seat?"

Perez turns to me. "I don't think so. Pull up that video again."

I reach over his shoulder and hit *Alt-Tab* to bring up the footage.

Perez points to the frozen panel of the woman leaving the car. "Look at the doors. It's a two-door."

"So?"

"So, a two-door with backseats is a coupe, not a sedan."

I had no idea. "Really? Makes you wonder how many people filling out the form know that."

Perez swaps screens back to the database. "Let's find out." He selects the *Coupe* option before clicking on *Search*.

9 records found.

"We can work with this." Perez scrolls through the names.

I follow his cursor. "I don't see many women."

"It could be her husband's or boyfriend's. You don't have to be the registered owner to—holy shit, what are the odds of that?" Perez points at the screen.

"What?"

"Look at the fourth one down."

I read the entry.

ROBINSON, JAMES D., BRECKENRIDGE COLORADO

"Are you thinking that's JD? Is his first name James?" I say, rapid-fire.

"I think so. Must be. They had that silver BMW the night after we left the bar, remember? Leanne driving after JD had all those beers?"

"I remember." I pause to give Perez time to respond. He doesn't. "There's no way. Quite a coincidence."

Perez frowns. "That's what they always teach us. There are no coincidences."

"You don't think—oh man, give me a moment here." I step back from Perez trying to put the pieces together. "I've got to think this one through."

"You do that. I'm going to review the other names. See if anything sets off alarm bells."

My thoughts are like pulling threads from a sweater. I can't extract them into anything usable. I'm approaching twenty-four hours without sleep. Every time I come close to a scenario where JD or Leanne would blow up a dam, my brain falls back to the *it's-just-a-coincidence* theory. Which doesn't really count.

I don't know the couple well—just what Perez told me, and our interactions last weekend. JD is obviously a stalwart community leader. And Leanne? The bombing devastated her. She was the one peppering me with questions and encouraging me to stay and help.

I hesitate. Leanne did have a ton of questions. How many times did I tell Leanne or JD I couldn't discuss the case? Especially Leanne. She wanted the inside scoop on everything. At the time, I assumed this was normal for the spouse of a local leader. She was expected to be *in the know* in her own community.

And the shower thing. The *call me if you need anything* innuendo. Shit. I shake my head. I was right the first time. I'm a middle-aged man with love handles. Leanne is married to the town stud. She didn't want me—she wanted to know whether she and her husband were in danger of getting caught.

"Rick?"

"Yeah?"

"We need to check those two. I know they're your friends, but—"

Perez interrupts, his eyes locked on mine. "We got leads, we follow them. No personal shit keeps me from doing my thing."

"Sorry, I just thought—"

"Think again. Where do you propose we start?"

"Probably show Leanne's picture to the bartender, Sandi?"

"What about Timmons? Think we should run their names by him?"

"He said he had friends in Breck. Good idea."

"What about motive? I just don't see why?" Perez is willing to investigate his friends but has the same misgivings I do.

"I'm thinking through that one," I say.

•　　•　　•

My head bobs with fatigue as we map out our next moves. Perez leaves a detailed email instructing the morning crew to investigate the remaining eight names on the license list. But Perez and I will point our investigation toward the Robinsons.

Perez pecks away on the computer, updating Sheriff Larkin on our discoveries. "I figure I'll tell the Sheriff everything we got. He can brief the Task Force."

While Perez types, I turn to Google. I start with *JD Robinson* and *Frisco* as search terms. When I click *Images*, a panel of photos—most of them taken of the JD Robinson I recognize—spreads across the monitor. Same thing when I replace *JD* with *Leanne*. Both the Robinsons feature prominently in the local community. The search results in multiple pages of photos. I save several of the images and send them via email to myself. Then I send a text to Sandi, the bartender:

Sandi, this is Tyler from earlier this afternoon. Could you check the attached photos and see if it looks anything like the woman you saw meeting Sullivan at The Rooster? Yes—no braid—but tell me what you think, OK? Also, have you ever seen the man in the picture? Kind of important, so I appreciate your quick response—Tyler.

I draft an email for Perez to send to Ron Timmons:

Ron, greetings from Buena Vista. I appreciated your offer to provide further assistance on the case we discussed and I'd like to take you up on it. I've attached photos of two people who we are interested in. Could you please review the photos and tell me whether you recognize them? Did you ever have a discussion with either or both of them about Colorado water systems?

I'm available on the number I gave you on my card and at this email address. It's urgent, so I appreciate your attention to this matter. I will follow up with a phone call in the morning.

Respectfully,
Deputy Sheriff Rick Perez
Chaffee County Sheriff's Office

When Perez finishes, I share my draft email. He sends it and the photos to Timmons.

He sighs. "We've got a lot to do and no one's awake. What do you think? Grab some sleep?"

"I'm wiped out," I agree. "What time you want to rally?"

"How about eight o'clock, here?"

"I'll be here." Things are happening.

•　•　•

I set the alarm for seven. My head hits the pillow just after three and I sleep a dreamless sleep. The clock reads six when my eyes pop open. I'm instantly wired. Like I've slept eight hours and already drank my coffee. I brew a pot anyway, the scent of fresh grounds enhancing my view of the sun rising over Four-Mile.

What would the Robinsons have to gain by blowing the dam—or cutting off Roberts Tunnel to Denver? Were they trying to collect on insurance? I try to recall whether Robinson mentioned any business ventures in Silverthorne. No—when that topic had come up at the brewpub, it turned weird. Leanne running to the bathroom, and JD explaining their frustration with Tolliver.

Leanne's visceral hatred of the developer gnaws at me. Robinson claimed Tolliver owned the other three towns and blocked competition. Therefore, Robinson couldn't own much in Silverthorne. Not until something loosened Tolliver's hold on the town.

Until something… My coffee mug freezes midway between the table and my mouth.

Damn. Bad pun. Dam—the dam happened.

Tolliver's development monopoly is centered in Silverthorne below the dam. If it goes, he loses hundreds of millions of dollars. Even if the engineers blow the south side to release the pressure, he'll lose those four condos by the river. I turn the issue over in my mind, trying to poke holes in my theory. It's insane—but so is any reason for blowing up a dam.

If JD and Leanne believe they won't get caught, then the destruction of Silverthorne is just the trigger event to get their foot in the door when they rebuild the town. I stew some more. If the Robinsons did it, then it's not environmental groups and the Colorado Cattlemen's

Association behind the plot. From what little I've learned of the Robinsons, neither involves themselves with environmentalists or ranchers. Even if they did, why would they take the risk for someone else's cause? Especially crapping in their own backyard for the main event. No. Far more likely are the oldest motives of all—money and power. The Robinsons are making a power grab.

I grab my overnight bag. I might not be back tonight. A half an hour later, I tuck into the Sheriff's Office computer, surfing up info on the Robinsons and waiting for Perez.

"I got an email back from Timmons," Perez barks, striding into the room. "That son of a bitch is pushing sixty. He probably can't sleep at night."

"What's it say?"

Perez takes the folding chair next to me and grins. "It says, and I quote." Perez reads the email aloud, "'*Sheriff Perez…*'" Perez pauses, a smile plastered on his face. "I like how that sounds, don't you? '*Sheriff?*'"

"Keep reading." I shake my head, but Perez's undisguised enjoyment almost forces a smile.

Yes, I recognize the pictures. The male is JD Robinson, a developer who lives up in Breckenridge. The female is his wife, Leanne. I've been friends with them for about six or seven years. I met JD when we stayed in one of his condos on a ski trip. We've been staying in his condos ever since.

Water systems? Yes, I discussed that with Leanne last winter, on my last trip to Breck. JD was off at some civic doo-hickey and my wife and I were having a drink with Leanne. The talk circled around to the Denver Water Authority and Leanne said she wanted to talk to someone there— I can't remember why. Anyway, I ended up telling her about my contact—Sullivan. Even gave her his phone number.

I think Leanne might drive a BMW. Either that or an Audi. Something small.

I'll call you later this morning but wanted you to have this information as soon as possible.

Perez lowers his phone. "How about dem apples?"

I'm quiet for a moment, as I struggle with the first confirmation we might be on track with the Robinsons. "That's pretty damning evidence. Even if Sandi at The Rooster doesn't recognize the pics." I pause. "I think I might have a little something as well."

"What?" Perez says.

"A motive."

"Do tell."

I lean back. "Name one person the Robinsons don't get along with."

Perez squints. "They get along with every—oh yeah. Tolliver. That developer guy, right?"

"Right. And where is all that water—" My phone vibrates in my pocket. I stop talking to check the incoming text.

Tyler, it's Sandi. I don't recognize the guy. But the pic you sent of the woman? That's her.

I hand the phone to Perez. "Not just motive. Now we got evidence."

SULLIVAN

Salida, Colorado-June 1st

Phil White isn't boosting Sullivan's confidence about this trial. Every visit opens with White describing a strategy centered on avoiding a life sentence by trading information about Sarah.

Sullivan doesn't change his strategy either. "Phil, I need to walk or maximum, serve five years. Quit with the life sentence talk."

"It's not my talk. It's the prosecution rumor mill. That's what you prepare for."

White doesn't seem to understand what Sullivan sees. Unless Sullivan talks, the state will never put the person responsible for this—Sarah—behind bars. Sullivan knows he's the brains behind the entire plan, but they don't need to know that. When it comes to taking responsibility for the bombs, he's just a patsy.

"They want Sarah, but don't know how to find her. They'll deal, Phil. We're holding the cards. Act like it."

White wags his head. "We're holding an okay hand. After tomorrow, we'll see."

"What changes between today and tomorrow?"

"The dam. They're doing the controlled blast today. Something that's never been tried before. If it works, then we can talk some more about you and your 'cards.'"

"And if it doesn't? Why do I care? They can't blame me when I'm behind bars."

White shakes his head like Sullivan doesn't get it. Like Sullivan is stupid.

"What?" Sullivan says.

"First off, the guys setting off the detonations won't be blamed. They're indemnified because this is all experimental. Second, the government won't accept responsibility. Do you know why?"

White is asking questions like Sullivan's in high school. Sullivan fumes.

"Because no politician is going to take the blame for something if they can shift it to someone else," White says. "As in you."

Sullivan forces himself not to speak. He won't give White the satisfaction of being right, but he gets it. If the controlled detonation goes badly, Sullivan is screwed.

ZAHN

Buena Vista, Colorado-June 1st

Perez and I try to poke holes in our theory.

Although Leanne met Sullivan at the Rooster, both of us agree JD must be behind the plot. He owns the resources. He stands to gain the most. The likely scenario here points toward JD using Leanne as an accomplice.

Perez raises the problem of confronting Robinson. How can law enforcement arrest him with no proof? My theory on motive sounds good. But it doesn't constitute evidence against JD—only Leanne.

If Perez and team bring JD in for questioning, he'll lawyer up. They'll be in the same situation as they are with Sullivan. Silence until the trial. At least for Sullivan, eyewitnesses link him to the crime.

The logical solution is to turn over our evidence to the Task Force. But Perez has no illusions about what will happen if we cede the case to the feds. The Task Force will bring in the Robinsons. They'll freeze the Sheriff's Office from the case. Perez will end up like Marshal Williams—driving around looking for something to do.

I respect Perez. Most of the time, he's your prototypical deputy sheriff. But he's willing to break that mold when necessary. I appreciate the side of Perez that thinks—and sometimes works—outside the box. In the bomb case, Perez boldly crossed county borders, acting first while coordinating later. He rappelled down a shaft to investigate a bomb, without calling it in first, then justified it to his boss. He hasn't thought twice about pivoting the investigation to focus on his friends, JD and Leanne.

But Perez's latest plan takes me by surprise.

"I want you to confront Leanne," he says. "Get her talking."

"Me?"

"Yep. If I do it, she'll lawyer up. She knows that you don't have the authority to arrest her or use anything she says against JD. You can use your conversational skills."

"What good will that do?"

"We'll wire you up. If you can get her talking, we'll have it on tape. And then we can use it against them."

I narrow my eyes. "Don't you need consent for a wire?"

"Yep." Perez grins.

"And how do you plan on getting her to agree to that?"

"We don't. We just need your permission."

"What?"

"Colorado is a one-party consent state. If at least one party knows it's a recorded conversation, it's not illegal."

"I'm the one party."

"That's the plan," Perez says. "Or part of it. The *wire* part is really more of a backup. Leanne probably won't talk. But you can bet your ass she'll call JD when she figures out we're on to her. I'll coordinate with the Summit County Sheriff." He squints. "Plus, Randall Williams is back up there, right? We'll have eyes on JD for the whole thing." Perez gives me a thin smile. "My guess? They're going to either lawyer up or make a run for it."

"I thought we didn't want them to lawyer up?"

"We don't. But they will if we arrest them or pull them in for questioning. Throwing you out there—a civilian—to question Leanne is a wild card. You might get something on the wire we can nab them on." Perez pauses a moment. "I'll liaison with the Frisco and Dillon cops as well. Probably should have someone on standby in case you run into trouble."

Outside-the-box thinking again from Perez. Way outside. He has definitely gone from black and white to gray.

"Timing?" I say.

"You got your overnight stuff?"

"Out in my car."

"Grab that and meet me in the back so I can wire you up." He checks his watch. "We got two hours." He pivots at the rear door. "I'll coordinate with Williams and the Summit cops on the way. You call Leanne and ask for another night in the condo. Tell her we're coming up for the blast and offer her a one-on-one update."

"She'll be all over getting the inside scoop," I say.

We're winding up the narrowing Arkansas River on the drive to Leadville, and Perez's phone rings from the dashboard mount. The deputy presses the button to take the call.

"Perez. Chaffee County Sheriff's Office."

"Deputy Perez? It's Jim Schork." Schork's voice carries over the Tahoe's speakers.

Perez raises his eyebrows at me. "Go ahead, Jim."

"Well, Carrie and I remembered something else."

"What do you got?"

"When the first guy, Sullivan, got back in the car at Twin Lakes? When he said the woman was going to be happy? Well, before that, he said they had enough. Enough for all three."

"And you think he was talking about—?"

"We're pretty sure he meant enough for all three bombs."

• • •

Perez spends the next twenty minutes coordinating the new lead with the Task Force and Summit County. He can't keep this information from the feds. The question now is whether the planned relief blast will go on schedule. While the alphabet soup of agencies jumps through hoops after Perez's revelation, we continue to plan my meeting with Leanne.

"I want distance between her and her husband. Let's see if she'll meet you in Frisco, and I'll just drop you off," Perez says. "I'll tell her I've got business in Frisco, so she'll have a reason to drive you to Dillon."

Perez runs through the plan again with me. When we pick up cell phone service again, I dial Leanne's number.

The call works. Leanne informs me that she and JD plan to join a group of community leaders at a viewing site north of the dam in Dillon. When she hears my offer of an update in Frisco on the investigation, she proposes an alternative.

"I can meet you in Frisco and you all can update me while we watch the dam release from that side. I'll take you to a better viewing area up the Old Dillon Reservoir trail."

Perez nods at me.

"Sounds great, Leanne. Perez has got stuff to do, so it's just me. Is that OK?"

"Sure. Where do you want to meet?" She draws out the *sure* like a cat's purr.

I'm not imagining it. "Walmart?"

Leanne agrees. I punch off the phone.

"That's a bedroom voice if I ever heard one." Perez smiles.

"Right?" I'm happy to get a confirmation on Leanne's tactics. "Might need those Frisco cops, after all."

Perez says, "They can use the dogs to check out her car at the trailhead while you're up the hill watching the show. Probably have the Dillon guys do the same thing with JD's car."

Perez's phone rings.

"Perez."

"Rick, it's Stan Muziak here in Dillon."

"Go ahead, Stan."

"Yeah, we swept the dam and found nothing. The engineers say the blast is a go. On schedule."

"Copy that, Stan. Thanks."

Perez glances at me. "Still a go."

•   •   •

The wire under my sweatshirt is already running when Perez parks next to Leanne's car, facing the opposite direction, and lowers his window. The last two numbers of Leanne's plate capture my attention like a neon sign—*24*.

"Leanne," Perez says. "Holding up OK?"

Leanne barks a short laugh. "Everything is crazy. Hope you guys are closer to figuring it all out."

"Well, I'm not sure about that, but our man Zahn offered to update you. Can you drop him off at the condo afterward?"

"Sure thing," Leanne replies. I climb into the passenger side of the BMW.

I fasten my seatbelt, inhaling the car's fresh scent. "So, Leanne, tell me about this better viewpoint."

ZAHN

Dillon Reservoir, Colorado-June 1st

Leanne drives to the Old Dillon Reservoir trailhead and parks the car in a dirt lot. She points to the small hill separating the parking area from the dam. "Mind ten minutes uphill?"

"I'm game."

Leanne exits the car and aims for the trail. "What update do you have? You guys figured out who's behind this thing yet?"

I hesitate before answering. Her reaction to the dam release might offer us some insight on her involvement, so I'm hesitant to ask my questions now.

"The altitude's killing me already," I say. "How about I fill you in up top?"

Leanne stops and tosses me a skeptical smile. "What the hell, Tyler? You and Rick live in Buena Vista. Only a thousand feet lower. You need to get your butt in shape." She runs her eyes over me. "Well, the butt's not too bad—but the gut."

"I know, I know," I say. I'm not completely out of breath, but she's not wrong. I need to get in better shape.

Leanne pivots and plows up the trail leaving me to admire the view.

My cellphone buzzes. A text. Perez.

The Frisco cops brought a bomb dog. It just alerted off of the BMW. Be careful.

I gape at the message, then jerk my head toward Leanne as she disappears around a bend. A bomb? Why the trailhead?

The top of the hill levels into a bluff, an ideal spot overlooking the release point. A crowd of spectators line the rock outcroppings on the far side of the dam. Their vantage point provides a closer view of Silverthorne. But they aren't as close to the blast site as we are. The engineering vehicles dot the east parking lot, the one where Sullivan launched his raft.

Leanne checks her watch. "We cut it close. They're supposed to blow it in four minutes."

How do I fill four minutes with updates for Leanne without accusing her husband?

"So, where are you guys at on this thing, Tyler?"

"You know we got Sullivan. He's in the jail in Salida."

"I heard he's not talking. Is that true?"

Damn, this woman has connections. "Yep. He's stayed quiet, at the advice of his lawyer. But, everyone's guessing he has information he'll spring at trial in hopes of reduced sentencing."

"So, he didn't give you guys a single clue?"

"Nothing. We also interviewed the Schorks again, hoping that Sullivan and Mandrake might have given something up in conversation."

"And…?"

"And nothing new." I peer over the bluff. "Looks like the demo team has cleared out."

"I can't believe you guys haven't made any progress." Leanne's voice is flat.

"We might have something, Leanne. I'll tell you about it after the release."

We both step to the edge of the bluff, waiting for the explosion. A billow of smoke blooms from the site. A deep vibrating rumble—deeper than thunder in a Colorado storm—crescendos up the bluff. The ground shakes.

"Here we go," Leanne yells, but she's not smiling. Her eyes hold that manic glow I observed the first night we met.

Smoke rises. The blast has triggered a landslide, but I can't spot its source through the mushroom cloud of billowing dust. The landslide tapers, transforming into a muddy torrent of water, small at first, then widening with momentum between the dam and the bluff. As the dust cloud clears, I point at a wedge blown from the dam's corner where reservoir water pours through the void. "See that?" I say, as if Leanne needs my commentary. "It'll release just enough hopefully."

Above the dam, the increased current pulls the chained buoys toward the gaping wedge. Everything sucks into the void from the blast. The reservoir water remains flat but a steady current rushes toward the release point. The glassy surface is the calm before a storm—in contrast to the scene at the dam's bottom, where chaos and destruction reign.

The surge of dirt, mud, and water hits the dry riverbed like the smart bombs on CNN we watched from our tents outside the Iraqi border. The sheer volume causes another dust cloud at the dam's base. Visibility clears enough to see water flowing past the valve control station at window-level. The chain-link fence surrounding the facility bends, then washes away. An abandoned bridge that once spanned the stream follows suit.

"Oh my God," Leanne yells. "It wiped out the bridge! See?" She turns to me, eyes wide.

I'm numb. I glance at Leanne, my mouth hanging open, before the irresistible pull of disaster forces my eyes back to the maelstrom. The engineers say the next bridge—the low span that routes I-70 over the Blue River—will hold. We'll find out in seconds.

The water wall surges through the valley, flooding the baseball fields and skirting the businesses near the river shore. Then it smashes into the I-70 bridge pillars. The water splashes halfway up the pillars to twenty or thirty feet. The highway stands tall enough to avoid the water. But will the pillars hold? As the mass of water continues its path of destruction through the town of Silverthorne, the silhouette of I-70 bridge emerges from the dust cloud.

"How high do you think the water will go?" Leanne yells. "It hit those stores and they're like a hundred yards away. Will it get higher?"

"I don't know." I really don't have any idea, but I suspect Leanne is asking because she's wondering if it will take out Tolliver's condos.

• • •

The initial surge disappears beyond the I-70 bridge, but the torrent of water continues to gush from the swollen reservoir. We gape at the flooded banks leading into Silverthorne.

If the entire dam had collapsed instead of the controlled release, I-70 would have disintegrated like a bridge made of toothpicks. The deluge would have taken out most Silverthorne residences and businesses.

It could have been so much worse. The release didn't kill or hurt anyone—at least physically. But economically? Time to discuss that.

The roar of the water has dulled, but I still have to raise my voice. "Leanne?"

"Yeah?" Leanne doesn't take her eyes from the water.

"Why did you and JD do it?"

Leanne's body tenses. She turns to me, her eyes frenzied. "What are you talking about?"

I move closer and raise my cell phone screen to her eyes. I twist the phone around and press play. When the grainy black-and-white video starts, I turn the screen back to Leanne.

"What is it?" she says.

The video shows a woman exiting her BMW at The Rooster and walking into the bar. "Recognize this?" I say.

"No. I don't."

"That's your BMW. We've identified the plates. That's you getting out of the car—your hair's a little different, but it's you. And this," I move my finger on the phone, fast-forwarding the video, "is Galen Sullivan arriving to meet you."

"I don't know Sullivan. Never heard of him before all this."

"That's not true, is it? Ron Timmons said he gave you Sullivan's contact info several months ago. You asked him for it." I pause. "Shall I fast forward some more and show you the video where you and Sullivan leave the bar at practically the same time? Do you want me to show you the ATM cam footage of the withdrawals you all made to pay Sullivan?"

I'm bluffing on this one—we don't have the financial evidence. But law enforcement has the bags of cash that I suspect came from Leanne or JD. I continue, "We're not trying to say you masterminded this whole thing. Things will go a lot easier if you tell us why JD did this."

Leanne shifts her eyes from the phone to me. The wild glow in her eyes dims, replaced with an expression of panic. Her lips move wordlessly as she takes in my sympathetic tone. She shifts her eyes below to the raging river. "You've got it all wrong—"

"We've got you both nailed with video and witnesses."

"No, you don't!" Leanne sobs. "You don't have *us both* nailed because you couldn't have video of JD. Or eyewitnesses for JD. Or financial transactions linking this to JD."

"How do you—?"

"Because it was all me!" Leanne shrieks. "I did the whole goddamned thing." Her eyes reignite. "That asshole Tolliver was keeping JD from his dream. I told you—JD told you—what JD could do for this county."

Leanne raises both arms. "He could transform this entire valley if he just had the freedom to build and establish himself. And that fucker Tolliver is freezing him out. Tolliver doesn't care about the future of Frisco or Dillon." Leanne points to the flooded town below. "Or Silverthorne. He just wants the power."

She sucks in a breath. "So, I had a plan to put him under. And let JD pick up the pieces." Leanne pauses like she's waiting for a reaction from me. It's all I can do to keep a blank face. "It was supposed to be bigger than this. I wanted water on Main Street. Tolliver has millions in Silverthorne, and if my plan had worked, it would already be gone. He wouldn't have any leverage to keep out other developers."

I can't keep my mouth shut any longer. "JD had no idea what you were doing?"

"Are you shitting me, Tyler?" Leanne pleads. "He's a Boy Scout. Just turns the other cheek and works hard at what he's got—but this? Never." Leanne takes another deep breath. "Sure, JD thinks I'm a little off. Like *oh-let's-fly-to-The-Bahamas-this-weekend* kind of flighty stuff, you know? But he has no idea of how far I'd go to help him."

Leanne's eyes shift again to her feet.

She shifts her eyes to me. "I'd do anything for him, Tyler. Anything."

My heart pounds. Her glance to the cliff's edge was brief, but it caught my attention.

Damn. She's losing it. She's not going to try to outrun me back to the car. She's thinking about jumping.

Leanne eyes move from me to the cliff. "If he knew, Tyler, he'd leave me."

If she breaks toward the edge and I go straight for her, she'll go over. Like a gridiron end-around sweep, I need to ignore where she is and anticipate where she will be if I want to tackle her.

"I can't live with that, Tyler. Seeing him after he finds out what I've done. I just can't!" Leanne's eyes shift from me back to the edge, and she steps away from the cliff.

ZAHN

Dillon Reservoir, Colorado-June 1st

I can't move at first. I was so sure Leanne was planning on jumping, I'm reluctant to change my position.

Leanne pulls her phone from her back pocket and presses on the screen with her fingers.

"What are you doing?" I realize it's a stupid question as soon as it leaves my mouth. Leanne's using her phone. I doubt she's checking the weather.

She walks backward, poking at the screen. "If you can't take out the asshole's property, the only thing left is to take out the asshole."

The third bomb.

I take two steps forward in front of Leanne before she even notices I've moved. I wrench the phone from her and step back, turning to shade the sun so I can read the screen. An open app reads *Detonation Options* and offers two choices: *Cellular* and *Countdown.*

Leanne hits me from the side and the phone flies from my hands landing just shy of the cliff's edge. Her full-on body blow knocks me to the ground in the direction of the phone. Her arms scrabble over the top of me as she grabs for it. I scramble on hands and knees toward the phone like an overzealous toddler, and Leanne slips off my back.

I stretch for it, but my legs are yanked backwards. My hand just shy of the case. A pain stabs the left side of my chest. The recording device is attacking me as I hit the ground. I use my arms to pull forward, dragging my legs and Leanne with me. We both reach for the phone. My outstretched hand connects but comes up short. The phone drops over the edge.

The pressure on my legs eases. I roll over. Leanne's eyes are wide, and she's on her feet. I rise, preparing to pursue her down the mountain, but she steps toward the cliff, away from where the phone disappeared.

Holy shit, she's going to jump.

I angle forward to cut off the attempt, nailing her midsection with my outstretched arms and lead shoulder. My momentum throws her off her path, leaving her upper body dangling over the cliff. I lock my hands around her midsection, but my feet have no purchase. She can take me down with her.

I wrap my arms around Leanne's body from her waist to her knees, and try to shift my weight back on the bluff without losing my grip.

Leanne's upper body drops further over the edge, arms scrabbling at the rock face. I dig the toes of my shoes in the dirt behind me to keep us both from toppling. Leanne screams as she struggles. But I've stopped all forward momentum. Half her body hangs off the cliff.

"Just let me go!"

I can't seem to get her under control. I squeeze my arms tighter around Leanne's ankles, trying to scooch toward a better grip on her lower legs without sending us both over the edge.

"Why won't you let me go?" Leanne wheezes while planting her arms on the side of the cliff. Arching her head, she shrieks, "What's it to you? God-dammit—let me go!" She kicks her legs. I squeeze her knees harder.

My breath finally slows. "That's not going to happen." I exhale. "Look down there, Leanne. Is that how you want to go?"

Leanne sobs. "I don't care. I can't face JD after this. He was never going to know."

I wedge the tips of my shoes into the rocks. Gaining traction, I pull my toes forward and push my heels and knees back. Leanne's body— and mine—move away from the cliff an inch. I do it again. Her body moves closer. Every time I move her further from the edge she whimpers. But she's stopped struggling, making things easier.

After several tugs, I peer over my locked arms and grab the waistband of her jeans, and yank with one hand while propping myself up with the other. I'm on my knees. I've got her.

As soon as Leanne's body is on the ledge, she tries to roll on her back. I release her jeans, and press my forearm against the back of her head, pushing her face in the dirt.

"What the hell are you doing?" Leanne's voice is muffled. "You got me."

"And I'm not going to lose you." I snake my other arm through her armpit and up behind her neck, using the half-nelson I learned in middle school wrestling. With my weight fully on Leanne, and her head immobilized, I release one arm from her neck and dig my phone from of my pocket. I enter my code to unlock the phone and speed dial Perez. Leanne reaches forward with her hands, so I press my free palm into her neck. Her hands return to her side.

Perez answers. "What the hell's going on, Tyler? The wire stopped. I've been calling."

"I need you to send the cops at the trailhead up to me. Leanne confessed. Pretty sure she's got her phone linked to a bomb. I'm lying on top of her right now."

"Where's the phone?"

"Over the edge of the cliff. Not sure if it's retrievable or not."

"We heard the confession. When the wire cut off, I sent the cops up."

"Where are they?"

"They should be close. I'm fifteen out. You're at the end of the Old Dillon Reservoir trail, right?"

"Yeah," I say, and shove my phone back in my pocket.

"Get off," Leanne grunts.

Without releasing my half-nelson on her neck, I drag Leanne ten feet away from the cliff's edge and turn her to face the town of Frisco. Then I reposition myself on her back and focus on the trail.

My jaw drops when a tall black man rounds the corner, weapon drawn. Holy smokes—the US Marshal is in town.

"Zahn?" Williams stops, raising his weapon halfway to the ready position.

"Hey Randall." I pull my arm up raising Leanne's head a few inches. "Meet Leanne Robinson. She confessed to planning the bombing." I toss my head in the dam's direction.

"The Frisco cops are right behind me. Did you hear what's going on in Dillon?" Williams says.

"No. What?"

"Bomb dogs have alerted on a parked truck on the Dillon side, next to that gaggle of folks watching the blast. They're running the plates now. They've got the entire area roped off."

Leanne stiffens in my arms. Her phone. The app. *Detonation Options.*

"Listen," I say. "Leanne's phone. It's opened to a detonation app. It went over the edge behind us. That truck might be one rabbit paw away from blowing up."

Williams moves to the cliff. Three officers call out from the trail. One of them takes custody of Leanne. Williams's voice calls out. "I see it. Ten yards down, next to that root."

"Yeah, I see it," one of the other two officers confirms.

The officer cuffing Leanne turns to me. "Sir, why don't you walk down with us?"

He's not really giving me a choice. With a last glance at Williams, I nod.

When we reach the bottom, the parking lot is empty, except for Leanne's BMW. I spot blinking red and blue lights in the distance. The police have cordoned off the lot. Another police officer meets us and we stroll over to the row of patrol cars by the main road. Williams's Explorer is visible beyond the flashing lights. The lead cop lowers Leanne's head and guides her into the backseat. Two men in green tactical gear jog toward the trail. A bomb team, most likely headed for Leanne's phone.

After they take Leanne away, I approach the remaining patrol car. "You Zahn?" the officer says.

"Yep."

The officer shakes his hand. "You've got a rep, man. Everywhere you go, there's an explosion."

I start to protest, but the officer stops me. "I meant that in a good way, brother. We all think you got balls of steel. We'd be cleaning up bodies right now if not for you." He claps his hand on my shoulder. "You done good. Take a load off. You can listen in with me."

I climb in the passenger seat, where the radio blares.

Team 3 is approaching the phone. That marshal guy found it. We're sending him back to the cars.

Team 3, Team 1 copies. The perimeter around the Dillon vehicle is clear. Plates came in. Registered to a Robert Tolliver. Break, Break. Frisco Police, can you confirm your vehicle is also clear?

The officer next to me keys his mic. *Team 1, Frisco Police confirms. Perimeter is clear around the vehicle at the Old Dillon Reservoir trailhead.*

Team 1 copies. Team 3, you're cleared to work the phone.

I take a breath and hold it. The officer pauses with the radio mic halfway between his mouth and the dash mount.

Team 1, Team 3?

Go ahead Team 3.

The phone is disabled.

I release my breath, raise my eyebrows, and look toward the officer next to me. "Fist bump?"

•   •   •

Perez is propped against the front wall of the station when Williams and I pull up in the Explorer. We exit the vehicle, and Perez strides toward me, hand extended.

"Psych." Perez pulls back the hand and wraps me in a hug. I feel him nod his head at Williams over my shoulder before releasing his grip. "Man hug. Five-second rule."

I laugh. "Four seconds too long, dude."

"You did it. You solved the son of a bitch."

I look at my feet, then back at Perez. "*We* solved it, man. *We* solved it. I just happened to be at the right spot at the right time, thanks to you."

Perez snorts. "Call it what you will. The fact is, you stepped up and it's over—thanks to you."

SULLIVAN

Salida, Colorado-June 7th

The good news? No one died. The bad news? Depending on how Sarah—although it turns out her real name is Leanne Robinson—and her lawyer strategize her defense, it looks like Sullivan might be implicated in an attempted murder. That crazy woman tried to kill a local developer with the explosives Sullivan left in the trunk of her car.

As each day passes, Sullivan's confidence he will be able to trade information for reduced sentencing fades. His testimony was designed to help law enforcement find Leanne. Now that they've found her, all he can do is confirm that Leanne masterminded the whole bombing scheme. And according to his lawyer, she's already confessed to that.

Sullivan's screwed, and thoughts of moving to a federal prison terrify him. His only visits are from lawyer Phil, and he's not coming by much lately.

"Sullivan. You've got a visitor arriving in twenty. Name of Michael Lee. Says he's here to talk to you about representation. That right?"

The duty officer's question catches him off guard. Sullivan opens his mouth, ready to explain he already has a lawyer, then pauses. He's so damned bored. "That's right."

"Our locals not good enough for you?"

Sullivan doesn't answer. The Sheriff's staff spares no opportunity to flip him shit, especially after his efforts to blow things up failed. He's got nothing to counter the jibes they throw at him.

It's thirty minutes before he's led to the same room where he spoke to Deputy Perez. Sullivan sprawls his legs under the table, trying to guess who this Michael Lee might be.

When an Asian man of medium height enters the room, Sullivan is no closer to figuring it out. Who is this guy?

"Mr. Sullivan. I am Mr. Lee." The man's voice is quiet, and he scans the room rather than meeting Sullivan's eyes.

Sullivan tilts his head toward the camera in the corner. "This room is considered public. What do you need, Mr. Lee? Did Phil White send you?"

Lee glances at the camera. "Mr. White is your legal defense, correct?"

"Yep."

"Well, if he's the one driving your case, think of me as the one riding in the passenger seat." Lee raises his eyebrows.

Regardless of his inevitable prosecution, Sullivan knows he's the smartest guy in the room. Lee is trying to tell him something.

Sullivan says nothing, holding the man's gaze while his brain churns. He laughs. Where he'd expected subtlety, Lee has surprised him with his direct message. This is the guy from the passenger seat of the drug guys' SUV. The mystery Asian man. "Phil and I can use all the support we can muster. What do you need to know?"

Lee continues, apparently confident Sullivan recognizes him, "Our legal team is impressed with your intelligence and tenacity. You came up with a brilliant defense strategy. If circumstances would have been different, you would have succeeded. We want you to know we recognize your talents and—regardless of the trial's outcome—want to stay in touch."

Sullivan's mouth drops, then turns into a smile. Lee is speaking in code, but it's pretty damn clear to Sullivan what's happening. Lee just told him that whoever he represents thinks Sullivan is smart, persistent, and would have succeeded at the dam except for circumstances out of his control.

Lee is correct on all accounts. It's nice to have someone who recognizes that. But it's too little, too late, if Mr. Lee can't help him with his looming prison stint. "Thank you, Mr. Lee. But I'm not sure how I can help. I predict I'll be out of touch in the immediate future."

"That's why I'm here, Mr. Sullivan."

"Why?"

"To let you know we see you. To encourage you to be patient. To remember there's a chance at redemption if you're willing to play the long game." Lee pauses. "Do you understand?"

Sullivan glances at the camera. Lee has dropped the code talk. Sullivan doesn't know who Mr. Lee represents or what he offers. But right now, he's the only person Sullivan knows who gets it. The only one who sees his talent. And all he's asking is for Sullivan to wait. As if Sullivan has any choice.

Sullivan meets Lee's eyes. "Yes. I understand."

ZAHN

Mount Harvard Trailhead near Buena Vista, Colorado-June 8th
My truck's headlights bounce across the rutted route to the Mount Harvard trailhead, flashing the trunks of the trees bordering the road in a strobe effect like the nineties dance clubs I seldom visited in college.

"Where the hell are we going, Zahn? We've been on this mountain goat trail for twenty minutes." Randall Williams's question comes from the rear bench seat of my truck.

Perez answers. "Randall, can your bladder handle five more minutes?" He turns to me. "Three middle-aged men? 5:00 a.m.? Hiking?" He pauses. "Well, two middle-aged men. You're past that, Z-man."

I laugh. Perez doesn't know another hiker younger than all of us is coming, too.

Kristee Li reached out after the case wrapped up and reminded me of our unfinished business above thirteen-thousand feet. Randall Williams came back out from Denver to join us. Our early start will ensure we summit—*if* we make it this time—before the afternoon thunderstorms sneak overhead. I smile. The crack-of-dawn start isn't so bad after only one beer and an early bedtime last night.

The road widens into the familiar parking area. Two other cars are parked in the lot, but not Kristee's 4-Runner.

"Gotta take a leak." Williams stumbles out of the backseat, flipping on his headlamp as he exits.

"Take your time," I call, grateful for the extra time to wait for Kristee. "We probably won't leave for another ten minutes."

Kristee pulls her 4-Runner next to my truck. We meet at the tailgate, our headlamps set on red beams to keep from blinding each other.

"Ready to hit it, old man?" she says.

Perez walks around from the other side of the truck.

"Perez, what's up?" Kristee grins. "You joining us?"

Perez smiles at Kristee before raising his eyebrows at me. "Thought I'd give it a shot. Didn't want you carrying Z-man's sorry ass up there alone." He glances at me. "Again."

Kristee laughs. "I thought you might be too tired from saving the world."

I pull my daypack from the truck bed and sling it over my shoulders. "How do you know about what we've been up to?"

"Well golly, Mr. Zahn," Kristee says in a tone that leaves no doubt she's joining Perez in dogging me. "The entire town knows what you and Deputy Rick did." She switches back to her normal voice. "But actually, the sheriff gave the Schorks an update, and the Schorks told some folks downtown. Then it showed up on Facebook."

"Who cares about Zahn and Perez? How about the US Marshals?" Williams pops around the truck.

Kristee jumps at his voice and looks at Perez and me with questioning eyes. "Who are you?"

"Randall Williams, US Marshal." Williams sticks his hand out in greeting. "And you had it right the first time. They pretty much solved the whole thing." He shakes his head. "I'm just concerned about it all going to their heads."

Kristee shakes Williams's hand, introduces herself, and turns back to me. "They said you dragged her off a cliff when she tried to jump." She aims her headlamp at me. "Is that true?"

I focus my beam on the ground. "She was making a break for it. That cliff was between her and wherever she was going. I just stopped her." I slam my tailgate shut.

Kristee closes the 4-Runner's rear hatch. The four of us start up the trail with Kristee in the lead. "That's badass, Tyler," she tosses over her shoulder,

She means it, otherwise she would have called me Z-man.

"So," Kristee says, "a little 14er should be no problem."

I snort. "We'll see."

I move to the rear after the first water break. I don't want Perez griping about me stealing all the Kristee time. Sure enough, Perez takes the place behind Kristee when we start climbing again.

We hike in the dark for another half an hour before the sun creeps up behind us, warming our backs. Small drifts of snow line the slopes of the valley, but the main trail is bare. When we reach the basin before Mount Harvard's steep incline, I'm not gasping for air like our first attempt.

Perez waits for me. Kristee lets Williams take the lead.

"Get any talking in up there?" I say to Perez.

"Some. She wants to meet me next week for coffee. She's been working on rewriting the SAR local operating procedures. Says she wants to ask me some questions about it."

"Well, hell." I grin. "Sounds like you got yourself a date."

We make good time, reaching the basin by six-thirty and passing Bear Lake by seven-thirty. The sun arcs above the trees behind us, spotlighting the ridges funneling our route. The south ridge looks almost higher than Mount Harvard. The jagged spine to the north connects Mount Harvard to Mount Columbia.

I'm feeling good. Good enough, that I start wondering if we should make the climb a twofer—Mount Harvard, then Mount Columbia. Perez is used to the altitude. It looks as if Williams isn't having any problem adjusting, either. He and Kristee have been talking nonstop for almost two hours.

I admonish myself. Just wait and see if you make Mount Harvard before considering a second 14er.

By nine-fifteen, the summit looms only fifty feet away. The last stretch is Class III climbing. We use our hands to rock scramble to the top.

My son, Jacob, would have loved this. Maybe Daria too—but I don't know what she likes anymore. I recall how her image flashed in front of me that night when I swam for my life. I vow to reach out to her soon.

Kristee calls me up to the front with Williams. I think she wants to keep an eye on us newbies. Spot our handholds and foot placement to make sure we don't slide our asses off the mountain.

Ten minutes later, the four of us summit and admire the tips of the neighboring Rockies visible below us as far as we can see. Taylor Park Reservoir shimmers in the distance. Behind us, the Arkansas Valley winds from Leadville through BV to Salida. Pike's Peak looms in the east, Colorado Springs hidden at the base. It's like the entire state of Colorado reveals itself within our view.

I snap pictures of the panorama before asking another climber to take a picture of our party. We settle into a wide crevice near the summit to escape the wind and eat. It's early for lunch, but we've been hiking for over four hours. I pull snacks from my pack and crowd next to the other three. We made it. I made it.

•   •   •

"Alright guys, spill," Kristee says.

I glance at Perez and Williams before answering. "You said it's all over Facebook."

Kristee shakes her head. "But I don't understand how this Breckenridge woman was involved in kidnapping the Schorks. What did the Schorks' drugs have to do with bombing a dam?"

Perez pops in. "Best we can tell, Leanne Robinson had zero connection with Jim and Carrie Schork. We're not pursuing the Schorks and their painkillers. They're going to get a second chance. Carrie Schork is exploring different options to help those with chronic pain."

"Good. They're good people."

"As for the rest," I turn to Perez. "Want me to give her the thumbnail sketch?"

Perez locks eyes with Williams. "Anything you want kept quiet?"

Williams smiles. "As long as you don't talk about the loving relationships between the Marshals, the FBI, and the CBI, then I don't care what you say."

"OK. Elevator version," I say.

Kristee leans back against a rock.

I tell Kristee about the Robinsons and Tolliver, and then about Sullivan and Mandrake. I explain the Schorks, the shaft, the drug guys who haven't been caught, and then the dam, glossing over my role in Leanne's confession since Kristee's already heard it.

I look around gauging my friends' reactions. "How was that?"

Perez cocks his head at me. "You forgot the third bomb."

"Right," I say. "Sullivan left his extra explosives with Leanne. The explosives found in Tolliver's truck matched the type used in the shaft. Leanne either put them there or had someone do it for her. We won't know until the trial. But it looks like she tried to kill Tolliver before she tried to kill herself."

Kristee's expression is priceless. "Dude, that's like a movie or something. Nothing like that ever happens here. I would expect big Randy, the marshal here, to be on the case. But local guys like you two?"

Randall grins at her. Perez and I trade raised eyebrows. *Kristee gets to call our US Marshal, Randy?*

Perez coughs, turning to Kristee. "Yeah, Z-man's involvement turned out to be a surprise for everyone. We didn't know about his superpowers." He turns to Kristee. "Don't you think he'd be a great cop?"

"Sure, I mean, how hard can it be?" Finally, Kristee is turning some of her shit-flipping Perez's way.

The more I'm around this woman, the more I realize how much I miss my own daughter. I remember Daria's quick wit as an adolescent. I can't imagine what she must be like now. "Perez has me looking at the Reserve Deputy program for Chaffee County," I explain. "A part-time deputy thing. Volunteer, just like Search & Rescue."

"You still got to complete six months of training. Just like I did," Perez adds.

Kristee's eyes widen as she turns to me. "You going to do it?"

"I might. The training for next year starts in the fall." I don't tell her what else I'm going to start. Drinking less. And, I'm going to reach out to my daughter and try to reconnect. These people and these mountains are changing me.

But I won't tell them. I'll show them.

Kristee climbs to her feet. "You guys ready to head down?"

The three of us don our packs.

Kristee grabs Perez's arm. "Why don't you lead the descent down this initial pitch so you can monitor Randy and Z-man? I'll bring up the rear."

"Got it." Perez grins at me.

Kristee turns to me as Perez and Williams disappear over the edge.

"Tyler, you've got to help me out here now that you've proven yourself as Mr. Initiative."

"You looking for help putting together those SAR procedures? Perez told me you're heading up that project."

"Not that," Kristee says. "I thought you could do a little matchmaking for me."

"It's about damn time, Kristee." I give her a grin. "I thought you two would never figure things out. But what do you need me for? Aren't you having coffee next week?"

Kristee peers over the edge, checking on Perez and Williams, then turns her head back to me. "What are you talking about? I'm meeting Perez for coffee next week. He's been in SAR forever. I need his help on the manual." She scrunches her nose while glancing from me toward Williams and Perez, then back to me.

"It's Randy, Z-man. We talked practically the whole hike up." She laughs. "I like him. A lot. How about you invite us all for beers after we get back or something?"

My jaw drops.

Randy?

Randall?

And Kristee?

. . .

I'm partially successful setting up the post-summit beer session. We agree to meet at the Eddyline brewpub that evening after post-hike showers.

My phone rings on the drive into town.

"Can't make it, Z-man," Perez says. "Just got called in for this Amber Alert down in Salida."

"Ah shit. Sorry. I know how much you wanted to spend more time with me."

"Screw you. Keep a watch on ol' Randall for me. Every time I tried to get a conversation going with Kristee, today, he was right there edging in our talk."

If you only knew. "Got it. Good luck tonight." And now it's just me, the third wheel at the start of a budding romance. I punch off the call and the phone instantly lights up again with an incoming call.

The name at the top reads: Daria Zahn.

ABOUT THE AUTHOR

Over a thirty-year Air Force career, best-selling author Cam Torrens delivered combat supplies and personnel across Europe, the Middle East, and Africa. He piloted the first mobility aircraft into Iraq during the Iraq War, served as the United States Air Attaché at the US Embassy in Beijing, China and spent four years as the professor of Aerospace Studies at Virginia Tech.

Father of six, Cam and his spouse live in Buena Vista, Colorado, where he serves as the Vice President of Central Colorado Writers and volunteers with the Chaffee County Search & Rescue team. He's admittedly weird—he likes to count things, like consecutive days running, books read, hiking miles, tennis/pickleball/ping pong matches, jacuzzi use, and so on.

Damaged is his fourth *Tyler Zahn* novel.

DON'T MISS BOOK 1 OF
THE TYLER ZAHN SERIES
CAM TORRENS
STABLE
SOMEONE IS TAKING THEM...
A TYLER ZAHN NOVEL

NOTE FROM CAM TORRENS

Word-of-mouth is crucial for any author to succeed. If you enjoyed *Damaged*, please leave a review online—anywhere you are able. Even if it's just a sentence or two. It would make all the difference and would be very much appreciated.

Thanks!
Cam Torrens

We hope you enjoyed reading this title from:

www.blackrosewriting.com

Subscribe to our mailing list – *The Rosevine* – and receive **FREE** books, daily deals, and stay current with news about upcoming
releases and our hottest authors.
Scan the QR code below to sign up.

Already a subscriber? Please accept a sincere thank you for being a fan of
Black Rose Writing authors.

View other Black Rose Writing titles at
www.blackrosewriting.com/books and use promo code
PRINT to receive a **20% discount** when purchasing.